Praise for Lis

'Chillingly believable and ut
Lucy Foley, No. 1 bestselling author of *The Guest List*

'A classic twisting mystery from the Queen of Suspense, Lisa Hall'
Woman's Own

'Brilliantly plotted ... a gripping read'
Alice Feeney, bestselling author of *Rock Paper Scissors*

'A classy thriller ... stylish, twisty and full of suspense'
Sarah Pinborough, No. 1 bestselling author of *Behind Her Eyes*

'Relentlessly pacy and brilliantly written ... A tense,
believable nightmare that you won't be able to put down'
Phoebe Morgan, author of *The Wild Girls*

'An unrelenting and scarily plausible story weaved expertly around
some very real characters. Good luck putting it down...'
Heat

'Compelling, addictive ... brilliant!'
B A Paris, internationally bestselling author of *The Therapist*

'Darkly addictive and impossible to predict'
Chris Whitaker, award-winning author of *We Begin at the End*

'A sharp game of cat and mouse with a brilliant,
twisty plot. Unputdownable!'
Candis

'Chock-full of menace, red herrings, and well-drawn characters
who pull you one way, then hurl you in the opposite direction'
Caz Frear, No. 1 bestselling author of *Sweet Little Lies*

Lisa Hall loves words, reading and everything there is to love about books. She has dreamed of being a writer since she was a little girl and, after years of talking about it, was finally brave enough to put pen to paper (and let people actually read it). Lisa lives in a small village in Kent, surrounded by her towering TBR pile, a rather large brood of children, dogs, chickens and ponies and her long-suffering husband. She is also rather partial to eating cheese and drinking wine.

Readers can follow Lisa Hall on Twitter @LisaHallAuthor.

Also by Lisa Hall

Between You And Me
Tell Me No Lies
The Party
Have You Seen Her
The Perfect Couple

The Woman in the Woods

Lisa Hall

ONE PLACE. MANY STORIES

HQ
An imprint of HarperCollins*Publishers* Ltd
1 London Bridge Street
London SE1 9GF

www.harpercollins.co.uk

HarperCollins*Publishers*
1st Floor, Watermarque Building, Ringsend Road
Dublin 4, Ireland

This paperback edition 2021

1
First published in Great Britain by
HQ, an imprint of HarperCollins*Publishers* Ltd 2021

To my girls: Izzy, Ruby, Olivia, Ivy, Pearl,
Lyra, Winnie, and Juno, with love

Smothering. The heavy press of a pillow against nose and mouth. That's the thought that swoops and swirls across my mind as I pause, one hand against the wall. My heart hammers in my chest, so hard that I can barely breathe as I glance up at the landing, the stairs a mountain to climb before me. I fight against the tightness in my chest, against the nausea that makes saliva flood my mouth and I step forward onto the first step, teetering on the edge. It's as if there is a voice whispering in my ear, telling me there's still time. I can take my foot off the step, lay it back on the solid floor and then turn and run. Or I can raise the other foot, take another step towards the inevitable. There is a roaring sound in my ears, similar to the noise you hear when you raise a shell to your ear to hear the crashing of the ocean. I can still feel the creak of the stairs underfoot even if I can't hear it, as I raise first one foot, then the other, climbing towards the top. By allowing myself to climb those stairs I have made my decision. There can be no going back, not now. Reaching the landing, a cold puddle of moonlight pools across the threadbare carpet and I feel the chill of it beneath my bare feet, feel the scratchiness of the worn carpet fibres against my skin. I take a moment, glancing out of the window to the darkness outside, my head feeling light and swimmy. My vision blurs slightly and blinking rapidly I try to clear my sight, letting my gaze be drawn to the white of the moon. I need to be able to see clearly, to do what must be done. My pulse skitters under my skin and I have to let out a long breath as I peer into the room ahead, seeing her tiny body in the bed in front of me, a frayed blue blanket laid across the foot of the bed as unfamiliar shadows dance across the ceiling. There is a breeze coming from somewhere, stirring the thick, heavy air; a window left open in another room perhaps. The cold brushes over my nose, my cheeks, my fingers and the frayed cuffs of my linen shirt hang limply over my wrists, tickling my sweaty palms. There is a thudding at my temples, a low-level nausea starting to swirl in my stomach, and I have to swallow, my throat painfully dry. Everything has already come undone, and there is only one way I can put things right. I can't stop now. There is no alternative. If they had just left me alone, none of this would be happening.

Chapter One

What did I do? The question is on my lips as I struggle my way into consciousness, my heart hammering in my chest, my nightshirt stuck to my damp body. The baby snuffles in the cot next to the bed, a faint intake of breath that turns into a squeak. I know cries will follow, and as soon as they do, my body reacts accordingly. Air hisses out from between my teeth as there is a sharp, almost painful tingle in my breasts, and the baby squawks in response, as if he knows.

'Al?' Rav nudges me gently, but I close my eyes, pretending I don't hear him. 'Allie, the baby. He's crying.'

I don't need to put the lamp on. A shaft of moonlight slices through the gap in the curtains and I see the soft curve of the baby's head, the tiny fists that pump the air as he prepares for a full-on wail. I should get to him before then, it's not fair for him to cry that hard. I lean over the cot and scoop him up, smelling that already familiar baby scent. I know that if the light were better in here, I would see his dark, almond-shaped eyes screwed tightly shut as he latches on, pain making me bite my lip. He's only four weeks old but I am cracked and bleeding, something I don't remember from when I had Mina. Or maybe I've just forgotten. I would see the dark, dark hair that covers his tiny skull, hair that no one apart from me was surprised to see. His sallow, olive skin, darker than me, lighter than Rav, a legacy of his Indian grandparents. I am the opposite. So white, so fair you could mistake me for a Viking. Or a milk bottle. There is nothing of me in the baby, he is all Rav.

I pull up my nightshirt and place him carefully at my breast, wincing as he latches on. Squashing down the faint whiff of resentment that rises as Rav lets out a sigh and rolls over, burrowing down under the duvet against the chilly draft that wafts in through the ill-fitting antique windows, I focus on the baby's head, the dark tufts of hair, the movement of his mouth as he squeaks and sighs contentedly against my skin. He takes his time, drinking greedily and by the time he is finished I am wide awake, my eyes gritty and dry. The baby unlatches and he lolls in my arms drunkenly, not even stirring as I reach over and lay him gently in the cot. Glancing at Rav, who slumbers on oblivious, I slide carefully out of bed, wincing as something inside tugs as I stand. Mina's birth had been easy, quick, a delightful first labour I was told by my midwife. This time, it wasn't so easy.

I slide my feet into slippers, big, cosy, fluffy monstrosities that Rav had laughed at when he saw them, but now I am grateful for them as the floorboards beneath my feet are icy cold, the chill wafting up around my bare legs. *A cup of tea*, I think. *That's all I need and then I'll go back to bed.*

Silently I move around the kitchen, tiredness tugging at my bones but feeling too unsettled to sleep. I pause as I pour boiling water over a teabag, a creak above me stopping me in my tracks as I wait for Mina or Rav to appear in the doorway. No one does, and I realize it must just be the house settling, the old beams and boards sighing as they move. Letting out my breath, I step over to the battered oak table, pulling my cardigan tighter around me. The kitchen is always slightly chilly, as is the landing at the top of the stairs. Rav says it's because the sash windows are old, that the house is old and we shouldn't expect it to be as snug as a new build, but I'm not quite so convinced. Surely then the whole house should be cold? I blow on the steaming hot tea and give myself a mental shake. I'm just feeling off kilter because of the dream. It was so vivid, so real. I could feel the creak of the stairs under my feet, the carpet under my toes as I walked across the landing, the cold spot in the moonlight as I paused and peered into the room, to where Mina was sleeping. The headache that thumped at my temples in the dream pulses there now, and I reach for the packet of Co-codamol that was sent home with me from the hospital, swallowing two down with gulps of hot tea that scald my throat. I watch the hands on the kitchen clock tick round towards four o'clock, the dark outside the kitchen window beginning to lighten now from velvety black to a deep purple. In the dream, it was dark, but with bright moonlight pouring in. Now, the moonlight that sliced through the bedroom curtains is gone and I can't see anything out of the window, just my own reflection staring dark-eyed back at me, my hair a tumbled mass of bright blonde, almost white at the tips where it has been bleached by the sun. I think again of the dream, the way my heart had hammered in my chest making it difficult to breathe, and I shiver, pulling the soft wool of my cardigan up high around my neck. It doesn't feel like a dream. It was too real, too intense to be just a dream. It feels more like a memory.

'Mama?' Tiny hands tug at me, and I pull myself up from the kitchen table, blinking in the bright light. My spine cries out as I stretch, muscles and bone untwisting from the slumped position I must have fallen into as I slept, and for one horrible moment I feel groggy and disorientated, my mouth patchy and dry from the painkillers I took.

'Allie? Al?' Rav appears in the kitchen doorway, awkward as the baby begins squirming and squawking in his arms. The sight of him, his dear, familiar face, his black hair tousled with sleep, and the fading six pack of his youth that has merged into the tiniest of paunches that peeps over the waistband of his pyjama bottoms is enough for me to shake the last vestiges of unease left by the dream. He watches me pull Mina up onto my lap, her chubby two-year-old fingers reaching up to pat my face as I try to blink away the exhaustion. 'I woke up and you weren't there. Leo needs feeding … I changed him but …' he gives a tiny apologetic shrug and I think I see a hint of irritation flit across his features. I kiss Mina on the top of her head before sliding her back down onto the floor and holding my arms out for the baby.

'Are you OK?' Rav's face creases slightly in concern and

I wonder if I imagined that shadow of annoyance. I turn my face away and concentrate on latching the baby on properly. 'I was worried when I woke up and you weren't there.'

'I couldn't sleep,' I say, reluctant to expand on anything in front of Mina, who tugs at Rav's pyjama leg as he switches on the kettle. 'Mina, leave Daddy. Hang on a sec and I'll get you some breakfast.'

'I would do it, Al, but I'm late already. The traffic will be a nightmare.' I feel a twinge of guilt at not being there when Leo woke, and I smile up at Rav as he pours himself a mug of coffee.

'It's fine. Don't worry. Mina can hang on until Leo finishes. I can manage. You'd better go and get ready – are you in court today?' Envy pierces my breast for a single fleeting moment, at the thought of Rav, in his gown and wig, striding into court to deal with another hardened criminal. It's not the criminals so much that I'm envious of, rather the idea of spending time with other adults. The idea of busyness, that doesn't revolve around nappies and nap time.

'Not today. We're still preparing.' Rav gives me a long look before checking his watch. 'Shit, I need a shower.' He thuds out of the kitchen, ruffling Mina's hair as he goes. I close my eyes, grateful for the early morning May sunshine that streams in through the window creating a puddle of warmth, and let the baby feed and feed, trying to ignore the gnawing thirst that has started up at the back of my throat. Rav didn't think to make me a cup of tea as well, his mind already on the difficult case that has crowded out everything else around him for weeks now. When Leo is finished, I lay him in the Moses basket and cut up some toast and fruit for Mina, tidy away the mug that Rav has left on the side, wipe up the sugar he has spilled across the worktop, and chug down a glass of water to ease the parched feeling in my throat.

When Rav comes back down, he looks gleaming and fresh, as if just unwrapped from cellophane. Feeling tired and faded, I watch as he bustles around, shoving papers into his briefcase, checking his pockets for his phone, his wallet, his keys, all while Mina dances around his feet, desperate for him to notice her.

Rav scoops her up for a quick kiss, his eyes on the clock on the kitchen wall. 'Hey, Mina, why don't you go and find the new dolly Avó brought for you?' He turns to me as she runs off into the hallway. 'Mum brought her a traditional doll, it's got a sari and everything.' He does a little eye roll and I push a smile on to my face. Rav's mother is lovely most of the time – I don't think she'll ever be entirely convinced I am the right woman for her precious son – but despite moving to Britain years ago with Rav's dad, she still loves to tell us stories about her old life in Goa and is keen to make sure that Mina knows about her heritage. Rav picks up his briefcase and then pauses, his eyes on mine. 'Al, are you really OK? You look tired.' He touches the back of my hand lightly with one finger, stroking along the strong blue line of my veins.

'I just couldn't sleep,' I say quietly. 'I had …' I had what? *A bad dream?* I sound like a five-year-old. That thick unsettling feeling comes over me again and I have to swallow hard. 'A nightmare. I had a nightmare and then I couldn't go back to sleep once I'd fed the baby. I thought I would make a cup of tea and I must have fallen asleep down here.'

'Oh, Al.' Rav lifts my hand and kisses it. 'You've not long had a baby; you need to make sure you get your rest. You can't be sleeping down here, it's freezing once the sun goes down. Your hands are cold.' He rubs my hand briskly between his palms.

'I didn't do it intentionally.' The thought crosses my mind that he could have got up with Leo, and I push it away.

'No, I know.' He looks at me oddly and drops my hand, moving past me to reach for his jacket that hangs on the back of the chair.

I feel horrid for snapping, but tiredness and that strange sensation of a dream that isn't a dream makes me feel on edge. 'Rav, I don't know …' I pause for a moment, my heart beating double time in my chest and reminding me of that feeling, standing on the stairs, peering into a room that felt both familiar and not, with my daughter sleeping soundly in the bed there. 'I thought it was a dream, but now I've thought about it, I'm not sure that it was.'

'What do you mean?' He is fussing with his cuffs, not meeting my eyes. Not listening, I think.

'I don't know.' My throat closes over, and I suddenly feel as though I might cry. 'Just not like a dream.'

'I think you're just really, really tired, Al.' He finishes fussing with his cuffs and pulls me towards him, wrapping his arms around me. 'I wish I could stay home, but this case

… I can't. I would if I could.' I lean into him, breathing in the fresh scent of his aftershave, but as he says the words his phone buzzes in his pocket and I can feel him fight to not pick it up, to not check the message. 'Can we talk about it tonight?'

I pull away. 'No, it's OK. I'm fine, really. You need to go in, I know this case is important to you. Naomi is only around the corner if I need help, and your mum is at the other end of the phone.' I'm lucky that both my closest friend and Rav's mother are close at hand, not that I want to rely on them too much. 'I've done this all before, remember? I just had a rough night, and I've got a busy day ahead today. I'm finally going to sort that stuff out in the attic.' I smile, hoping that it stays fixed on my face and doesn't wobble off.

Rav's relief is evident as he smiles back and shrugs on his jacket, leaning down to kiss me hard on the mouth before pulling his phone out. 'I have to go,' he sighs. 'You have a good day, OK? And be careful up in that attic.'

'I will,' I say, shooing him towards the door. 'I need to get ready too — I have to take Mina to nursery. I'll take a slow walk up there, and it'll do the baby good to get some fresh air.'

'OK. Great. It'll do you some good as well.' Rav frowns. 'I might be late tonight. I'll try to be back before Mina goes to bed, but we have a lot to get done today. I love you.' He leans over to kiss me again, and what he says next makes my blood run cold. 'I was worried about you, you know. When Leo was crying last night, you were just lying there, with your eyes open, not moving. I didn't know what to think when I woke up and you weren't there.'

'Sorry,' I say quietly, but he is already rushing down the path, towards the car, his mind already moving past us to the day he has ahead of him. What does he mean, I was lying there with my eyes open? Wasn't I asleep? And if I was awake, how could I have had a nightmare? An icy finger runs up my spine as I turn his words over in my mind, dread settling on my shoulders. Because if it wasn't a nightmare, then what was it? The words on my lips last night swim before me, as if written in neon. *What did I do?*

Chapter Two

I get Mina washed and dressed, and by some miracle manage to get us out of the house only five minutes or so late for nursery. The morning air is already warm, and I lift my face slightly, letting the sun brush over my cheeks. By the time I have handed Mina over to the nursery staff and started the short walk back, I am hot, sweat tickling the nape of my neck and the idea of heading up into the stuffy, humid attic doesn't feel quite as appealing as it did.

I walk past the village sign that proudly denotes Pluckley as the most haunted village in England, a gossamer thin cobweb hanging from one corner, blowing in the slight early summer breeze. A ripple of unease runs down my spine. I had laughed when Rav told me that Pluckley was known that way, the idea of ghosts seeming ridiculous and fanciful, but this morning I am tired and unsettled by my dream and something prickles on the back of my neck.

'Allie?'

A voice behind me stops me in my slow plod towards the house and I let out a tiny sigh. I can see the hedge that masks our house from the road, the wonky chimney stack that sits atop our roof, the post of the small, wrought–iron gate that leads up the path to the front door. I turn, glancing into the pram as I do so, to make sure that cessation of movement hasn't woken the baby.

'I thought that was you. How are you feeling?' Naomi pulls me into a hug, and I wince slightly as my back twinges. 'Oh God. Sorry. Did I hurt you?'

'No, just a twinge. I fell asleep at the kitchen table, believe it or not.'

'Oh, you poor thing, no wonder you're feeling stiff. Did you have a rough night?' Naomi squeezes my shoulder in sympathy.

'I just didn't sleep too well, that's all.'

Naomi's face creases in concern. 'You do look tired. I was coming to see you later, if that's OK, just to catch up and see if you wanted anything. If you need to rest, I can look after Leo if you want to go to bed for an hour? I'm just on my way into the shop but we're not too busy so I'll be done by lunchtime.'

I feel a pang of envy at the image of Naomi standing in the florists where we both work, her nimble fingers twisting and tying wire around sprays of roses and chrysanthemums. I find myself missing the sweet scent of freesias and lavender, the cloying perfume of stargazer lilies, the earthy scent every time I step inside the shop. 'That would be nice, to catch up I mean. You don't need to look after the baby.' I force a smile onto my face, the thought of an hour of uninterrupted sleep calling to me like a drug. *What did I do?* I shiver, the image of the gloomy, dark staircase of my dream rising in my mind and laying a blanket of dread over my shoulders.

'Oops, somebody walked over your grave.' Naomi frowns. 'Are you sure you're OK, Al?'

'Yes, fine. Like I said, just tired.'

'I suppose you want to get this little one back before he wakes up. I'll walk up the road with you.' I let Naomi lead the way, her arm bumping against mine as we walk and she chatters about the shop, the customers, the flowers.

Naomi and I had met when we were both training to be florists. We hit it off straight away, my quiet, insular nature drawn to Naomi's lively, more outgoing one. She helped draw me out of my shell, and we were inseparable until I married Rav. Naomi was the one I went to when Rav and I had our first date, and then our first fight, the one I went to when I took Rav home to meet my mother for the first time, and things didn't go the way I thought they would. Naomi is the first person – after Rav – I told when I found out I was expecting Mina, and she was the first person I rang when my water broke. She is the one who has mopped up my tears, made me laugh until I cried, listened without judgement to all of my secrets. She is, quite simply, my best friend. I thought us moving to Pluckley, after making the decision that we didn't want to bring Mina up in the city, might mean that our friendship would stutter a little – she had finally settled down with Jason and they were trying for a baby – the distance between us, although not great in miles, meaning that we wouldn't get to spend half the time together that we used to. But not long after Mina was born, when I had gone back to work as the manager of The Daisy Chain, Naomi had arrived in

Pluckley, without Jason, and before I knew it, she had a job working under me.

'… so, do you think that would be OK?' I realize Naomi has been talking to me and I have no idea what she was saying, so intent was I on thinking about the past.

'Oh, yes. I'm sure.' I smile, hoping I haven't accidentally given her terrible advice. 'Listen, I've got a few bits to do today … I told Rav I'd sort out those boxes in the attic, and I only have a few hours before I have to pick Mina up again. Pop over tomorrow instead?'

'I'll bring cake.' Naomi grins and I let her kiss me on the cheek, inhaling her sweet, floral perfume and watching her walk away for a moment before wheeling the pram up the path and bumping it over the threshold into the hallway.

Taking advantage of the baby sleeping, I tuck the monitor into my back pocket, and slowly ascend the rickety ladder that leads to the attic space. If I'm honest, the attic was never going to be my favourite place to spend the morning, but I had told Rav I was going to clear some of the boxes out, and now I felt obliged to follow through on it. When we moved into the cottage, just a few months before Leo was due to be born, we had piled boxes of our belongings into the attic, Rav swearing that he would go through them once we got settled. He hadn't, just as he hasn't yet filled in the pond in the garden as he promised, his position as prosecutor on a high-profile case taking every moment of his time.

Now, I sit back on my haunches, wiping dust and grime from the ladder onto my jeans and survey the dingy space ahead of me. Rav has stacked our boxes neatly to one side, but the attic is filled with years of other people's possessions, left abandoned and unloved as they have moved on. I pull out a box marked 'Summer' and peer into it, seeing some of Rav's summer shirts, Mina's armbands, an old sari of mine that I bought in India years ago. I flip the lid over and push it back into place. As I reach for the next box there is movement ahead of me, an activity to match the movement of my own arm and I freeze, my heart hammering in my chest before I let out a laugh, a breath that wheezes its way out of my chest. *A mirror.* Crawling forward, careful not to bang my head on the beams, I see it propped up against the far wall, clearly left behind by a previous occupant. I scooch along the floorboards, aware that I am getting covered in cobwebs and grime, past the overhead beam into a space where I can stand. It's a full-length mirror, the glass spotted and dirty but with the most beautiful ornate frame. Getting closer, I run my finger over the whorls and curls of the frame, my skin coming away black with dirt, and I wonder why anyone would leave anything so beautiful behind. *It would be perfect in the hallway*, I think, and I move closer, testing the weight of it. It's heavy, but I think if Rav gave me a hand we could get it downstairs. Get it cleaned up. Hang it in the hallway. I imagine myself, checking my reflection in it on the way out of the house every morning and have to suppress a smile. It feels like unexpected treasure.

It doesn't take long to pull down a couple of boxes of books and one containing cushions and throws. At the top of the stairs, the landing is cold even though the sky outside is still a brilliant blue, and I feel a sense of déjà vu tickling at the base of my spine, the memory of my dream close and heavy. I peep into the bedroom to make sure the baby still has his blanket over him. As I lean over the cot, taking in his tufts of dark hair, the way his hands ball into fists on either side of his head, he stirs and I hold my breath, before leaning down and scooping him up. He nestles under my chin, his head bobbing as he roots around looking for food. Sinking into the nursing chair, I draw him close and let him feed, forgetting about the contents of the boxes that now need to be put away. Trying to forget about the creak of the stairs, the cold spot on the landing.

Twenty minutes later, I groan inwardly as I push the pram towards the preschool building. There is a large gathering of mothers outside, which tells me I am early and will have to wait until they open the doors. Usually I wouldn't mind – I'm used to spending time chatting with customers as I create their bouquets – but I don't want to make conversation today, the shadow left by the dream making me feel unsettled, as if a storm is brewing inside me. I wish now that Rav had a job where he could have stayed home from work.

'Ahhh, let's have a peep.' A woman I think I vaguely recognize from previous pick-up and drop-off times peers into the pram, her hands clutching the handles of her own designer travel system. 'Beautiful. How old is he now?'

'He's errr … he's four weeks old now.' I clutch the handle of the pram a little tighter, unnerved by her familiarity. I haven't spoken to her before, I don't think.

'Rav back at work, is he?' She smiles, showing perfect white teeth. 'It's nice to get into a routine, isn't it?'

I stare at her for a moment, before nodding. 'Yes. Always good.' Rav must have been chatting to the mums when he dropped Mina off the first week I was home after having Leo. The one week that he could spare away from work. That would explain her familiarity. I peer over into the pram she is holding. 'How old is your little one?' I can't tell if it is a boy or a girl.

'Oh, he's three months old now. Sleeping through the night already like a little angel. I'm going to start weaning him soon.' She fussily tucks the blanket tighter around the gurgling baby. Weaning at three months (and sleeping through the night) seems a little early to me, but that isn't what is making me feel unsettled. Before I can think it through, before I can try and figure out what it is that has made an icy fist clench low in my stomach, the doors are thrown open and 'Aunty Linda', the preschool manager, is ushering us all inside.

Mina stands patiently, her rucksack on her back, until she sees me and starts waving and calling to me. I park the pram up and go to her, making sure she has all her things.

'Mrs Harper?' Aunty Linda stands behind me, a stern expression on her face. 'I know you've only just had a baby, but if you're going to send Mina in wellies, can I please ask that you pop some plimsolls in her bag? We can't really have children running about in wellies, not on this slippery floor. It isn't very comfortable for the child either.'

My cheeks flaming red, I apologize and grasp Mina by the

hand, eager to get out onto the street and get home. *What on earth was I thinking? She must have put them on while I was rushing to get out of the door on time. It's May, for heaven's sake.* As I struggle to manoeuvre the pram over the step out into the car park, feeling sweat start to bead on the back of my neck, the weaning woman appears beside me, letting go of her own pushchair to help me get it over the step.

'There,' she says smiling, and I have no choice but to say thank you and smile back. 'It's always a nightmare trying to get over that awful step. I'm Tara, by the way.'

'Allie.'

'Listen, Allie, I don't know if you would be interested but there's a mother and baby group at the village church on a Thursday morning. I go most weeks and so does Karen.' She gestures to another woman with shiny dark hair, a baby in a spotlessly clean Babygro on her hip. 'We'd love it if you could join us.'

I can't respond for a moment as I realize what it is that had me so unsettled outside the preschool.

'Allie? It's literally right next door to the preschool here, so you wouldn't be far away if they needed you for any reason.'

'Um … yes, thank you. I'll definitely think about it.' I smile weakly and place Mina's hand on the pram, eager to get away, but it's not the proximity of the toddler group that has me feeling shaken. The blanket. The blue, handmade blanket that covered Tara's baby in the pushchair looks unnervingly like the one that lay on the bed in the darkened bedroom in my dream.

Chapter Three

'I've found something,' I say the moment Rav walks through the door. Mina is already fed, bathed and tucked up in bed, Rav failing to come through on his promise to be home in time to help out.

'What?' He sounds tired and distracted, as he shrugs off his jacket and lays his briefcase on the table.

'Up in the attic. Remember I said I was going to go up and sort the boxes out? Well, I found something.' Ignoring the frown on his face, I feel a little buzz of excitement at the thought of the mirror. 'Come on, I want to show you.' I reach for his hand, but he pulls back.

'Can't it wait? I've only just walked in the door, Al, I'm shattered.'

'Oh. I suppose so.' I deflate like a popped balloon. 'I did want to show you before the light goes but I guess it can wait until the weekend.'

Rav pauses, his hand on the knot of his tie. 'What is it?'

'I'd rather show you,' I say, and this time when I reach for his hand, he lets me take it. I lead him upstairs to the landing and stop under the loft hatch. 'You might want to change out of that suit.'

Rav sighs, but his eyes go to the hatch, and I know he won't argue. 'OK. I'll change, you go on up.'

I pull down the ladder as quietly as I can, aware that Mina is sleeping in the room next to mine, that the baby is tucked up in the cot in my bedroom. A waft of warm, musty air hits my face and I cough discreetly into my elbow before climbing the ladder, pulling myself up into the dusty space. The light is different in here now, later on in the day. The small round window at the front of the house lets the sun in in the morning, and when I came up earlier there was a shaft of sunlight beaming in, lighting the attic. Now, the sun has disappeared over the other side of the house and although the air is stiflingly warm, the attic is shrouded in shadows. I shiver, despite the heat, scrubbing my hands over my arms.

'What it is that you've found then?' Rav's voice in my ear makes me jump and I press my hand to my mouth.

'Bloody hell, Rav, you made me jump.'

He laughs, tracing a finger over the bare skin at the back of my neck, making me shiver in a different way, and I decide to forgive him for being so snappy. 'Come on then, Al, show me what you've found. I'm starving and I've still got a ton of paperwork to go through tonight ready for tomorrow. Unless you've found something rare and valuable that we can sell for a fortune, and I can retire in the morning?' His mouth quirks upwards into a smile.

'Don't be daft. Over here.' I step forward, catching

movement ahead of me as I do. I stop for a second, my pulse speeding up, before I remember this morning. My actions mimicked in the mirror ahead of me, and again now as I move towards it, Rav close behind me.

'Look,' I say. 'I found this mirror. Isn't it beautiful?' I run my finger over the carved frame again, just as I did hours before.

'Yeah, it's nice,' Rav says. 'Really nice, actually. I doubt it's worth much though.'

'I don't want to *sell* it,' I say, horrified at the thought. 'I want us to use it, Rav. It would look amazing hanging in the hallway, don't you think? It just needs a good clean and then it would finish off that space perfectly.'

Rav runs his eyes over it again. 'Yeah,' he says eventually. 'Yeah, it would look good. You clever thing. I suppose you want me to help you move it?'

'Would you?' I flutter my eyelashes at him, and he laughs. 'Here, you take that side, and I'll grab here.' I clamp my hands firmly around the frame, one midway and one at the bottom. Together we manage to inch it towards the opening of the attic. It's surprisingly less heavy than I first thought, but I am still sweating when we reach the space down to the landing below.

'I'll go down first, and then if you slide it towards me, I think I can manage to get it down. Just be careful,' Rav instructs, before he starts to descend the ladder. As his head disappears through the opening, the shadows seem to gather and I feel the air stir, as if someone has walked up behind me. My arms breaking into goosebumps, I turn slowly, suddenly sure that there is someone, some*thing* up here with me, just waiting for Rav to leave, but when I look over my shoulder there is no one there.

Idiot. I whisper it under my breath, as I spot something poking from between the boards where the mirror was stood. Rav calls up to me that he is going to grab some water, something about dust in his throat, so I slip silently over the dusty floor to look closer. The tip of a white feather emerges from the crack in the floorboards and I crouch down to pick it up. *It was just a bird, that's what disturbed the air.* I scan the beams but it's too dark to see if a bird is trapped up here. My fingers pull at the tip, fumbling at the slick fibres. A white feather. Isn't a white feather good luck? Or spiritual? Something like that anyway. I try to remove it, but something prevents it from sliding out. Something that feels heavier than a feather should.

'Al? Are you ready?' Rav's voice wafts up from the landing below. 'I really need to get on with some work so can we get this done if you want it down here?'

'Coming,' I call back, letting the feather fall back down between the cracks until just the tip is showing. Together we manage to manoeuvre the mirror out through the hatch to the attic, down the stairs and into the hallway without dropping it or arguing. Rav props it against the wall, but there are two fixings in the middle of the wall, in the exact space where I pictured the mirror hanging.

'Wait, Rav, can you just help me hang it on these hooks?' We take a side each and get the grimy, age-spotted mirror hung. 'Thank you.' I blow Rav a kiss as he hurries away to the kitchen to grab his laptop and briefcase, his mind already back on work. I stand back and survey the mirror. It looks perfect, almost as if that was where it was meant to hang.

We eat dinner in the living room, Rav surrounded by papers, his hair sticking up on one side where he keeps running his hands through it. I know better than to ask if he is OK, if there is anything I can do, and instead I eat in silence, my thoughts going back to the feather in the attic, wondering what it was that stopped it from being pulled out completely.

'Al? Allie?' Rav's voice snaps into my thoughts and I lower my fork to my half-eaten dinner. 'The baby. He's crying, didn't you hear him?'

I look to the baby monitor, where red arcs across the buttons and then I register the thin wail coming from upstairs. 'Sorry,' I say, 'I was miles away. He probably needs feeding.' But Rav doesn't respond, already lost in legalese. I run upstairs to where the baby shouts in the cot, his tiny face growing red and sweaty and I scoop him close to me, latching him on before I've even sat in the nursing chair. 'Shhhh,' I soothe him, running my finger over the tiny dome of his bald head as he suckles greedily. I close my eyes, just enjoying the weight of him in my arms, when a thin breeze wraps its way around my ankles, and I remember the loft hatch. It's still open. Rav was so eager to get back to his laptop that neither of us thought to close it. I let the baby finish feeding, change him, and tuck him back into the cot before heading out onto the landing and stepping onto the ladder.

The attic space is a little cooler now, and I half wish I had worn a cardigan as I crouch on the floor beside the tip of the feather. I'm not sure why it seems important to find out why the feather won't just slide out, but as I tug at it again, I meet the same resistance. Something thunks against the underside of the floorboard, the feather stopping dead. Shining the flashlight of my phone onto the feather, I see there is what looks like a piece of string tied around the bottom of it.

Curiouser and curiouser. A beat of excitement pulses through me and I scrabble for the edge of the floorboard. When we moved in, I hoped that we would find something hidden away somewhere, a little piece of the past, and maybe this is it. *Or maybe it's just a feather and some string, a bit of old rubbish that slipped down between the floorboards.* My fingernails bend back slightly as I tug the loose board away, almost losing the feather in the gap as it slips free, driving a splinter into my forefinger.

'Shit,' I whisper under my breath, raising my finger to my mouth. I taste blood, wrinkling my nose as I swallow. Sliding my other hand into the gap I pull out a tangle of string. Attached on one end is the feather and at the other is a stone with a hole in the middle, carefully tied to the bottom. *Hag stone.* The words feel familiar as they rise to my lips, as if I have heard them many times before. In between the hag stone and the feather sit two iron keys, spotted with rust. I turn them over in my hands, the keys leaving orange smudges on my fingers, the tang of metal in the air.

'Allie? Are you up there?' Rav calls and I slide the

floorboard back into place, tiptoeing across the attic to the hatch.

'Yes. I'm coming down now.' I make my way down the ladder, careful not to slip, the keys in my hand, as blood snakes its way down my finger from the splinter.

'What did you do? You're bleeding.' Rav takes my hand but I shake him off.

'Just a splinter.' I hold out the keys. 'Look, I found this under the floorboards. It was poking out from where the mirror was. What do you think it is?'

Rav takes it, his nose wrinkling a little in distaste. 'God knows. It looks like ... well it just looks like some old keys.'

'What about the stone?'

'It's probably just a souvenir someone picked up on the beach and used as a keyring.' Rav tosses them up in the air and catches them in one fist. 'We have keys to all the doors here, so they can't be anything to do with the house. They're just a bit of old junk, Al, nothing exciting.'

'Do you think?' I feel doubtful, but I don't know why. Maybe I just really wanted to find something exciting.

'Yes, I do. Isn't the mirror enough of a find for one day?' Rav yawns, not bothering to cover his mouth. 'I'm going to bed; I've got a long day tomorrow. Are you coming?'

I nod, following him into the bedroom where he throws the keys onto the chest of drawers and then heads back out into the bathroom to brush his teeth. I wait my turn, then slide into bed beside him, the covers already pulled up around his chin and his eyes tightly closed. I wait a moment, sure by his breathing that he's not yet asleep.

'Rav, those keys …'

'Allie, they're junk,' he says, his voice muffled by the duvet. 'Come on, babe, get some sleep before Leo wakes up again. Love you.'

I settle back into the pillow and close my eyes, hoping I can sleep before the baby wants another feed. When I do sleep, I dream I am in the attic, tucking the feathered keys into the floorboard as I mutter to myself, the stone warm against my skin as breath whispers at the back of my neck.

Chapter Four

Naomi appears as I finish making Mina's lunch, tapping lightly on the front door so as not to wake the baby.

'Hey!' She slips into the hallway and takes off her cardigan and shoes before handing me a tiny hand-tied bunch of alstroemeria – *symbol of devotion and friendship* – fronds of dark fern woven in between the stems. 'I brought you these. Ooh, nice mirror.'

'Thanks.' I smile, a genuine smile for the first time today, as I accept the flowers. I am tired and out of sorts, after another restless night. I dreamed of the attic, and then again of my feet on the stairs, the weight of a pillow in my hands. 'Can you believe I found it in the attic?' I have spent the morning while Mina is at nursery scrubbing the mirror, using an old toothbrush to get into the grooves of the carving. The glass is still spotted with age, but it looks perfect hanging on the hallway wall.

'What a find. Did you clean it all up?' Naomi says as I nod. 'You look tired. How is Leo sleeping?'

'OK, I guess. Feeding every couple of hours or so.' With that I stifle a yawn. 'God, sorry. To be honest it wasn't the baby that kept me up all night last night.' My heart bangs a double thump in my chest at the thought of vocalizing the dream, the image of myself creeping up the stairs, the way it made me feel.

'Really? Not Mina?' Naomi strokes a hand over Mina's dark head as she sits at the table, crumbling breadsticks onto her plate, a small stick of cheddar in one chubby fist.

'No, not Mina.' I incline my head towards Mina, letting Naomi know I'll tell her when she is finished eating and out of earshot. 'Are you done, sweetie?' I lean down and wipe Mina's hands and face with a baby wipe and she shoots out of her chair and into the sitting room, and we hear the television go on.

'CBeebies.' Naomi rolls her eyes and I feel a twinge of guilt before I shake it off. It won't hurt to let Mina watch telly for half an hour while I get things off my chest. 'So, why didn't you sleep?'

'I had a bad dream,' I say, not meeting her eyes, 'only it didn't feel like a dream. Did you ever have a dream so vivid that it felt real? So real that it was more like … a memory.'

'Vivid dreams, yeah. But so real as to be a memory … can't say that I have.' Naomi frowns. 'The baby is only a few weeks old, Al. Your hormones are all over the place. Do you want to tell me about it?'

I shake my head, not wanting to go through it all again. In the excitement of finding the mirror, I had pushed it out of my head, and I don't want to think about it now. 'I just worry I suppose … It felt so real, as if I was really there, and I woke up wondering what on earth I had done.'

Only I hadn't woken up the night before, had I? Rav had told me that my eyes were open, that I was awake. 'You're right, it's probably just hormones racing around, you know how it is.' Immediately I want to bite my tongue. Because Naomi doesn't know how it is. That's part of the reason why she and Jason separated. Naomi can't have children, and after several miscarriages, and then complications, which led to the doctors telling Naomi children would never be possible, Jason left her.

Naomi says nothing for a moment, and I open my mouth to apologize but she speaks before I can say anything. 'I think maybe you're overtired. Shall I take Leo for a bit and you go and have a lie down?'

'I'll be fine, honestly. You don't need to …' I protest, but Naomi is already leaning over where the baby sleeps. She gently lifts him from the Moses basket in the corner of the kitchen and tucks him into the crook of her arm, murmuring softly under her breath. I let her take him, guilty relief washing over me and head up the stairs to the bedroom.

Jolting awake with a gasp, my eyes go to my phone on the bedside table and I lift it, lighting the screen. Four o'clock. I've been asleep for almost three hours. I strain my ears but can't hear either of the children, just the muted sounds of the television. *Shit.* I push my way out of the duvet, getting to my feet so quickly that for a moment I feel dizzy, light-headed, and I have to take a deep breath, holding on to the bedside table.

'Mina? Naomi?' I call out softly, anxious that the baby will be asleep and my shouts will wake him. There is no response, so I run down the stairs, suddenly sure that I will get downstairs and the house will be empty, the children will be gone. As my feet thud on the stair risers, an image appears in my mind of a chair overturned, cups and plates left covered in crumbs and remnants of tea on the table, the back door swinging open in the breeze. *A domestic* Marie Celeste. A chilly breeze strokes my legs with icy fingers as I step off the bottom stair, and I peer into the sitting room. The room is empty, Mina's toys scattered across the floor, the television playing to itself.

'Naomi?' I call again, and swivel on my heel as a clatter comes from the kitchen. I trip over Rav's trainers left lying in the hallway as I fly along the passageway to the kitchen, the ancient quarry tiles slippery and cool beneath my bare feet. As I reach the kitchen door I slow, one hand pressed against my chest.

'God, Allie, are you all right? What's wrong?' Naomi sits at the kitchen table, her mouth a perfect O of shock, as the baby still snoozes contentedly in her arms and Mina draws a picture using a packet of fresh, unbroken crayons that Naomi must have brought with her.

'I thought …' I let out a wheeze that could be mistaken for laughter. 'I thought you were gone. I woke up and looked at the clock and I'd been asleep for ages. I couldn't hear anyone …' I enter the room fully, stooping to kiss Mina on the head, wanting to pull her close and squeeze her tightly. Almost as if the sound of my voice has reminded him that he hasn't fed for hours, the baby stirs and makes a mewling cry and I feel a tingle as my milk comes in.

'Let me take him,' I say, as Naomi fusses with him, trying to calm him. 'He needs feeding.'

'Oh, of course he does,' Naomi says in a baby voice, but to the baby, not me, and she hands him over. His face is hot and crumpled from being pressed against her arm. 'Here, Leo, go to your mum.'

I take him, his tiny Babygro feeling damp against my skin where he has got hot in Naomi's arms. I expect her to pick up her bag, eager to get back to the shop but she settles back into the chair opposite, watching me. 'Sorry I slept for so long. I must have needed it. If you have to head off, I understand, you were only supposed to pop in for an hour.'

Naomi shakes her head and her mouth turns down in what is a now familiar gesture. 'No, no. Nothing to rush back for.' She pushes a huff of air out from between her lips, a sad attempt at a laugh.

'Oh, Naomi.' Leaning forward I reach for her hand. 'I'm sorry, I'm so selfish. I just dumped the kids on you and didn't even ask how you were.'

'Pah.' Naomi shakes her head. 'It's fine. I'm fine.' But her eyes fill with tears and she blinks them away rapidly, so I pretend I haven't noticed. Naomi used to laugh all the time, one of those girls who was always fun, upbeat, always knew the right thing to say to make others feel better. Until Jason broke her heart.

'Have you heard from him?' I ask gently. It's been almost

a year, but Naomi hasn't met anyone else, hasn't moved on at all.

'Nothing,' Naomi replies, 'although … I did see on Facebook that Tracy is expecting.' Her face crumples slightly and I shift out of the chair, reaching forward to hug her.

'The bastard,' I say, letting her lean against me even though it is awkward to hold the baby and comfort her at the same time. Jason left Naomi for Tracy, after Naomi discovered she couldn't conceive, and then it was my turn to be there for Naomi. To listen as she vented, to mop up her tears, to make sure she was eating enough to soak up the wine we drank together, and then to make sure she didn't text him while she was drunk. Now every time I think Naomi is managing to get herself together, something else happens to knock her back.

'No, he's not.' Naomi sits up and wipes her eyes on the sleeve of her cardigan. 'He's moving on, it's me that needs to sort myself out. Why am I even bothered? I have you and Rav and the kids … I don't need him. Let's not talk about it anymore.' She blinks again, sliding a finger under one eye to catch an errant tear.

The baby shouts a shrill, brief cry and I sink back into the chair and pull up my top. 'He's the one who missed out. The right guy is out there for you, we just need to find him. Did you try that new dating website Rav mentioned?'

'Ugh, not yet. I can't face it. I just want what you guys have – is that too much to ask for?'

'What – no sleep, Rav farting next to you all night and Avó telling you regularly how you're doing everything wrong?'

'Exactly that.' Naomi laughs, but her face is pinched, her smile not meeting her eyes. 'I should probably leave you to it. Do you need anything before I go? What time are you expecting Rav home?'

'Oh, who knows?' I say, as the baby begins to feed hungrily. 'He's said every night this week that he'll try and be back for Mina's bath, but he hasn't.'

I half hope that she's going to offer to stay until Rav arrives home but then she says, 'I better get off.' Naomi flicks her wrist to check her watch. 'Are you feeling a bit better now?'

'Much.' I smile at her gratefully, and I do feel better, a little less fuzzy anyway. Maybe all I needed was to catch up on some sleep. 'Thank you for watching the children.'

'I can come again tomorrow, if you like?' Naomi reaches out a hand and smooths the baby's head as he feeds. 'He was an angel. They both were.'

'Oh no, it's fine, honestly. You must be busy at the shop. All those weddings coming up. I wish I was there to help you.'

'It's not so bad.' Naomi gives me a quick grin, which tells me it probably is. 'If you don't want me to come over, then give me a call if you need anything or you change your mind, OK?'

'Yes, of course, but I'll be fine. Don't worry.'

And I am fine. I don't dream that night, and even after getting up four times with the baby, when Rav goes off to work the next morning, dropping a kiss on my cheek, I feel positive. It's not until I have dropped Mina at preschool and returned to the house that my doubts start to creep in.

I feed the baby, finally starting to feel as though I am getting used to having him attached to me at all hours of the day. He goes down for a nap and I sneak downstairs, wondering for a brief moment if he sleeps too much. Should he spend so much time asleep? Do I remember Mina sleeping this much? Worry gnaws at my gut, and at the bottom of the stairs, when I pause and turn to look back up towards the landing, I am swamped by a feeling of déjà vu. The image of the moonlight puddled across the landing fills my mind and my heart starts to knock hard against my ribcage. There is that claustrophobic feeling again that something awful has happened, something dark and overwhelming. I feel grubby, as if the dream has left some kind of dirty, oily stain on my skin that I can't scrub out, and I have the urge to wash my hands, to scrub them until my nail beds are sore and my knuckles bleed.

Feeling shaky and sick I walk into the kitchen, reaching under the cracked, old butler sink for a clean cloth and a bottle of bleach, directing the urge at the house instead of my skin. I'll clean until I stop thinking about it. I scrub at the sink, the draining board, the work surfaces, even thinking about wiping over the old horsehair plaster walls, the only thing stopping me is the fear of the plaster coming away completely. I finally stop when sweat beads my temples and my throat is scratchy and dry with thirst. Taking a moment, I pour myself a glass of cold water from the tap, letting it run for a few minutes to make sure it is as cold as possible. It is unseasonably warm for May so making sure the baby monitor is at full volume, I open the back door and, clutching my glass, step out into the sunshine.

I feel calmer now, as through the scrubbing action and acrid smell of the bleach has washed away my feelings of doubt and fear. Closing my eyes, I let the sun warm my cheeks, before I open them and look out onto the garden. There is thick woodland at the bottom of the garden, once you have crossed an expanse of green lawn, the grass thick and lush in most places before it thins in the shade of the trees. I need to remind Rav to mow it at the weekend, I think, my gaze drawn to the thick herb borders that line either side of the garden. There is a pond at the back of the lawn, not far from where the woods start, the water a murky green with reeds and water plants crowding the surface. Rav talked about filling it in when we first moved in, worried that it was unsafe for the children, but he hasn't done it yet, despite my nagging. There is something about it that I don't like, maybe just the idea of an open expanse of water, albeit small, where the children play. Whatever it is, I'll tell Rav again this weekend. I'll tell him it's got to be filled in. The garden, and the woods beyond it are partly the reason why Rav wanted the house so desperately. Having grown up splitting his time between the Kent countryside and Colva Beach in Goa, Rav can't bear to be kept indoors. When we met in Goa, Rav there with his elder brother and his parents, visiting his aunts and uncles, and me with Darron and Sue, two backpacker friends I'd picked up in Thailand and travelled on with, I'd been drawn to his infectious energy. The way the sunlight, the sand, the crashing waves as we sat in a shack on the beach eating hot, crispy prawns and oily, garlicky naan bread seemed to bring him to life. Later, when we were living together in a flat on the outskirts of Ebbsfleet with no outside space, I saw that energy fade as I watched him grow more and more weary and fed up, so I couldn't turn him down when he brought me to view this cottage.

'Al, just look at this garden. Think about Mina, and the new baby.' He nudges me, and I smile even though there isn't a new baby, not yet. We've only just started trying, not even three months ago. 'You're so close to work, it's perfect. I don't mind a bit of a longer commute, although really it isn't going to be that much longer, and it's not too far from my mum's new house. She'll be about to help with the kids.'

'It'll be a lot of work,' I warn him, casting my eyes over the bushes, the unkempt lawn, the woods throwing dark shadows out across the bottom of the garden. I shiver slightly, as though someone has walked over my grave.

'I'll do it.' Rav turns to me with pleading eyes. 'It's perfect, Allie. And look at the cottage – what's not to love?'

I turn back to look at the house, Rav keeping an eye on Mina as she stumbles over the cracked slabs of the patio. She's only just started walking and I want to tell him to scoop her up, that she'll fall. The house is lovely, a four-hundred-year-old cottage, Grade II listed, with a solid oak front door and mullion windows. From the front, it is a perfect picture of country living – a Kent peg tiled roof sits above those beautiful windows, a slightly crooked chimney reaching up towards the sky. A tangle of pale pink roses – *a symbol of friendship and love, or secrecy and confidentiality, depending on the occasion* – with thorny green stems climb around the door, winding their way around the small, run-down porch. All secured behind an ancient-looking hedge, and a small, rickety, wrought-iron gate. The chimney needs re-pointing, the roses need pruning, and the porch needs to be knocked down completely, but Rav doesn't see this. All he sees is the solid, old oak door, the beautiful windows, the chimney that means there is an open fire. I look up now at the back of the house, at the arched mullion window that looks out over the garden, sure that I saw movement there, but the window is dark, the only movement the reflection of the clouds that swoop briskly across the grey sky, and I tear my eyes away. I must have been mistaken.

Inside, the ceilings are low, crossed with sturdy dark oak beams, with a wide, open brick fireplace that Rav has already fallen head over heels for. The bedrooms are damp-free, thank goodness, but the time-worn wallpaper is peeling in soft, thick strips and despite being crammed full of original features, like the deep, claw-footed bathtub and the ancient butler sink, both the bathroom and kitchen have seen better days. The house hasn't been lived in for a long time, and it shows. Everything needs a lick of paint, proper repairs to be done, and a good clean to scrub away the residual soot from the fireplace and the mould that creeps into the corners of the kitchen and bathroom. It's liveable and with a bit of TLC it could be amazing. It is a beautiful house, there's no doubt about it, but as I stand and stare at it, I can't help but rub the tops of my arms as if cold.

'Is it the ghosts?' Rav puts his arm around my shoulders,

pulling me in close, as Mina sits on his opposite hip. 'They do say Pluckley is one of the most haunted places in Britain.'

'Oh, shut up!' I nudge him, and he laughs before pressing his mouth to mine.

'Just think about it, Allie. Away from the dirt and noise of the town, friendly village life, this amazing garden for the kids to grow up in. We can take our time doing it up, there's no rush if it's our forever home. And it's a bargain.' He pauses for a moment, the smile dropping from his face. 'I can't live there anymore, Al. All I think about is getting away from it all, so it's here or back to Goa.' Rav laughs to show he doesn't mean it, but I know that a secret tiny part of him does.

I look back at the house, and let myself imagine it tidy and freshly painted, full of our things, our longed-for second baby lying in my arms, and I feel a fizz of excitement in my veins. Rav is right, this could be our forever home. 'It looks like it's Pluckley then.'

Now, I sip my water and look over the herb borders, one ear open for the baby monitor. The beds are full of sage, lavender and chamomile, mixing with the heady perfumes of roses and jasmine, clashing with the harsher scents of rosemary and mint, all tangled together with weeds. I should work on them, I think, I'm a florist. I can tame them and make the borders less bedraggled and sad-looking while I'm at home on maternity leave. It's not fair to expect Rav to do it all, not with the hours he's doing at work. There is a chirp from the baby monitor, and I take another mouthful of water before draining the rest of the glass into the herb bed. As I straighten up a flash of white catches the corner of my eye and I pause, half leant over the scraggly border. There is someone in the trees. I stand stock still, watching the dark shadows of the woods. The branches sway in the light breeze and I think for a moment I must have imagined it, when I see it again, a flash of white moving through the trees at a pace, a glimpse here and there before it vanishes and doesn't reappear.

Shit. I swallow hard and on shaking legs turn and run into the kitchen, slamming the door behind me. A wail comes from the bedroom and I rush up the stairs to the baby, eager to have him safe in my arms. Why would someone be in the woods? The estate agent told us that technically the woods belong to whoever owns the cottage – a sign on the other side of the trees tells visitors it is private property – and as they are effectively in our garden, no one actually enters them, preferring to use the less dense woodland on the other side of the village. In the months since we moved in, I have never seen anyone in these woods – we are just that little bit too far out of the village. Our nearest neighbour is a quarter of a mile away, at the end of the village High Street, which is exactly what we were looking for when we bought the house. Peace and quiet. Only right now, it just feels isolated and lonely. I stop on the landing and stare out through the window, jiggling the baby as he fusses in my arms. I need to feed him, but I can't relax, not until I know there is no one out there. Cautiously, I make my way downstairs and out through the back door, stopping to make sure my phone is in my pocket and to slide trainers onto my feet in place of flip flops.

'Hello?' My voice isn't as strong as I would have liked as I approach the darkened area of grass where the trees cast their shadow. The weather has changed, and the air feels electric as there is a gust of wind and a thick cloud scuds across the sky, blotting the sun from view. Goosebumps rise on my bare arms and I hold the baby closer. 'Is anyone there?' Nothing. No flash of white, no movement apart from the glossy, bottle-green leaves of the trees. I scan the woodland again, shifting the baby to my other arm, anxiety leaving a small lead ball in my belly. A crow shouts, a loud, harsh bark and I turn and hurry back to the house, sure I can feel eyes on the back of my neck.

Chapter Five

'I'm not saying there was definitely someone there,' I say irritably, as Rav and I sit in the living room, the television playing some mindless soap opera. For once, he has put his laptop away and the baby lies on Rav's chest, his tiny body rising and falling with Rav's breath.

'You said you saw someone in the trees.' Dark circles ring Rav's eyes and his tone is short.

'I said I saw some*thing*,' I say firmly.

When Rav got home the first thing I did was tell him about the flash of white I saw streaking through the trees. I had spent the afternoon feeling unsettled and when Mina had asked to go outside, I had refused, locking the back door and making her cry. I had tried to tell myself that it was nothing, just someone out for a walk, but there was something sinister about it that left behind a rattling sense of dread. I can't put my finger on whatever it is, but I still feel it now, a pregnant cloud of unease hanging over me.

'It was probably just … a seagull or something.' Rav stifles a yawn, before lowering his hand to cup the baby's head. 'And the wind. They're saying there's going to be a storm tonight.'

'It wasn't a seagull, Rav. It was too big to be a bird. I don't know what it was, but it scared me.' I press my fingers against my temples, where a headache thuds, dull and heavy. I don't know if it's from frustration at Rav or the thick, stormy air.

Rav reaches out awkwardly, careful not to wake the baby and entwines his fingers with mine. 'I just think you're over-reacting a bit, Al. I can take a look out there if you want?'

I sigh. 'No, it's OK. Don't worry. Whatever it was will be long gone by now.' *I hope.* 'Maybe you're right. Maybe it was just my imagination playing tricks on me. I'm sure it's probably nothing.' I'm not, not entirely, but I don't want to talk about it anymore, don't want to keep thinking about it. 'Do you mind if I go up?'

'No, of course not. You go, I'll bring him up when he wakes.'

A loud rumbling yanks me from sleep, my heart crashing in my chest as I wonder what it is that has woken me so abruptly, before realizing it is thunder. The bedroom fills with a flash of bright white as lightning streaks across the sky, and I glance towards the cot where the baby is starting to stir. Rav mumbles next to me, reaching out in his sleep to brush his hand over my hip and I feel horrid for being so snappy and irritable with him earlier. His dark hair is mussed up where he has tossed and turned, and I can see Mina in his sleeping face. The baby lets out a short cry, and I slide from the bed, leaning over the cot to pick him up.

Maybe Rav was *right*, I think, as the baby starts to feed. Maybe it was just a bird, or a small animal, perhaps. Maybe I was seeing things. I am tired, more exhausted than

I remember feeling with Mina. Perhaps it was just the storm making me feel unsettled; don't people say the weather can have a huge effect on emotions? Goosebumps rise on my arms as I think of the way the white flash moved through the trees and I shake the image away, telling myself again that Rav was right, that it is nothing out of the ordinary, nothing sinister, just a bird. My mind wanders back to the keys, the way they were tied to the stone, the feather carefully attached. I don't think it is some form of old keyring, despite what Rav says. There was something about them that feels different, odd. As if sensing the tension that floods through me, the baby unlatches with a tiny sigh and I gently place him back in the cot, laying one hand lightly on his stomach as he fusses for a moment before dropping off to sleep.

'Such a good baby,' I whisper, and my eyes fill inexplicably with tears.

'You OK this morning?' Rav asks over the breakfast table. He gulps from his coffee, slams his cup down. 'I thought I heard you wandering around last night, but Leo was in the cot.'

'Just a bit restless.' I smile, handing Mina some toast and a plastic beaker of orange juice. 'The storm woke me, and I couldn't get back to sleep.' I don't tell him that once I put the baby back in the cot, I stood at the landing window, letting the cold draught there chill me until I could barely feel my fingers, watching over the woods just in case. Just to make certain.

'Are you sure?' He runs his eyes over my face, and I feel

as if I am under a microscope. I don't blink, waiting for him to look away first.

'I'm fine. I'll sleep later while Mina is at school.'

'I'm not going to school,' Mina announces cheerily.

'Yes, you are,' I say, 'how else will you learn all the exciting things you're going to come home and tell me about?'

'Avó said she didn't used to go to school.' Mina's face screws up, her mouth scrunched into a pout, and I glance at Rav and raise my eyebrows.

'That's because Avó had to stay home and feed all the pigs and chickens. Is that what you want?' Rav scoops her up into his arms and throws her over his shoulder, fireman's lift style as she shrieks and giggles. I shoot him a grateful look as he marches her upstairs and feel a pang of love shoot through me. Everyone said we wouldn't last, that I didn't know him when I married him. Which was true to some extent – after all, we had met on a beach by the Indian Ocean, in a place that felt magical. Within three months of being home, I was living in his tiny cramped flat in Ebbsfleet, and we had discovered we were about to have a baby. One hastily arranged marriage later, much to his mother's horror and many of my mother's Gallic shrugs, we were married in the Archbishop's Palace, our union sealed, a true whirlwind romance.

Thirty minutes later, Mina is ready for preschool, and I remember today to make sure she is wearing plimsolls. Rav is at the door as I hustle the baby into the pram, his fingers tapping at the screen of his phone.

'You're late leaving this morning.'

Rav looks up in surprise, although how he couldn't have noticed us all piling into the narrow hallway, I have no idea. He slides his phone quickly into his pocket, something like guilt crawling across his face.

'Rav? Everything OK?'

'Yes, fine. All fine.' He fusses over the pram, leaning in to kiss the baby on the head, almost as though he doesn't want to make eye contact with me.

'Sure? Who was that you were texting?'

'Oh, no one. Just … just Gareth. He has to take Robbie for a college interview, so he'll be in the office late. I have to go.' He reaches behind me for his jacket. Even though the storm has passed and left a shiny, new day, the pavements still glittering with rainwater as the sun creeps its way up a clear, blue sky.

'Oh. OK.' Maybe I was imagining the look that crossed Rav's face as he stuffed his phone away.

'I'll see you later, I won't be late.' I don't respond. He's said that so many times recently and then failed to follow through on it that I don't believe him for a second. I watch him hurry down the path, before turning back to get the baby. My eye catches my reflection in the mirror and I suppress a smile, still feeling that tickle of love for it, spotted glass and all.

'Come on you,' I say to Mina, taking her tiny chubby hand in mine as we walk out of the gate and onto the main road into the village. We haven't got far when ahead of us someone waves, and as we get closer, I see that Tara is waiting on the corner for us, with the baby and her eldest, a boy whose name I can't remember. Mina starts to race ahead to catch up with them and I shove away the exhaustion that seeps into my bones, pushing a little speed into my stride.

'Allie! How are you this morning? You look great.' Tara leans in to kiss me on my cheek and I resist the urge to pull away.

'Really?' Last time I looked in the mirror I wouldn't have said I looked great. Fat, tired, with dark circles around my eyes and if my hair wasn't so blonde, at least an inch of grey roots.

'Really. It suits you, how you've let your hair grow out.' I lift my hand to my head, smoothing down my hair as I wonder how to respond, but she is already talking again. 'How is this little chap? Sorry, I've forgotten his name. Baby brain sticks even after they're born, you know.' Her cheeks flush and realizing I never told her his name, I open my mouth, but the word sticks in my throat for a moment.

'Leo,' Mina shouts. 'His name is Leo, Leo, Leo the Lion.' She twirls on the spot, making her summer skirt whoosh out around her in a circle. Tara turns to start the short walk to the preschool, and I realize that she was waiting so we could all walk together.

'So,' she says as Mina and her boy, James, walk ahead, holding hands. 'You still on for the baby and toddler group? It's on Friday so a nice way to end the week.'

'Mina still has preschool on Friday.'

'That's fine. Just bring the baby. We have coffee and biscuits and complain about how tired we are.' She laughs, seemingly unbothered but there is a hint of a rough edge to it. 'Then usually, Karen and I go back to either her house or mine and we have lunch. A glass of wine, before the babies came but you know, maybe later. After the summer, once I've started weaning.'

Her words create a slight panicky feeling low in my stomach. I quite like the idea of going to a baby group, or meeting some of the other mums, but I still have so much to do at the house. All those boxes in the attic to unpack. The garden to sort out. The thought of it makes me feel anxious and I don't know why. I glance discreetly into her designer pram, where baby Rufus sleeps soundly snuggled under his blue blanket. *The* blue blanket.

'I can't,' I say eventually, trying my best to look regretful. 'Mina finishes at one o'clock and then I'd have to get home to make her some lunch. Thank you for the offer though.'

'No lunch then,' Tara says, insistent. 'You can at least come to the baby group and meet a few of the others. It'll do you good to get out.'

It'll do you good to get out. The same advice I keep hearing from Rav, and Naomi, and even from Rav's mum after she spoke to him a few nights ago. Along with, *sleep when the baby sleeps, get into a routine.* Everyone seems to be forgetting that the baby is only a few weeks old. We haven't had time to get out or get into a routine.

'Everyone is super nice,' Tara is saying, 'and I've picked up loads of tips from the other mums about how to get the baby sleeping longer at night, weaning tips, things like that.' She peers at me closely, concern now working its way across her features.

'Yes, OK,' I say eventually. 'OK. That would be nice.' The boxes, the unpacking, the garden. It can all wait.

Later, in the afternoon sunshine, I play with Mina on the lawn as the baby snoozes on a blanket in the shade, always keeping one eye on her in case she heads towards the pond.

'Mummy, look.' Mina toddles towards me, something pinched between her fingers. 'A jewel.'

I peer closely at her fingers, holding my hand out for whatever it is she has found. She drops it into my outstretched hand – a small misshapen pearl, its creamy sheen masked with smudges of dirt. 'Where did you find this?'

'Over there.' She points towards the edge of the woods, where shadow branches reach their bony fingers across the lawn.

Strange. I roll the gem between my finger and thumb, fancying I can feel the heat of it against my skin. This isn't the first one found in the house. I think back to the day we got the keys, Mina seeming so much smaller than she is now, the baby a solid five-month bump in my belly.

Rav swings the keys from one finger before inserting it into the lock and pushing the oak door open, the hinges creaking from lack of use. The air in the hallway is damp and musty and I cough as dust hits the back of my throat. Leaving damp footprints on the brick-red tiles from the rain outside, I follow Rav into the kitchen where he fiddles with the dials on the ancient boiler in an attempt to bring some heat into the house. There is the sound of a gas flame igniting and Rav lets out a whoop.

'Come on, let's explore our new place.' Rav's giddiness is infectious as he pulls me towards the staircase, and I am glad we have left Mina with Avó. Ascending the stairs, I try not to grimace as I notice the swathes of dark cobwebs that hang from the ceiling.

'It's like a haunted mansion in here,' I say, cringing at the thought of having to deal with them. 'You're going to have to sweep those down; I wasn't expecting to be five months pregnant when we moved in.' We had taken the test a week after having our offer accepted on the house, and I had had to break both bits of news to Naomi in one go, that we were leaving, and that we were having another baby.

'It's just a bit of dirt,' Rav says. 'It's all structurally sound.' He bangs a fist against the wall, coughing as a white shower of plaster dust bursts from the wall.

'Let's have a look at the bathroom,' I say, 'see if it's as bad as I remember.' I push open the door, watching Rav's reflection in the dark spotted mirror ahead of me. A brief flicker of doubt brushes over his features before he rearranges his face into an enthusiastic smile.

'This bathroom is going to be amazing,' he says, running his hand over the lip of the claw-footed bathtub before surreptitiously wiping it on his jeans. I take in the mould-spotted walls, the rust that stains the bottom of the tub, the black ring that sits in the toilet bowl.

'Really?'

'Really. I promise.' Rav wraps me in his arms and I lean contentedly against him as the baby swoops and swirls in my stomach. 'I'll clean up that tub, re-enamel it if we have to, and that mould will scrub right off. In fact, I'll do that tonight, before you and Mina sleep your first night here.'

'So, we haven't made a huge mistake?' I grin into his chest, knowing that despite the mould, the cold air that doesn't seem to be warming up despite Rav lighting the boiler, and the huge cobwebs, Rav is exactly where he needs to be.

'Absolutely not.' He kisses the top of my head and releases me, heading into the bedroom that will be Mina's. I wait for a moment, smiling into the stained mirror until the electric bulb overhead flickers, making me jump.

'Just dodgy old electrics,' I laugh under my breath, one hand pressed to my chest. I turn to leave, to follow Rav into Mina's room when I spot it, a glint of light reflecting back from the cream shell. A pearl. A single pearl, lying just to one side of the bathtub, as if spilled from a broken necklace. I stop to pick it up, feeling my back give a twinge, and hold it up to the bare bulb. It's real, I can tell by the way its shape is imperfect, an almost round circle of off-white. I squeeze it between my fingers, wondering briefly where it came from before I tuck it into the pocket of my jeans. Maybe it'll bring us luck.

I think of that other pearl now, as I wrap my fingers around this new one. It has to be a new one, the original pearl is tucked into the jewellery box my mother gave me for my sixteenth birthday. *How strange.* A vision pops into my head of a woman, dressed in dark clothing, pearls hidden against her skin, standing in the doorway to the cottage. It's so real, my eyes flick towards the doorway, but it's empty. Of course it is. *Ridiculous.* The sun dips behind a cloud, blocking the warm rays and making the bare skin on my forearms prickle. Shaking my head, I close my fist over the pearl, and just as I did with the first one, I tuck it into my pocket.

'Daddy!' Mina shouts, and I look up to see Rav striding across the lawn, his arms open for her to jump into. He scoops her up and brings her over to where I sit, leaning down to kiss me. He smells like sweat and the train, and I think for a moment as his mouth leaves mine, maybe a little like alcohol.

'Sorry I'm a bit later than I planned. Aren't you getting cold out here?'

I hadn't realized that the sun has started to disappear behind the trees, the shadows from the branches long and stretched across the lawn. I scoop up the baby, his tiny hands cold after lying in the shade and pull him close to warm him up. *Terrible mother.* The words flash neon in my mind and I blink for a moment, feeling a little unsteady on my feet.

'Allie? Are you all right?' Rav's hand is warm on my arm.

'Yes. Sorry, just got up a bit quick.'

'Let's get you lot inside. I'll give Mina her bath, shall I?'

I follow Rav into the house, eager to get out of the chill of the shade cast by the trees. How did I not realize the sun had gone down? What if the baby gets a cold? Pneumonia? A knot of anxiety builds in my chest as I picture him still and blue, his breath rasping in his chest, and I have to force it down, smiling at Rav as he climbs the stairs with Mina. A few moments later I hear the creak of the old bathroom tap and water starts to thunder into the chipped enamel bath.

The baby fusses and I lay him in his Moses basket, tucking

him in tightly even though he has warmed up now, making small shushing noises in the hopes that he will fall back to sleep, just for a few moments so I can make Mina some dinner. His eyes grow heavy, and I lay my hand gently on his tiny chest, about to creep away when I hear it. A scratching noise. Cocking my head on one side I strain my ears, trying to figure out where it is coming from, but there is only silence. *Maybe I imagined it?* I take a small backwards step away from the baby, ready to turn towards the kitchen when I hear it again, a faint *scratch scratch scratch* like a pencil on a board. The baby's eyes fly open and I think, no, I didn't imagine it. The baby heard it too. My legs feel wobbly as I step back towards the Moses basket, holding my breath. *Scratch, scratch, scratch.* It's coming from the chimney. Without waiting to hear if the noise comes again, I scoop up the baby and hurry up the stairs to Rav.

Chapter Six

'And how are you sleeping?' The health visitor at the baby clinic doesn't look at me as she speaks, concentrating on laying the baby gently into the large weighing scale on the table in front of her.

'Fine,' I say, as a yawn pulls at the back of my throat. The baby pumps his fist as the health visitor logs his weight and then tells me I can pick him up.

'Lovely healthy boy,' she says, finally looking at me with a grin. 'You didn't need to bring him in just yet though. Has your midwife discharged you?'

I know I didn't have to bring him in, and part of me didn't want to; the thought of the doctor's waiting room filled with sick and vulnerable people breathing all over my baby was not appealing, but I needed some fresh air. I heard the scratching again last night, after the baby had fed at three o'clock, the sound even more eerie in the thick darkness, and this morning, once Rav had left the house. 'Yes, she's passed us over to the health visitor,' I say as breezily as I can, the jollity sounding forced to my ears. 'She was happy with everything … she said it was all fine.'

'I'm sure she did.' The health visitor pushes her glasses back on the top of her head and rubs her hand over the baby's soft, downy hair. 'He's lovely. No concerns from me at all. But how are you feeling?'

'I'm fine. Busy. We've not long moved into our house, so I've been trying to get on top of that, but Mina is at nursery now so that helps.' I quickly dress the baby in a fresh nappy. 'Tired, obviously. But apart from that I'm good.'

'Try not to overdo it,' the health visitor says, scribbling in the baby's red record book and handing it back to me with a smile.

'Of course not,' I say forcing a matching smile onto my own face. I move over to the other table and start tucking the baby back into his sleepsuit, as the health visitor moves on to the next tired, weary mum. As I lay the baby back into the pram, tucking a blanket over him despite the sunshine outside, a sound rips through the air that makes me freeze in my tracks. A *scratch* that makes my blood run cold. I hang over the pram, as if making sure the baby is comfortable, inhaling deeply before I muster the courage to turn around, to see where the noise is coming from.

It's a zipper. I exhale, feeling sweat start to prickle under my arms, a hysterical bubble of laughter growing in my throat. It's the zipper on a huge green changing bag, the woman bent over it rummaging for something. As she straightens up, I realize it is Karen, the other woman from the preschool.

'Gosh, sorry,' she says, pushing her hair out of her eyes. 'I didn't mean to make you jump. This bloody zip sounds like a plane taking off. You're Mina's mum, aren't you? Tara said you might be joining us at the baby group on Friday?'

'Yes. I hope I'll be able to make it,' I say non-committally, relief making me feel oddly shaky. I pick up my own changing bag and drape it across the handles of the pram. My feet take an involuntary step towards the door. 'Maybe, I'll have to see how …' I gesture vaguely towards the baby and rush towards the automatic doors of the doctor's surgery, keen to be outside. Once out on the pavement, I gulp in great, deep breaths of hot, stale air, thick with the scent of the fresh tarmac they are laying across the street before I start to laugh. *Idiot. Fancy jumping at the sound of a zipper.*

Naomi brings over a gypsy tart and a packet of my favourite posh teabags later in the afternoon and I am pleased to see her, grateful to her for making time to visit. She moves into the kitchen, switching on the kettle and slicing two big sections of tart for the both of us as if it's she who lives here, not me. An image rises in my mind of a cuckoo, thrusting its way into a nest, before I blink and it is gone, and there is only Naomi, wiping her hands on a tea towel before she places a mug of tea and a plate in front of me. There's something comforting about it – maternal almost – and pity makes the gypsy tart taste stale in my mouth. Naomi would have made a wonderful mother.

'So, tell me again what you saw?' The baby wails as Naomi settles in the chair across from me, not bothering to avert her gaze as I unsnap my top and place the baby at my breast. The wailing stops abruptly and I feel my shoulders lower, tension leaving my body.

'I didn't see anything really. Nothing concrete.' I feel silly, Rav's reaction making me half convinced that there wasn't anything out there other than a seagull or something equally as benign. 'Something white. That's all. I thought it looked like a person, rushing through the trees, but Rav says that's ridiculous. And I suppose it is. I mean, in the months we've lived here I've never seen anyone in those woods.'

Naomi takes a bite of her tart, chewing slowly and I get the impression she is mulling over my words before she speaks. 'Well,' she says eventually, 'Rav does have a point. You haven't seen a single person in those woods since you got here. But then, it's not really been the weather for outings in the woods 'til now, has it? I mean, winter was so horrifically wet, and there was all the flooding, and it's only really been the last few weeks that things have dried out enough for anyone to want to walk in the woods.'

'I suppose.'

'Look, Al, even if there was someone in the woods – which there might have been, it's possible – it doesn't mean anything. You guys knew when you bought the house that potentially you would have ramblers and dog walkers cross-ing the bottom of your garden.'

'Yes, I know. I guess I just thought because there *hadn't* been anyone, that there *wouldn't* be anyone.'

'It's natural for you to freak out a little bit. I mean, you're at home on your own with a tiny baby, with no neighbours close by …' Naomi breaks off, hastily grasping at her mug and taking a swallow of tea, as if she realizes that perhaps she isn't helping. 'But honestly, Al? I think Rav is right. It's nothing for you to worry about.'

I nod as if in agreement, but I don't mention the fact that I was sure the figure was standing watching me, before turning and rushing through the trees as soon as whoever it was realized that I had noticed them. 'It just felt a bit weird, that's all. Almost like it was moving *too* quickly.' *Scuttling.* The word pings into my mind and I stuff another bite of tart into my mouth.

'Maybe it was The Colonel or the Pluckley Witch.' She rolls her eyes and waggles her fingers at me, making a 'woooo' sound, falling silent when I don't laugh. 'You know the stories, Al: the Colonel who hung himself from a tree and still wanders the village at night, the white lady who haunts the church, the highwayman who died in a sword fight at Fright's Corner and re-enacts it – the village is full of them. It's all a load of rubbish. I'm sure if The Colonel really did hang himself in the woods, he hasn't stuck around to terrorize the people of Pluckley.'

'I thought I heard scratching, coming from the chimney,' I say with a forced laugh, trying not to let my apprehension show as Naomi places her mug back down and eyes me carefully.

'Scratching?'

The baby unlatches with a pop and an audible sigh, and I hand him to Naomi while I sort out my top. 'Like a scratching noise coming from the chimney. As if something is up there.' Something *insistent*, is the word that comes to mind when I think of the repetitive scritching sound. 'I know it's probably nothing, but it shook me a little, coming so soon after I saw something in the trees.'

'It's probably a bird.' Naomi leans down and sniffs the baby's head. 'God, Allie, he smells so lovely. I don't know how you're not sniffing him all day long.'

I do laugh at this, and I feel another pang of loss and longing for Naomi, wishing more than anything that she and Jason could have conceived. Wishing that she could be sitting opposite me now bouncing her own baby on her knee before going home to her husband, instead of back to her tiny, cramped flat with a ready meal for one.

'Sorry.' She smiles, but it's tinged with sadness as she traces one finger over the baby's soft, milky cheek. 'It probably was just a bird. We had a fireplace when I was a kid, and my dad was forever having to shove things up or down the chimney to get rid of the birds that fell down it. Your pot on the top might be damaged and that's how it got in.'

'Of course.' Relief is swift and welcome. I think of the movement in the air when I was in the attic. 'It must be a bird – I think there might be one trapped in the attic; I thought I heard it when I was up there getting the mirror.' I did see something in the trees, but the more I talk about it, the more I am sure I am just trying to convince myself that it wasn't a person.

'Well, I'm not surprised,' Naomi says. 'It doesn't help that there's a full moon tonight. Flower Moon, believe it or not. How appropriate for us. That's probably got your emotions all over the place as well.'

'Flower Moon?'

'That's what the May full moon is called … you didn't know?'

I had no idea that full moons had names. Blue moon, yes, I had heard of that but not any other. 'No, I had no idea. It is very apt for us.' Thinking of the florist, the scent of the flowers, the moist air that keeps the plants damp and makes my hair frizz, I feel a twist in my stomach. 'How on earth do you know this stuff, Naomi?'

She shrugs. 'I store shit information that is rarely, if ever, needed, but I can't remember what I went to the shops for. Maybe I should go on a gameshow or something, try and make use of it.'

'Remember that dreadful pub quiz we did, at that holiday park in Devon?' I say, a bubble of laughter tickling the back of my throat. 'I'll never forget your face when that guy accused you of cheating.'

'Oh my God, I'd forgotten that. It wasn't my fault his quiz was absolutely shit. Mind you, the Robbie Williams tribute act that night was worse.' Naomi laughs, and the baby jolts in her arms, his face crumpling.

I feel my shoulders rise up towards my ears, tension creeping back in as I will Naomi to stay quiet, for the baby to sleep for just a little while longer. Naomi rocks him gently and he seems to settle again.

'Are you busy at work?' Talking of the Flower Moon, thinking of the shop makes me want to catch up on everything. 'I miss it, you know.' The summer months are my favourite, the busiest time of year. I wake up early for the markets and stay in the shop long after others have all gone home, working my way through bridal bouquets, buttonholes, funeral arrangements, declarations of love all tied up in ribbon and ferns.

'So busy, you wouldn't believe it.' Naomi rolls her eyes, 'I'd much rather be at home with a baby.' Her face clouds over and she shifts the baby up onto her shoulder, resting her cheek against his tiny head. 'Enjoy this time at home with him. You'll be back in the shop before you know it.'

There is something sharp in her tone, her words stinging a little and I want to tell her that I *am* enjoying it – trying to anyway – but that she doesn't understand how becoming a mother strips away a part of your identity. I can never say those words to her. Instead, I change the subject slightly. 'Are you sure you can spare the time to come and visit me? Don't forget I know how rushed off our feet we are at this time of year, so if you're too busy, don't feel you have to come over.' Even as I say the words, I don't mean it. I've loved having some adult company and being with Naomi reminds me of the old me, the pre-baby me.

Naomi looks down, her finger dabbing at crumbs from the tart on the table. 'It's fine. We've … they've taken someone else on to help out while you're off.'

'Oh.' I sit back in my chair, the spindles on the back digging into my spine. 'Oh, well of course they would. They can't be a man down during the summer, it's not practical.' There is a sharp twist in my chest at the idea of someone else opening up, someone else drinking tea out of my mug, or using my pliers, and I shake it away, feeling silly.

'Listen' – Naomi leans forward, her cheeks flushing, and I wince waiting for the baby to stir – 'why don't I take Mina out for a bit this afternoon? I could take her to the park, and you could sleep for a bit while Leo naps. I can put him in his Moses basket now, and I'll take Mina for an ice cream. No offence, Al, but you look like shit. You must be exhausted. I know all this stuff about someone in the woods has upset you.'

'Naomi …' I am not offended by her words; I probably do look like shit. 'What about work? You just said you're really busy.'

'I … I can take the afternoon off. It's fine. You need me more than they do.'

'Well, I suppose I could get the rest of those boxes down …' Before I can finish my answer, the doorbell rings and I get to my feet, rushing along the hall to answer it before whoever it is rings again and wakes the baby.

'Avó!' I am surprised to see Rav's mum on the doorstep. 'I wasn't expecting you …'

'I did tell Rav I would come and see you today.' She gives a heavy sigh as her tiny frame pushes past me into the hall. 'I have to see my grandchildren. I've hardly seen the baby since he was born! Ravi says you're too tired. But it's fine. I will take the bus all the way over here to see you, if Ravi won't bring you to me.'

I bite back my frustration and let her brush past me into the kitchen, without saying a word. We moved here partly to be closer to Avó, but it still isn't close enough for her – she is only a short bus journey away, a walkable distance for Rav and me, but she would only be truly happy if we were living in her spare room, or failing that, in the house next door. She already has the baby in her arms by the time I appear in the kitchen doorway. I call to Mina, who rushes downstairs and throws her arms around her grandmother's legs.

'Allie, you do look tired. Ravi was right. This won't do. You need to sleep when the baby sleeps.' Avó frowns at me as she reaches down to stroke Mina's head and I feel the weight of her judgement as if it were a ton of bricks.

'I was just telling her the same thing, Mrs Harper.' Naomi gets to her feet, snatching up her bag from beneath the table. 'Allie, shall I take Mina to the park, get her an ice cream and then ...' she casts a quick glance towards Rav's mother, 'you could get some sleep while we're gone?'

Avó's face is already creasing into a frown, her mouth open to say something, and I speak hastily. 'Oh no, Naomi, honestly it's fine. We're fine. But thank you for coming over, it was good to see you.'

'OK. If you're sure?' Naomi raises her eyebrows and I nod.

'Absolutely sure. Mina, say goodbye to Naomi.'

I see her to the door, and by the time I get back Avó is already tucking the baby into a knitted cardigan that she has magicked from somewhere, and Mina is sitting on the kitchen floor, pushing her trainers onto the wrong feet.

'Did I miss something?' I say with a tired laugh. 'What are you doing?'

'Your friend Naomi offered Mina an ice cream, so I am taking Mina for an ice cream,' Rav's mother says briskly. 'I am taking the baby too, so you go upstairs now and go to bed.' She peers closely at me, her face only inches from mine. I can feel her breath on my cheek, smell the scent of the Indian sweets she eats. 'Rav is right, you are very, very tired.'

And she is right, too. I am far too tired to argue.

Chapter Seven

The house is quiet once Avó has bustled out with the children, and I try not to let her forceful interference grate too much, telling myself she's only trying to help. I close the door behind them, smiling and waving, and head back towards the kitchen. Passing the mirror, I pause, eyeing my reflection closely. Naomi is right, I *do* look tired. I peer closely, tugging at the skin beneath my eyes, a flicker in the mirror drawing my gaze away from myself to the hall behind me. *Movement.* I thought for a moment there was movement in the mirror, to one side of my own reflection, but when I turn to check, the area behind me is empty and silent. *Of course, it is,* I think. *You're alone in the house. There's no one else here.* My thoughts return to Naomi's comments about The Colonel and the Pluckley Witch. It's just superstitious nonsense but it still makes my skin prickle to think about it. *If I go outside now,* I reason, *the fresh air will make sure I sleep tonight.*

The sun is still warm as I venture out onto the patio, heading towards the border filled with herbs. I run my fingers through the trailing stems of thyme, rub my fingertips together on a sage leaf before bringing them to my nose, inhaling the fresh, herby fragrance. The white starburst buds of jasmine are partially closed, ready to bloom as the sun goes down and fill the garden with its heady scent. I get on to my knees, not bothered about the dirt and grass that will stain my jeans and start to push through the mass of tangled plants that meld together. I've spotted the thyme and sage, and as I part and separate them, I find woody stems of rosemary at the back of the border, the last remnants of dried purple flowers still clinging on desperately. I suppress a smile at the scent of rosemary, as I remember my mother cooking roast lamb on a Sunday, the smell filling the kitchen and creeping up the stairs to where I sat in my bedroom, eventually lured down by the scent, and the banging and crashing coming from the kitchen. I would sit on the kitchen counter as she cooked, a glass of red wine to hand. Sitting back on my haunches I feel a wave of longing for my mum, imagining her in her tiny flat in Paris, cigarette in one hand, the other crumbling a croissant into nothing as she flicks through the paper. It wasn't all bad growing up with her, and now, at a time when I wish I could see her every day, I feel her absence keenly. We were close when I was young, being just the two of us, but she never really approved of Rav and once Rav and I were married our relationship stretched thinner and thinner as I struggled with her disapproval, until we reached a point of barely speaking at all. She hadn't been happy about me leaving her behind to go travelling in the first place, and when I came home with Rav in tow

I should have known she wouldn't have been ecstatic about it. It had started the moment I brought him home to meet her – I'd been nervous, especially anxious as I already felt so strongly about Rav. It had been just me and my mum for such a long time, that it was important that she liked him, that she accepted him. But the moment he walked in and I had introduced him to her, hiding my shaking hands behind my back, I could tell by the way she narrowed her eyes that she didn't like him. Rav, to his credit, battled his way through stilted small talk with her, whispering to me as he kissed me goodbye at the door that he thought he might have frostbite. I had laughed, a soft laugh that died on my lips as I closed the door and turned to see her watching us. It had only got worse. The more serious Rav and I got, the tighter my mother tugged on her maternal cord, until I felt suffocated, breathless with the weight of her neediness. On our wedding day, she had been rude to Avó, and barely spoke to Rav when he greeted her, turning her face away when he bent to kiss her cheek. She had told me at our wedding dinner that she was only concerned that Avó would never accept me, that none of Rav's family would, that we were from two different worlds, but I knew it was more about the fact that she felt I was leaving her. I had finished my wedding day crying in a crappy Portaloo, eventually coming out to find my mother had left without saying goodbye. After that, I had tried to keep our relationship going, my heart breaking at the way she shut me out, but it was almost as if she were punishing me for marrying Rav. When she wouldn't visit when Rav was home, refused invitations to birthdays and Christmas, and rarely returned my calls, it made things almost too difficult to bear.

Now, I feel an intense longing to hear her voice, and I pull out my mobile and scroll until I find her name, stabbing at the button to connect. It rings, the long, single tone of the international call, and I hold my breath, waiting. It clicks to voicemail, my mother's voice flying down the line speaking rapid French that I still understand, even though I haven't spoken it for so long, and then the beep of the message.

'Mum. It's me, Allie.' I pause, not sure what to say. 'I just wanted to say … I miss you. And I wish you were here.' My throat thickens and I have to swallow. 'Things are … I just wish you were here, that's all. I could do with your help.' I hang up before the tears can leach into my voice.

My trawl through the border reveals chamomile, mint and a rose bush, tucked away into the corner. I snip off the dead parts, clearing away the weeds that surround it and hope that I've done enough to encourage new growth before the summer is out. Picturing a vase of fresh roses on the kitchen windowsill, or a tiny jar of blousy peonies in the spare bedroom, brings a smile to my face as I snip, and prune, and weed, my head feeling clearer for the first time in what feels like weeks. I should have let Naomi take the children out before when she offered. Much as I love being a mother, being alone in the garden without the worry of them I feel as though a fog has lifted. Being among the plants reminds me of why I chose to do the job that I do, and I feel almost like the pre-children Allie again. Straightening up, I pull the weeds together into a pile, glancing along the border as I do so. I have cleared quite a large section, but the end that is in shadow, towards the woods, is still overgrown and rambling, and there is still the matter of the pond to be dealt with. I throw the weeds into a pile in the opposite corner of the garden and step towards the shaded area. A cool breeze washes over my bare arms as I lean down, the shadow from the trees casting a cold shawl across my shoulders. Things are less organized this end, as though whoever planted it had run out of patience, had hastily stuffed the plants into the ground without care and attention. I see green fronds of coriander, emitting a faint washing-up liquid smell when I stroke the leaves, interspersed with previous years' dry stems, brown seed pods still attached. Glossy, smooth basil leaves evoke memories of fresh pizza, Rav and I sitting in our favourite Italian restaurant, sipping red wine for him, Coke for me, Mina growing in my belly. I feel a buzz of excitement, keen to tell Rav the treasures I've discovered growing in the garden, when I catch sight of a plant that makes my stomach drop away a little.

The purple flowers of wolfsbane stand out against the wild, tumbling green of *vinca major*, a plant I haven't seen for a long time. Stepping onto the edge of the border, I carefully peer into the wild plants, the outline of a white oleander bush taking shape at the edge of where the sunlight meets the shade, its white flowers standing out in stark contrast to the vibrant purple of the *digitalis* that grows alongside it. An uneasy feeling snakes its way along my spine, as I glance back towards the end of the border closest to the house, the innocent herbs planted there taking on a more sinister feel as I realize what has been planted at the opposite end where I now stand. All of these plants, in this chilly, shadowy end of the bed are poisonous, all capable of causing serious illness from stomach pain to dangerously low blood pressure if ingested, some of them too dangerous to even touch. I step back, rubbing my hands over my arms, realizing as I do so that I stand in the exact same spot as I did when I made this motion before. When Rav brought me to see the house. Only this time, I don't feel that tingle of excitement for what the future may hold. Instead an unsettling feeling bubbles low in my stomach. I scrub my hands over my now baggy maternity jeans, even though I didn't touch any of the poisonous plants, telling myself it's just a border, it's nothing unusual, nothing special. Glancing back towards the house I strain my eyes for any sign of movement, in the hope that Avó is back with the children, but there is nothing. The house is still and silent, the air thick and heavy as if waiting for something. I feel dizzy for a moment, the image of my own feet on the stairs, the blue blanket draped at the end of the bed from my vision swirling in front of my eyes.

'Ridiculous.' I mutter the word aloud, swiping my hand across my sweaty forehead. 'You're being ridiculous.' There is a small thud as I collide with something behind me, and I turn to see the peeling, slippery bark of a birch tree. I have backed so far up from the border that I am on the very edge of the woods. The sun doesn't reach here, the trees casting long shadows, and as I turn and peer into the woods, the branches of the trees seem to connect overhead, turning the world a dim, greenish dark. I step forward, the last thick blades of grass bouncing beneath my feet as I step into the dark, onto the bed of dry leaves and twigs that have lain here for summer after summer, following their winter deaths.

'There's no one here,' I whisper under my breath, ignoring the chill that has followed me in. Tiny spots of sunlight are all that can fight their way through the thick boughs above me, and the sweat that trickled down my spine as I crouched over the border makes my T-shirt cling to my back like a cold, sticky hand. I let out a laugh, a rush of breath that loosens the tightness in my chest. 'There's no one here. It's just a wood, nothing else.' I let myself step further in, running my hand over the gnarled bark of an oak tree, spotting the bent, crumpled stems of bluebells that would have just finished blooming. Now I have been brave enough to set foot inside the border of trees that mark the start of the wood I feel silly, the cold, sinister sensation fading to leave me feeling almost drained. There is nothing to be afraid of, no flash of white or disturbed earth. I step further in, with one quick glance back towards the house, enjoying the relief that comes from the cool, earthy air on my face after the heat of the sun in the garden. A bird, a crow or magpie maybe, caws somewhere deep in the trees and I suppress a shiver, laughing at myself, before something catches my eye and the laugh dies in my throat.

A flash of white. I blink, my tongue sliding out to lick at my suddenly dry lips, before I see it again, a flash of white moving at speed through the trees away from me. As if whoever it is was watching me and fled before I could realize.

'Hey!' Without thinking, I start to run towards the white, a shambling slow run, feeling hefty and unfit as I stumble over twigs on the uneven path, but it's no use – I can't keep up and the flash of white disappears from view. Stopping, I bend at the waist trying to suck in enough oxygen to soothe my burning lungs, rasping and gulping. Tears spring to my eyes and I swallow hard as I straighten up, trying not to be sick. My stomach muscles hurt, my legs hurt – everything hurts – and I place one hand on my chest, achingly aware that the baby will need to feed soon. I wait for a few minutes, despite my legs wanting to turn back towards the house, to the sunshine and hopefully Avó and the children wondering where I am, but I force myself to wait, to make sure that I am entirely alone before I start to walk back. I am almost at the end of the trees, my eyes fixed on the house ahead when I stumble over a partially buried tree root, my hands flying out to brace my fall.

'Shit,' I hiss under my breath, brushing the debris from my palms, sure that beneath the denim of my jeans my knee is skinned. I look up, scanning the woods for any sign of movement, suddenly sure that I will see her, the woman I visualized before standing in the doorway of the cottage. *Don't be ridiculous, Allie.* There is a growing sense of foreboding and the air seems to thicken around me, making it difficult to draw breath. There is no sign of movement, no flash of white, but as my gaze comes to rest back on the tree stump, I see the patch of disturbed leaves, as if someone has stood there recently.

Someone was here. I wasn't imagining it before, and I definitely didn't imagine it today. They were stood where I am now, a clear line of sight to the house, and to the patch of bent blades of grass where I was kneeling just a short while ago. I turn on the spot, trying to narrow down the path that whoever it was might have taken through the trees to stand here. A flattened shrub to the right, along with a pile of leaves that look as though someone has scuffed through them lures me in and I walk closer, expecting to see further evidence that someone has walked through here, loitered here, something concrete that I can show Rav when I tell him that I wasn't imagining things. Because I wasn't imagining things … was I?

It's too late for the children. I can feel it. Goosebumps ripple along my arms, tugging the hairs on my skin to attention as the icy breeze brushes past me, laying cold clammy hands on the bare skin of my feet. I think if I breathe out, I will see my breath in front of me in plumes of smoky grey, swirling ghostly clouds to watch over me as I do the unthinkable. My bare feet are numb as I take another step along the staircase, sliding my hand along the pitted, rough plaster of the walls. Glancing down I see the ragged edges of my shirt, greying and pilled, and I pause to pull the sleeves further down over my hands, trying to stop the chill that embraces my skin. The fabric is too thin, too worn. I'm so cold. I feel as if I have forgotten what it is to feel the heat of the sun on my body. I let myself remember, just for a second, the feel of warm sun on my face, the sweat collecting at the base of my neck as it beats down overhead, before shaking it away. I have a job to do. I can see into the room at the top of the stairs, the moonlight that puddles on the landing casting an eerie silver glow. I can see the slight hump in the bed, the blanket that drapes over the foot, the fronds of her dark hair that spill across the pillow. The blue knit of the wool, the fraying-edge ribbon picked out by the thin light that illuminates the room, trickling in from the open landing.

I stop, a rabbit on red alert, my ears pricking. Is there someone else here? I thought I was alone; I need to be alone in order to do this. My muscles ache as I hold my position, listening, but there is only silence. I strain my ears, sure that there should be some noise, someone else in the house, convinced I heard a door somewhere, the creak of a hinge, but nothing. Just the faint breaths coming from the room ahead of me. I know, without really knowing, that it is just them and me in the house, and no one is going to disturb me. No one is going to stop me, not if I act fast.

I trail my fingers over the smooth wood of the bannister, the wood warm beneath my cold fingers, almost as if it's still alive, the air around me so icy cold. The feel of the wood under my fingertips feels familiar, an action I have carried out a hundred times a day. I feel as if I should know this place inside out, but it is strange, unnerving, as if I have walked through the looking glass and I half wish I hadn't come here. I don't recognize the shadows on the wall of the bedroom in front of me as I reach the threshold, my hand pushing the door all the way open, even as they rearrange themselves to form some sort of picture on the otherwise bland walls.

The smell in the air catches at the back of my throat, and I raise my hand, covered with the sleeve of my shirt, to my nose, the thin cotton doing a poor job of blocking it out. It is thick, laying heavy in the air, like a layer of oil on water. My temples thud, sharp pain pulsing through my head and my stomach does a long, low swoop, my mouth filling with saliva. I struggle to keep focus on my *thoughts, on what I am about to do. Fog descends and I fumble wildly for the doorframe to steady myself. I'm not sure what I am about to do, but I know it has to be done. That this is the only solution. The baby shifts and mutters, his tiny fists punching the air, and I close my eyes.*

Chapter Eight

Rav doesn't come home until long after the children are asleep and I am in bed. I mumble at him as the mattress dips with his weight, waiting for him to ask how my day was, but he doesn't. He slides into bed, landing a kiss on my hair before he rolls over without a word. Inhaling, I open my mouth to speak, to tell him about what I saw in the woods, but before I can say anything his breath rasps in a light snore and I close my mouth again. With the faint thud of a headache starting behind my eyes, I will sleep to pull me under, before waking two hours later with Leo's cries, my nerve endings prickling with the remnants of the dream. *The same dream.* I shiver as I hold the baby close, Rav still snoring beside me. I can see myself, my feet on the stairs, knowing that the children are asleep above me, knowing that once I reach that room something is going to happen, something awful. *But it's not me*, I think, letting my forehead wrinkle in a frown, that nagging feeling still in the pit of my stomach. *Whoever it is, it's not me.*

Rav is gone when I wake in the morning, the headache still there, pulsing at my temples as the baby begins to murmur in his crib. I didn't think I would sleep again after the dream, but I did, deeply and thankfully dreamlessly. Now, I feel groggy and disappointed that Rav didn't wake me before he left. I wanted to tell him about what I saw in the woods. My eyes go to the dresser, combing the piles of junk that have accumulated on the top for the feather and keys, my palm remembering the weight of the stone when the baby shouts, a sharp, angry yell to remind me that he is the priority, not a figure in the woods, not junk found under the floorboards.

The morning is another bright and sunny one, the sun warm on my shoulders as I walk Mina to nursery. I plan to come back and head into the garden, determined not to let the figure in the trees put me off what needs to be done there. The baby can lie on a blanket in the shade, and I will rid the borders of the weeds, and maybe even mow the lawn when the baby goes upstairs for a nap. I have shaken off the uneasiness that I woke up with, driven away by the cloudless blue sky and brilliant sunshine. My plans change though, when I arrive at the nursery and realize it is Friday – and that I had said I would go to the baby group with Tara and Karen. Tara hasn't forgotten, and when I reach the door, waving madly at Mina who ignores me, she smiles.

'I'm glad you agreed to come, it's nice to have a new mum in the group,' Tara says as we walk across the car park. 'Karen has gone on ahead to make sure the tea urn is on and we have biscuits in.' She goes on to tell me that she started the baby group herself, when her eldest was born as there wasn't one around here. I nod politely, telling myself that this is what I wanted – I wanted adult company during the day. It's either this or back to the cottage and the figure in the woods.

The small room to the side of the church is filled with mothers and babies, ranging from newborn up to around toddler age. Small plastic toys litter the floor, along with baby mats, baby gyms and a couple of play pens, both occupied with chubby older babies.

I take my thin cardigan off, sweating in the heat of the small room, the chatter around me louder than I was expecting, reminiscent of a school hall at lunchtime. I scoop the baby out of the pram and carry him across to where Karen has saved us seats.

'I put the baby mat down for the babies,' Tara says pointedly, as she stands in front of me, clutching two mugs of tea. I glance down, noticing a tiny patch of dried sick on the corner of the mat, and hold the baby a little closer.

'I think he'll cry if I put him down,' I say, and Tara shrugs, passing the mug that I assumed was for me to a woman I don't recognize. Tara takes her own seat and then starts introducing me to the other women, as I frantically try to remember names, quite unsuccessfully.

'And this is Miranda.' Tara gestures to the woman she handed the mug to. Miranda is slightly older, her hair greying at the temples although she can barely be forty, the bottom half of it tinted a faded greeny-blue. She wears a patchwork-style dress and a pair of battered Doc Martens, the kind of uniform I wore as a teenager. I feel a moment of kinship with her, recognizing in her an inkling of the same lost feeling I am experiencing. I give her a small smile and she looks down at the mug in her hand, before raising it to her lips, not returning my smile.

I don't say much, as the women chatter as if they haven't seen each other for months, rather than a few days. There are comparisons between babies at every stage – which ones are weaning, which are sleeping through the night (the majority of them, by the sounds of it), which can sit up, roll over, crawl. I lower my face to the baby's, breathing in his soft, milky smell and thank my lucky stars he's not old enough to be judged on any of this yet.

'I've seen you somewhere before, haven't I?' Miranda's breath smells like coffee as she leans forward to speak to me in an urgent whisper, as if she doesn't want to be overheard.

'Maybe?' I say, sure I don't know her. 'I work … well, I'm on maternity leave, but I work at The Daisy Chain. I'm a florist.'

'Yes.' She eyes me closely, before her gaze flickers down to the baby. 'Maybe that's where I've seen you. Have you been in the village long?'

'Allie only moved here a few months ago,' Tara butts in, 'with her husband and daughter.' She has answered before I can even open my mouth to speak. She comes and sits next to me, leaning against my shoulder chummily and I realize Tara is almost staking her claim as my friend. 'How is Rav?'

'Oh, fine. Working. Busy, you know.'

'Where do you live in the village, Allie?' another woman asks, a polar opposite to Miranda. This woman is like

Tara, well groomed, her hair sleek and she sports a perfect face of make-up.

'Gowdie Cottage, at the end of the lane. We're on the outskirts, really.' Miranda mutters something under her breath, something I can't quite catch.

'Oh.' The woman sits forward in her chair, suddenly intent on the plastic ring her baby is chewing on.

'Allie hasn't been here long, she probably hasn't heard the stories,' Tara says blithely. 'Although surely the estate agent must have told you, I mean, it's common knowledge round here. Everyone knows the stories about Gowdie Cottage, that's why it was on the market for so long. Ray Watts must have been over the moon when you two put an offer in.'

'Sorry, Tara, I have no idea what you're talking about.' I look between her and the other women in confusion. 'I mean, I've heard things about Pluckley, who hasn't, right?' I push out a small laugh. 'The Colonel who committed suicide in the woods and still roams about the village? And you can't really miss the ghosthunters, but there isn't any story about Gowdie Cottage. Not that I've heard.' Miranda keeps avoiding my eye, and any sense of kinship I had with her drifts away. Surely whatever it is can't be that bad – wouldn't the estate agent have had to reveal it if something dreadful had happened in the house? An uneasy feeling begins to prick its way up my spine, and I nudge my bag with my foot, checking it's close by, already anxious to leave.

'The witch house,' Miranda says quietly. 'You're living in the witch house.'

Chapter Nine

'It's called Gowdie Cottage after Agnes Gowdie. She lived there,' Miranda says, drawing breath to say more but Tara shoots her a look and her mouth snaps closed.

'The witch house!' I laugh, looking from Tara to Miranda and back again. 'You're … are you serious?'

'It's just a story,' Tara says, but Miranda looks down at her hands, picking at the skin around her nails without saying anything. 'A silly village legend like the others. You'll hear all sorts of ghost stories now you're here. It's up to you whether you want to believe them or not.'

'Right. A legend. Of course.' I smile, but I am thinking of the scene that popped into my mind before, of a woman, dressed in dark clothing, standing in the doorway to my cottage. 'I don't believe in all of that.' I pause. 'Not really.' As I say the words, I feel that same unsettling feeling wash over me, the way it did when I woke this morning, the dream etched behind my eyes. 'Tara, it was lovely of you to invite me – us – this morning, but I should probably get going. I've still got a lot to do – unpacking, you know …' I get to my feet and place the baby back into his pram, laying the blanket loosely over him and, raising a hand to the other women, I call out, 'Lovely to meet you!' and walk quickly towards the door.

'Allie, wait.' Tara follows me as I reach the door, one hand already pushing it open. 'I hope we didn't upset you. Miranda can be … well, she can be a bit intense sometimes.'

'I'm not upset,' I say. 'I forgot Mina has … a doctor's appointment. I have to go and collect her early. Sorry, it totally slipped my mind.'

Tara looks at me for a moment, head on one side. 'Are you sure? It's just a story you know, and it's just what it's like around here. Everyone has a ghost story to tell.'

'No, of course, I know it's just a story.' I turn back to where Miranda is talking to one of the other mothers. As if she feels my eyes on her she looks up and I look away quickly, back to Tara. 'I hope I haven't offended Miranda, saying that I didn't believe.'

Tara shakes her head. 'Ahh no, she'll be fine. She's the only one out of all of us who is really invested in it – the rest of us don't take it quite so seriously. It's just part of living here. I'll see you at drop-off on Monday?' I nod and wheel the baby out of the too-warm hall, round to the door for the preschool, trying to shake off the cold feeling that wraps its way around me every time I think of Miranda saying *Agnes Gowdie*.

After giving the nursery workers the same excuse – that Mina has a doctor's appointment – I decide to walk us home the long way through the village, on the road that takes us along the High Street. Knowing what I know now about the cottage, I am in no rush to head home, Miranda's words about the witch house tumbling over and over in my mind. There is an itching under my skin when I think about it, the jumble of feathers and keys, weighted by the hag stone springing to mind. *Legend,* I tell myself, as Mina chatters along beside me, *that's all.* I think of the flash of white moving through the trees, moving in a way that seems, the more I think about it, unnatural, not right.

I meander up the road with Mina until we reach the front of The Daisy Chain. Naomi has put buckets of fresh flowers outside, so many that they are crowded together, the flowers jostling against each other as a heady scent rises in the late morning sunshine. Tulips rub up against cabbage roses, freesias snug against the nodding heads of white daisies, while bright sunflowers stand guard over them all. Longing sweeps over me, so fierce I can only describe it as a kind of homesickness, and I manoeuvre the pram through the doorway into the tiny floor space inside. Naomi is serving a customer, but she looks up as I enter and flashes me a quick smile, wiggling her fingers in a wave at Mina. I wait patiently, jiggling the pram to keep the baby sleeping, and gently tapping Mina on the wrist as she tries to stroke the delicate petals of a stargazer lily, while Naomi wraps brown paper and string around the pot of a pink azalea and hands it to her customer.

'Allie, what are you doing here?' She comes around from behind the counter and embraces me. I relax into her hug and inhale the earthy, woody scent that comes from her clothes. So familiar, I used to come home smelling the same.

'Mina, come here to me.' Naomi lets me go and scoops Mina up onto her hip and we all follow her through into the back room.

I cast my eyes around as Naomi fills the kettle and switches it on, dropping a teabag into two mugs without even asking me if I want one. It's changed slightly since I left eight weeks ago. It is untidier, more chaotic, with wire clippings littering the floor and rolls of brown paper stacked on the metal work surface, next to a tangled ball of brown garden string. My fingers itch to start tidying, to put things back in their proper place, but it's not my job at the moment so I accept the mug Naomi hands me and say nothing.

'Where's the new girl?' I ask. I wasn't expecting Naomi to be on her own and had been hoping we could get some lunch together. I want to bounce Miranda's witch house comment off her, to see what her reaction is.

Naomi shrugs. 'She called in sick. She's not been too reliable to be honest. I can't see her lasting.'

'I can always help out.'

Naomi laughs. 'Don't be silly, Al, you've got enough on your plate with these two to look after. Not that I wouldn't swap with you tomorrow if I could.' She sobers, and I know what she's going to ask me. 'Are you OK? You look a bit pale.'

'Mina, you want to watch Peppa?' Ignoring Naomi's frown, I hand Mina my phone and she sits cross-legged in the corner, immediately enthralled by a little talking pig. 'A woman just referred to my house as the witch house.'

'Huh? What do you mean?'

'A woman at the baby group … she said Rav and I are "living in the witch house".' I sigh, peering down into my mug at the milky brown liquid. 'She said it's called Gowdie Cottage after someone named Agnes Gowdie.'

'Who is Agnes Gowdie?' Naomi frowns as she wraps a length of brown twine into a ball.

'I don't know.' I shrug. 'A witch?'

Naomi lets out a peal of laughter that makes the baby jump in his sleep. 'Oh God, Allie, that's hilarious. The witch house.' She shakes her head, her laughter dying away as she realizes I'm not laughing with her. She looks at me askance. 'You don't believe them? Allie, come on. I didn't think you were the type to buy into all that kind of thing.'

'I *don't*.' My words are petulant, her laughter stinging my skin. 'It's just … a bit unnerving, that's all. She was deadly serious.'

'People believe in that stuff round here; they've all grown up on it,' Naomi says matter-of-factly. 'It's all rubbish, Al, all of it. I've never seen anything in the village, have you?'

I pause, hesitant to say it out loud. 'The person in the woods?'

'Just someone out walking. You know the woods aren't secure; they might be attached to your house but anyone can walk through them.'

'I know but … I saw them again, the person in the woods.' I shift in my seat, suddenly uncomfortable. 'The way they moved … it was …' *Frightening*, is what I want to say but I don't. 'And then there are the keys.'

'Keys? What keys? You didn't tell me about any keys.'

Naomi puts the ball of twine on the counter, where it immediately rolls to the floor and unravels. She tuts and rolls her eyes but leaves it, taking a seat opposite me.

'You know I found the mirror? There was something in the floorboards underneath it.' I tell her about the way I had tugged at the feather, the weight of the stone and how the keys didn't fit any doors in the house. 'Rav says it's an old homemade keyring but I don't think so.'

Naomi is quiet for a moment and then she says, 'I think you're exhausted, Allie. I think you're tired, your body has been through a huge upheaval, and on top of that you're still getting used to living here. You don't have support from your mum, and Rav is working hard.'

When Naomi puts it like that, without that undertone of scepticism that I get from Rav, it feels almost rational.

'Maybe I should take the kids off your hands for a few hours,' Naomi says when I don't tell her she's wrong, 'when the new girl is back from being sick. I can look after them for the day, even overnight if you want. Mina can sleep in with me and the baby can go in the Moses basket; they can stay at the flat. There's plenty of room. Then you can get some sleep and start feeling more like your old self. No one said you have to do this on your own.'

'No.' I am shaking my head before she has even finished speaking.

'Or I could stay with you,' she offers, hope written all over her face. 'We could get a takeaway, then I'll get up with Leo in the night.'

'I'm OK, Naomi, honestly. You're probably right, I just

need to get a good night's sleep. I'll ask Rav to get up with the baby tonight.' As if on cue Leo wakes with a thin, reedy cry and I lift him from the pram and attach him once again.

'Maybe you should consider seeing the doctor?' Naomi says, watching as the baby gulps greedily. 'Just to … I don't know, check everything is all right. That you're all right.'

'I told you I'm fine, Naomi.' The words tumble out of my mouth as sharp, angry knives. 'I don't need to see a doctor.'

'OK, OK. I just thought, you know … if you're not sleeping very well with these nightmares, and then seeing things …'

'I'm not "seeing things". I did see someone in the woods.' I unlatch the baby before he is finished and call to Mina to give me my phone as we're going home, ignoring her grumbling response.

'But what Miranda said to you about Aileen Gowdie seems to have really unsettled you.' Naomi stands in the doorway as I try to squeeze the pram past her.

'*Agnes* Gowdie,' I snap. 'I was just feeling emotional. It's nothing. Look, I feel better already for speaking to you about it.' I manage to get past her and out on to the street, the scent of the flowers on the pavement hitting me as I step out. Once outside I stick on a conciliatory smile. 'It did unsettle me a little, but I know it's only a story. I'm OK, promise.'

'Well, you know where I am. The offer still stands.' Naomi rests her palm on the handle of the pram before I can walk away. 'I'll see you after the weekend and … take care, OK?'

I am in bed not long after Mina, and asleep pretty much straight away after Rav agrees to stay up with the baby and do the night feeds for me. I don't dream of the staircase, of the thick, heavy air or the shadowy pictures on the wall. Instead, I dream of bones, of dried herbs twisted together, of blood splashes in a pestle and mortar, a strange smoky smell in the air. The cry of a child jolts me awake a little after three o'clock in the morning, my nightshirt stuck to my body with clammy sweat, the piercing sound ringing in my ears. I reach out for the baby only to find the cot empty. The space in the bed next to me, the sheets cold, tells me that Rav isn't there either.

I slide out of bed, shivering as the chilly air of the cottage hits my skin. I pull the open bedroom window closed and creep downstairs to the living room where a puddle of golden light seeps out into the hallway, shadows dancing across the living-room wall ahead of me.

'Rav? Are you down here?' My heart does a painful double thump, as I step into the living room, suddenly afraid that it won't be Rav sitting on the sofa but someone else, someone dressed in white. But it is Rav. Of course it is. Heat prickles under my arms and I feel stupid, over dramatic. I tiptoe into the room, noting the open laptop on the low coffee table in front of Rav as he snoozes on the sofa.

'Rav, wake up.' I shake him gently, and he stirs, blinking awake sleepily. 'Come upstairs, it's cold down here. Come to bed.' Rav sits up and I step back, nudging into the coffee table and bringing the laptop screen to life.

Rav rubs his hand over his eyes, his gaze also drawn to

the laptop screen, the glare seeming overly bright in the dimly lit room, before he looks up at me. 'Allie. I must have fallen asleep. I was looking at ...' He gestures to the screen and I turn to look at it.

'Oh.' My face flushes hot as I see the last website I pulled up on the screen before I had slammed the lid closed when Rav came back down after kissing Mina good night. 'I can explain.'

'I hope so, because this is all a bit fucking weird.' Rav is wide awake now, his eyes never leaving mine.

'I was researching the house,' I say flatly. After Miranda's revelation about us living in 'the witch house', I resisted the itching urgency to investigate until I couldn't bear it any longer, and I opened the laptop and started googling. It turned out that she was right. Gowdie Cottage *was* the witch house, known to the villagers by that name. I found a tiny mention in a badly written website, which said that Agnes Gowdie had lived here, way back in the 1600s, and was the sister of Isobel Gowdie, a well-known Scottish witch burned at the stake. Agnes had fled Scotland when her sister was condemned to death, and the locals believed she had brought her witchcraft with her. She gained a reputation in the village as a healer and as a witch, and it wasn't long before rumours started to circulate about her, although I couldn't find much more information than that. It seems that Isobel Gowdie is of more interest than Agnes, the article focusing more on her history than on Agnes'. There was a two-sentence paragraph on Gowdie Cottage and how strange things had been happening here for years. The words made my skin crawl, and I had slammed the laptop lid down without shutting the browser. I think now of the borders in the garden, the range of plants and herbs there that could all be used for either healing or harm, none of them, I think, planted just because they look pretty.

'It's ridiculous,' Rav says. 'Who put all of this in your head?'

'No one … a woman at the baby group called it "the witch house" so I came home and did some research,' I whisper angrily, not wanting to wake the baby. A single scratch comes from the chimney. 'I hardly think you can blame me for wanting to know why she would call it that, and now I know. Rav, the reason this house was such a bargain is because the previous owners just upped and left over fifty years ago. Overnight, they just *left*, disappeared. And they weren't the first ones. There have been weird things happening in this cottage for years. You would think the estate agent would have said something to us when we put in an offer.'

Rav says nothing, reaching for a small bottle of water by his feet. He takes a long swallow and stands. 'Allie, I need to go to bed, and I think you should too.'

There is something about the way he says it that makes the hairs on the back of my neck stand on end. 'You knew, didn't you?' A bubble of red-hot fury pops low down in my stomach, making my veins fizz. 'Bloody hell, Rav, you knew the history of this place and you never even mentioned it!'

'Because I knew you would react like this,' Rav hisses back at me. 'I knew you wouldn't want to live here if you thought it had a past, but seriously, Allie! A house this age will always have a past, and I knew it might creep you out. I was trying to protect you; I didn't want you to worry.' He moves towards me, putting his arms out as if to embrace me but I take a step back. 'Allie, please. We both love this house. I knew it would shake you up if you knew it had a reputation as a witch's house but come on. It's just a story, none of it is real. Let's go to bed, it'll all look so much better in the morning.'

'You can sleep down here.' I march to the understairs cupboard, pulling out a set of blankets. 'Or I will. I need to be on my own.'

Rav sighs, and for a moment I think he's going to apologize, but he just says, 'Fine. I'll sleep down here,' and holds out his arms for the blankets.

It's only a short while later, when I have tucked the baby into the cot and climbed into bed, too wired and hurt by Rav's decision to keep the history of the house a secret to sleep, that I realize I am cold, chilled to my bones. The sun is already starting to rise on the horizon, and I roll over onto my side, burrowing down into the duvet, my heart freezing in my chest as I see that the bedroom window – the window that I closed when I woke earlier – stands wide open.

Chapter Ten

Early morning sunlight is peeping in through the window when I open my eyes to a gentle pressure on the bed next to me. Rav is perched on the edge of the mattress, a mug of tea in his hand. My eyes feel gritty and sore. The open window had played on my mind until some time after the sun had appeared over the horizon. The shrill cries of a child had been ringing in my ears, but when I checked on Mina she had been sleeping soundly and then the baby had needed another feed. My head thumps as I struggle into a sitting position and take the mug from Rav.

'I'm sorry,' he says, his eyes not quite meeting mine. 'I should have told you about the house before we put the offer in.'

'Yes, you should,' I say and then, 'I'm sorry if I came across as overdramatic.' It's not a straight apology, but it's all I can bring myself to say in light of things. The keys. The person in the woods. Agnes Gowdie.

'You know I only did it to protect you?' Rav asks, linking his fingers through mine on my free hand. 'I didn't want you to worry about anything, but I realize now I made the wrong decision.'

Tears sting my eyes and I blink them back, not taking my gaze away from our linked hands. Rav did make the wrong decision, and the fact that he kept things from me hurts, but I don't want to fight with him about it. The baby squawks and I feel a twist in my chest. It's not worth ruining the weekend over. And maybe, I think, maybe Rav does have a point. Maybe I am reading too much into things, letting myself get upset over things that don't really matter. I want that to be the case, anyway.

'I know,' I say eventually, 'seeing someone in the woods … trying to find out about the history of the house … it freaked me out a bit. Can we start again?' I lean forward and kiss him now, properly, not a chaste peck on the cheek. He looks as tired as I feel, and I can hear the faint strains of canned laughter from the television downstairs that tells me Mina is already up and awake.

'Good idea,' he says. I think I see a flicker of irritation cross his face when I mention seeing someone in the woods but it's so fleeting, I can't be sure. 'So, no more about witches, or people in the woods?'

I shake my head. 'No more.' But even as I say it, I picture the flash of white, moving at speed through the trees, Miranda's words ringing loudly in my ears.

The weekend passes in a flash, and I manage to get through most of it by trying not to think too hard about the house, and the strange things connected to it. It helps that the weather is beautiful, so we spend Saturday away from the house, away from Pluckley. Rav promises not to work for the whole weekend and we take Mina and the baby to the beach – Rav wants to go to Joss Bay, but I can't bear the anxiety of all the sand, whipping up into the baby's face or getting in Mina's swimsuit and making her skin sore, so we compromise, ending up at Deal for chips on the pebbled beach, Mina running in and out of the waves as they brush the shoreline.

Avó comes to visit on Sunday, much to Mina's delight, and I am relieved when Rav uses her presence to go out on his pushbike for an hour. It is worth putting up with Avó's thoughtless comments for a while if it means I have a little space from Rav. We might have agreed not to talk about it, and I might have told him I have accepted his apology, but I still have that unsettled feeling when I think about him knowing the history of the house and not telling me. It hasn't helped that I have woken the last two nights with my heart pounding my chest, sure that I can hear a child crying somewhere outside, even though the baby and Mina have been sleeping. Avó sits, rocking the baby at the kitchen table, while I start to prepare the leg of lamb for dinner.

'I can make the dinner for you, Allie,' Avó says. 'You should rest. You should be letting me do it.'

'Avó, I can do the dinner. I make the dinner every night for all of us.' I open the oven door, letting out a huge plume of hot steam into the already stifling kitchen.

'Hmmm.' Avó frowns, her black eyes on me as I move about the kitchen. I am about to give in and ask her to peel some potatoes, when she says, 'That lamb won't taste of anything you know, not if you don't put some herbs in there.'

Resisting the urge to roll my eyes and tut, I smile graciously at her. I should have known whatever I did it wouldn't be right in Avó's eyes. 'How about you keep an eye on the baby and I go out to pick some rosemary for the lamb?' Without waiting for her to answer, I walk out to the unruly border, weeds already beginning to grow back in the area that I cleared. I avert my eyes from the cluster of trees at the edge of the wood, sure that if I look directly into the forest I'll see that flash of white, feel the prickle of someone else's eyes on me, and suddenly, irrationally, I wish Rav were here to do his mother's bidding. I snap off the rosemary stalks, releasing their pungent scent into the air and raise a stalk to my nose, breathing it in. *Rosemary gets rid of negative energy.* The words rise unbidden into my mind alongside an image of a bundle of rosemary twigs tied together hanging upside down in the kitchen doorway. I don't know how I know this. Did I learn it at college when I was training? Or did I read it last night, when I stumbled down the internet rabbit hole trying to find more information on legends and tales about Gowdie Cottage? I blink and the image vanishes as the sun disappears behind a cloud, leaving me feeling chilled and, once again, a little spooked. That creeping sensation that we are not safe, that the children need to be protected from something washes over me. Maybe I should try and contact Ray Watts, the estate agent, myself – he might know more about the history of the cottage, he might be able to put my mind at rest, seeing as I've agreed not to talk about it with Rav. Some of the stories on the internet might be exaggerated, if Miranda's reaction is anything to go by. I jump as the gate to the garden crashes open and Rav wheels his bike in, his face hot and sweaty under his helmet.

'Allie, you all right?' He frowns as he tugs his helmet off, and I swallow before pasting on a smile.

'Yes, fine.' I hold up the sprigs of rosemary. 'Just getting some herbs for your mum.' I look towards the kitchen window – she's taken over and started preparing us dinner. I roll my eyes good-naturedly and without looking back at the woods, follow Rav into the house.

Later, when we've eaten and Avó has refolded the baby's vests, done a pile of ironing that didn't really need to be done, and told me all about her neighbour's daughter who has a new baby and still manages to cook a three-course dinner every night, Rav drives his mother home. I get Mina to bed and lay the baby in the cot, relieved at no longer having to stifle my annoyance at Avó's interference. It's hard work trying to keep Avó happy and keep my temper, and exhaustion tugs at my bones as I sink onto the sofa, tucking my feet underneath me, as Rav heads upstairs to work, his promise to leave it for the weekend forgotten now he's spent time with us. I've barely slept again all weekend, the open window from Friday night playing on my mind, but as I promised Rav I wouldn't mention it again I've kept it to myself, like a worry doll living deep at the back of my mind, that I keep taking out and turning over. A worry doll, full of uncertainty and sinister ill-feeling.

A yawn pulls at the back of my throat and I get to my feet. I'll make Rav a cup of tea, try and persuade him to come to bed. I step out into the hallway, my feet cold on the quarry tiles as I catch sight of my reflection in the mirror. I step closer, smoothing my hair down, wishing I didn't have such huge bags under my eyes, when I see it. Movement again, from the corner of my eye as if someone has walked past the mirror behind me. The air stirs, and the tiny hairs on the back of my neck stand up, as I think I see the shadow of a figure on the stairs.

'Rav?' I turn, suddenly feeling cold. The hallway behind me is empty. I turn back to face the mirror, my mouth dry, looking not at my own face, pale and tired in the glass, but behind me, waiting to catch that glimpse of movement again, but there is nothing. A pulse starts to beat in the soft hollow of my neck, a double beat that makes my breath come faster. There is a creak overhead and for a brief, dizzying moment I am back in the dream, seeing my bare feet on the carpet of the stairs, hearing the floorboards creak beneath them. I close my eyes, the world feeling strangely off kilter, resting one hand against the frame of the mirror to steady myself. The silver is warm beneath my palm, despite the chill in the air. After a few seconds, the feeling passes, and my eyes go to the glass again but there is just the reflection of the empty staircase behind me. The only sound is the shower running overhead, the hot water pipe giving out an intermittent bang as the creaky old plumbing tries to keep up.

Water. I head into the kitchen and pour myself a glass of water from the tap, swishing a mouthful around to ease my dry throat. Rav's mobile sits charging on the kitchen worktop and, straining to hear if the shower is still running upstairs, I tap in the passcode intent on looking up Ray Watts's email. I don't get as far as Rav's email account. The screen unlocks on his messages screen, and the third message down is not what I was expecting to see. It's from Naomi, received at 1.14 p.m. on Friday, not long after I went to see her at the florist. The message has already been read by Rav and I quickly swipe to open it.

Rav, call me. I need to talk to you. It's important.

The shower goes off abruptly, and I hear Rav's footsteps thud overhead as he walks from the bathroom to the top of the stairs.

'Al?' His voice drifts down the staircase and I lay the mobile back on the worktop with shaking hands.

'Be right up.'

I feel sick, the roast lamb dinner from earlier sitting heavy in my stomach. Why has Naomi texted Rav a message like that – what could be so important that she needs to speak to him so urgently? And why wouldn't she tell *me* what was so important? I know we talked mostly about what Miranda had said about the house, but wouldn't she have mentioned to me if she was worried about something, or had something urgent on her mind? A thought settles in my mind, pressing down as sure as a hand on my shoulder. *Maybe it's something she doesn't want me to know about. Maybe it's something that neither of them wants me to know about.* Rav lied to me about the house, by hiding the fact that he knew the history behind it. Lying by omission is still lying, isn't it? I remember the faint scent of alcohol on his breath after work, the floral scent that I thought might be incense, but now that I think about it could have been Naomi's perfume, the one I bought for her birthday last year because it reminded me of the violets she loves. Have they met without me, behind my back? And if so, why? If he lied to me about the house, what else is he lying to me about?

Chapter Eleven

Monday morning can't come quick enough, and I am glad that Rav has left by the time the baby wakes me. I feel odd about the text on his phone from Naomi, not sure what they could have to discuss without me – they are friends, but not close. Not close enough to meet without me being there. Rav's name flashes up on my phone as I strip my clothes off in the bathroom, steam from the running shower blurring my reflection in the mirror, and I let it ring out before stepping under the water, ignoring the beep that tells me he's left a voicemail. I have decided to keep Mina home today, to let her bunk off preschool. As much as the house is unsettling, the idea of walking through the village to school, having to face Tara and Karen after the baby group on Friday is all too overwhelming, giving flight to panicky flutters in my chest like a thousand tiny butterflies. I have an indescribable itch to find out more about the house, telling myself that if I can just find out more then maybe it will put my mind at ease. There is a tiny bookshop on the other side of the village, with a whole display dedicated to local authors. If I time it right, I can get over there and see if they have any books that feature the cottage, without bumping into Tara or Karen. I shower quickly, all too aware that Mina is downstairs, albeit glued to CBeebies again, and dress in jeans and a clean T-shirt, taking a moment to brush my hair and twist it up into a clip before I snatch up my phone, listening to the voicemail Rav has left.

'Hey, Al, you're probably on the way to preschool.' I feel a tiny pang of guilt that I squash down into nothing. 'Just wanted to tell you that I might be late again tonight. Something has come up with the case. I won't bore you with the details. Go on and eat without me, I've no idea what time I'll make it back.' I dither in the entrance to the living room, watching Mina as she plays with the Indian doll Rav's mum gave her, the television chattering away to itself in the background, debating whether to call Rav back or not. He won't answer even if I do call him; it'll just go to voicemail. There is a clanging chime from the old-fashioned doorbell that Rav has installed, and I tuck my phone into my pocket.

Angela, my health visitor stands on the doorstep, lanyard around her neck and a harassed look on her face. Her cheeks are flushed a bright pink and wisps of mousy hair escape from her ponytail. 'Hi, Allie. I'm so sorry I'm late – I know we said nine o'clock, but this morning has run away with me already.' She steps into the hall and I move to let her past into the living room.

'No, not late at all.' I had completely forgotten that she was coming, the events of the past few days driving every-thing else from my mind, but now she is here I'm glad

I managed a shower and some clean clothes. 'Can I get you a cup of tea?'

'Thanks, but it'll have to be a quick one.' After a surreptitious glance at her watch, she gives me a grateful smile, before turning her attention to the baby who slumbers on in the Moses basket.

Stepping through into the kitchen I wait until the kettle is boiling noisily before taking in a few deep breaths. I had completely forgotten Angela was coming, and my eyes sweep over the kitchen, glad that I had cleaned up after last night's dinner and tidied the living room of all Mina's toys. When I walk back into the living room, a mug in each hand, Mina is lining up her dolls, demanding that Angela listen to all of their names.

'Mina, not now, darling.' I hand Angela a mug and glance towards the sleeping baby, worried that Angela will judge me for leaving the two children alone in here while I made the tea.

'Let's have a look at him.' Angela holds out her arms and I place the baby in them gently, holding my breath as I wait for him to let out a wail, but he just stirs, his mouth pursing into little kisses. 'Oh, what a good boy,' Angela coos, and I watch as she removes his clothes, checks him over, and weighs him before handing him back to me to clothe again as she writes up her notes. As she finishes writing she peers over the top of her glasses at me. 'You look very well, Allie. How are you feeling?'

'Oh, fine.' I jiggle the baby now he is back in his sleep suit, hoping he'll go back off to sleep for just a little while longer. He pumps his fist, his face reddening.

'Sleeping OK? As well as can be expected at this stage anyway.' Angela lets out a small laugh and she is already packing her things back into her huge bag.

'Yes,' I lie, lowering my face to the baby's head to hide the red flush that creeps over my cheeks. 'All fine. He's a good baby.'

'Well, you look great.' Angela is on her feet, and I can tell by the distraction in her voice that she's already on to the next appointment in her head, already thinking about the next mum. 'It's not often I get to mums this early in the morning and they're already showered and dressed. I think we can discharge you, if you're happy?'

'Yes, I'm happy.' I follow her to the front door, the baby starting to grizzle in my arms. 'Thank you.' She waves as she runs to her car, already even later than before, and I call to Mina to come and get her shoes on. We're going to the bookshop.

The village is quiet, and as I approach the threshold of the bookshop, I am relieved that I have made it along the High Street without bumping into anyone I know. Mina sighs impatiently as I wrangle the pram through the narrow door into the quiet calm of the store, before slipping past me and heading towards a squashy beanbag arranged in one corner.

I glance anxiously towards the woman behind the till, an older lady with dishevelled curly hair tied up in a headscarf, big silver earrings hanging from her ears. She flaps a hand and smiles. 'She's fine.' She comes out from behind the till and crouches beside Mina, pulling out a handful of picture books from the shelf behind her. I smile my thanks as she gets to her feet, Mina already engrossed in the colourful pages. 'Is there something I can help you with?'

'Ermm … I'm looking for something about local legends … maybe something on the houses in the area?' I feel my cheeks flush a hot red as I stumble over the words.

'Oh, something like this?' The woman leads me towards the display of local books and pulls one down with a dark cover, a ghostly apparition on the front. The title is *The Legend of The Black Horse*.

'This one is about the pub,' she says, 'written by a local author. All about the ghosts you can share a room with if you spend the night.' She gives a short laugh and I take the book. 'Have a browse, there are plenty there. There's a sofa over in the corner, if you want to take the weight off.' She peers into the pram with a smile. I thank her, and keeping one eye on Mina, I return to the shelf in front of me, hoping to find something about Gowdie Cottage. I browse the books, hoping to find something dedicated to the house, but although there are mentions here and there, there is nothing more than that. Flicking through a book entitled, *Pluckley and its Ghostly Residents* – not exactly the snappiest title – I find reference to the Pluckley Witch and my fingers still, holding the book open. *It must be Agnes*, I think as my eyes scan over the page, barely registering the tinkle of the bell as the door to the shop opens. *Agnes must be the Pluckley Witch.*

I tuck the book under my arm and face the shelf, my eyes returning to the one title that keeps jumping out at me: *An Introduction to Witchcraft*. Something stirs inside me, and glancing towards the woman behind the till, I pick it up and begin tentatively flicking through the pages, not entirely sure what I am looking for.

'Oh, hello. Fancy seeing you here,' a voice says in my ear, making me jump. I shove the book hurriedly under my arm with the others, and turn to see Miranda standing beside me, the scent of sandalwood surrounding her. She wears a thick silver necklace with a moon hanging from it and her lips are painted a vivid purple. 'How are you?'

'Good, thank you. What about you?' I peer around her to check on Mina.

'Fine.' Miranda nods, a small, awkward smile on her lips and I get that feeling again, of kinship. I get the sense that we both feel the same, as if we aren't quite sure we fit in.

'I was just …' I hold up *Pluckley and its Ghostly Residents*. 'Are you going to buy it?'

I frown, my eyes going back to the sinister-looking cover. 'I don't know … I was hoping for a bit more information on my house and Agnes Gowdie, but there's not much in there. And anyway, it's all just superstition really, isn't it? Surely no one believes all that stuff. I'm not sure if this book …' I push away the flicker of white rushing through the trees that rises in my mind.

'Only I wrote it.'

'You wrote it?'

'Yes.' Her cheeks flushing a startling pink, Miranda takes the book from me and points at the author's name. 'M. I. Richards. Miranda Isobel Richards. I wrote this book. Some people do believe in this stuff, actually.' She puts the book back on the shelf, a tinge of hurt in her voice.

'Wow. You wrote it.' *Shit. Talk about putting my foot in it.* I take the book back, deciding that I will buy it, when a thought strikes me. 'Miranda, if you wrote this, then you must be a bit of an expert on all this stuff, the stories and legends in Pluckley?'

'Well, obviously. Yes. I grew up here, it's part of my family history. I'm named for Isobel Gowdie, we're descended from her on my grandmother's side.'

'Then I think … maybe you're the person I need to speak to.'

'What do you want to know?' Miranda asks, before she says, 'I was waiting for you to ask me, if I'm honest. I knew you would, I could feel it.'

'Errm, well I suppose I wanted to ask you about what you said at the mother and baby group,' I say, wrong-footed by her saying she could *feel* that I wanted to ask her. 'You … you said I live in the witch house, and in this book, there is a mention of the Pluckley Witch. What I'm asking is …' I break off and swallow, fear suddenly making my mouth dry, and I'm not sure I do want to know after all. 'I guess I just want to know more about her. If she lived in my house then I almost feel as if …'

Miranda is nodding before I even finish speaking. 'There's a connection between you? I absolutely understand what you're saying. People often say they can feel a connection between themselves and the spirit, especially when there's something unfinished about it all.'

I wasn't going to say that, I was going to say, *I almost feel as if she is still there*. Now I'm glad I didn't. Part of me is starting to wish I hadn't asked Miranda at all, but she carries on speaking, not picking up on my apprehension.

'Agnes Gowdie – also known as the Pluckley Witch – fled Scotland when Isobel, her sister, was burnt at the stake, taking only two things with her. She arrived in Pluckley a short while later, and it wasn't long before rumours started to fly. Her reputation for using herbs quickly became well known, and while Agnes used them as healing agents mostly, the village didn't see it that way, especially after she delivered the landlady's baby. Strange things started to happen, people began to fall ill, all after Agnes arrived here. People who had crossed her, called her names, accused her of things, a lot of them fell sick, and then of course, the other stuff started.'

'Wow.' A shiver runs down my spine, at the thought of Agnes standing over a stove, stirring and muttering under her breath, cursing the people living side by side with her. I think of the herbs sprouting merrily in the border of my back garden.

'That's how it was back then,' Miranda says. 'Of course, once they found out she was Isobel's sister it just reinforced their idea that she must be a witch.' I must have looked sceptical, as Miranda says, 'They might not have had the internet back then, but news still travelled.'

'What happened with the landlady's baby? Why did that make things difficult for Agnes? Surely using herbs alone wasn't enough to suspect her of being a witch?'

'You'd be surprised,' Miranda says drily. 'Agnes delivered

the baby, but it was stillborn. Devastating, of course, but made worse by the fact that the landlady swore she heard the child cry as it was born. She said she saw a black shadow hovering over Agnes's shoulder as the baby was delivered, and that he uttered a single cry before Agnes handed her a dead baby.'

'Oh my gosh, that's heartbreaking.' I blink rapidly, seeing the flit of a shadow brush past the door the night I thought Rav was downstairs, a knot growing in my stomach. 'You said she fled Scotland with only two things, what were they?'

'A baby in her belly – Agnes was six months pregnant when she arrived.'

'Oh.' My eyes drop to the baby, sleeping soundly in the pram, his wispy hair just visible above the blanket. 'A baby?' *A connection.* I blink, imagining an invisible cord linking me to Agnes, one that feels rotten and decayed. 'What was the other thing? You said there were two things.'

'Isobel's pearl necklace,' Miranda says. 'She hid it under her clothes, close to her skin the day they came to take Isobel away.'

'What?' It feels as though the floor has dropped away beneath my feet, and I lower myself gently onto the sofa, my legs suddenly like jelly. I think of the pearls that nestle in my jewellery box in my bedroom at the cottage. Both of them found in and around the house. Coincidence, surely.

'A pearl necklace, and a baby,' Miranda goes on blithely. 'Things got worse. Several years after the birth of the stillborn baby, Agnes's own child – a little girl – went missing. Agnes blamed the landlord, but the villagers were convinced that

Agnes had done something to the child herself, especially in light of the dead baby she had delivered a few years before. Agnes spent weeks roaming the woods behind the cottage, searching for her lost child, telling everyone she knew she was in there, that she could hear her crying for her.'

'Oh my God.' My blood runs cold, the hairs on my arms rippling to attention. The shrill cries that have dragged me from sleep echo in my ears and I have to resist the urge to cover them with my hands. 'What happened to her? What happened after her child was lost?'

'The children started disappearing.' Miranda's voice is barely above a whisper and I can smell her shampoo as she leans in close to me. 'One by one, the children of the village began to disappear. Some went to the market for their mothers and never returned, others went out to play and vanished. The parents tried keeping them home, and then they started disappearing from their beds. The villagers … they said Agnes took them, in revenge for the loss of her own child. More than one parent said they had seen her, hanging around watching the children before their child was taken. She was burnt at the stake as a witch less than three years after Isobel. Strange things have happened in and around Gowdie Cottage ever since – it's believed that Agnes still haunts her old home to this day.'

My throat feels thick, and I can feel the hot sting of tears behind my eyes. The baby stirs in the pram and I know I won't have long before he starts to shout for a feed. 'Did they ever find any of them? Did they ever find Agnes's child?'

Miranda shakes her head. 'No, they never found the

children. Locals believe that Agnes's daughter still calls for her mother from the woods, wandering barefoot and lost, wearing a white dress with long, blonde hair. I've never heard or seen anything, but others have said they have. Are you all right? You look very pale.'

I get to my feet, the book sliding from my lap, sure for a moment that I will fall as my vision blurs and I feel dizzy. I think I can hear her, the child, crying in the distance, and I see her in my mind, crouched beneath the trees, shrouded in white. It passes as quickly as it comes on and I let out a shaky breath, my hands gripping the handle of the pram tightly. 'I'm fine. It's just … I wasn't expecting quite such a story.'

Miranda is on her feet beside me, pressing her book back into my hands. 'Interesting, isn't it? It's not the most well-known legend around here, The Colonel can take the credit for that, along with the Highwayman and the White Lady, for haunting Frights Corner and the church, so I'm really looking forward to working on a book about Agnes next.'

'It's … yes, interesting. Fascinating, actually.' Although *fascinating* is not quite the word I would use to describe the feeling I had in the hallway, with the tickle of eyes on the back of my neck from an empty staircase.

'You know, if you want some more information on the house, you could always ask Mrs Sparks. She's the woman I've been talking to for my next book. She lived in the house as a child. She was one of the last people to live there, as a matter of fact. Until you guys showed up, anyway,' Miranda says. 'I'm sure she wouldn't mind.'

'Where can I find her?'

'She lives on the outskirts of the village. Here ...' Miranda takes out her phone and taps out a text. 'This is her address. Pop your number in and I'll send it over.'

I tap quickly, something like nerves fluttering in my chest. It feels like a lot to take in and I wish I had just asked Miranda before, instead of trying to find things online. 'Thanks. Mina, we should go,' I call, holding up the book, before slipping the one about witchcraft underneath it. 'I should go and pay for this. The baby will need feeding soon.'

'Take care, won't you, Allie?' After I hand over my money at the till, Miranda follows me out on to the High Street. 'Be careful near the woods.'

Now, as I hurry into the house, I keep my eyes averted from the woods, the trees visible through the window on the upstairs landing as I head up there to the nursing chair to feed the baby, Mina following behind me with her new book. It's no use though, as I pass by the glass, the air around me growing distinctly chillier as it always does up here, my eyes flicker towards the rustling green leaves, suddenly sure that I will see that flash of white moving quickly, silently, searching for something lost.

I rock the baby gently in the nursing chair as he feeds, my mind turning over everything Miranda said in the bookshop. I think of the pearls, imagining them at the throat of Agnes Gowdie, four hundred years earlier, and shake my head. There is no way the pearls I found around the cottage could ever have belonged to her. *Agnes Gowdie. A witch.*

A murderer. Still here? Movement from the hallway catches my eye, a flicker of something swift and fleeting, and my heart leaps into my throat, my arms tensing. The baby is still feeding but his suckle has slowed and his mouth gently falls open. Something isn't right. I blink stupidly, waiting for my brain to catch up, before I realize what it is, what is wrong. Mina is no longer at my feet. *She's gone, just like Agnes's child.* A spluttering flame of fear ignites as the realization dawns, as I lay the baby in the cot, and walk into the hallway, the air around my ankles chilly and brisk as if a draught is blowing.

'Mina!' I call, peering into her bedroom. Empty. *Shit.* I was expecting her to be sitting on the floor, playing with her doll, but she's not there. I shove open the bathroom door – also empty, the faint drainy smell that occasionally oozes from the bathtub making me swallow hard.

'Mina!' I shout as I barge my way into the spare bedroom, and then into my bedroom, hoping I would see her curled up on my bed with her thumb in her mouth, but she isn't there. My chest heaving, panic leaves an acidic taste in my mouth as I race across the landing, looking out into the trees, down to the grass below, to the pond, desperate for a glimpse of her small, dark head but she isn't there. I sprint downstairs, my legs like jelly, trying desperately to remember if I put the chain back across the door, knowing that I didn't, I wouldn't, it's the middle of the day. *Oh please, please, don't let Mina have gone out the front door.* I skid to a halt on the cold tiles in the hallway, Mina's tiny feet visible as she sits snuggled on the sofa, her blanket under one arm, her thumb in her mouth. *Oh, thank God.* She is glued to the TV, a wash of primary colours tumbling across the screen and once again I feel a pang of guilt at being such a shit mother for letting her watch telly for hours every day.

I scoop her up from the sofa, ignoring her protests as I hold her close, burying my face in her hair so she can't see my tears. I thought I had lost her. *I thought Agnes had taken her for her own.* I shake off the thought, the image of Mina following a shadowy figure out of the house, towards the woods, so dark and vivid in my mind that I hold her even tighter, so tight that she begins to wriggle and squirm in my arms.

I set her back down, kissing her hair, drawing in a deep breath to fight off the nausea. I'll let her do playdough, I think, just for a little bit while the baby is sleeping. I open the understairs cupboard, reaching in for the playdough Rav's brother bought her for Christmas, catching sight of someone sitting at the kitchen table as I do. *There is someone here, there's someone in the kitchen. Fuck.* I pause, silent, waiting to see if whoever it is has noticed that I am downstairs, my fingers reaching for an old umbrella in the cupboard before I start to tiptoe towards the kitchen. My heart feels as if it is going to burst out of my throat as I slip soundlessly along the hallway, my useless weapon clutched in one fist. Sending one worried glance back over my shoulder to where Mina sits on the sofa, I slide my phone from my back pocket, typing in the triple nines ready to hit connect. As I step into the kitchen, I see who is sitting at the table and my phone flies from my hand, dropping to the tiled floor with an ominous crack, the umbrella following after it. My hand flies to my mouth.

'Mum?'

Chapter Twelve

'Mum. Oh my God. What … why …?' My words tangle in my throat at the sight of my mother, sitting at my kitchen table as if I only saw her last week, instead of months ago. She looks just as she did the last time I saw her – her hair still a shiny conker brown, her figure an impressive size eight. She has been complimented on her slim figure more times than I can count over the years and she behaves as though it is effortless. Only I know that she is slim because she doesn't eat, preferring to smoke to stem her appetite. There is an unlit cigarette in her hand now, the telltale rim of pink lipstick on the filter telling me that she has already been tempted to smoke it. Tiny lines around her mouth are the only sign that she is in her early sixties, all other wrinkles botoxed away. Seeing her sitting there, chic and well dressed, I feel frumpy and fat, my stomach still wobbly and bloated from the pregnancy.

'Mum,' I say again, feeling hot tears sting at the back of my eyes. I blink rapidly, not moving from where I stand in the doorway. My instinct is to go to her, to throw my arms around her tiny frame and breathe in the familiar scent of her Shalimar perfume and the faint smoke on her skin. But my mother isn't a hugger and never has been, so I stand where I am, still unable to believe she is actually, really here.

'I did knock but there was no answer, so I let myself in through the back. You left it open,' she tuts.

'I can't believe you're really here.'

'Alys, I am your mother. Haven't I always been there when you needed me?' Her hand goes to her mouth, the cigarette at her lips before she remembers and lowers it.

'No one calls me Alys. It's Allie.' I feel that old familiar spark of irritation that she ignites in me, the one that reduces me to a teenager, before I make an effort to mentally blow it out, the sheer fact that she's here dampening it. 'How did you … ? You got my voicemail?' I hadn't expected her to answer the phone when I called the other day – deep down I *knew* she wouldn't – so the fact that she is here, in my kitchen, feels unreal.

'Yes, I got your voicemail.' She smiles, and finally I move to sit in the chair opposite her. 'Of course, I would come if you need me. You're my daughter, Allie, even if we don't speak often.'

'The baby is sleeping at the moment, the health visitor just came and discharged us. Do you want to come and see Mina? She's in the living room …' The words tumble out of me. I have so much to say to her and I don't know how much time she'll give me to say it.

'You, Allie,' she interrupts. 'What about you? The baby will be fine, and I will see Mina in a moment. You would have said already if there was a problem with the children.

It's you that I am most worried about.' I have missed her soft French accent, the gentle slur on some of her words, the dropped h's and short vowels.

'I'm OK,' I say, a lump filling my throat. I swallow, but it stays lodged there. 'Oh God, Mum, it's been *so* long. I've got such a lot to tell you. I can't believe you're here.'

'I am here. Of course I am. I think you are not. OK, that is.' My mother makes no move to comfort me but pulls a clean tissue from her sleeve and places it on the table. 'Also, I do not think this is to do with the baby. Is it that husband of yours? Are you leaving him? You can come to Paris, stay with me. We can be there by this evening.'

'No, no it's not Rav. I'm not leaving him, and I'm not coming to Paris.' I blow my nose hard into the tissue. 'I don't even know where to begin. Things have been … strange, I suppose.'

'What kind of things?'

'Silly things, really. There was someone in the trees, or so I thought. Watching the house. Watching me.' My thoughts go to the pearls that I have hidden upstairs in the drawer next to my bed, the jumble of keys and feathers that sit on the top of the dresser, tangled with receipts and spare change, hairbands and make-up bottles. 'Noises coming from the chimney. Naomi said it was probably a bird, but how long can a bird live inside a chimney? I closed the bedroom window the other night but when I went upstairs it was open.'

'You are tired, Allie. Exhausted even, from the baby. Does he sleep?' My mother stands and moves to the open back door, the cigarette going to her mouth. She lights it, sending a stream of blue-grey smoke out into the garden.

'He sleeps as much as your average newborn,' I say, tightly. 'You sound like Rav, he said exactly the same thing, that I must be imagining things.'

Mum tuts at the mention of Rav's name. 'I never said you were imagining things.' *Were* comes out as *wear*.

'Miranda – this woman I met at a baby group – she called this house the witch house.' I have to pause for a moment, my mouth suddenly dry. 'There's this whole legend about a Pluckley witch who used to live here. And although I know it's ridiculous, there is something about it all that is unsettling. A feeling, you know. There was someone in the trees, I saw them, I saw the path they made through the grass. And I found some keys, tied together with feathers in the floorboards.'

'Keys?' My mother frowns. 'For the house?'

'No, not for the house. That's what is odd – the keys don't fit the house and along with the feathers they're tied to a stone,' I say. 'I showed them to Rav, and he said it's probably just an old homemade keyring but there's … something about them. I keep thinking about them. It's just unnerved me, that's all. And then all Miranda's talk of witches …'

'Witches.' My mother lets out a snort, before drawing on her cigarette, ash floating to the floor.

'I met Miranda in the bookshop earlier today, while I was looking for more information on the house. According to her, this cottage was home to a witch four hundred years ago and weird things have happened here according to the few stories I could find on the internet. People disappear, die, go bonkers. I don't know. It's all just … If I'd known then what I know now, maybe I wouldn't have agreed to put an offer in on the house.'

'And Rav? Did he know?' She puts out the cigarette, running the butt under the tap and throwing the damp end in the bin. A thin trickle of smoke follows her into the kitchen, and I wonder how I will explain it to Rav if he smells it later.

'Yes,' I say quietly and watch her mouth twist into a moue of distaste. She has never approved of Rav. 'Rav knew about the history of the house but he didn't tell me. He said he didn't want to upset me. But I am upset, and not just because he knew. He knew the history behind this house, and now when I tell him about these things, he just waves them away, says they're nothing. Why doesn't he believe me when I tell him that something doesn't feel right?'

My mother opens her mouth to speak, and I know it will be something derogatory about Rav. I narrow my eyes and she pauses, as if thinking, proving me right.

'Witches aren't all bad, you know,' she says eventually, as she sits back at the table. 'Most of the time they were just healers, nothing sinister, but people did not understand them. I did not bring you up to believe in fairies and magic and fanciful things. But I am not agreeing with Rav, that you are imagining things.'

'I'm not saying I believe in it,' I snap, that spark of irrita- tion reigniting. 'I'm saying that since I brought the baby home, maybe even before but I didn't notice it, things have been … off. When we first moved into this house, I was so excited to be here, so looking forward to building a home with Rav for our children, but lately I feel … I feel as though something, or someone is here, in the house. As if someone is *waiting*.' I pause for a moment, before voicing my real fear. 'I'm worried that the children aren't safe. That I'm not safe.'

My mother shrugs. 'I had these same feelings when you were born. It is a difficult time for a woman – you lose your sense of identity. You are a wife, a mother, you are not just Allie anymore. Children, they are a big responsibility. You are tired, your body has been through so much. It can be overwhelming.' Her face darkens, and I think back to my childhood, growing up tiptoeing around her. I don't want to be like that with Mina and the baby.

'Do you think I'm being overly dramatic? That it's just hormones playing havoc with my emotions? That's what Naomi thinks.'

'Possibly, I don't know.' My mother shrugs. 'I only know how I felt when you were born. Naomi doesn't know about these things; she hasn't had a baby, has she? Are you happy with Rav? Maybe it's your mind trying to tell you that he is not the one.'

Bloody hell. I should have known that she would start on Rav, that it would be Rav's fault. 'Mum, I am perfectly happy with Rav.' And I am, most of the time. I don't think about the way he never told me about the history of the house, the smell of perfume on his clothes, the text from Naomi on his phone. A faint cry comes from upstairs and

I raise my eyes to the ceiling. 'The baby is crying. Let me go and get him, and Mum, don't go anywhere, will you?'

When I walk back downstairs, my mother is sitting on the arm of the sofa, next to where Mina sits curled into the cushion, one hand stroking Mina's dark curls.

'Is everything OK?' I ask her, jiggling the baby as he fusses in my arms, his little face scrunched and sweaty. 'Was Mina crying?' It's been so long since Mina saw my mother, I'm not sure she wouldn't confuse her with a stranger.

'No, she is sleeping.' My mother gives Mina's hair one last stroke before she gets to her feet and brushes past me back to the kitchen. I step into the living room and see she is right. Mina is curled on the sofa, her head resting on a cushion, her mouth slightly open as her breath whistles in and out. It's unusual for her to sleep this early in the day, but maybe the baby woke her last night with his cries. I decide to leave her for half an hour and follow my mother back into the kitchen, shivering as a quiet scratch comes from the chimney.

'So, you have something else you want to talk about?' My mother gazes at me, her blue eyes clear and bright and I get the sense of being under a microscope. She used to look at me the same way when I was young, and unease makes my shoulders tighten.

'We could talk about what you're doing here,' I say, my words sharp. I lay the baby in the Moses basket, then turn to fill the kettle and throw teabags into mugs, avoiding meeting her eyes.

'I don't want tea. I am here to see you, you know that.

You asked me to come. Leave that. Come and sit with me. Anyone would think you're not pleased I am here.'

I sit, as directed. 'I am pleased, Mum, of course I am. I just wasn't expecting you. You didn't answer the phone when I called, and you never called back, or even sent a message. I didn't even know whether you'd listened to the voicemail.'

'Allie, you know I am not good at keeping in touch. Neither of us are, not anymore.'

Her words sting with the ring of truth. 'Where are you staying?' I feel a flicker of panic, suddenly sure that she'll say she's staying here but I don't see any sign of a bag.

'Canterbury. I have work to do at the university.'

Does that mean that if she hadn't had work here, she wouldn't have responded to my voicemail at all? I push the thought away, trying to believe that she wants to repair our relationship, that she has missed me as much as I have missed her. 'Right. How long are you here for?'

She shrugs, 'I don't know. A week or two. If you need me, I will stay longer.'

I want to tell her that I don't need her, that I've managed fine without her so far, but I don't. After all, I did leave her a voicemail begging her to help me. A scratch comes from the chimney and my mother's eyes go to the chimney breast.

'There is something else bothering you,' she says, looking back at me.

'I'm not sleeping too well,' I confess. 'I had a dream … or a nightmare. Some sort of *vision*,' I blurt out. 'A dream, but it was so real it felt like it happened. It really happened.'

'I see. What was this dream?' My mother fumbles for

another cigarette and moves to the back door again. I had forgotten how much she smoked.

'I was on some stairs, at the top, by the landing. Looking into a bedroom … the children are there, sleeping in the beds and there is a funny smell in the air. Weird shadows on the walls.'

'But what does this have to do with anything? Surely it is just a *cauchemar*? A nightmare?'

'I don't know.' Blood beads on the broken skin of my lower lip as I bite it. 'I can't see the children properly, but I know they are Mina and Leo …' I break off, my breath tight in my chest. 'All I know is that I am about to do something awful, *terrible*. And I have no way to stop it. But at the same time, it isn't me. It's not me that is about to do this awful thing.'

'Oh, Alys.' I let the name slide, as my mother's mouth twists down into an expression I haven't seen for years. Sadness. Or disappointment, maybe. 'It's a dream. OK, you have this strange feeling about the house, but you just had a baby. We all feel strange when we have a baby.'

'Maybe.' I blink, hot tears stinging behind my eyes. I don't want to cry in front of her.

'Perhaps the history of this house is playing on your mind, this is why you have the strange dreams,' my mother says. 'Maybe you need to speak to this girl in the bookshop again, to find out what she knows. If you can find out more about the house, then maybe it will set your mind at rest.' She hands me a tissue from the table. 'Better?'

I nod, sniffing. 'Better. Sorry. Maybe you're right. Perhaps

I should find out more – Miranda said there is a lady in the village who used to live here. Maybe I should go and see her.'

'That sounds like a good idea.'

'Would you …' I pause, strangely reluctant to ask the question. 'Would you come with me? If the lady will see me? I'd rather not go on my own.'

'Of course.'

'Brilliant.' I let out a breath. 'Thank you. Will you stay now? I would like Mina to see you properly when she wakes up.'

But Mum is already shaking her head. 'I can't stay, Allie. But I will be back, I will come with you to see this lady who lived here.' She glances at the clock on the kitchen wall. 'I should be going.'

It's because of Rav, I think. Even though we're married with children she doesn't want to accept him, to accept that I'm happy with him.

'Look, Mum, don't worry about Rav.'

'What do you mean?' The look on her face tells me she knows exactly what I mean.

I sigh. 'I know … the two of you don't get on. You don't like him.' She opens her mouth to speak but I raise a hand. 'I'd love nothing more than for you to just accept that Rav and I are together, but I kind of know that isn't going to happen now. I suppose what I'm trying to say is … I'm glad you're here. And if you don't want to come over when Rav is here, then it's fine with me. I'm just happy to be able to spend some time with you. I've missed you.'

My mother smiles and presses her cold hand to my cheek.

'I am glad to see you too. And I do have to go, but I will come over again, tomorrow perhaps.'

I walk her to the front door and watch her walk away up the path towards the village, towards the train station. The baby shouts, awake again, and I turn to listen, then when I look back she is gone, the street empty. As I close the door, I hear it again, a low scratch coming from the chimney, before a door upstairs closes with a bang as if a window has been left open.

Chapter Thirteen

The slam of the door frightens the baby, his shouts getting louder as I hurry along the hallway, unease prickling under my skin. My phone buzzes on the table with a text message from Rav as I scoop up the baby, the smell rising from his Babygro telling me it's time to change him. Wearily I head for the stairs, ignoring the text, and lay the baby on the changing table. As soon as he is clean and dry his cries stop, and I stand over him for a moment, just watching as his tiny fists pump the air, his legs kicking. He gazes up at me, trying to focus on my face before his eyes move past me to a spot over my shoulder. There is a thud in my chest as my heart does a double beat. I can feel it again, the cold draught across the back of my neck, that needle-like sensation of eyes on me. *Breath on the back of my neck.* I squeeze my eyes closed, suddenly so sure that there is someone behind me, close enough to touch, peering over my shoulder at the baby. I gently lay a hand on his chest and whip my head round, only to see an empty room. There is no one there. I let out the breath I am holding and look towards the window, but it is shut.

The window is shut. I quickly put the baby's arms and legs back into his Babygro, and pick him up, holding him close as I walk on shaking legs through the open door into Mina's room, and then through the open door of the bathroom. All the windows are shut, and every door stands open. I close my eyes and try to count to ten, only getting to five before they fly open, adrenaline making my hands shake. If the windows are all closed and the doors are open, then what was it that made a huge bang as I waved my mother goodbye? I didn't imagine it, I'm sure of it, the baby woke and started crying. Making small shushing sounds to the baby as he begins to fuss, I head back downstairs to the living room, where Mina still sleeps on the sofa, her cheeks now flushed with pink. I settle in the armchair across from her and latch the baby on before he can begin to wail properly. All is quiet now, the only sounds the snuffling of the baby and Mina's breath as she snores lightly, sounding slightly congested. I feel myself begin to relax, my shoulders lowering as no sound comes from overhead, and the chimney is silent. My pulse slowing, I allow myself to think over my mother's visit, now I am over the shock of seeing her sitting at my kitchen table. I can't believe she was here. The sight of her, sitting there as though it hadn't been months and months since I last saw her, was something I never expected but I am relieved she came. I still feel unsettled, and although she didn't give me much sympathy – which is not unusual, that's just how she is – I feel as though she believes me more than Rav. Rav is convinced that it's exhaustion that is making me feel so on edge. But I am still no closer to understanding what the vision I keep seeing could mean. If I'm honest I played it down a little, not telling her that I didn't just dream it whilst asleep, that it plays on my mind in the day too.

I wake Mina for lunch, trying to push any thoughts of my mother, and the slamming of the door upstairs, from my mind for a while. She struggles into consciousness, her cheeks still flushed and her eyes bleary. She grumbles as she comes into full wakefulness and raises her arms for me to lift her. I carry her through into the kitchen, her small body warm against mine, and prepare her some soup and fingers of bread. Mina picks at the bread listlessly, letting the soup spill in bright orange spots onto the table.

'I'm not hungry,' she whines, and slides off the chair, heading back towards the sofa. By the time I clean up and follow her, she is asleep again, tucked into the armchair this time and I feel a faint prickling of worry. *She's just off colour*, I tell myself. *All kids get a bit under the weather sometimes.* I resist the urge to call Naomi and ask her what she thinks, still feeling uneasy about the text from her that I saw on Rav's phone, and instead I close my eyes and decide to do what they all keep telling me to – I try to sleep.

Scratch. Scratch. The noise from the chimney wakes me from the light, troubled doze I have allowed myself to fall into. I open my eyes without moving from where my head rests on the cushioned arm of the sofa, and stare up at the cracked, yellowing ceiling as the noise comes again, seeming louder this time. Turning my head, I see Mina is awake, but her eyes look too bright and her cheeks are flushed a deeper pink. The scratching comes again but Mina makes no sign that she has heard it.

'Min?' I whisper and she turns to look at me. 'Are you feeling poorly?'

'I don't feel well, Mama,' she says, before sliding from the armchair and coming to me, climbing up to lie on my chest. She is hot, too hot, her skin dry and burning.

'Oh, darling.' Holding her close I struggle to sit up, trying to ignore the insistent scratching from the chimney, a shard of guilt slicing through me. Did I cause this by keeping her home and saying she was unwell, when just this morning she was fine? Did I call some higher power into play when the lie tripped off my tongue? *Witchcraft. Strange things have happened around Gowdie Cottage ever since.* I shake the thought away, chiding myself for being ridiculous. 'Let me get you some medicine.' Laying her down, I get to my feet, noticing as I do that the sun is lower in the sky than I was expecting, the puddle of sunlight that was in the middle of the room when I sat down earlier has now almost disappeared, just pale fingers reaching the edge of the windowsill.

In the kitchen, I rummage in the cupboard searching for the infant paracetamol, but to no avail. The bottle we have doesn't even contain enough for one dose, and I am pretty sure Mina has a temperature, probably an ear infection the way she tugged on her earlobe as she climbed onto my lap. Picking up my phone to call Rav, I see the last text message he sent still sitting unread. I swipe to open the screen, revealing the message.

Just checking in, haven't heard from you all day. I'll probably be late again tonight. Don't wait up.

x

I imagine him quickly tapping out the text between calls or clients, then sliding the phone into his desk drawer, forgetting about us for the rest of the afternoon.

I tap on his name to call his office line, glancing at the clock to see with a shock that it is almost six o'clock. Hovering my finger above the icon to connect the call, I pause for a moment. There isn't much point in calling him. I probably won't get through, and even if I do, he'll be brusque and snappy, annoyed at me for disturbing him at work. And anyway, I can't wait for him to pick up infant paracetamol on the way home if he's going to be really late. I tap my fingers on my chin as I think. The time on my phone ticks over to 5.56 p.m. and I think of Naomi. The shop closes at six o'clock, but the phone rings out when I call. Swiping to call her mobile number, I wait, anxiously tapping one foot on the tiled floor but it goes to voicemail. She must be on her way home already. Sighing, I stoop to pick up Mina's trainers from the hallway and grab her little jacket from the coat stand by the door.

'Come on, darling, let's go and get you some medicine.'

There is a hint of a chill in the air, despite the sun still being above the horizon, and I walk briskly, glad that I thought to attach the weird buggy board contraption that Avó bought us so Mina can ride along instead of walking. The small supermarket in the village is still open and I hurry inside, glancing at the darkened windows of The Daisy Chain as I pass. I had half wished that Naomi was working late and hadn't answered her phone because she was occupied with floristry tape and ferns, but the complete darkness even at the far end of the shop tells me otherwise. Snatching up the medicine, I pay quickly and once outside lay my hand on Mina's forehead. She is still warm, so I open the package and hastily squirt a syringe of sticky pink liquid into her mouth, hoping it will start to work by the time we get home.

'Daddy,' Mina mumbles as I tuck the blanket a little tighter around the baby, before turning the pram in the direction of home.

'Yes, Daddy will be home soon,' I murmur, laying one hand on her head as I try to steer with the other.

'No, *Daddy*,' Mina's voice is thin and whiny as she raises a finger to point to the small area outside the village pub. I look to where she is pointing, my heart seeming to stop in my chest. Rav's car is parked in a narrow space outside the pub. I pause, then slowly step towards the pub window, peering in through the glass into the bar. Rav sits there, a pint next to one elbow, as Naomi sits beside him, talking animatedly. It's such a familiar scene that I can almost hear her voice, the only difference is that I am this side of the window. Shut out. Rav keeps his eyes on her as she talks, and I realize I can't remember the last time he paid so much attention to me when I am speaking. Naomi moves closer, her knee resting against his as she nudges Rav in the arm, shaking her head with a faint hint of a smile on her face before she raises her hand in a gesture to the barman to bring her another glass of wine.

I watch, my pulse thudding loudly in my ears, unable to tear my gaze away. Mina shifts impatiently beside me, as Rav leans in close to Naomi, his lips grazing her hair as he talks in her ear. Turning her face so that she is gazing into his eyes, Naomi reaches out a hand and twines her fingers with his, before Rav slides off his bar stool completely and stands beside Naomi, wrapping her in his arms. I turn away, bile burning the back of my throat, my eyes hot and sore with unshed tears as I grasp Mina tightly by the hand.

I start to walk briskly, ignoring Mina's cries, almost running across the pedestrian crossing and narrowly missing a cyclist who raises a middle finger in my direction.

'I want Daddy,' Mina cries, her hot face red and sweaty.

'It's not Daddy,' I lie, 'it's just the same car as Daddy. He has to work late but he'll come in and kiss you goodnight, OK?' The lie tastes bitter on my tongue and I store it away, to think over later when Mina is bathed and in bed, her temperature finally lowered, when the house is quiet, and I can turn it over in my mind.

'Al? I'm home.' It's close to nine o'clock when I hear the front door slam closed, and then Rav walks through the bedroom door.

'Some meeting,' I say, not looking up from where I am leaning over the cot. The baby is sleeping but I don't want to make eye contact, don't want to watch his face as he lies.

'God, it really was.' Rav lowers his voice, stripping off his jacket, throwing his tie on the chair in the corner of the bedroom. 'Sorry I'm so late. Did you eat?'

'Yes, I ate with Mina,' I lie. I watched Mina eat a small bowl of spaghetti hoops, if that counts. 'Sorry I didn't save you anything.'

'Oh, don't worry. I grabbed something after the meeting.' He walks towards the bathroom, snatching up a bath towel and I follow him, my skin prickling.

'Did you? Where did you go?' I wait expectantly, giving him the chance to redeem himself without knowing.

'I stopped for a pint with Gareth, so we grabbed some chips while we were there.' He turns the shower on, the pipes clanking.

'Oh.' My stomach drops away, as if on a rollercoaster and I tense as Rav turns and wraps his arms around my waist, his bare skin warm against my body. 'Mina isn't well, I think she's got an ear infection.'

'Really? Poor thing. Keep her home from nursery tomorrow.' Rav kisses the top of my head and I bury my face against his chest, the hairs there tickling the end of my nose.

'We had no Calpol. I had to take her out to buy some – I did call Naomi to ask if she could get me some because it was almost six, and I knew she would have been leaving work, but she didn't reply.'

Rav stills, almost imperceptibly, before pulling away from me and yanking back the curtain to the shower. Steam fills the room and wraps around his body, creating a blanket between us.

'Sorry. I didn't mean to be so late. I wanted to miss the traffic back from Bromley, so I didn't leave the pub till gone eight.' He's lying, and the ease with which he does it makes the blood in my veins run cold.

Three o'clock in the morning. The real witching hour, not midnight as I always believed. The sensation of someone sitting on the bed wakes me from the light, troubled doze I have fallen into and I blink myself awake, sure for a moment that I can feel a hand on my chest, the warmth of a palm lingering on my skin. I lie still, Rav's snore rumbling in my ear as he sleeps the dead slumber of the deceitful, waiting for *something*. I have the feeling that I was not alone while I was sleeping. That someone was there, watching me. I lie there, trying to keep my breathing even and regular as my heart crashes in my chest and my skin prickles with goosebumps, but there is no movement, no longer any sense that there is someone in the room other than Rav. *A dream, that's all*. But even as I think the words, I know I don't believe them. The baby stirs and I feed him quickly and silently, before placing him back in the cot and going to stand at the landing window, the chilly draught around my legs. Rav still snores lightly and I am alone. I can't sleep, visions of feathers, a figure on the stairs, a flash of movement in the mirror, my mother, Rav drinking in a pub forty miles closer to home than he said he was, all dancing in my head as soon as I close my eyes. I look out on to the woods, strain behind my eyes causing the faint thud of a headache at the bridge of my nose. Why were Rav and Naomi meeting at the pub? And why would he lie? Is this something to do with the text she sent him about needing to talk to him? They looked like they belonged together, I think, picturing them in the pub, they looked like a couple. Is that what this is? A prickle of unease runs down my spine, as a fox appears at the edge of the woods, his head raised as he sniffs the air. *Wily, cunning, sharp*. Can these words apply to Rav too? The fox steps towards the pond, his nose close to the ground now, hunting something that has scurried along this same path. There is a shriek from the woods, a high, keening sound that makes my breath stick in my throat and my hand flies to my mouth, a pulse roaring in my ears. *Just an animal*, I tell myself, an owl, or a mate to the sleek, red fox that works its way towards the water now, the lumpen, dark body of *something* rustling in the reeds, before slipping into the water, ripples spreading across the broken surface. *An animal, nothing more.* I close my eyes to the image of a small body, huddling in the trees, the moonlight casting a blue-white aura around her blonde hair. *Agnes's child, still waiting, still lost.* The shriek comes again, and I turn from the window, anxious to lie next to Rav's warm, lying, deceitful body. It sounds unnervingly human.

Chapter Fourteen

Rav seems overly attentive this morning, bringing me a cup of tea before the baby has even woken for his six o'clock feed, and sitting on the edge of the bed as I sit up to drink it.

'Aren't you going to be late?' I bury my face in my cup, the steam hot on my cheeks. My head still thuds with a dull ache after only a couple of hours' sleep and I wish he hadn't woken me.

'Yes, Probably. I didn't get to see you last night.' He reaches for my hand, but I move, scratching at a non-existent itch at the top of my arm. It was his choice to come home so late. His choice to meet Naomi instead of coming home to us. The image of the two of them, sitting so close together, looking so *intimate*, rises to the front of my mind and I feel suddenly sick.

'Well, I need to get up.' I push back the covers, cold air hitting my legs and feet. 'I need to get Mina ready for preschool.'

'You're not sending her today?' Rav frowns, shifting out of the way so that I can get out of bed. 'I thought she was ill? I checked on her when I got up and she was still a little warm, so I don't think she should go in today, Allie.'

I had forgotten that Mina was ill yesterday. How could I have forgotten? I sink back down onto the bed, taking back the mug that Rav holds out. 'Of course not. Of course, I'm not going to send her.'

'Al, are you sure everything is OK? You seem … I don't know. Not yourself.' Concern sits on his face and I wonder just how sincere that concern is.

'Everything is fine. I saw the health visitor yesterday, she was happy, she's discharged us.'

'Really?'

'Yes. Really. I should get up, and you need to get going. You don't want to have to make up any time at the office.' *Because I know you didn't stay late for a meeting last night*. The words hang unspoken in the air, but it's only me who is aware of them.

'How about I try and get home a bit early tonight? I'll pick us up Thai on the way back and maybe we can sit out by the pond and have a glass of wine when the baby goes to bed?' His fingers inch towards mine, reaching out, stroking my palm and I feel my pulse slow.

'Maybe.'

'If you pump, I'll give Leo his late feed too. That way you can enjoy some wine and relax for a couple of hours.'

I want to believe that he'll do this, but bitter experience tells me he won't. Something will come up at work, and he'll text to say he's going to be late – that's what usually happens. I wonder if it is guilt that is making him unusually patient and attentive this morning. It's on the tip of my tongue to ask him to tell me where he really was yesterday, to tell him that I saw his car parked outside The Black Horse last night when he says he was over forty miles away in Bromley. That I know he was with Naomi, not Gareth. But there is a part of me that thinks – *hopes* – that it wasn't what I imagined, and a part of me that doesn't want to know if it was. 'You should get going,' I say instead, letting him kiss my forehead and watching as he walks towards the door. 'See you tonight.'

Mina wakes not long after Rav leaves, followed by the baby, his shrill cries making my hairs stand on end as I remember the noises coming from the woods in the dead of night, the noises that sounded like a crying child. *Agnes's crying child*. I feed him urgently, shoving my breast in his face in order to stop the crying, then feeling guilty as he snuffles and wrenches his head away.

'Sorry, baby.' I kiss him on his soft, downy hair, closing my eyes and inhaling his scent, feeling the sharp pinch as he finally latches on and begins to feed. Mina comes to sit close by me, her colour back to normal now and as I press my hand to her forehead, it feels cooler.

'No nursery today,' I tell her, as she presses herself against me, her weight a small, suffocating cushion as her sharp elbows dig into my ribs. 'We're going to see a lady.'

I had texted Miranda after my mother had left, asking her about visiting Mrs Sparks. It had been less than an hour later when she had replied, telling me that Mrs Sparks would see me this morning. I feel apprehensive now, as the baby finishes feeding and I tuck him in the pram, before helping Mina with her trainers, and I am glad when a knock on the door signals the arrival of my mother. Stepping out onto the path to the pavement, I pause for a moment wondering whether I should turn back and pick up the keys from where Rav threw them onto the dresser.

'Allie? Are you ready? We don't want to be late.' My mother stands waiting for me under the small amount of shade cast by the yew tree in the front garden.

'I'm ready.' I help Mina onto the buggy board, making sure her hands are holding tightly to the handle of the pram and start walking. 'You shouldn't stand near that tree, it's poisonous you know.'

'Tree of Death.' Mum rolls her eyes. 'I didn't touch it, don't worry so much.' She falls into step beside me and we walk in silence towards the outskirts of the village. I don't have much to say, anxiety squeezing my stomach as I wonder what Mrs Sparks will tell me about the house, if anything at all. It's only a short walk to her house and when we reach it, I realize I have walked past many times on the way to take Mina to the park.

'Here,' I say. 'This is it.' We stop, and I take a moment to catch my breath. 'OK. Let's knock on the door and see what she has to say.' I lift the knocker and drop it twice, the thud sounding abruptly loud in the quiet of the street. A few moments later the door swings open, and a woman with a lanyard around her neck appears.

'Allie Harper? Mrs Sparks is expecting you.' She stands to one side and I manoeuvre the pram awkwardly into the dimly lit hallway. 'I'm Mrs Sparks's carer. Follow me, I'll introduce you to her.' Mina steps off the buggy board and slides her hand into mine. The baby is sleeping, so I pull his blanket a little lower – the air is stifling – and leave him in the pram. I shoot an anxious look at my mother, but she nods and makes a shooing motion for me to follow the nurse. We step through a doorway into a cluttered sitting room. Ornaments cover every inch of available surface, as thin sunshine battles its way through yellowing nets and Phil and Holly talk soundlessly on the television. An elderly lady sits in a high-backed armchair, a hand-knitted shawl over her legs. She looks frail and fragile, other-worldly almost.

'Elsie?' The nurse crouches in front of her. 'This is the lady Miranda was telling you about. This is Allie Harper. She's come to talk to you about the old house.' She flashes me a reassuring smile and makes a discreet exit.

'Hello, Mrs Sparks, thank you for agreeing to talk to me.' I perch on the edge of the sofa opposite, Mina sliding to stand between my knees. 'This is my mother, Sophie.'

'It is nice to meet you, Mrs Sparks.' My mother steps forward into a thin shaft of sunlight that forces its way through a gap in the net curtains.

The elderly lady's gaze drifts towards my mother, and then back down to me, her blue eyes clear and bright. 'Elsie. Call me Elsie.' Her voice is quiet, and I lean in to hear her. 'So, you live in the cottage? At Gowdie Cottage?'

'I do, yes. We moved in a few months ago.'

'How are you finding it?' Her eyes fix on mine.

'Oh, we like it. I mean, the cottage is beautiful … the garden … the garden needs some work, but luckily I'm a florist.' My mouth feels dry, and I raise my gaze to where my mother has retreated to the doorway, giving the old lady some space. 'Tell her,' she mouths. I nod and turn back to Elsie.

'Is it quiet?' Elsie asks.

'Quiet?'

'At night. Is it quiet? Or are you woken?'

I think of the child's cries that have woken me almost every night this week. 'Sometimes.'

My mother shifts impatiently in the doorway and I take a breath. 'Listen, Elsie, I found something in the cottage, and I wanted to ask you about it. It was a set of two iron keys, tied together with feathers and a stone with a hole through the middle.'

'The hag stone,' Elsie says quietly. 'You found it?'

'Yes,' I say. 'I found it under the floorboards in the attic. There was a mirror, and when I moved the mirror I saw the feather. You don't know anything about it, do you? I told Miranda and she said you used to live there, that you might have some more information about the house.'

'Agnes Gowdie's house,' Elsie says. 'She's still there, they say. What did you do with the keys?'

'They're in my bedroom. I've hung the mirror on the wall in the hall, it's like it was supposed to be there.' I smile at the thought of it. 'So, you do know about the keys?'

'I put them there,' Elsie says, her face growing serious. 'I hid them under the floorboards. They're a charm, you see. To protect the house.' She looks at Mina. 'Things quietened down after I hid the charm, but by then it was too late.'

Ice water trickles through my veins and I shiver as if

someone has just walked over my grave. 'Quietened down? What do you mean?'

'My mother had the gift,' Elsie says. 'She said I had it too, and I've always wondered if that's the reason why it all happened.'

'The gift?' My mother steps back into the beam of sunlight next to Elsie's chair, one hand outstretched to rest on Elsie's arm. 'What do you mean, gift?'

'The house was always … active,' Elsie says, 'but it got worse after my little brother was born. I would hear crying in the night, but he would be sleeping. We would feel as if someone was in the room with us, but there was no one there. Things moved of their own accord. I saw her, you know. Agnes. After the baby was born. That's why I had to make the charm.' She waggles her fingers at Mina, but her face is dark. 'Do you just have this little one?'

'No,' I say. My throat feels thick, closing over as fear tickles at the base of my spine. 'I have a little boy. Leo. He's four weeks old.'

Elsie looks up at me sharply. 'You have to put it back,' she says, a quiver in her voice. 'The charm, you have to put it back under the floorboards. It's there to keep you safe. Promise me you'll put it back.' Her voice rises and the nurse bustles her way into the room.

'You're upsetting her. I'm going to have to ask you to leave.'

'I'm sorry, I …' I get up, squeezing Mina's hand tightly. 'I'll put it back, OK? Just please, tell me what happened in the house. Tell me what Agnes did.'

'Put it back,' Elsie says. Her eyes move down to where my mother's hand still rests lightly on her forearm. 'You've disturbed things. It's there to keep the children safe.'

'Allie, what the hell are you doing?' Rav walks into the bedroom as the light is fading.

'Looking for the keys,' I say, pulling out T-shirts and vests from the chest of drawers. I had hurried home from Mrs Sparks's house, dread lodged like a stone in my stomach. My mother had wanted to come in and talk over what Elsie had said, but she had had to leave, late for a meeting at the university, and I had rushed upstairs only to find the charm missing from where Rav had left it on the dresser. Now, Mina and Leo are in bed, and I am tearing the bedroom apart looking for it, Mrs Sparks's words reverberating in my mind.

'What keys? Your keys are in the front door, I just found them there.' Rav holds up a hand, my house keys swinging from the end of his forefinger. 'Do you want us to get burgled or something?'

'Not those keys.' I stop, my hands on my hips, scanning the room for anywhere else the charm could be. 'The ones I found in the attic, with the feathers and the stone.'

'Oh.' Rav watches me as he lays my keys in the spot on the dresser where the charm was. 'I threw them out. They were rubbish, Al.'

'You threw them out? When?' Already I am pushing past him, down the stairs to the kitchen.

'I don't know … last night? The night before?' Rav

follows me, his feet heavy on the stairs. 'Allie, fucking hell. What are you doing?'

I pull the lid off the bin and yank out the half-full bin bag. Grimacing, I reach in and start to rummage in among the food scraps and tea bags. 'I need to find it, Rav. You shouldn't have thrown it away, not without talking to me first.'

'Allie, stop. Jesus Christ.' Rav pulls the black sack from my hands. 'They're not in there. The bag was full, so I took it to the outside bin and the bin men came this morning. The keys are long gone.'

'Oh no.' I slump back against the kitchen sink, suddenly aware of the tea leaves and tomato sauce staining my hands. 'Rav, you don't know what you've done.'

'I've thrown out rubbish, Al, that's what I've done!' Rav briskly ties the top of the bin bag in a knot. 'What the hell is all this about? Has that woman been filling your head with more crap about witches?'

'No ...' I say, but Rav carries on, his voice raised.

'Because if she has, I'm having words with her. I don't need to come home to you rifling through the bin because some mad woman has told you some crazy story. I've got enough shit on my plate at work without this as well.'

Tears spring to my eyes and Rav's face softens. 'Al, what's really going on here?'

'It wasn't Miranda. It was the old lady who lived here before, years ago. She ... she said that it was a charm, to keep the children safe. I just wanted to put it back, that's why I was looking for it.'

'We don't need a charm to keep the children safe, Allie.' Rav pulls me towards him, seemingly not caring about the filth on my hands as he wraps me in a hug. 'That's what we're here for.'

But you're never here. I think the words, but don't say them out loud. We stand that way for a few moments, Rav's arms around me as I cross my wrists behind his back, careful not to get dirt on him. As he pulls back to drop a kiss on my forehead, the shadows in the hallway move, as if a figure has pulled back just out of sight.

Chapter Fifteen

'He threw them away,' I say, as my mother slips into the chair opposite mine. We are meeting at the village café, the morning after we met with Mrs Sparks. 'Rav threw the charm away, Mum. He said they were rubbish, that we don't need them.'

'How do you feel about this?' My mother toys with the sugar packet in her hands, turning it over and over, the thin paper wrapper crumpling.

'I don't know,' I say. The waitress appears beside me and I pause to order. 'A peppermint tea for me please, and ...' I look towards where my mother sits across from me. '... a black coffee?'

Mum nods and the waitress scribbles on her pad and whisks away with a smile.

'A pot of cream,' my mother calls after her. 'Bring a small pot of cream too, please.'

'I feel like it should be rubbish, that Rav is probably right and it's all just superstitious nonsense,' I say, keeping my voice low, even though the waitress is out of earshot. 'But then there is part of me that thinks about what Mrs Sparks said, that it was there to keep us safe, to keep the children safe.' *Active*, that was the word she used. She said the house was active before she hid the charm. 'I feel ... unsettled, I suppose. I wish Rav hadn't thrown them away.'

My mother suppresses a smile. 'Allie, it probably is just superstition. Perhaps. What do you feel in your gut?'

I am silent, slightly hurt by the ghost of a smile that still sits on her lips. Everyone, my mother, Rav, they all seem to find this a little ridiculous, funny, something to laugh about. 'My gut tells me she is right, that the charm was protecting the house,' I say finally. 'Things have been ... odd in the house since I found it.' *Hands on me while I sleep, that unnerving feeling that someone is watching me, movement in the glass of the mirror.*

The waitress appears, placing the peppermint tea in front of me, hesitating a moment before setting the coffee down in front of my mother. 'Enjoy,' she says, slipping a small silver plate onto the table with the bill attached.

'She forgot the cream,' my mother mutters under her breath, flapping a hand at me when I look after the waitress and raise my hand to flag her down. 'Leave it. It's better for me to not have the cream. Perhaps it is for the best that Rav throws away the keys, the charm, whatever it is. You said yourself he doesn't believe in any of these things. So maybe, it can be a fresh start for you both.'

'Perhaps. Although I just wish he would listen to me, instead of brushing everything aside like it's nothing. I mean ...'

'Listen, Allie. I think you must just focus on the children, and yourself. You told me before you are not sleeping properly, and you have to take care of yourself, so you can take good care of the children. Tell me, how is everything with Rav?'

'Fine,' I say darkly, 'apart from he's coming home late. Every night. We barely see him at the moment although ...'

'Although?'

Reluctantly, I let the words come. 'He found time to meet Naomi for a drink.' Mum says nothing but waits expectantly. 'And she texted him to say she needs to talk to him about something. She never mentioned it to me, though.'

'You think something is going on?' Mum leans forward, lowering her voice. I bet she would love that, if Rav were cheating on me. 'Surely not.'

'No. Yes. Maybe. I don't know. They looked ... close.' I push my mug away from me, feeling slightly sick. 'It might be nothing, I don't know. Honestly, Mum, I don't think I can even think about it at the moment.'

'All the more reason to look after yourself. You know I had to take care of you alone after your father left us. It's difficult, Allie, you know that, but you also know that you can come to the apartment in Paris anytime.'

'Yes, Mum, I know how hard it was for you.' *Not just for you, either.* 'And I told you, I'm not coming to Paris. It might be nothing. She might have financial problems or something that she doesn't want to worry me with, I don't know.' Wishing I hadn't mentioned it to her, I get to my feet, sliding the strap of the changing bag onto my shoulder. 'Look, I have to go, I need to go and get Mina from school.

I'll see you later?' I throw a five-pound note and some small change into the dish on the table and leave my mother sitting in front of her slowly cooling coffee.

'You stay there, poppet.' After lunch, snuggled together on the sofa, I slide out from under Mina's bony elbows and take the baby upstairs to the cot, swapping his tiny body for the plastic heft of the baby monitor. I step lightly down the stairs, ignoring the chill that permeates the landing, a basket of laundry under my arm, a sense of normality descending. As I shove the clothes into the machine, I wonder if I have been overthinking things. I didn't sleep last night, but I also didn't have the dream. I am tired, but what new mother wouldn't be? The health visitor didn't seem to see any problems with me, or the baby, so maybe that's all it is, a dream. Maybe my mother is right – I should forget about all of it and start over with Rav. The washing machine begins to turn slowly, the dull whirring a comfortable, normal sound. I spritz over the kitchen counters, change the bin, bleach the sink, inhaling the chlorine-y scent that hangs in the air reminding me of the pool, of hours spent in my teenage years doing lengths until my arms hurt and my breath felt raw in my throat. Mrs Sparks's words don't mean anything, I tell myself as I scrub, and wipe, and mop. It's just superstition, a story made up to draw in the tourists like all the other ghost stories. She never actually said what happened in the house, just that it was active, which realistically could mean anything. Maybe her parents didn't get along and that was the crying she heard at night when her baby brother was sleeping. How could anything awful happen in a house that smells so fresh, that houses a happy family? I blot out the image of the tied rosemary hanging over the kitchen doorway, ignore the thought of the rusty iron keys that had lain jumbled in a tangled heap in the piles of junk of the top of the dresser, as I scour and clean, my positivity fading, and I jump as the doorbell rings.

'Shit.' I wipe my hands on the tea towel that hangs on the Aga, the skin feeling cracked and raw from the cleaning products, and open the door to the postman. 'Thanks.' I take the mail from him, scanning through the envelopes as I push the door closed with my shoulder. 'Oh … wait!' There is an envelope marked with an address in the next road over, that has slipped in between two of ours. Opening the door, I call out, hurrying along the path to the road, hoping to catch the postman before he gets back in his van. Too late. He is already driving away as I reach the pavement. I shrug and make my way back up the path towards the front door, past the huge yew tree in the front garden. At first, I don't notice them, it's only as I get closer that I do a double take, registering that there is something in the tree that doesn't look right. Moving closer, I frown, the envelopes in my hand forgotten as I step towards the pile of leaves and squashed berries, my hair tangling in the low hanging branches as I almost walk into them. Raising my hand to my mouth, I stifle the shriek that bubbles up in my throat, before I snatch a tissue from my pocket and wrap it around my hand. Bones. Tiny, fragile bones tied together with what looks like garden twine and hanging carefully at eye level in the branches of the tree.

Hurrying back into the house, I slam the door without thinking, dropping the mail to the floor where it scatters. Adrenaline courses through my body and for one unnerving moment I think I am going to be sick. Forcing deep breaths in through my nose and out through my mouth, I wait until the nausea has passed before I open my hand and gingerly peel back the tissue to reveal the creamy off-white bones.

As I bend my head to get a closer look, I feel it. Eyes on me, making the hairs on the back of my neck stand on end. Raising my eyes, I look into the mirror, something dark and fleeting darting out of sight the moment my gaze hits the glass. There it is, that unmistakable feeling of being watched. I stand up straighter, my senses on high alert, certain that there is something, something awful, just waiting for me to drop my guard. Squeezing my fist tightly closed I step back, my knees feeling as if they will give way beneath me, my eyes never leaving the glass. Slowly, silently I turn to look behind me at the staircase. It is empty. As I exhale, my breath steams slightly in the mirror, and I am suddenly, inexplicably cold.

'Mummy?' Mina's voice calls from the sitting room, and immediately the chill dissipates, leaving me tired and confused, standing in the hallway with the bones tightly clutched in my fist.

'Mina?' I peer into the room where she sits on the floor, the TV blaring a nonsensical tune as creatures dance across the screen. 'Are you OK?'

Mina nods, seemingly oblivious to anything but the television. 'Watching the lady,' she says, pointing at the screen.

'OK. OK.' Looking down at the small bundle in my fist, I resist the urge to wipe my hands, moving into the kitchen away from Mina. I feel dirty, the bones in my hand giving off a thick, clinging aura that makes saliva spurt into my cheeks. Wrapping them back up, I call Rav on instinct, cutting the call before he gets the chance to answer. He won't see any threat in it. He'll just tell me that I'm exhausted, that it means nothing, that it's a prank by local kids to try and psych me out, but the goosebumps rising so hard on my arms that it is almost painful tells me otherwise. Instead, I dial Naomi, forgetting about her sitting with Rav in the pub, calling The Daisy Chain directly instead of her mobile.

'Good morning, The Daisy Chain. Evie speaking.' The voice on the other end of the line is unfamiliar and I stumble for a moment, before remembering what Naomi had said about taking on a new girl.

'Can I speak to Naomi, please?' My voice is thin and reedy, and I have to clear my throat before the words will come out. There is a pause, a muffled exchange of words and then Naomi's voice rings out in my ear.

'Hello?'

'Naomi, it's me.'

'Allie? How are you? You sound—'

'Are you busy?' I ask, cutting her off. 'I need to talk to you.'

'Well, busyish …' I hear her murmur something to

someone in the background. 'I can come over in an hour or so, if that helps? Is everything all right?' She lowers her voice. 'Al, are the kids OK?'

'What? Yes, of course they are. They're with me. So, you can come over?' I turn the bundle over in my hands, almost expecting it to burn my skin. 'I found something. Something horrible,' I say before she can answer me.

'Something horrible? Al, you're not …'

'Naomi, I found bones. *Bones*. I told you … remember I told you I found the keys? Well now, there are bones.'

'Yeah, you told me. But what—'

'The bones were tied together, in the yew tree in the front garden. Just now. Whoever was in the trees, whoever was watching me from the woods has been to the house, right into the front garden. Maybe even while I was here, while I was asleep.' Spinning around, I peer into the sitting room to check on Mina, who is sitting just as I left her. I press the baby monitor to my ear, but there is no sound. 'They left it here so I would know.'

'I'll be over soon.' Naomi's voice is soothing in my ear, and I feel the adrenaline begin to drain, leaving me feeling weak and shaky. 'Just … don't do anything. Stay there, and I'll be there as soon as I can, OK?'

I hang up and go to the front door, unlatching the lock and taking the chain off, before tentatively opening it the tiniest crack and peering out into the street. Fear whispers in my ear, drowning out the thud of my racing pulse as I peep out, sure that I will see something, *someone* watching from the shadows. But the street is empty, except for Charlotte

Elliot, the barmaid from the pub, who raises a hand. I throw a wobbly smile in her direction and close the door again, heading for the stairs. The baby still sleeps, his eyelids moving rapidly as he dreams. I lay a hand on his chest, reassured to feel the fabric beneath my hand rising up and down, and move to the window to look out onto the garden, and the woods beyond.

Please be quick, Naomi, I whisper under my breath, my eyes fixed on the trees. There is no unusual movement, only the soft swaying of the branches as the wind ruffles through the leaves of the trees. My fingers are wrapped so tightly around the bundle of tissue that my nails dig into my palm and I open my hand to look closely at the bones. I had yanked them from the tree without stopping to think, the yarn fraying now in my hand as I turn them over to inspect them. They are bleached white, tied tightly together with garden twine, a small dark stain on the end of one bone. At first glance they could be finger bones, and I shudder inwardly, trying to tell myself that of course they're not finger bones, probably chicken bones. But why? I turn them over and over, resisting the urge to wipe my fingers on the fabric of my jeans. Why would someone tie bones up in a tree? No matter how much I try and tell myself that it is just a prank, kids maybe, I can't shake the feeling that there is more to it than a simple trick. It's left a feeling behind, a dark, sinister feeling that winds its way round my legs like a cat, furry fingers slinking up my thighs, around my ribcage where they squeeze tightly.

I rewrap the bones, tucking the end of the tissue in tightly to leave no part of them exposed, and place it on the dressing table to show Naomi when she arrives. As I turn towards the door there is movement in the garden, and I step towards the window again.

White. I think I see a flash of dark hair, white fabric catching the sun as someone steps between the trees, the outline partially blocked by the branches and the tops of the reeds that surround the pond. Anger rushes through my veins and I run down the stairs and out of the back door, my bare feet damp as I run across the dew-covered lawn.

'Hey!' Stopping at the edge of the pond, I peer into the darkened tunnel of interlocked branches ahead of me. 'Who's there? I saw you just now.'

There is no reply, just the caw of a bird overhead, sharp and harsh. I rub my hands over my arms, wishing I had stopped to pick up a sweater or at least stuck my feet into flipflops. 'Hello?' My call is quieter now, and I realize that maybe I was mistaken after all. I blink, letting my breath calm and slow. The woods are quiet, the only movement the rustle of the glossy, green leaves. Maybe it wasn't a person – perhaps that flash of white was something else, feathers or fur belonging to a bird or another small, unknown animal living in the woods. There is a squawk from the baby monitor, and I feel my shoulders slump, my cold feet feeling leaden as I turn and walk back towards the house, the small cry of the baby in stereo now, floating out from the open bedroom window, mirrored through the monitor. *Is this what Agnes heard?* I wonder, *night after night, the cries of her lost baby? Is she still here now?* I feel the prickle of eyes on me, suddenly sure that Agnes is here, watching me. That it was her moving through the trees. With one backward glance towards the pond, and the woods beyond it, I hurry back into the house, locking the back door and rushing up the stairs to fetch the baby before he erupts into a full-on wail. He is quiet as I reach the landing and, crossing the bedroom quickly, I reach down into the cot, ready to hold him close, to nuzzle my cheek against his head, but the cot is empty. The baby is gone.

I no longer feel scared. I have felt afraid for so long, fear constantly brushing against the very edges of my nerves, fraying them, until I feel I might dissolve. But not now. I try to picture his face, but it won't come, my mind's eye is just a blank. It's gone, like I don't know who he is. As if I never knew who he was. All I can see is the anger, the fear, the suspicion. I don't want to think about what he has done, what has gone before. What has led to this moment, led to me on the stairs, icy cold and broken. I catch sight of myself in the darkened glass of the window. Dark eyes in a white face. Tangled hair. A smudge of something on one cheek. Battered. Broken. That's what I see in the reflection shining back at me, but not fear. I am not afraid. I whisper it under my breath over and over, careful not to disturb the sleeping girl in the darkened bedroom. My heart still bangs hard in my chest, my breath raw and bloody as it rattles from my throat. I am not scared, but I am still anxious. Anxious to do what I must, before they come. They won't be long; I am sure they are already on their way. If I don't do this, everything will tumble down around me, fracturing. Like soldiers made of glass. Everything splintered and shattered. I think of my mother, of how she will respond when she finds out. I picture *her house, so far away, everything in its place, neat and tidy. The smell of wine on her breath. After, when all this is over, I will go there, to my mother's house, back to the beginning, as if none of this ever happened. To my home. And I will crawl beneath the heavy blankets and my mother will sit on the edge of my bed, the way she always does when I am upset. She will hold me, and stroke my hair, and murmur little familiar sayings to me, telling me I never should have left, that she was right. I will be home, and she will make everything all OK again. My hands shake, but my feet are steady on the stairs, one step, then another, climbing towards the top. This is not who I planned to be — not what I planned to be — but this is my only option. Fate, if you like. There is only so much a person can stand before you have no choice but to take steps to protect yourself. I tried to tell them. I tried to warn them all. Shadows crowd in the entrance to the room, where soft breaths hum in and out, and they feel familiar, warm, egging me on. Telling me this is how it is; this is how it should be. This will mark the end of what has come before, will herald a new beginning. Darker, more unfamiliar shapes dance across the back wall, goading me, taunting me. I am an outcast, that is what they have made of me. But after all this, I won't be anymore. I'll be free. Fear rises like bile in my throat.*

Chapter Sixteen

I stare into the cot and yank back the blanket that lies there, crumpled on the empty sheet. The baby is gone. The monitor lies silent in my hand, and I drop it into the cot without thinking before turning and running down the stairs, my heart in my mouth.

'Mina!' I shout her name as I tumble the last three or four steps down into the hallway, landing awkwardly on my ankle. 'Shit.' Pushing myself back onto my feet, I wince, pain shooting up my ankle as I put weight on my foot. Maybe I did see somebody in the garden. Maybe they were watching the house, maybe they left the bones tangled in the tree. *No.* I shake the thought away, fear plucking at my nerve endings.

'Mina!' Calling to her again, I notice that the front door is ever so slightly ajar. Fuck. I know I closed it properly after I came back into the house after finding the bones. Didn't I? What if I didn't? What if someone – whoever was watching the house, watching *us* – has taken the baby, snatched Mina? Images flash through my mind of Agnes Gowdie frantically searching for her baby, of a flash of white through the trees, of a hand reaching out and grasping Mina's, leading her away down the path towards the road. A sob catches at the back of my throat, and I limp towards the door as fast as I can on my sore ankle.

'Allie. Allie, it's OK, I'm here.' Naomi appears in the doorway to the living room and it takes me a moment to see that the baby lies snuggly in her arms. 'Jesus, what did you do?' She looks at my foot, and I follow her gaze to see a fat, blue swelling appearing on my ankle bone.

'You've got the baby.' Snatching him out of her hands, my nail catches the delicate skin on his cheek, and he lets out a cry. I pull him close to me, kissing the red welt that rises on his cheek before turning my fury on Naomi. 'What the hell do you think you're doing?'

'What?' Naomi blinks. 'What are you talking about, Allie? He was crying …'

'You took the baby. Took him out of the cot without even telling me. How did you get in here anyway?' My eyes go to the door, the thin line of light peeping in where the door doesn't meet the frame. 'You let yourself in.'

'You told me to come. The baby was crying.' Naomi looks close to tears herself. 'I knocked and knocked and there was no answer. I knew you must be home because I could hear the baby crying.'

'I could have been in the bathroom.'

'Allie, the door was ajar. It wasn't latched. After you called me this morning, I was worried about you. When I got here and saw that the door wasn't closed properly, I thought that something might have happened to you.'

I had forgotten that I called Naomi, had forgotten my panic on opening the door earlier. The image of bones tied neatly in the branches of the yew tree comes to mind and I have to fight to suppress a shudder. Naomi reaches out, her hand coming to rest on my shoulder. 'I'm sorry,' she says. 'I shouldn't have let myself in. I thought … I was worried, that's all. Look at you, you're shaking. Come and sit down and you can tell me about what you found.'

Naomi holds her arms out to take the baby, but I ignore her, stepping towards the living room. My ankle throbs as I press my weight onto it and for a moment my vision goes cloudy, nausea causing my stomach to lurch and roll.

'Let me take him, come on, Al. You're in pain.'

Reluctantly I pass the baby to Naomi, my arms feeling empty and cold without the heft of his weight. She presses her cheek to his head before gently taking him through to where the Moses basket sits empty next to the fireplace. As she lays him down, I feel an itching urge to move the basket away from the chimney, but before I can Naomi takes my elbow and helps me hobble to the sofa. 'There.' She arranges my foot on some cushions, ignoring my wincing as her fingers brush my sore ankle. 'Let me get you some tea. Do you have anything to bandage this up?'

'There's a first aid kit in the medicine cupboard in the bathroom.' I have no choice but to let Naomi bustle around, taking care of me. Now the shock of her appearing in the doorway with the baby in her arms after I thought someone had taken him has faded, having her here comes as something of a relief. Mina scrambles up on to the sofa next to me, her thumb going to her mouth and I lean down and kiss the top of her hair, smelling the apple shampoo I used to wash her hair last night.

'Here you go, I brought you some painkillers too.' Naomi hands me the packet of Co-codamol I brought home from the hospital and crouches at my feet, the green first aid box in her hands.

'Aren't these a bit strong?' I turn the packet over in my hands, remembering the thick, suffocating drowsiness that came over me the last time I took them, sitting at the kitchen table. The vision, dream, memory that followed. I tuck the packet down the side of the sofa, feeling the sharp corner of the box against my thigh.

'They'll do you good,' Naomi says without looking up from where she is expertly wrapping a gauzy bandage around my foot. 'Let me know if this is too tight.'

I try to flex my foot, wincing again as the sharp pain shoots across my ankle. 'It's fine,' I say, feeling it throb beneath the gauze.

'Hand me those tablets if you're done with them.' Naomi gets to her feet and holds out a hand. I slip my fingers down between the sofa cushions and hand them to her, feeling like a scolded child. 'I don't want you to forget about them, Mina could get hold of them. I'll put this stuff away and make us some tea, OK? And then we can talk.'

'Don't you need to get back to the shop?'

'Evie is in charge; I don't have to hurry back.' Naomi smiles, 'I'm hardly going to rush away and leave you in this state, am I? I wouldn't be a very good friend.'

I muster a smile as she heads out to the kitchen, feeling like a pretty shitty friend myself.

'Here you go.' I take the steaming mug of tea that Naomi holds out to me, shifting Mina from where she lies awkwardly against my ribs. 'Here, Mina, come and sit with me.' Naomi pats the armchair she now sits in and Mina scrambles from the sofa, jabbing me hard in the stomach as she does. She climbs onto Naomi's lap as Naomi gives her an indulgent smile, tucking her arm around her. They look the perfect picture of mother and child and I blink, looking away.

'So,' Naomi says, 'do you want to tell me what happened this morning?'

'I'm sorry I shouted at you.' My cheeks flush at the memory of the way I lost my temper, although I am not entirely sorry. Remembering Naomi sat next to Rav in the pub, a little flare of anger pops in my belly. It is on the tip of my tongue to tell her that I saw them, to demand that she explain herself, but this isn't the right time. 'I thought someone was out there and after finding the bones, I thought someone had taken him, taken Mina.' *I thought Agnes had reached out with one hand, pulling Mina in close, a replacement for her own lost baby.*

'It's all right, Allie, I would have freaked out too. If it had been my baby.' An expression, something heartbreakingly close to pain crosses Naomi's face and I feel my gut twist.

'I just panicked, I guess. I was expecting him to be in the cot.'

'Sorry.' Naomi looks down, sheepish, before changing the subject back to the reason why I called her. 'Tell me what happened this morning, Al. You sounded terrified on the phone.'

I feel the flutter of butterfly wings of fear in my chest, as I think about the bundle of bones wrapped in tissue upstairs in the bedroom. 'It's silly, I feel ridiculous,' I say, but even as I say the words the butterflies take flight, panic lodging in my throat.

'Don't feel silly. Whatever it is has clearly got you rattled.' Naomi leans forward, awkwardly with Mina still in her lap, her eyes on mine. 'What happened? Tell me everything.'

I take a deep breath. 'I thought I saw someone, out there in the trees. Rav thought I was imagining it but … I really do think there is someone watching the house.' I let the words fall out in a steady stream, worried that if I stop talking, I won't be able to start again. 'I was sure I saw someone out there, in the woods, and when I looked there was a patch where all the grass had been tamped down, a place where if somebody wanted to, they could watch the house in relative safety. I wouldn't have been able to see them from the window. And then I started to find things.'

'What things?'

'Do you remember when Rav and I got the keys, I found a pearl in the bathroom? Mina found another one in the garden. They look old,' I say.

'Oh, Al. It could have been there for years …' Naomi catches sight of my expression and falls silent.

'No. Maybe, I don't know. Miranda told me this whole

story about how the Pluckley Witch came here with just a baby in her belly and a string of pearls, but …' I shake my head. 'I don't know. Don't you think it's odd that Agnes Gowdie had a string of pearls when she came here, and now I'm finding them in the house?'

'Well, it is funny,' Naomi says, 'but could it not be a coincidence? I mean, I've heard of the Pluckley Witch, but I don't know the full story. Even so, Al, four hundred years is a long time for some pearls to be knocking about in a house and not be found before now. It's probably, I don't know … a bit of old costume jewellery.'

'They don't *feel* like costume jewellery.' Naomi's mouth opens but I raise a hand, letting her know I'm not finished yet. 'I was prepared to try and ignore it, to ignore the pearls and the idea of someone watching the house, to let Rav convince me that I was just overtired, but when I went out into the front garden this morning, I found the bones, hanging in the branches of the yew tree. And that wasn't a coincidence – someone deliberately put them there.' I shudder, the idea of there only being an oak door between me and some lurking stranger (*witch*) making my nerve endings sing.

'Bones. Now that is creepy,' Naomi says quietly, her long, thin fingers tapping at her chin. Her nails are polished a bright coral, unchipped despite her hours spent tying florist wire and clipping stems and I resist the urge to curl my bitten fingernails into my palm. 'Allie, it sounds obvious but are you sure you're not missing pearls off anything you own? A decorative button off a cardigan or anything? One of those fancy purses you used to use?'

'No,' I say bluntly. 'Naomi, I am not hysterical, no matter what Rav might be thinking. I am perfectly rational.' I'm glad now that I didn't bring up seeing the two of them together in the pub, suddenly sure that Naomi would use my words against me to convince Rav that I'm going mad.

'Yes. It is strange, and I'm not disputing that, but they are just pearls. Someone probably snapped a necklace and they've just ended up turning up around the place.' *A man's hand reaching out to Agnes's throat as she is marched away, grasping the pearls and pulling, the gems bouncing across the floor as her mouth twists in a snarl.* I blink and the image disappears.

'What about the bones?' Anxiety makes me jittery, and I want to get up and pace the floor, my swollen ankle holding me back. 'Who the hell ties bones into a tree? Miranda called this place the witch house.' I pause. 'Maybe the bones appeared because of the charm.'

'Charm? What charm?' Naomi looks confused, her brows burrowing into a sharp V.

'Remember the keys, and the feather in the attic? I went to see the old lady who used to live here – she told me it was a charm, hidden to keep the house quiet.'

'Could the bones be some sort of charm? Something similar?'

'No.' I shake my head. 'It's hard to explain. They feel … different.' Darker, somehow. 'They feel like a threat, a warning. I don't know. Maybe I need another charm to hide back under the floorboards.'

'Superstition?' Naomi raises an eyebrow at me. 'Come on, Allie, you're the least superstitious person I know. You don't believe in charms. I bet this Miranda has pink hair and wears tie-dyed dresses.'

I let the corners of my mouth lift in some semblance of a smile. 'You're not far off.'

'See? I bet she makes it her life's mission to bring up witches and throw them in people's faces every chance she gets. I bet she carries a sage stick in her mirror-covered knapsack.'

I let out a short bark of laughter at that. Naomi hasn't even met Miranda and she's got her down to a tee, not that I see anything wrong with a sage stick or mirrored knapsacks. I think of the shrieks from the woods, the scratching in the chimney, the way I was convinced I could feel eyes on me, and my smile fades. Even if Naomi is trying to make things seem normal, I still feel unsettled and on edge. As if there is danger lurking just around the corner, just out of sight. I can smell it, almost taste it on the air but there is nothing substantial for me to grab hold of and confront.

'I wish my mum was here.' A wave of longing washes over me, and I wonder how long she'll leave it before she turns up again.

'Oh, Al, do you miss her?' Naomi comes to sit next to me on the sofa, leaving Mina in the armchair still glued to the phone. The baby murmurs in the Moses basket and Naomi tenses, straining to see into the cot. I shake my head, and we wait, the baby eventually settling again.

'Yes, I do miss her, more than I expected,' I say, the memory of my mum sitting at the café, coffee in front of her, dancing in front of my eyes. I open my mouth to say that she was here yesterday but close it before the words come out. I haven't told Rav yet that I saw her, and while he says he doesn't have a problem with her, I have to admit that life is easier when she isn't around. And it's easier for me to deal with her when Rav isn't around. If she decides to stay longer than planned then of course I'll tell Rav she's here, but until then I don't see any reason for Rav to know — he'll only insist on inviting her for dinner out of politeness, and I'm not sure I could cope with the strain of the two of them in the same room at the moment.

'You kind of get used to it, don't you?' I say. 'When you grow up and leave the family home, you get used to not being around them all the time, but at the moment it feels odd not to see her every day. I always thought when I had a child I wouldn't be able to get rid of her.' I blink rapidly, picking at the sore skin around my bitten nails, as I think of the way she was so suffocating to me as a child. The way she wouldn't leave me alone. It all changed, once I left to go travelling and met Rav, almost as if she wanted to punish me for leaving her behind.

'But I thought you weren't that close? Growing up, anyway.'

'Hmmm. It was complicated, growing up with her as a mother. We were close when I was younger, it was just the two of us, so we stuck together. After I met Rav, she didn't approve and we kind of … fell out. But everything changes when you have your own children, you sort of see things in a different light. You see things the way your mother might, you know?' I could kick myself. Of course, Naomi doesn't know.

'And I just wish I had a child for my mother to fuss over,' Naomi says, her words tinged with bitterness.

'I'm sorry.' I hate the way Naomi's face changes, grief etched into her features.

'No, I am. I shouldn't have said that. I'm sorry. It's just difficult sometimes, you know …' She breaks off, sighing. 'But I have you guys, right? I told you before, Al, I can help with the children anytime.'

'I know. I do appreciate the offer but I just …'

'There's something else bothering you, isn't there?'

I wait a moment, uncertain whether I want to be this open and honest with her. I haven't forgotten that she told me she hadn't spoken to Rav, even though I saw her name in his messages. That she was with him in the pub, when he told me he was working late.

'Al?' she persists. 'What is it?'

'Remember I told you about the … dream I had? The one that seemed so real. I've had it again. More than once.'

Chapter Seventeen

Naomi fixes her dark eyes on me, a slight frown creasing her brow. 'It's just a dream, Allie. It's nothing to worry about it.'

Oh, but it is, I think, seeing my feet on the stairs, that unfamiliar room, feeling the chill swirl around my body.

'It's just a dream,' Naomi goes on. 'I think you're having some sort of weird lucid dreams, maybe because of your hormones, or perhaps when you do sleep, you're sleeping deeper than usual? I don't know.'

'It feels so real, not like a dream at all.' I stand, forgetting about my bandaged ankle, ignoring the pain that bolts up my leg. 'I keep waking up after it, with this … sense of dread. As if it's going to reach out into real life and take over all of this.' I sweep my arm to encompass the room. 'What if everything is all connected? What if I did something really awful?'

Naomi is shaking her head, her hair falling over her face so I can't see her expression. 'No, Allie. It's just a dream. You're not an awful person, you're not the kind of person to do awful things. Look at you, you uprooted your whole life to follow Rav to Pluckley, you gave up your life in London, even though you loved it because you love Rav more. Those aren't the actions of a horrid person. Those are the actions of a selfless person, a kind, decent person.'

I think of the way the stairs creaked beneath my feet, the way I had peered into the darkened room to see Mina and Leo asleep, and I shiver, rubbing my hands over my arms.

'Al, I think you've freaked yourself out over nothing.' Naomi stands next to me now, taking my hands in hers. Her palms are cool against my clammy fingers. 'Look at what you've got – two lovely kids, a nice house, an amazing husband. Stop focusing on the bad stuff and appreciate what good you have in your life. Come and sit back down; you're going to make that ankle even worse.' I let her guide me back to the sofa, sinking slowly back down onto the cushions. 'Drink this, you haven't even touched your tea.' She hands me the lukewarm cup and I take a sip, grimacing as the cool liquid hits my lips.

'Honestly, Allie, I think you're more likely to be living in a haunted cottage, haunted by witches no less, than you are to have done something so dreadful that you can't sleep over it.' Naomi grins, and I utter a small laugh.

'Maybe. Maybe Miranda was right after all.'

Naomi laughs, her face lighting up, illuminating her flawless skin and perfect make-up. I feel shabby again, fat and frumpy, and adjust my T-shirt to cover my still lumpy belly. 'I'd take a haunted house over my cramped, empty flat any day of the week. Why don't you let me look after the kids for a day?' Naomi says, the smile fading from her face. 'There's no shame in asking for some help if you need it, Al. I'm your best friend, you should ask me if you can't cope.'

'I can cope.' The image of her name in Rav's phone swims in front of my eyes, my gut twisting with the sense of betrayal. 'I can cope fine. I just let Miranda's superstition get to me. You're right. Rav is right.' I watch her face for clues, to see if guilt crosses her face but there is nothing.

'How is Rav?'

'Fine,' I say shortly, not wanting to talk about him, even though I am the one who brought him up. 'Working hard.'

'I bet. He's a good guy.' Naomi takes my cup from my hand, still full. 'Let me get us a fresh one and then we can change the subject, OK? Talk about something else.'

I nod and sit back to wait for her to return. Maybe I am reading too much into Naomi seeing Rav behind my back. After all, they get on well, I made sure of that. When I came back from India with him on my arm, my mum was so dismissive, so adamant that he wasn't the right one for me, that Naomi's opinion became even more important. I hadn't known her long before I went travelling but she was the first friend I made at college on the floristry course I took after school. Her opinion of Rav was important to me, important to the survival of our friendship, so when she had turned to me in the pub while Rav was in the loo and squeezed my hand, I knew she approved.

'Allie, he's perfect!' she had breathed excitedly, 'and you met him on the beach. That's so romantic.' She had faked a swoon, making me laugh so that I almost choked on my vodka and tonic. 'I wish Jason and I had a more romantic meeting than crashing trolleys in Costco.'

I had laughed even harder, loving the way we all clicked

as a foursome. We'd go to dinner together, to the theatre, Naomi and I would talk books, both of us swapping recommendations on new releases and old favourites, and Rav and Jason would talk films and music, neither of them being big readers. We were good friends, all four of us, and when Jason left Naomi, it was us she called on to come and help her move her stuff, me and Rav who helped her redecorate the tiny flat she found on the outskirts of Pluckley. I don't know why I thought a text from her in Rav's phone would be anything more sinister than her perhaps checking up on him – on us – to make sure we didn't need anything. Hormones. All of this can probably be put down to hormones. But then I think of her fingers linking with his, the way Rav lied to me about where he was and then, once again, I'm not so sure.

'Cheers.' I gratefully take the steaming mug of fresh tea from Naomi, determined this time to at least get more than a mouthful before the baby starts to grizzle in the cot. 'Sorry for dragging you away from the shop. I didn't mean to be so weird, I was a bit shaken up.'

'You've always been weird.' Naomi grins. 'I just want to know that you're OK, that's all.'

'I am,' I lie, burying my face in my cup. 'I am honestly OK.' The baby wails and I jump, spilling hot tea on my shirt. 'Oh, shit.'

'Let me get him.' Naomi is already on her feet, her hands reaching into the Moses basket for him. 'Oh, baby, come on. Al, he still smells delicious … but he's definitely hungry.' The baby is twisting his head, rooting at her chest as she holds him close for a long moment before handing him over to me.

'I didn't even ask, is everything OK with you?' I say, stuck where I sit now until the baby has finished.

'Fine,' Naomi says, 'busy at work, and I went on the most awful date the other night, but apart from that everything is fine.'

'Right. Well. That's good.' I run my hand over the baby's head as he feeds, my eyes on his perfect peachy skin. 'I just thought I should ask, you know. In case there was anything you were worried about or wanted to talk about. I know I've chewed your ear off.'

'No.' Naomi gives me a puzzled smile. 'Everything is fine. You know I would tell you if I had something on my mind. Shall I get Mina a snack?'

I nod and Naomi takes Mina by the hand into the kitchen, as I think again about the text from her on Rav's phone, telling him she needed to see him. I don't know what to think. Am I seeing things that aren't there? I can't confront either of them until I am absolutely sure. I hear the fridge door open as I gingerly drink down the rest of my tea, careful to twist my head away from the baby. I get a fierce image in my head as I drink, of the cup slipping out of my grasp, the no longer boiling but still hot liquid scalding the baby's delicate skin. Nausea rises in my gorge, warm liquid bracing the back of my throat and I lean over the arm of the sofa, letting the virtually empty cup fall to the floor.

'Everything OK?' Naomi appears in the doorway, glancing

towards the tiny puddle of tea that has spilled onto the floor where I dropped the cup.

'Couldn't quite reach the floor.' I offer up a wan smile, the image of the scalded baby still bright in my mind. Naomi mops up the small drops of spilled tea, talking about the new girl, Evie, how they went for a drink at The Black Horse, but I'm finding it hard to follow the conversation, my eyelids drooping.

Scratch. My eyes fly open and my shoulders tense. The baby unlatches and I freeze for a moment before I tug my top down. *Scratch, scratch.*

'Did you hear that?' I interrupt Naomi, who is still talking about Evie. 'Did you hear that noise?'

'What noise?' Naomi says, but I think I see her eyes go to the chimney.

'A scratching noise. Coming from the chimney. Just the same as the one I was telling you about.' I watch as Naomi's eyes glance towards the chimney again, before realizing she is looking at Mina who sits to one side of it, a small plastic tub of circles of ham and cheese with crackers in front of her.

'Allie…' Naomi's voice is calm, quiet. 'I can't hear anything.'

'Really? You didn't hear that scratching sound? Like …' I flounder for a moment. 'Like claws, or fingernails or something?' My voice rises as Naomi shakes her head.

'No, Allie. There wasn't a noise.' She points another meaningful glance towards Mina, who sits oblivious. 'You looked like you were starting to doze off. Maybe you imagined it.'

I sit back, letting Naomi take the baby. 'No. I don't think so.' As she takes Leo upstairs to change his nappy, I strain my ears, taking shallow breaths and listening as hard as I can but the noises don't come again.

Voices wake me, a low murmuring from the kitchen. I have fallen asleep on the sofa, and now I push myself into a more upright position, feeling the low throb of my busted ankle as I do. Mina is no longer sitting beside the chimney, and the sun has disappeared behind the house leaving the sitting room in cool shadow.

Where are the children? And Naomi – is she still here? Panic flutters in my chest and I stand, aware that the throbbing in my ankle isn't as fierce as it was. The box of Co-codamol sits on the mantelpiece above the fire, and I slide the packet out. Eight tablets are missing. Did I take them? I don't remember, and I am unsure of how many were missing from the packet before. I don't remember taking any, sure that I gave the packet to Naomi, but the dryness in my mouth, the fuzziness in my head tells me that perhaps I did take them after all. I follow the sounds of muted voices into the kitchen, where Naomi and Rav are talking. I hover in the doorway, watching as Naomi leans against the worktop, a glass of wine in her hand. Rav is at the stove, stirring something that smells like his signature dish – spaghetti bolognaise. He obviously changed his mind about Thai.

'... the children,' Naomi is saying. 'Just a feeling that something isn't quite right – Allie! You're awake.' She smiles at me, the smile not sitting well on her face, wine glass in her hand. One of the wine glasses Rav's uncle bought us for a wedding present. We don't use them very often; they are irreplaceable, and I worry about breaking them.

'What isn't right?'

'Oh … nothing. Just talking politics.' Naomi glances at Rav, then sips at her wine.

'Al.' Rav turns, leaving the sauce-covered spoon on the worktop but he doesn't move towards me. 'I thought I was going to have to wake you up.'

'You came home early.' I wasn't expecting him, so to see him cooking and drinking wine with Naomi feels strange. As if she is his wife, and I am just a visitor.

'Naomi told me you fell down the stairs?'

'Just slipped off the bottom steps,' I say, unsure as to how much Naomi has told him. 'Nothing too dramatic. It's just a bit sore, that's all.'

'Well, you should probably stay off it,' Rav says, looking down at the neat white bandage. 'Come and sit down.'

'Easier said than done, eh?' Naomi gives a bright laugh before she turns her eyes to me, her cheeks flushed from the wine. 'Are you feeling better?' A seemingly innocent question, but to me it feels loaded with meaning.

'Much better. All I needed was a nap,' I say brightly. 'I should get Mina and the baby ready for bed. Rav, you should have woken me.' I look about the kitchen, as if the children will magically appear. 'Where are they?'

'Naomi got Mina up to bed while I bathed the baby. They're all sorted. All you need to do is relax and rest that ankle.'

'Oh … right.' I feel disconcerted, a little off balance. My gaze goes to the open wine on the worktop. It's a bottle Rav's work bought us when the baby was born, one that I thought we were saving for a special occasion.

'Well, you two lovebirds, I had better be off.' Naomi drains the rest of her wine in one mouthful, snatching up her cardigan from the back of the chair.

'You don't have to, does she, Al?' Rav says, picking up the wooden spoon again. 'I've made loads, we'll be eating it all week otherwise.'

'Was I asleep for long?' My mind whirrs slowly, trying to catch up.

'Only a couple of hours or so,' Naomi says. 'Don't worry, I sorted Leo out, and I gave Mina one of those little pizzas in the oven for her tea. Not that she wanted much of it.'

'It was the snack,' I say, frowning. 'She doesn't usually have anything that big in the afternoon.' My tongue feels a little too big for my mouth, my throat dry.

'I'll let you guys have your dinner in peace.' Naomi shrugs on her cardigan, picks up her bag and moves to the doorway.

'Are you sure you won't stay?' Rav asks, and my heart sinks. I don't want her to stay for dinner, don't want her to mention to Rav about the bones. Naomi glances towards me and seems to read my face.

'Better not. I've got to go back to the shop and make sure Evie kept on top of everything. I told her I would only be gone for an hour or so.'

'I'll see you out.' I follow Naomi along the hallway, and apologize for keeping her so long, for falling asleep.

'It must be those tablets,' Naomi says as she rummages in her bag for her shop keys. 'They do say on the side of the box that they can cause drowsiness. You need to be careful when you take them, Allie.'

'Oh, I didn't think ... I mean, I wasn't sure ...' I don't know how to formulate the words without sounding like I'm going bonkers. In the end I settle for, 'Yes. Probably the tablets. Sorry, they've made me feel a little bit foggy.'

'Make sure you get some rest.' Naomi leans forward and kisses me on the cheek, her floral scent wrapping around me. The same scent I am sure was on Rav's clothes the other night. 'And you know you can give me a call if you need a rest – if your ankle starts playing up – and I'll come and look after the kids for you.'

I am already shaking my head. 'I'll be fine.'

'I know you will.' She winks. 'I just don't want you to think you have to be a superhero, that's all. I'll text you in the morning, see if you need anything, OK?'

'OK. Thank you for today.' I glance behind me, to where the sound of Rav's whistling comes from the kitchen. 'Listen, Naomi, you won't say anything to Rav, will you?'

'About what?'

'Well ...' I shift my weight on my aching ankle, looking at the floor. 'About the noises from the chimney. The bones. Or ... how I fell down the stairs. I don't want him to worry. Maybe I was imagining things, you know, after taking the tablets.' The tablets I don't even remember taking, but I don't mention that. 'I will tell him about the bones, just … not yet.'

She hesitates for one tiny moment. 'My lips are sealed.'

I'm not tired that evening, my short nap tricking my body into thinking that I am rested, I can carry on. After we eat, Rav and I take the rest of the bottle of wine he and Naomi opened out to the garden and sit by the pond, although I don't drink more than a mouthful or two. We talk – or rather he talks – about work, the case he's working on, the kids, whether or not we have time to take Avó out for dinner at the weekend, while I nod and murmur in all the right places, my mind not fully with him. I am still thinking over the snippet of conversation I overheard between Naomi and Rav. They weren't talking politics – Naomi *never* talks politics. The fact that she lied about it, the words *'something just not quite right'* on her lips, makes me think that she could only have been talking about me, about what happened today. A ripple of fear brushes over my skin as I remember the way I felt as I looked down into the baby's empty cot. I wrap my cardigan tighter around my body, across my swollen, sore breasts and my lumpy stomach, waiting to hear the sound of crying coming from the trees ahead of us, but there is only the rustling of the leaves overhead. Rav doesn't seem to notice as he finishes the bottle of wine and when we move inside, he falls asleep the moment his head hits the pillow. I lie awake, my head less foggy now as the pain in my ankle returns to a sharp throb. I don't want to take more medication, instead I lie still, embracing the pain as Rav snores softly next to me.

The baby wakes and I feed him again, on autopilot, not bothering to wake Rav to give the baby the tiny amount of breastmilk I managed to express after dinner. I worry as he drinks, imaging the tiny sips of alcohol in the wine passing from me to him, before shaking my head. It's been hours, and I barely had more than a mouthful. Sated, I lay him back down and slide out of bed to the window. It's becoming a tradition now, I feed the baby, then stand at the window and watch, keeping guard, sure that I will see that flash of white slinking between the trees. That I will see a fresh set of bones swinging from the yew tree that stands on the very edge of the garden.

The moon shines on the pond, a fat circle of unbroken white, shimmering on the surface of the dark water and I wonder how it would feel to step into the water. Icy cold lapping at my sore ankle, the feel of mud between my toes. Our chairs still sit by the edge, one slightly askew, the other tilted precariously on a small mound of earth – a mole hill perhaps, only I am too far away to see. An owl calls somewhere in the trees, a haunting, lonely sound and I shiver, aware again of the cold draught that swirls in through the badly fitting windows. London was never this noisy, I am sure. The fox returns, streaking across the lawn from between the trees, catching the tilted chair as he runs. It falls, landing silently on the grass and I turn away. How easy it is, one touch and everything tilts.

Chapter Eighteen

Mina is crying, not wanting to go back to preschool although I'm sure she is fine now, her temperature back to normal. I struggle to get her trainers on her wildly kicking feet, resisting the urge to snap at her. I drop her off, still crying, sure that the other mothers are judging her behaviour and my response. Tara calls my name as I walk towards the village, but I pretend I don't hear her, something I regret when it is time to pick Mina up again. I have spent the entire morning running through everything in my head, trying to figure out what Naomi could have meant by what she said to Rav. She definitely lied about talking about politics, and I wrack my brain, trying to recall exactly what I heard. I'm sure before she said that something wasn't quite right, she mentioned the children. What did she mean? The fact that Rav didn't say anything also makes me feel odd, out of sorts. *And then there was the message on his phone, saying she needed to talk to him.* About what? About me? I think about the things I told her yesterday, thinking that perhaps I could still trust her. About the charm, the bones, the scratching in the chimney, the pearls that I feel sure are connected to Agnes Gowdie. Is she just humouring me? There is something about the tone of her voice as she spoke to Rav that makes me think she doesn't believe me, that she *is* humouring me. That she thinks I'm mad. Maybe they both do. I can't help it; I imagine all sorts of things as I sit feeding the baby. The scratching starts up in the chimney the minute I sit down to feed, a persistent *scratch, scratch, scratch* that makes my body go rigid, my shoulders aching with tension as I wait for it to stop.

'Allie!' Tara catches me up as I cut through the almost empty car park after collecting Mina, who, as it turns out, was absolutely fine in the end. 'Allie, how are you? I've missed you.'

She has? 'Mina had a temperature; I thought I should keep her home.' I think of the nursery Mina went to as a baby in Gravesend. None of the mothers and carers there would have noticed if we hadn't turned up for a day or two.

'Oh, poor thing. She seems much better now.' Mina is hopping on one foot beside me. 'I did try to catch you this morning, but you were in your own little world.' Tara cocks her head on one side, and I get the feeling she knows I heard her. 'And what on earth did you do to your ankle? Are you sure you're OK to walk on it?'

'Oh. Yes, it's fine. A little bit sore. I slipped coming down the stairs.' My ankle throbs as if in response, and I shift my weight slightly to ease it. 'I should get back; I have to try and keep the weight off my foot.'

'Oh no, don't rush off.' Tara flicks her head to the left and I see Karen approaching, baby strapped to her front. 'Karen and I are going for lunch at that little café at the end of the High Street. Come with us? It's on the way to your house and you can put your feet up and have a coffee. Would you like that, Mina? Having cake with James?'

Mina shouts in delight and starts skipping around the pram, while I think for a moment. It's either suffer an awkward lunch with Tara and Karen or go back home to scratching in the chimney. 'Sounds lovely,' I say finally.

'Karen, you can manage the pram for Allie, can't you?' Tara dictates. I grip the handle so tightly my knuckles turn white.

'No,' I say bluntly. 'No, I'm fine. It helps to have the pram to lean on slightly as I walk.' I wonder if Miranda will be at lunch as Tara falls into step on my left and Karen takes my right side, making me feel as if I am being frogmarched to the café.

'I was going to text you if you weren't at school today,' Tara is saying as we approach the café, Karen going ahead to hold the door open for me. I don't remember giving her my number, but then I don't remember taking the painkillers yesterday. The smell of hot coffee and butter wafts out from the open door of the café and my mouth starts to water. I didn't eat breakfast, my stomach feeling heavy and nauseous after yet another sleepless night, and now it rumbles, reminding me of the fact. 'Oh look, everyone is here!'

Awkwardly, I manoeuvre the pram through the doorway to see a large table in the centre of the café, taken up by other mothers from the baby and toddler group, Miranda included. She waves her fingers at me, a blush creeping up her neck. She is wearing what looks like a maxi dress, tie-dyed green and orange and the tips of her hair are now pink. I think of Naomi describing her perfectly and wonder if Naomi has seen her around the village.

'There's a seat next to me,' Miranda says quietly, tapping the chair beside her as Tara and Karen are squealing and air kissing the other women. Straightening my skirt and fussing with the nappy bag, tucking it out of the way, I take the seat next to Miranda, peering down the table and raising a smile at the other mothers.

'Thanks,' I say. 'I've been meaning to catch you.'

'You have?' Surprise flashes across Miranda's face.

'Yes. I wanted to thank you for speaking to Mrs Sparks – I went to see her.' I lower my voice. 'She told me about the cottage. About it being "active".'

'Oh? She did?'

'She didn't go into detail though. I wondered if you knew any more … if you'd spoken to her about it for your research?'

'Um, not yet, no. I'm planning on seeing her sometime next week.'

I peer down the table, and once satisfied everyone is preoccupied, I open my mouth to ask Miranda about the bones, my heart banging in my chest at the thought of it, but Miranda carries on before I have a chance to get the words out.

'Do you have any comfrey in your garden?' Miranda's voice is muted, and I have to strain to hear her over the chatter of the other women.

'What? Comfrey? No, I don't think so.'

'It helps with sprains. Or arnica. You could put arnica on it too.' Miranda's blue eyes are fixed on mine and I shift in my seat slightly. 'Sorry, I wasn't being rude.' She reaches for the slab of cake on the plate in front of her and the tension is broken. 'I just saw you had your ankle strapped up – comfrey is good to help with repairing damaged tissue.'

'Oh, I didn't know that. Thank you.'

'How did you get on with the book?' Miranda flushes an even deeper pink. 'I'm not asking as the author, I just wondered if you found what you were looking for?'

'I didn't get much chance to read it yet. Listen, you could come over, if you wanted? To have a look at the house, I mean.' I don't know why I didn't think of this before. Miranda believes in witchcraft and ghosts. If she visited me at the house, maybe she would feel the same unsettling feelings that I do. Maybe she would see movement in the mirror when she looks at her reflection. I could show her the bones.

'No, I'm not sure—'

'Miranda, are you telling Allie your good news?' Tara's voice calls shrilly, piercing above the other women's voices and interrupting me before Miranda gets a chance to reply.

Miranda opens her mouth, but before she can speak Tara butts in. 'Miranda is pregnant again, Allie. Isn't that wonderful news?'

I glance towards the small child on Miranda's lap. I can't remember if it's a boy or a girl, but it can't be much more than ten months old. 'Wow. Congratulations.'

'Thanks.' Miranda cheek's flush red again and I realize she hates being the subject of Tara's attention just as much as I do.

'Let's hope it's just as easy as when Arlo popped out, eh?' Tara raises her mug in a toast and so begins a whole conversation of birth stories, something I am definitely not comfortable sharing with a bunch of women I barely know.

Mina's birth was a breeze – everything was textbook perfect from the moment I felt the first contraction until they laid her on my chest, tiny hands curled into fists, lusty cries pouring from her angry, red face. She was beautiful. Rav had cried a little, and then FaceTimed Avó (something I wasn't fully on board with, but I was too exhausted to say so), and after kissing me repeatedly and gazing in wonder at the tiny creature we created, he left, and the room emptied of nurses and it was just us. Me and my tiny daughter.

'Allie, what about you?' Karen is saying and I look up with a start. Mina is holding a chocolate cornflake cake in one hand, chocolate smeared across one cheek.

'Oh no, you don't want to hear about that.' I shake my head, reaching into the nappy bag for a wipe to clean Mina's face, rummaging longer than necessary in the hopes that they'll move on to someone else.

'Come on, Allie, we're all sharing,' Tara says loudly. 'We've all been through it. Nothing none of us haven't heard before.'

It seems Tara is not going to take no for an answer. 'Tara, I'd really rather not …'

'Pfffh.' She flaps her hand. 'Don't be silly, we're all friends here.'

Hot tears sting my eyes and I blink them away, hoping no one will notice. 'It wasn't the best experience with Leo, to be honest, Tara. Things were a little bit frightening for a time, so if you don't mind, I'd rather not share.'

'Oh, darling, you poor thing.' Tara reaches for my hand. 'I'm so sorry. Those of us who have an easy time often forget that it isn't that simple for others. I mean, Rufus just *shot* out. But here you are, Leo's a lovely, strong little thing and you both got through it. Did you have him at the William Harvey?'

Miranda mutters something as she picks at a plate of seed cake in front of her, but I can't make out the words.

'Yes, I did.' I take the remains of the cake from Mina's hand and wipe her sticky palms, before picking up the nappy bag and hanging it over the handle of the pram. 'Miranda, did you say something?'

Miranda shakes her head, but Tara steps in. 'Yes you did, Miranda. What did you say?' She looks around at the rest of us, letting out a trill of laughter. 'Don't leave us all in suspense.'

'It's nothing.' Miranda shakes her head again, and I feel a twinge of pity as she shifts uncomfortably in her seat.

'Oh, come on,' Tara presses, oblivious to Miranda's embarrassment. 'We're all friends here, just say it, Miranda.'

Miranda throws her napkin down on the table as if accepting defeat. 'I said' – her cheeks burn a bright vivid pink as she speaks – 'it's a good job Allie didn't have him at home.' Her eyes meet mine. 'Not in that cottage.'

I make my excuses, keen to get away after Miranda's unsettling words, and I drag a briefly grumbling Mina out onto the street, bribed with promises of an ice lolly when we get back. It *was* a good job Leo wasn't born at home, although Miranda's words caused a shiver to run down my spine, the hairs on the back of my neck pricking to attention. The baby's birth was the complete opposite to Mina's. Things had started well, but I didn't progress as I should have done – things were taking longer and longer, and I was growing more and more exhausted. Everything fades to a blur when I try to think back now, walking home to the cottage with Mina skipping along beside me. Rav told me after that the baby wasn't in the right position, that his tiny body inside mine was stuck. Hours after my waters had broken, hours spent pushing and pushing with nothing happening, I vaguely remember being so tired that I barely noticed when a contraction came. My hair was stuck to my face and there was a raging thirst burning in the back of my throat, nausea bubbling up after every hit of gas and air, before there was a flurry of activity that Rav tells me later was a whole team of midwives and doctors that rushed into the room. There is tugging, pulling, a feeling of somehow being violated although I can't feel anything thanks to an expertly timed epidural. The only scene that stands out, clear and bright in my mind, is the sight of the baby in the midwife's arms as she carries him to the baby station, trying to shield him from my view. In addition to his getting stuck, the cord was wrapped tightly around his neck, a deafening silence filling the room as he was finally yanked from my body. The image of his small limbs hanging loosely, his skin a terrifying bluish-white, crowds my vision and I blink hard, looking down into the pram to his fat, pink cheeks. He was fine, obviously. The doctors did whatever it was he needed and seconds that felt like minutes later, he was crying angrily as if enraged at being pulled from his warm, soft space into clinical white light. They placed him in Rav's arms as I was stitched up and cleaned up, all while feeling as if it was happening to someone else. When they eventually gave him to me, I couldn't reconcile the shifts and squirms in my belly with this tiny white creature with two marks either side of his head where he had been wrenched from me.

'Look, Mama, a parcel,' Mina races up the path to the front door, where a small box sits.

'Wait,' I call, 'don't open it.' Dread creeps along my spine as I remember the bones tied to the tree. 'We don't know who it's from.'

'Yes, we do.' Mina ignores me, pulling open the cardboard flaps to reveal a Tupperware container. 'It's from Avó.'

Of course, it's from Avó. Once we get inside, we open the box to find a tub of Rav's favourite curry – enough for one generous portion – a pot of spiced potatoes for dosa (even though Avó knows I don't know how to make the thin, crepe-like pancakes that Rav loves for breakfast), and a large packet of chocolate buttons for Mina. Sighing, I stack the tubs on the work surface and pull out my mobile to call Avó to thank her, even though none of the gifts are for me.

'Hi, Avó,' I say when she answers, trying to inject some enthusiasm into my voice. 'Just calling to say thanks for the package you left.'

'Make sure Rav gets his dosa in the morning, eh?' she says,

and I am glad we are having this conversation over the phone, not face to face as I roll my eyes at Mina and she giggles.

'I will, and I'll give him the curry tonight, OK?' I'll have toast; my appetite seems to have shrunk to nothing anyway. 'It's his favourite.'

'Eh?' she squawks into my ear, 'the potatoes are for Ravi. The curry is for you.'

'For me?' I feel the sharp sting of tears behind my eyes. Avó has never brought food for me before – Rav and Mina, all the time, but never for me.

'For you. It's good for the milk. And good for the baby to taste the flavour, so he won't be a fussy eater when he grows up.' She sniffs.

'Oh. Well, thank you.' I don't know whether to laugh or cry and I'm not sure whether the gift is for me or really for the baby. Movement outside catches my eye and I move closer to the window, craning my neck to peer out into the garden. 'Avó, thanks so much, it was very thoughtful of you, but I have to go. There's someone … at the door.' And there is someone here, out in the garden by the border.

I hang up, promising I'll try my best to make dosa for Rav's breakfast (as if I don't have anything else to do) and pull open the back door, stepping out into the sunshine that warms the patio. 'Mum.' She stands from where she is crouching over the border plants, a waft of Shalimar surrounding her.

'Ah, you are home. I didn't think you would be long. I thought I would wait.'

'I'm glad you did. How was your meeting yesterday?'

I ask, stepping towards her with a brief glance back towards the kitchen. I don't have the baby monitor, although the baby is still asleep in his pram and I'm sure Mina has parked herself in front of the television while I am distracted.

'Eh. Busy. Full of men explaining things I already know. How are you today?' Mum looks at me closely, as she rubs a rosemary stem between her fingers releasing the pungent scent. 'This smell reminds me of Paris.'

'Oh, you know. Tired.' I force out a laugh. 'I found bones tied to the tree outside, and I think Naomi might think I'm going mad.'

'Bones? What is this?'

I tell her what I found, that creeping sense of dread tickling between my shoulder blades as I picture the bones upstairs in the drawer. It's as if there is a tie between us, something dark and tangled that makes my skin crawl and I swallow hard at the idea of touching them again, but the thought of throwing them away makes my pulse skip and a knot tie in my belly. 'I haven't told Rav yet that I found them. I'm not sure that he'll be very happy about it.' He'll tell me to throw them out, or worse he'll throw them out himself. I don't want him to touch them, and I can't explain why but I feel too frightened to let them go until I know why they were left there, what significance they hold.

My mother shrugs, hand going to the pocket of her tailored shift dress, to the bulge of her cigarette packet. 'You say that you think Naomi thinks you are crazy.'

'I don't know that, I just get that feeling, after she sent that text to Rav, and they met in the pub without me. I think she thinks that there's something wrong with me.'

'But she didn't say this? This is only what you think, but perhaps you need to be careful what you say to her. Just in case.' She shrugs again, lighting her cigarette and blowing the smoke in my direction, causing me to flap my hand to wave it away. 'Have you looked at these plants?' my mother says, turning her attention back to the borders. 'I can see why your friend called this place the witch house. Look, sage, rosemary, lavender. All healing plants.'

'There are others, too.' I guide her towards the far end of the borders, to the shadows of the woods beyond. 'Oleander, vinca major, digitalis. All less than healing.' She reaches out a finger to stroke the leaves on the oleander tree, and I put out a hand to stop her, my fingertips millimetres from her skin. 'Don't touch them. They're poisonous. Oleander will give you nausea and vomiting, diarrhoea too if you're unlucky.' I point towards the others. 'Digitalis will give you stomach pains and dizziness, and vinca major will give you dangerously low blood pressure. I think they were all planted here deliberately.' An image of the woman in dark clothing, Agnes, bending over the borders rises in my mind.

'Really? It is possible I suppose. Are you still having the dream, or vision, whatever you are calling it?' My mother speaks bluntly, her eyes on mine.

'Yes.' I wish I could tell her differently.

'Hmmm. You are a good mother, Allie. Remember that.' She looks back at the border, a frown on her face, before she turns and walks towards the house. 'Come. Let's go inside.'

I follow behind her, afraid that if I let her out of my sight, she'll vanish like the cigarette smoke that surrounds her.

'Do you want to hold him?' When I enter the kitchen a few steps behind her, she is leaning over the pram, her face close to the baby's.

'No, no. Leave him while he is sleeping.' Her eyes roam around the kitchen, eyeing the tubs of food from Avó on the side, waiting to go in the fridge. 'You are being well looked after.'

'It's just from Avó, you know she's a feeder.' The baby stirs in the pram then, and I lean in to pick him up. 'Are you sure you won't hold him?'

'No, let him sleep.' She leans closer though, stroking his head with one finger. 'Listen, I only stopped by to see how you were. You seemed upset when you left the café, and I wanted to tell you that I did enjoy spending time with you and the children.'

I wait, sure now that she'll tell me she's going back to France. She never admits to enjoying my company. We've barely spent any time together at all since I married Rav. It's as if she can't bear to be near me after I refused to listen to her when she told me she didn't like him, that I was making a mistake. 'Is this where you tell me you're leaving?'

'Only for the post office,' she laughs briefly, as the doorbell rings. 'I have to go and send some things to my office, but shall we have coffee again soon?' She rests a hand against my cheek briefly before she picks up her bag and moves to the back door. I can smell her perfume. 'You are not going mad, Allie. But I do think you should get those bones out of the house.'

Chapter Nineteen

'I'm so sorry, Allie, I rang the bell and then you didn't answer and I rang again, and then I thought, oh, maybe she's feeding Leo, or he's asleep ...' Tara starts talking the minute I open the door to her. 'I didn't wake him up, did I? I should know better, it's not like I don't know how annoying it is when someone wakes the baby up.' She eyes the baby in the fancy travel system she is holding, the top of his head peeping out from the blue blanket.

'Tara, it's fine. Do you want to come in?' Pulling the door open further, I stand aside to let Tara in, her face shiny with sweat.

'Thanks. I'm not disturbing you, am I?'

'Honestly, it's fine.' I gesture for her to follow me, calling to Mina that James is here to play. The two toddlers run upstairs to Mina's room and I lead Tara along to the kitchen. 'Come and have a drink. It's a shame you weren't here five minutes earlier, you could have met my mum.'

We step into the kitchen, empty apart from the baby and my mother's crumpled cigarette packet left lying on the table. The baby lies in his pram, kicking and waving his tiny fists, and the chair where my mother sat is still pulled out at a slight angle. 'Sorry,' I say, as Tara takes a seat in the chair opposite, after parking the travel system in the hallway and sliding the baby out. 'I haven't had a chance to clean up from this morning yet.'

Tara looks around the kitchen, to the empty box on the worktop that held the food from Avó, the empty mugs in the sink. 'Are you kidding me? This place is spotless compared to mine!' she laughs. 'This little chunk is nearly five months older than Leo and you're far more organized than me.'

I turn to the kettle, filling it noisily as my cheeks flush a hot red, although I'm not sure why. I make tea for both of us and sit in the chair recently vacated by my mum, the wood cool against my bare legs.

'I wanted to apologize for earlier,' Tara says, jiggling her baby on her knee. The baby, a boy, has more hair than Leo and his mouth makes a surprised 'O' shape as he bounces. Ralph, I think he's called. Or maybe Robert. 'If I made you feel uncomfortable.'

'Oh, no.' I shake my head. 'No need to apologize.'

'I should have left it, not nagged at you to tell us your birth story. Shhh, Rufus.' The baby lets out a grizzly cry and Tara bounces him harder. 'I always go too far, I'm sorry. Karl is always telling me when enough is enough. That's my husband.'

'It's OK, Tara, I'm fine. It's just not that easy to talk about, you understand. It was a pretty scary experience.'

She nods, pursing her lips and for one brief, dizzying moment I think she's going to press me on it again, that she's going to try and cajole me into telling her the whole horrifying tale. Instead, she says, 'How are you feeling now, though? I mean, an easy birth can take it out of you, right? It must be even harder when things don't go according to plan.'

'Oh, I'm fine.' *Just not sleeping, dreaming of something terrible happening when I do manage to sleep, and worried I'm sharing my house with something that shouldn't be here.* 'Just a bit tired, you know.'

'Oh, I know,' Tara says emphatically. 'I had postnatal depression after I had James. It was the most horrendous time of my life. I honestly wouldn't have been able to cope if my mum and Karl hadn't been around. You haven't ...' She breaks off for a moment, shifting in her seat. 'You haven't been feeling down or anything, have you?'

'Um, no. Nothing like that at all.' The conversation has taken a serious turn and I get up, moving to the sink to rinse out my cup, even though I am only halfway through my tea.

'Sorry, I didn't mean to make you feel uncomfortable. No one ever asked me that, that's all. This time they've been all over me, asking if I'm OK, how I'm feeling, but the first time, nothing.' Tara offers up a small smile. She's not as confident as she makes out, I think. A lot of it is bluster and noise.

'I'm sorry. That must have been awful for you.' I am not like that. I am tired, yes, but I am not depressed.

'Anyway. Let's not talk about that. As long as you feel all right, that's the most important thing. And it's nice that you have your mum to support you at the moment.' Tara picks up her cup, Rufus still balanced on her knee and I have that frightening image again of the cup dropping, the hot tea spilling all over the baby, scalding him.

'Here' – I hold out my arms – 'let me hold him while you drink your tea.' Rufus feels different in my arms, a solid hefty weight, with rolls at the tops of his chubby thighs in contrast to my baby.

'I wanted to apologize about Miranda too – well, not apologize as such. Explain, I suppose.' Tara greedily swigs at her tea, and I recognize that feeling. The urge to drink it all while it's hot, and you have a free hand, if only for a moment.

'Miranda? Yes, she's a bit of a character, isn't she? She seems nice, though.'

'Oh, she is. Very nice. She's just a little … involved, shall we say, with all the witchcraft and paganism thing. She can't help it.'

'She told me that she writes those books about the legends of the village. Is she …' I want to laugh at what I am going to say next. 'Is she a practising witch?'

Tara snorts, and I let a bubble of laughter leak out. It all seems so ridiculous, until I think about the icy chill at the top of the stairs, the cries from the woods, Mrs Sparks describing the house as *active*. Then it doesn't seem so funny after all.

'No,' Tara says, 'she's not a practising witch, but she definitely believes in all that. She's Pluckley born and bred. Her mother was a supposed witch, and she reckons she can trace her lineage back to Pendle Hill and to the Scottish witches.' Tara rolls her eyes. 'Her mother reckons they're related to the Gowdie sisters. Hence Miranda's middle name being Isobel. No proof though.'

'Yes, she did mention that when I spoke to her about … some of the stories around the village,' I say. I don't want to tell Tara that I was asking about Agnes specifically and how she is connected to the house.

'I hope she didn't scare you too much?' Concern crosses Tara's face. 'She can be a bit full on with it all. The thing with Miranda is that she's grown up with it all as a big part of her life, so she can come across as a bit odd when you first meet her, but she is honestly harmless.'

I think of Miranda's face as I left the baby group earlier today. *Good job he wasn't born at home. Not in that cottage.* A shiver runs down my spine and I have to fight the urge to shudder.

'We've all got used to her, and lots of the others don't think too dissimilarly to her, to be honest.' Tara sniffs. 'I'm from North London originally. I don't hold much stock in all this talk of the supernatural, to be honest, all those bloody ghost hunters clogging up the village just get on my wick.'

'You're from London?' Although London is barely sixty miles from Pluckley, the difference in the pace of life, the attitudes of the villagers compared to Londoners is at such odds that it often feels like a different world to me down here. We spend the rest of the afternoon talking about the things we miss about living in a big city – the regular public transport, the lack of Deliveroo and Uber Eats in the country.

'I miss the theatres,' I say. 'Rav and I used to go to the West End a lot, we'd go for a quick dinner somewhere – The Ivy if it was a special occasion – and then go and watch a show.

What I wouldn't give for a plate of shepherd's pie from The Ivy for dinner tonight.'

'Borough Market,' Tara says with a groan. 'Saturday morning spent wandering around the market, then a walk along the river and a few beers in the sunshine.'

'Oxford Street,' I say with a grin.

'The MAC counter in Selfridges.'

'The space,' I sigh.

'Space? Surely you have more space here?' Tara says.

'Space from people, I mean,' I say, thinking as I say it that perhaps she isn't the right person to be saying it to. 'I'm used to being ignored on the Tube, not being questioned by people in the village shop as to how Rav is doing at work.'

Tara laughs. 'Sorry, you probably thought I was a right nosy parker when I started chatting to you that day soon after the baby was born. You'll be surprised how quickly village intimacy becomes the new normal.'

Village intimacy? Like, walking through the woods that back onto my garden? 'Tara, what do you know about the woods?'

'The woods?' She looks past me, out of the window to the trees. 'What about them?'

'I know they belong to us technically and they are private property, but do many people use them? I haven't really seen anyone in there, but it has been a really long, wet winter. I just wondered if many people walked through there, seeing as they do back on to the garden.'

'Not that I know of.' Tara frowns. 'I mean, maybe some people might use them, but I wouldn't really understand why. They don't cut through anywhere into the village, so they aren't used as a footpath, if you see what I mean. Most people use the land on the other side of the village for dog walking and stuff. That's where all the ghost hunters go, when they're on their ghost tours.' She is quiet for a moment. 'Why do you ask? Is there something worrying you?' She leans in close, letting Rufus grab hold of her finger. 'Have you seen someone in there? Heard something?'

'Oh, not really. Maybe.'

'Maybe?'

'OK, I thought I saw someone, just a flash of white as I was standing in the garden.' There is a faint double thump in my chest as I picture the unmistakable flash of movement through the trees, the sounds of a child's cry on the air.

'Maybe someone out for a walk.' Tara shrugs, finishing the last of her tea. 'I wouldn't worry about it too much, if I were you. Perhaps someone got lost, or they just fancied a change on their walk, they didn't realize that this side of the woods backed on to your garden.'

'Perhaps.' Should I mention the bones? Is that too weird? I mean, Tara has all but said that she doesn't believe in any of the witchcraft stuff that Miranda is so caught up with.

'You're not worried it's the Pluckley Witch, are you, come back to check on you?' A smile hovers around Tara's mouth.

'No!' I let out an awkward laugh, the lie squeezing out between my teeth. 'I did feel as though perhaps whoever it was might have been watching the house. Maybe.'

Tara looks closely at me. 'Watching the house? Have you told Rav?'

'He thinks I was probably imagining things.' *Scratch.* Scratching comes from the chimney and I have to concentrate on keeping my eyes on Tara. *Ignore it, Allie.*

'Like I said, someone might have just been a bit lost, wandered too close to the house. If you're worried you could call the police but I'm not sure they could do much.'

Scratch, scratch. I give in and let my gaze go the chimney breast. Tara doesn't seem to notice the scratching and before I can ask if she can hear it, Rufus goes rigid in my arms, his face turning a deep beetroot and then an unmistakable smell fills the air.

'Oh, blimey, Allie, I'm so sorry. I've changed his milk. Give him here.' Tara is on her feet, holding out her arms and I pass the baby to her. 'Can I change him somewhere?'

'Of course. Top of the stairs, the door directly facing you, there's a changing mat and table in there.'

Tara rummages under her travel system for what she needs and heads upstairs. I hear the sound of the floorboards creaking under her feet as she moves across the landing, her voice murmuring quietly above me as she deals with Rufus. Shrieks and laughter come from Mina's room, but I still can't quite allow myself to relax. I wait for the scratching to come again, but there is only silence. Tara isn't as overwhelming when she is alone, and I feel bad for ignoring her when she called to me outside preschool. I hadn't realized either that she had suffered postnatal depression with James, and I wonder if I was too quick to judge her – perhaps her image of perfect clothes, perfect hair, perfect make-up is all just a façade, a way of controlling the world around her. Maybe

I shouldn't be so suspicious, perhaps Tara and I could be proper friends, like me and Naomi, only without that underlying awkwardness that sometimes rears its head when the subject of babies and pregnancy arises. It was easier to make friends when I was travelling, the idea that I would spend time with other backpackers, drinking, dancing, swimming, and then they would move on, or I would move on, making it easier to allow myself to open up. I've always found it difficult to make friends – me and my mum were always a solid unit of two when I was growing up and she never saw any real need for friends – Naomi is the only person I've ever really allowed myself to be friends with. Maybe now it's time to take another step, to let Tara in. She's not as bad as my first impression of her. I paste a smile on as I hear her descend the stairs, James whining as she reaches behind her to hold on to his hand.

'Sorry, Allie, I think we had better go. Rufus is a little under the weather. It's the milk, I think.' She rolls her eyes and I laugh.

'I understand. I'm glad you came over.' I help her to the front door, promising to meet her for coffee after the preschool drop-off at least once this week, and waving with Mina until they disappear around the corner.

'That was nice, to play with James at home,' Mina says, before she scurries back upstairs to her toys and I have to agree, ignoring the *scratch, scratch* that starts up again from the chimney as I pass by, heading back towards the kitchen to check on the baby.

It's not until later, much later, after Rav has come home

(late, again) and sleeps soundly, snoring as usual, that I see Tara left something behind. While changing the baby I notice a scrap of fabric, peeping out from under the changing station. I lay the baby, clean and fed, back in the cot and then, wide awake, I tiptoe towards the changing mat, careful not to disturb the rest of the household. Reaching down I pull at the scrap, holding it up in the thin light that comes from an almost cloud-covered moon. The blue blanket. The one I have seen in my dream, my vision. There is a loose edge, the satin ribbon coming away from the knitted part, and I run my fingers over the stitching, my heart cold.

Chapter Twenty

Creeping downstairs, I silently take the bones and the pearls from where I have hidden them in the drawer and take the blanket with me, not wanting to leave it in the same room as the baby. Rav carries on snoring, and I peep in on Mina as I pass her bedroom. The nightlight casts a warm glow over the room, her tiny, dark head just visible on the pillow, her duvet tucked in close around her.

The living room is all in darkness and I reach for the switch on the lamp, chasing away the shadows that lurk in the corners, filling the room with a dim light. Goosebumps rise on my arms, the night air chilly, and I want to laugh. In any other circumstances I would wrap the blanket in my hands around my shoulders, or drape it over my lap, but instead I lay it on the coffee table, my heart pounding hard in my chest. I can hear my breathing, fast and loud in my ears and I draw in a deep breath and hold it, trying to calm my racing pulse.

When I first saw the blanket draped over a sleeping Rufus as Tara stopped me in the doorway to the preschool that first morning, I thought it was just a coincidence. Lots of babies have blue blankets – there are so many ones in a similar style to the blanket that sits in a heap in front of me now. But when I picked it up from where it had fallen beside the changing station, I noticed the fraying edge, where the satin strip had come away. In my dream, my vision, whatever it is, the same strip of frayed satin lies across the bed, the image burned into my mind. What does this mean? I reach out and finger the soft, silky edging, the bobbled, worn knitted main section of the blanket. This blanket isn't new, bought especially for baby Rufus. It is old, worn, well loved. How could this be the blanket I saw in my dream?

I get up and start to pace, tiredness tugging at my bones. I don't have time to waste on sleeping, I need to figure out what this means. Laying the bones on the table, I place the pearls next to them, and then fold the blanket alongside. I feel it again as my eyes wander over the small pile of items. That thick, oily draw that comes from the bones, the sensation that I need to lay my hands on them while simultaneously feeling nauseous and faint at the idea of my fingers touching them again. I reach out, picking up a pearl. Naomi was wrong, I think, they aren't some cheap bit of costume jewellery, they are real. An image flashes into my mind as I let the pearl sit, warm and hard in my palm, of the pearls bursting as a man grabs a woman (Agnes?) by the throat, the pearls scattering across the room. The image is so real that my hand flies to my throat, sure I will feel the beginning of a bruise. Laying the pearl back down my attention goes back to the blanket. Was Tara telling the truth when she said she doesn't believe in ghosts and spirits? How could I dream of a blanket that I had never seen before?

I wrap the bones and pearls back up in the blanket and begin to pace again, the puzzle feeling too big, too complicated to figure out – the only logical answer that I can find is that something is here, something that shouldn't be. *Haunting*.

Scratch. Scratch. The noise from the chimney stops me in my pacing and I freeze on the spot. 'No,' I whisper, hoping that I will hear Rav's footsteps on the stairs. Silence for a moment, then, *scratch, scratch, scratch*.

'Enough. That's enough now.' My voice is loud in the thick quiet of the room, the tiny Turkish lamp in the corner giving out barely enough light to see by. Rav complains about it, says there is no point in a lamp that barely gives out any light, but usually I like it. It's cosy, warm. Now though, I wish I had a lamp of surgical levels – especially as the overhead light bulb blew the day that we brought the baby home, and neither of us have remembered to buy a replacement. The noise comes again, and I feel it as well as hear it this time, as if tiny hands are digging tiny claws into my skin. I move to the fireplace, creeping silently, waiting for it to come again. As I move across the room, something – *someone* – rushes past the doorway into the hall, a black blur in the corner of my eye. Freezing on the spot, I turn towards the doorway, aware as I do so that the air around me is disturbed and scented with the faint smell of rosemary, a perfume that seems to grow stronger as I breathe in.

'Rav?' I whisper, barely able to hear myself over the banging thud of my pulse. 'Rav, is that you? I'm in here.' I don't know why I'm whispering, who I am afraid of disturbing – the children wouldn't hear me upstairs. There is no response, but the rosemary still lingers in the air, thick and heavy, so strong I can almost taste it. I inch my way towards the empty doorway on silent feet, pausing as I reach the threshold. I peer out, into the darkened hallway, making out the outline of the coat stand by the door with Rav's coat and Mina's tiny jacket hanging from it. There is no one there. The hallway is empty, but I would swear on Mina's life that someone rushed past the doorframe just seconds earlier. I stand there, my bare feet cold on the ancient quarry tiles, waiting in the dark, but there is nothing. Not even the scent of rosemary on the air now, almost as though I imagined it. Turning back to the sitting room, my feet glad to be leaving the cold tiles of the hallway, I realize if it had been Rav in the hall then I would have heard his footsteps, but there were none. Whatever I saw moved silently.

Scratch. Just one barely there scratch, but it's enough. Crossing the room almost at a run, my nerve endings taut and singing, I pick up the wrought-iron poker that sits in a set of fireside tools (another gift from Avó) on the hearth and angle my body so that my shoulder is under the chimney. And then I shove, upwards, quick and hard, swearing under my breath as the poker meets resistance. There is something up there, and I thank God that although the winter was long and wet, Rav had stuck to his guns on not lighting the fire too much until we could arrange for the chimney to be swept. A smattering of soot and ash, and grains of dirt tumble down into my face and I close my eyes, spluttering, before I push the poker up again. I am gentler this time, pushing it insistently into whatever is lodged there, wriggling the poker as more and more dirt and soot tips down onto my hair, my face, grit flying into my eyes. Coughing, I cover my mouth with a grey and dusty hand as I give the poker one last shove and whatever is blocking the chimney comes tumbling out onto the hearth, grey dust showering the hearth and floor in front. Leaning away from the mess, I cough, hard and sharp, my mouth feeling dry with grit. Finally able to catch my breath, I wipe my hand over my face and crouch down to inspect the detritus that has fallen from the chimney. There is nothing alive, thank God, I didn't see anything scurry across the room and out of sight. Although what does lie in the heap of soot and dirt is not terribly reassuring either. Among the ash and the remnants of what looks like a nest of some sort, there is a tiny carcass, something that on first sight I think might be a bird. I snatch up a crayon, left on the coffee table by Mina, and poke gingerly at it. Tiny, bleached white bones, covered in soot and dust are tangled together and once I have prodded them and turned them using the crayon, I think that maybe it's not a bird after all. A tiny squirrel perhaps. My eyes go back to the now silent chimney. A squirrel would make sense … maybe. Their tiny claws would definitely make a scrabbling noise, although I'm not sure how likely a squirrel would be hanging around a chimney pot. *And how could a squirrel, so long dead he is only a set of bones, scratch at the inside of a chimney?* But it is not the set of miniscule bones that set my teeth on edge. Rather, it's the other item of any substance that has fallen out on to the hearth that makes my blood run cold.

Witch's ladder. I don't know how I know, but I know that

this is the name for what I am holding in my hands right now. A thin braid of hair tied together at the top and bottom with what looks like garden twine. Entwined in the cord of hair are black feathers – some tiny, others large and ragged, the fibres coming away from each other into uneven clumps. These are accompanied by several tiny bones, all tied to the braid and similar to the ones I found hanging in the trees. I drop it as if it has burned me, and I fancy I can feel the branding of it on my fingertips, an oily film left on my skin. The hair is dusty, but the same bright, pale blonde as mine. My hand creeps to the base of my neck and I finger my hairline, sure I will find the stumpy ends of tresses snipped clean off. An image of myself, sleeping the thick, heavy sleep of painkillers on the sofa, while Naomi looms over me with a pair of scissors in her hand rises bright and clear in my mind and I shake my head, feeling my legs begin to tremble. Naomi wouldn't do something like this. I don't know where the image has come from, but it has the same suffocating feel as the dream. The dream that feels like a memory.

'Allie?' I tear my eyes from the coil of hair on the floor, something sinister emanating from it. Something almost solid and real on the air. A smell, thick and haunting, worse than anything emitted by the bones. 'Allie. What the hell is going on?'

Rav is standing over me, his hair mussed up and wearing only a pair of striped pyjama bottoms. Glancing towards the window I see the darkness outside is no longer thick and complete, purple and peach hues rest on the horizon as the sun begins to climb in the sky, another day breaking.

Looking at up him from where I crouch on the floor, I say, 'It was in the chimney.'

'What?' Rav crouches next to me, seemingly not caring about the dust and grit under his bare feet. 'All this was in the chimney? Allie, it's four thirty in the morning, what are you doing down here, poking about in the chimney?'

'I heard … the noise, I heard that scratching sound that I told you keeps coming from the chimney.' I glance down again at the heap of dust, the witch's ladder laid on the top. 'I thought if I shoved the poker up there, I could dislodge whatever it was that was making the noise.' *It's driving me crazy*, I want to say, but don't.

'What the hell is that?' Rav's hand reaches for the witch's ladder and I grab his arm, my fingers locking over his tanned skin.

'Don't touch it,' I say. 'Can't you feel it?' Malevolence oozes from the twined hair, so thick I can almost taste it. It's like a heavy shroud on my shoulders.

'Feel it? Allie, it's just some grubby trinket that some mad old woman has shoved up the chimney. There's nothing to feel, and there won't be anything to see in a minute.' He snatches it up and a gasp sticks in my throat. I follow him through into the kitchen, Rav holding the witch's ladder between finger and thumb, until he opens the pedal bin and tosses the hair inside.

He turns to face me, dusting his hands on his pyjama bottoms and I fancy I can see traces of black dancing across the fabric, the stain of the witch's ladder. 'Allie, what's going on? I'm worried about you.'

'Nothing,' I say shortly, desperately averting my eyes from the bin. It's as if the witch's ladder is calling to me, a low tugging in my stomach. 'Nothing is going on.'

'It's four thirty in the morning – you should be in bed, next to me, making the most of the fact that you have another two hours of uninterrupted sleep until Leo wakes for a feed, if you're lucky.' He cups my face with his hands, and I try not to flinch. I can smell the dust and dirt on his fingers. 'I don't understand why you're down here, digging around in the chimney. I don't know what's going on with you.'

Just not quite right. I recall Naomi's words to him. 'I'm fine, Rav.' I pull away from him, opening a nearby cupboard and pulling out a frying pan. 'I couldn't sleep, that's all. I came downstairs and I heard the scratching and I thought I would sort it. I've been waiting for months for you to call the chimney sweep and get the chimney done and you've always been too busy. Nothing more than that. You don't need to worry.'

Rav comes to stand in front of me, still not content to let things go. 'You could have just called a chimney sweep, instead of waking the whole house up.' His tone is brusque, his impatience impossible to hide. 'Allie, you're going to make yourself ill if you don't start sleeping.'

'I am sleeping. I'm sleeping in the day, when Mina is at school and the baby naps,' I lie, reaching for the olive oil.

'What are you doing?' Rav grabs me by the wrist, shocking me into stillness. I look down at his fingers, tanned and strong, wrapped around my pale wrist and he drops it, looking away.

'I'm making you dosa.' I splash oil into the pan. 'Your

mum left you spiced potatoes, she said I was to make you dosa for breakfast.'

'I don't want dosa.' Rav grabs my hand again, more gently this time, and pulls me close to him, his arms wrapping around my waist. I lean against him, suddenly tired, breathing in the faint scent of the remains of yesterday's deodorant and something vague and sleepy on his skin. 'I want you to sleep, Al. I want you to rest, and I want you to stop freaking out about witches and spirits, OK? It's a load of old nonsense, rumours, that's all. The whole village plays on it.'

The village you brought us to, I think, but I nod my head against his chest. 'OK,' I say, 'I'm sorry. I … I got carried away.'

'Go up to bed, go on.' Rav moves to the sink, fills the kettle. 'You go up and get some sleep. I have to be up in an hour anyway, there's no point in me going back to bed.'

'Thank you.' I say it quietly and wait until his back is turned before I slip my hand inside the bin and pick up the witch's ladder, wrapping it in the blanket as I pass by the sitting room. Alone, in the bedroom, the baby snuffling in his cot, I slip the witch's ladder into the drawer, alongside the bones and pearls, my lip curling involuntarily with distaste, before I fold the blanket and tuck it on top. Now the items are hidden from view, I feel safer. Climbing into bed, I toss things over in my mind: Tara, the blanket, Naomi, the bundle of tied hair and what it could all mean, but before I can make sense of any of it, a blackness descends, and I tumble down into sleep.

I am in the room this time, my feet on the bare floorboards of the bedroom. No longer on the worn carpet of the landing. The wood beneath my feet is warmer than I expected, and I feel a prickle of heat spark through my body. Too hot now, the faded grey linen I wear feels too tight around my neck, a noose poised and ready to tighten. I run a finger around the collar, pull my sleeves up. Sweat beads on my forehead and I have that overwhelming sensation again that I might be sick. I stop, wait, breathing steadily until it passes. I can't throw up. That wouldn't do, not now. Ahead of me, she lies huddled in the duvet, a dark head stark against the white pillowcase. A figure I know so well. A cup of water lies on the floor beside the bed, empty, on its side. A few drops of water have collected in a tiny puddle beneath the lip of the cup and my tongue flickers out and runs along my top lip, collecting the salt that collects above it. Thirsty, my throat is dry and scratchy, air burning as I draw it deep into my lungs. She shifts in the bed, emitting a small sigh, dislodging the blue, frayed blanket that lies across the end of the bed and I pause, afraid to move a muscle. Settling, her tiny frame is still again, the room silent once more. I am steady now, my mouth dry but my head clear. I am ready. Moonlight is the only light in the room, a small, cold puddle that leaks in from the landing. It's not enough to see by properly, and I raise a hand as if about to grope for the light switch before I let it drop. I don't need light. It's better in the darkness. It will be easier in the dark. In the dark, they won't see me coming.

A cloud scuds across the moon, briefly leaving the room in thick, inky darkness and for that one moment I am relieved, before the sharp pincers of fear grasp me tightly. I don't want to see clearly but the dark, this thick, velvet cover of obscurity is disorientating, and my heart beats a frantic tattoo of alarm against my ribcage. I don't want to do this, I've changed my mind, are the panic-driven words that flutter across my mind before I push them away. I tried to find an alternative, I tell myself, but there isn't one. There is only this. A tangy taste lies in the back of my throat, something filled with iron filings, sharp and metallic. Fear, maybe, if fear had a taste. I strain my ears, listening hard, the fight or flight urge keeping me on the balls of my feet, as that persistent thud batters against my temples, a drum being beaten in the back of my skull. It's not too late, a voice whispers in the back of my mind. Oh, but it is, I reply silently. I have no choice. The only way to be safe is to finish this. As if he knows, the baby lets out a squawk, a shrill, brief shout.

A door slams somewhere far away and my heart rate accelerates, my breath sticking in my throat as that cold, chilled feeling sweeps over me again, leaving me covered in a clammy sweat. There is no more time. This is it. Quickly, quickly before it is too late.

Chapter Twenty-One

I wake briefly as a door slams somewhere distant, but the lure of the deep, embracing slumber I have fallen into pulls me back in and when I finally awaken properly the sun is streaming in through a gap in the curtains, the room hot and stuffy.

Silence. I sit up, peering into the cot only to find it empty. The first stirrings of panic flicker in my gut but my phone screen lights up with the buzz of an incoming message from Rav.

> You were exhausted, so I took Mina to school and dropped Leo off at Mum's. We need to talk tonight.

I sink back against the pillow, the final sentence in the message lodging like a stone in my stomach. Things never go well when someone says, *we need to talk*. I lie still for a moment, the events of a few hours ago heavy on my mind, and I think I smell rosemary in the air again. I feel rested physically, but my mind still feels drained. I had the dream, the vision, whatever it is again, after a few nights' respite. It's as if the moment I let myself sleep I am back there, creeping along the hallway to that darkened room, the thick scent of fear and something else, something darker in the air. *Me, but not me.* I shiver, despite the stuffy heat that fills the room, sliding out of bed to throw open the window. I lean out, the sun warm on my cheeks as I breathe in deep lungfuls of fresh, country air. Something splashes in the pond, ripples casting out across the water and the trees at the bottom of the garden shake their branches. I can hear the whispering rustle of the leaves, thick and glossy green, and I tense as the faint cry of a child carries on the slight breeze. Feeling on edge, I pull my head and shoulders back inside, scrubbing my hands over the tops of my arms. I pull on a thin T-shirt and a summer skirt with an elasticated waist from before I had the baby and move downstairs, snatching up my phone from the bedside table as I go. My mouth is dry, my tongue feeling too big, and I head to the kitchen, downing a cold glass of water. My breasts ache and I stuff a pad into each cup of my bra. I didn't feed the baby, didn't even wake when he cried, and when I check the fridge the last of the pumped milk is gone. *The baby.* I have to call Avó, make sure he is OK.

She answers on the first ring, as if she has been waiting for my call. 'Avó, it's me. Allie. I just wanted ... is everything ...' I can't get the words out. My thirst is gone, but I don't know what explanation Rav has given her for dropping the baby with her.

'It's fine, fine, all fine,' she singsongs down the line. I think I can hear the baby gurgling when she says, 'He's sleeping.

Such a good boy. So like Ravi. He is just like his daddy, that thick, dark hair. So handsome. No one would ever guess from looking that you are his mother.'

I tell myself that it's just because the baby has Rav's dark hair and olive skin, that's all. She doesn't mean anything by it. I picture a dark-haired woman, rocking in a nursery chair the same as ours, an opposite to me. Her arms are empty, her baby gone. 'Yes, just like Rav,' I breathe, blinking the image away. 'Did Rav bring the milk? Should I come and get him?'

'No. I don't need you to come.' Avó is as blunt as ever, and I picture her standing in her tiny hallway, arms folded across her chest as she talks into the landline. She's the only person I know who still uses one. 'No, you rest, Allie. I can take care of my own grandchild.'

'Of course you can.' It's such a tightrope with Avó, she can take offence at the slightest thing. 'Would it be OK to leave him with you until I pick Mina up? Did Rav bring enough milk?' At the thought of the baby's little mouth working at the bottle teat, I feel a tingle and dampness seeps into the pads in my bra. I'll have to pump, whatever Avó says.

'Yes, yes, I told you already he brought it. He brought too much, probably. I'll see you then.' And she hangs up.

I pump, transferring the milk to the fridge and then pull out the laptop from the cupboard. If I have some time to myself for a few hours, there is no way I am going to waste it sleeping. Moving into the sitting room I falter for a moment, sure that I will see the grit and dust, the tiny bones from the chimney scattered all over the floor, but it seems that

Rav has been busy this morning. There is no trace of the filth that covered the hearth last night. I type Agnes Gowdie into the search bar on the computer, but it doesn't bring up anything new. I try different variations, using her name, the village, Pluckley legends, but there is nothing that I haven't seen before. Thinking for a moment, my fingers hover over the keyboard before I type in, 'Elsie Sparks, Gowdie Cottage, Pluckley, witch.' The usual sites come up, and I scan down them quickly bypassing all the links marked in purple that I have already clicked on. On the third page, I find a link I haven't seen before. It's to a small, badly made website that hasn't been updated for a long time by the looks of things. There is a picture of the house, my house, in black and white. The roses around the door aren't as tangled and thick as they are now, the roof not quite so covered in moss, and I realize I am looking at the house as it was years ago, when Elsie was a child. The article accompanying it is brief, and there is no author name attached, but I hold my breath as I read the scant article. It says that in 1949, a young family by the name of Sparks was one of the last to live in the cottage before it was abandoned.

Despite claims made by Elsie, the Sparks's eldest child, that the house was haunted by an entity known as 'the Pluckley Witch' there was never any evidence of this. Following the death of baby Christopher, Lillian Sparks, the child's mother, was removed and committed to a psychiatric hospital, after local police arrested her for the death by smothering of her youngest child.

Pressing a hand to my mouth I sit back, my limbs suddenly feeling heavy and numb. A child died in our house – not just a rumour, it really happened. I think of Elsie, how she had been watching Mina as she told me about the charm. How she had warned me about replacing it to keep the children safe. She doesn't believe her mother did this, she believes Agnes is responsible.

I re-read the article, realizing that the implication is that Lillian Sparks was suffering some sort of postnatal depression. Tara's confession springs to mind and I shake my head. I don't feel like that, I can cope fine with everything. My house is clean and tidy, my children are well cared for, I get out of bed in the mornings no matter how tired I am. Something flutters in my belly when I think of Naomi's message to Rav, the way she told him something 'just isn't quite right'. There is something dangerous in my house, but it is not me.

I don't want to read the article again, the words leaving a nasty taste in my mouth. Instead, I search for Tara on Facebook, clicking on her completely open profile. She has hidden nothing, her page filled with photos of herself with the boys and Karl. She tags herself everywhere she goes, giving the entire world a run-down of her day.

My phone pings on the table next to me, startling me, and I switch it on to silent, not wanting to be disturbed. Glancing down I see Tara's name on the screen, her unread text waiting, and I feel a hot prickle of guilt before I squash it down, telling myself I have nothing to feel guilty for, everybody snoops on Facebook. I carry on looking through

Tara's photos, stopping as I reach one with Miranda and a couple of the other women from the baby group. The caption is, 'BIRTHDAY DRINKS AT MINE WITH THE GIRLS'. They are all sitting cross-legged on the floor, a drink in their hands, smiling at the camera. All except Miranda, who looks mildly terrified. One of the women has moved at the time of the picture being taken, her face a blur, although there is something familiar about the way she is sitting. But it isn't the women who have caused me to pause. In the background, there is a blue-grey spiral of smoke coming from the table behind them. My first thought is cigarette smoke, or maybe incense, but the plume is too thick. Frowning at the screen, I enlarge the photo, zooming in on the smoke. It's not a cigarette, it's a bunch of sage. A cleansing stick. Why would Tara have a cleansing stick burning, if she doesn't believe in witchcraft? I check her profile page, just in case her birthday is on Halloween, a perfect excuse for one of the women to burn sage at her birthday for a joke. But Tara's birthday is in July.

Maybe it's nothing, I tell myself, sitting back in the chair. Maybe one of the others brought it to the house and Tara burnt it to be polite. *Or maybe,* I think, *she lied to you and she does believe in witchcraft.* A shiver runs down my spine and I think of the witch's ladder shoved up into the chimney, before raising my eyes to the ceiling, to the bedroom above, where the book, *An Introduction to Witchcraft,* lies hidden beneath the mattress. Shoving the laptop to one side, I run up the stairs and pull out the book, carrying it carefully back to the sitting room.

The pages fall open naturally, as if the book has been thumbed through before, and when I look down my blood chills. The book has fallen open to a page entitled *The Witch's Ladder — an introduction*. The accompanying photo shows a braided cord, similar to the one I found last night. Taking a deep breath, I let my eyes drift to the text, suddenly afraid of what I will discover.

The Witch's Ladder usually constitutes a spell, each step on the ladder counting towards an incantation. I pause, absorbing the words, my hands feeling clammy and shaky, before reading on. *The Witch's Ladder may have many uses, but it is believed that witches of old used this method to cast a death spell, by tying knots and then hiding the cord where it was unlikely to be discovered.*

I slam the book closed, my heart pounding so hard in my chest that I can barely breathe. *What the fuck?* Questions flash through my mind. Who left the ladder in the chimney? Why? And what do I do about it? I throw the book onto the table, as if it will scald me, inadvertently nudging the laptop screen back into life. Tara's photo of the smiling women appears, with the grey smudge of smoke in the background.

Sage. Sage is a healing plant, a cleanser. I reach for the book, flicking through until I find the correct pages and start reading about how to cleanse my home using sage, ignoring my mobile as it buzzes on the table. I find a section about how many rituals involve beginning by sitting in a circle and something registers in the back of my mind. I click back onto the photograph of Tara's drinks and pay attention to how the women are sitting. They are all cross-legged on the floor, in a circle.

I stop, scrubbing my hands over my face. Did Tara lie to me? The positioning of the circle of women, the sage, all say yes, but I don't know why she would. Her friends list is long when I click back on to it, over 1,200 people have access to her account. How does she even know 1,200 people? Scrolling through the names, I'm hoping that I will recognize the women from the photo – I can't remember any of their names apart from Miranda – and maybe if I click on their profiles something will become clear. I scroll, clicking on some, scrolling fruitlessly through other people's life events, all to no avail, until I reach a name that I do recognize. A name that I wasn't expecting to see, alongside a familiar profile picture. Naomi Byrne. Naomi and Tara know each other.

Chapter Twenty-Two

My phone buzzes again and tearing my eyes from the screen I see I have four missed calls. The screen lights up again, Rav's name appearing overlaid on his photo. Frowning, I press the green icon to accept the call. Rav never calls during the day.

'Hello?' My eyes wander to the screen again as I click on Naomi's name to go through onto her profile picture. The blurred face of the woman in Tara's picture, I think it could be Naomi.

'Allie? Where the hell are you?' Rav's voice is loud in my ear. 'Have you only just woken up?'

'No, I've been awake for a while. I called Avó.' I pull my phone away from my ear to glance at the time on the screen. 1.45 p.m. Shit. 'God, Rav, I have to go, I'm late for Mina.'

'I know, that's why I'm calling you. Why didn't you answer your phone? The preschool has been trying to get hold of you for over half an hour.'

'I'm sorry. I'm sorry I just …' I slam the lid of the laptop down and run into the hallway, grabbing my keys and shoving my feet into my trainers. 'I'm going there now, can you call and tell them I'm on my way?'

Rav agrees and cuts the call before I have time to apologize again. I slam the front door closed behind me and start walking as briskly as I can on my aching ankle towards the edge of the village, towards the school. As I half march, half limp along, my breath coming hard in my chest and making my lungs burn, I toss over everything I have learned this morning in my mind, which doesn't seem to amount to much.

Something terrible happened in my house — has been happening for years if the stories are true. There is something in my house, something that is always just out of my eyeline. Something or someone that is dangerous to me and my children.

The blanket. Tara is in possession of the blue blanket — something I thought was a coincidence originally, until I saw the same unravelled piece of satin. How does she have the exact blanket I have been dreaming about? And why did she leave it at my house? I still don't know if that was an accident, a simple case of the blanket sliding off the changing table and she had forgotten it in the rush to get Rufus home, or something else. She brought up the topic of post-partum depression, practically asked me if I thought I had it. She possibly lied to me about believing in witchcraft. Whoever left those bones tied to the tree, whoever pushed the witch's ladder into the chimney believes in that kind of thing. And she knows Naomi, who also thinks that something is wrong with me.

This is the part of it all that I can't seem to make sense of. Naomi is my friend, and until I saw her sitting with Rav in the pub, with her knee pressed against his, I would have trusted her with my life. We've been friends for years, since before I met Rav, before I finished my floristry course. We've been through so much together. We've spent birthdays and Christmases together, been on holiday together, been through break-ups and weddings together. The vision of Naomi looming over me as I half doze, scissors in her hand, appears again and I shake it off. That didn't happen, there is no way Naomi would entertain the idea of witchcraft, she's far too sensible. Isn't she? Maybe she didn't even realize the significance of the sage, the seated circle. Naomi loves me, Rav, she loves the children. The children even more so, given that she can't have any of her own.

My steps slow as I approach the car park to the preschool and I battle tears, blinking hard and taking deep breaths. I don't know what to think anymore. Maybe Rav and Naomi are right, and there is something the matter with me, I am going crazy. Maybe it's just nothing, and I am being a drama queen. But then I think of the twined hair, the feeling of foreboding that I had when I first held it, the way the air had changed around me. I think of Rav lying directly to my face about where he had been the night that I saw him and Naomi in the pub, her name on his phone when she told me she hadn't spoken to him. No, I think, someone is out there, and all of this is connected, somehow. As I reach the steps to the preschool the door swings open and Naomi steps out, holding Mina by the hand.

'Mummy!' Mina rushes forward, flinging her tiny arms around my waist. 'You are *so* late.'

'I know, darling, I'm so sorry.' I kiss the top of her head and raise my eyes to where Naomi stands awkwardly at the top of the steps. 'What are you doing here?' I feel a bubble of irrational anger rising in my throat, ready to pop and spill out fury across the pavement. I think of the blurred picture, trying to match it with Naomi's face.

'I came to fetch Mina. Rav called me.'

'Rav called you?' I snatch up Mina's hand, gripping tightly as she tries to twist away from me. 'Why the hell did he call you? I was coming to get her, I was just a bit late.'

'You're nearly an hour late, Al,' Naomi says quietly, her gaze drifting down to where Mina is pouting, still tugging away from me. 'The school tried to call you and you didn't answer your phone. They called Rav, who also couldn't get hold of you, so he called me and told the school I would be collecting her.'

'And you were just ready to step in,' I say bitterly.

'What?' Naomi steps forward and I glare at her, pausing her in her tracks. 'Allie? What's that supposed to mean?'

'Ready to step in and be a perfect mother, just like the other day when the baby was crying and I was out in the garden.' Mina tries to pull her hand away again, starting to cry when I hold it tighter.

'Allie, don't be so ridiculous. I picked Leo up because he was crying, that's all. I was just trying to help.'

'By taking him out of his cot and away from where I left him, so I didn't know where he was? What would you have done today? What would have happened if I had arrived to pick up Mina and she was gone because you had already

227

taken her?' My breath hitches in my chest and I realize Mina is not the only one about to cry. It's as if everything I know has changed, morphed into something unrecognizable. The sight of Naomi here now, holding Mina by the hand has rattled me even more.

'Allie, please calm down.' Naomi does step towards me now, reaching out to rest one hand on my arm. 'Look, if you hadn't arrived, I would have taken Mina back to the shop and called and texted you to let you know she was there. I didn't know you were on your way, I didn't know what had happened. I just did what Rav asked me to do. I only wanted to help.'

'I don't need any help,' I say, but the words come out weakly. 'I was just … I lost track of time.'

'We all do that occasionally,' Naomi laughs, an effort at normality, before her face turns serious again. 'Al, what really is the problem? You seem a little … I don't know. Off. On edge. Have you seen something again?'

'No. Nothing. I had a late night, that's all.' I don't say anything about the witch's ladder. Not in front of Mina. 'Sorry, I didn't mean to overreact. I wasn't expecting you to be here, that's all.'

'It's fine, I understand.' Naomi holds her arms out to Mina for a goodbye hug. 'I'm your friend, Al. I'm here to help you. I told you, you can always ask me, and I'll do whatever you need.'

There is a look on her face that I can't quite read, and I feel prickly and irritable again. 'It's fine, honestly. I can manage, time just got away from me today.'

Naomi nods. 'I'll see you later, maybe? We'll catch up properly soon.' She chucks Mina under the chin and steps past me, walking away in the direction of The Daisy Chain.

'Naomi,' I call out, 'how do you know Tara Newman?'

'Who?' she calls back, pausing and turning to face me. She shrugs, raising her palms to the sky and pulling a face, before she waves and walks away.

Mina and I stroll in silence through the village to the out-skirts where Avó lives in a house much smaller than ours. No witchcraft attached to hers though, hers is a brand spanking new build, complete with all magnolia walls and a badly laid herringbone paved driveway. Mina is sulky, annoyed that I grabbed her so hard and that I didn't let her go to the shop with Naomi. I try to push away the shards of guilt I feel at hurting her tiny hand, concentrating instead on the photo on Tara's Facebook. Maybe it wasn't Naomi in the photo? She doesn't seem to know who Tara is. I try to recall the blurred face in the picture, but now I am doubting myself, thinking that perhaps I was seeing things that weren't really there.

Avó is waiting for me on the doorstep when we turn into her road. She scoops Mina into her arms, and I follow her into the small, white kitchen. The baby snoozes in the pram, and I reach in and pull the blanket lower down. It's warm in here, the air rich with the scent of spices as something bubbles away on the stove.

'Thanks for having him, Avó,' I say, scooping up the empty baby bottles on the draining board and tucking them into the nappy bag that hangs from the handles of the pram.

'It's no problem,' Avó says. She peers closely at me, before taking my face in her hands. I can smell the hand lotion she uses, and the floral oil in her hair. She looks up at me, her black eyes intent on my face. She is at least five inches shorter than me and I feel like a giant beside her. 'You are not happy,' she says. 'There is something wrong.'

'I'm fine.' Her fingers are cold on my face and I resist the urge to pull away. 'Just tired, like Rav said, I had a late night, and he wanted me to sleep.'

'Hmmm.' Her eyes are bright with suspicion. 'You always say you are just tired. I don't think so.'

'I am, Avó, I swear. There's nothing else.'

'You are sure?'

'Yes.' I squeeze out a laugh and, uncomfortable under her scrutiny, give in to the urge to pull back. 'I'm sure.'

'You seem agitated, like someone has upset you,' she needles on.

'I said I'm fine,' I snap, regretting it immediately. 'Sorry, Avó, I was late for Mina, and I got upset, you were right. Please don't mention it to Rav? I'm OK now, I promise.'

Avó follows me to the front door, watching silently as I struggle to get the pram over the threshold. I get the feeling that there is more she wants to say to me, but she says nothing, instead reaching up to kiss me on the cheek as I turn to say goodbye. She has never done that before, and I don't really know what to make of it.

I can feel it the moment we step back into the hallway, Mina running upstairs as the baby starts to grizzle in the pram. The air is disturbed, and I know someone is in the house.

'Rav?' I call out cautiously, even though I know it would be nigh on impossible for him to get home before me unless he'd already left when he called. 'Is that you?'

My mother appears in the kitchen doorway, watching as I wrestle a now screaming baby from the pram. She looks as chic as ever, this time wearing a white shift dress that I remember from my childhood. She used to wear it through the summer to pick me up from school, with a pair of hot pink wedges and huge sunglasses on her face. I was always mortified when she turned up to collect me in her glamorous outfits, my tiny ears not immune to what the other mothers were saying about her. I thought I remembered her throwing the dress out with a bundle of other things when she moved into her Paris apartment, but clearly not. She looks cool and fresh, while I am sweating, the baby cross and red-faced in my arms, my trainers covered with dust from the walk home along the country lane.

'You left the back door unlocked again,' Mum says in answer to my unasked question. I brush past her into the kitchen, sitting in the chair closest to the door and latching the baby on. 'You could be murdered in your beds.'

'It wasn't me,' I say, sighing as a cool breeze wafts in from the garden, lifting my hair off my face and winding its way round my bare legs. 'Rav must have opened it this morning.'

'You need to be more careful.' My mother's face is serious. 'You don't know who is out there.'

'Did you see someone?' My shoulders tense, and the scent of lavender and mint wafts in through the open door. I struggle to turn to look out on to the woods, the baby squirming as I move my body.

'No. I'm just saying you need to be careful. What's the matter? You look pale, something has happened.'

I should have known that she would know, without me even mentioning it. She has always had a knack of reading me like a book, an open book with fully illustrated pictures. I wait until the baby has finished feeding and I have laid him in his bouncy chair, before I go upstairs to the drawer of trinkets. I pause for a moment, the drawer opened in front of me, not wanting to put my hands inside, not wanting to touch the bones and hair secreted away in there, before I shake myself.

Ridiculous, I mutter under my breath, *it's just bones. Hair. It can't hurt you.* Even so, I wrap the items in the blue blanket before carrying them down and laying them on the table in front of my mum.

'What is that? This ... horrible thing.' She points at the witch's ladder, the 'h' sliding from 'horrible'.

'I found it in the chimney. It's some sort of ... witchy ritual. Curse. Witches used to use them to cast spells.' Looking at it, a familiar chill creeps up my spine, that thick, oily *badness* seeping from it into the air around us, and I can't bring myself to use the word *death*. 'Mum, I wish we'd never come here. I wish I'd told Rav I wanted to stay in Ebbsfleet.' Tears make my throat thicken, making it hard for the words to come out. 'I don't care about the garden, the village life, the space. I don't want a garden full of toxic plants and a house with a history of witchcraft. It wasn't supposed to be like this.'

'But this was what you wanted. You were excited to move here,' my mother says quietly. 'I thought you wanted what was best for the children.'

'Yes, of course I do, but honestly, Mum, this doesn't feel that great.' I feel sulky, like I did as a teenager when she disagreed with me. 'At least if we had stayed in Ebbsfleet none of this would ever have happened.'

'And what if Rav had refused to stay? If he had said he would come here alone and leave you? Would that be better?' She stalks to the open door and lights a cigarette. 'Remember, Alys, I brought you up alone after your father left. I wouldn't go with him when he wanted to go back to France, I stayed in England for you. Believe me, it is harder to be alone.'

And then the minute I showed you I could stand on my own two feet, you hot-footed it right back to Paris anyway, I think, a bitter worm turning in my stomach. It feels odd to hear her defending Rav, when usually she disagrees with everything he says. 'If I had stayed in the flat, no, things wouldn't have been ideal, but at least I wouldn't have been dealing with stuff like this.' I throw my hand out towards the bones, the twined hair. 'Witchcraft, Mum. Someone has been watching the house. I hear things, see things and then they vanish, like they were never there. I feel as though something has cursed me.'

'Something?' Blue smoke hazes around her perfectly

bobbed hair. 'Allie, there is no *something*. Don't you think it makes more sense that this is the work of *someone*?'

'Yes,' I say, 'of course it's the work of someone, not something. That's what I meant.' I just don't know if that *someone* is a woman accused of terrible things four hundred years ago.

'Then you need to figure out who it is.' My mother gives one of her Gallic shrugs, as if finding out who is responsible will be easy.

'I think I should show this witch's ladder to Miranda,' I say carefully, hoping that she'll give me something to go on this time. 'She might be able to tell me what it's for, what I should do with it.' Quickly, before I can change my mind, I snap a photo of it, laid out on the table, and check the image, suddenly irrationally sure that there will be a blank space in its place.

A wail comes from upstairs and my mother glances at her watch. 'Well yes, maybe that's where you start. Be careful who you trust, Alys.' Another wail comes and then there is a thud. *Mina.*

'I have to check on her.' Hurrying up the stairs into Mina's bedroom I find it is nothing serious, and I spend ten minutes soothing her, putting a cold flannel on her finger where she has pinched it in the hinge of a plastic box of bricks. When I step back into the kitchen, sweat pooling at the base of my spine in the mid-afternoon heat, my mother is on her feet, bag on her shoulder.

'Do you want me to come with you, to show this thing to the girl, Miranda?'

'No, it's fine,' I say, fingering the edge of my phone, aware of the photo of the items in my camera roll. I don't want to touch the bones again, to have to carry them with me to show her. 'You look as if you need to go. I'll let you know what she says.' I see her to the door and then sit alone at the kitchen table, the ash rolling around the back door the only sign she was ever here.

Chapter Twenty-Three

Rav eyes me cautiously when he comes home, tiptoeing around me as if I am a bomb about to go off. He bathes Mina and I hear the rumble of his voice overhead as he reads her a story. I find myself hoping he'll eke it out, knowing that when he comes downstairs and we are alone he'll want to talk over what happened this morning – why I forgot all about our daughter.

By the time he comes downstairs I have thought of the perfect avoidance technique, and my bag is already over my shoulder, his car keys in my hand.

'What are you doing? Where are you going?'

'Nappies,' I say, with a bright smile. 'We need more nappies. When I put the baby to bed, I realized we were down to the last pack.'

'We've got enough to last us til the morning,' Rav says, reaching for the strap of the bag. 'Come and sit in the kitchen. I'll make dinner.'

'I'd rather go now.' I pull away, brushing past him towards the front door, trying not to limp on my bad ankle as I wait to feel his hand on my arm to stop me, but he just follows me to the door.

'Allie, it can wait. Please, we need to talk.'

'Rav, I'll be ten minutes – twenty tops.' I look down at the keys in my hand. 'Please, let me go. I just need a bit of fresh air. I won't be long.'

'OK,' he sighs after a long moment. He steps away from the front door, a resigned look on his face. 'I'll start cooking. But when you get back, I really think we need to talk about what happened today with Mina. Please, Allie. I'm worried about you.'

'OK, Rav. I said I'll be back in ten minutes.'

I don't look back as I get into the car, fumbling for the ignition before driving the short distance to the local Co-op. As I park up, a gaggle of ghost hunters hurry past the car, clutching their cameras and phones to their chests, one of the girls giving a shrill, nervous laugh as they pass. They head along the High Street, past the pub and towards the outskirts of the woods and I wait until they have stepped into the darkness of the trees before I exit the car. Stepping inside the store, the lights are bright and I squint, half wishing I'd stayed home and faced Rav's questions. I browse the aisles, not in any rush, tucking a packet of newborn nappies into my basket alongside a jar of fancy coffee. Neither Rav nor I drink it, but my mother practically lived on black coffee and her trusty cigarettes while I lived at home. Turning into the dairy aisle, I see Miranda standing in front of the yoghurts, holding a carton in one hand as she stares unblinking into the fridge. She is alone, no sign of the baby, and I quickly turn and move into the sweet aisle, not sure if I should approach her or not. Lurking over bars of Dairy Milk, I dither as she hovers in indecision, before snatching up another carton and heading to the till. Suddenly panicking that she'll leave, I hurry past the chocolate, towards the bottles of fizzy drinks so I can catch her. As she stuffs her purchases into a compostable carrier bag, Miranda looks up and sees me.

'Hi, Allie,' she says quietly, and I nod in her direction. She takes her receipt and steps towards me. 'No baby, eh? It feels odd, doesn't it. Did you put some comfrey on that ankle?' Her words tumble over one another as if she is racing to get them all out before I make an escape.

'No, no baby. And no comfrey either. I don't think I have it in my garden.' I smile and move past her to the till.

'There used to be,' she says, her blue-streaked hair shining under the glare of the lights. 'Maybe you could ask her, across the road.' She nods in the direction of the automatic doors and I follow her gaze out across the street to the darkened windows of The Daisy Chain. 'She could probably get you some.'

'Maybe.' Frowning I lay the basket on the self-scan machine and start swiping. 'Speaking of the cottage, I was sort of hoping I might run into you this week. I wanted to talk to you about Elsie.'

'Oh?' A wary look flits across her features but she steps closer.

'Did you speak to her yet?'

'Yes, I saw her this morning, actually. We talked about

her childhood, growing up in the cottage.' Miranda looks away, shifting from one foot to the other.

'I know what happened,' I say bluntly. 'I know her baby brother died, and her mother was put away.' Miranda opens her mouth to speak, but I carry on. 'I know Elsie thinks Agnes was responsible.'

'They said her mother was depressed, that she couldn't cope with the baby,' Miranda says reluctantly. 'I don't know how true that is.'

'Elsie didn't believe that,' I say. 'Here, I wanted to show you something.' I shove my purchases into a carrier bag and pull out my phone. 'Look at this.' I open up the image of the bones that I snapped with my phone and hand it to her. 'I found this.'

'In the house?' Miranda looks for a long moment at the image, before raising her eyes to mine. Her face is pale and there is something in her tone that stops my hand in mid-air as it reaches for the phone.

'Yes, in the house. At first, I thought maybe it was another charm, like the one Elsie Sparks hid in the floorboards, but there was something about it ...'

'It's not a charm,' Miranda says bluntly, pushing the phone back into my hands. 'It's a witch's ladder.'

'I know. I bought a book on witchcraft.'

'Get rid of it, Allie. You have to get it out of your house.'

'Get rid of it?' I knew there was something off about it, the way it felt dark and sinister, even before I read about it, and Miranda's reaction has confirmed that what I read is true. There is something bad attached to that coil of hair and feathers. 'I found bones too, in the trees, tied together. What is it, Miranda?'

She leans in close. 'It's a curse,' she hisses. 'A witch's ladder is a curse. The knots have to be untied and a new spell spoken over it to break it, or you must destroy it. Allie, this witch's ladder, it doesn't have to be a curse on you.'

'Miranda, I don't—'

'It could be a curse on your house.'

My hands shake as I slide back behind the wheel of the car, tucking my groceries into the passenger footwell. A curse. On me, or on our house, possibly. Part of me can't believe what Miranda says – the rational part of me that knows it is all superstitious nonsense. Then there is the other part of me, who sees movement in the mirror, figures on the stairs, hears the cries of a child coming from the trees. A child who disappeared four hundred years ago. *Idiot*, I try to laugh, the sound raw and catching in my throat. *Superstitious nonsense. There's no such thing as ghosts.*

My laughter dies as I pull up outside the house. I have to face Rav now and explain to him properly why I was so late to pick up Mina. He's going to be cross, I think, when he finds out I took the witch's ladder out of the dustbin. He's going to ask me why, and I can't explain it. All I can say is that I feel drawn to it, as if the black, twisting fingers of whatever spell has been tied to it are drawing me in. I sit in silence, watching the house, sifting over in my mind a way of explaining things to him that don't make me sound as if I am going mad. I'll have to tell him about what happened before. About Lillian Sparks and her dead baby. As I sit, I see the Turkish lamp go on in the sitting room at the front of the house, Rav appearing in the window with a glass of wine in one hand, about to draw the curtains. As he pulls the second curtain across, I see the silhouette of someone else in the house, standing in the doorway of the sitting room. Rav pauses for a moment, his face solemn, before pulling the curtains all the way shut, blocking my view.

Someone is there, in the house with Rav and the children. My skin prickles and I automatically look up at the windows on the top floor. There is a soft light glowing in the hallway, as if one of the bedroom lights has been left on and a shadow moves across it, gliding quickly. I slide out of the car, closing the door as quietly as I can. Walking up to the front door, I change my mind and swerve off to the left, taking the path that leads along the side of the house. I unlatch the gate, wincing as it creaks and step into the shadows, my eyes on the kitchen window. The lights are on and Rav now stands at the old-fashioned Aga-style range, stirring something in a copper saucepan. He says something, his lips moving but the sound muted through the glass of the windowpane, his brow furrowing. He stops stirring, turning his back to me as he faces whoever he is speaking to. I inch along the side of the house to get a better view, stumbling over the beginning of the border at the edge of the house. Scents of jasmine and chamomile rise on the mild night air, and raising my hand to cover my mouth I think I can smell the fresh, apricot scent of the oleander bush. For a moment I don't know if it's on my skin or in the air. I move to the back door, peering in through the window to see who is making Rav frown like that. She sits at the kitchen table, my baby on her lap. He lies in the crook of one arm, her other hand cupping his tiny head. His mouth opens in a muted wail, and her hand reaches for the bottle of milk on the table, silencing him as she gently places the teat in his mouth. Naomi, sitting at my table, talking to Rav, feeding my baby. Tears prick my eyes. They look like a family. A real family, with a mum who is happy and well rested, not fretting about people watching the house and witch's curses. *This is what she wants*, I think, the thought suddenly clear in my mind, only I'm not sure if I'm talking about Naomi, myself or Agnes. I can hear their voices now I am close enough and I catch the end of what Rav is saying, his face still carrying that shadow of anger.

'… more than just "not quite right"! I've been reading up on it.'

'The article I sent you?' Naomi's voice, quieter as she sits further from the door.

'Yes, the article. Postpartum psychosis. I feel like … like this is what it could lead to, you know that?'

'I know that …' Her voice fades and I have to strain to hear her. '… Keep the children safe.'

I reel back into the shadows, my legs suddenly feeling numb. *They think I'm mad*. Naomi thinks I'm mad. Rav thinks I'm mad. I press my hand to my mouth, biting down on the skin to stop the sting of tears behind my eyes. I'm *not* mad. On leaden feet I move back towards the door, the handle moving more easily than I thought. I tumble into the domestic scene playing out in front of me, Rav's mouth opening in surprise.

'Allie, you're back. What are you doing coming in the back way? Did you forget your keys?' He moves past me and pushes the door closed. I stand for a moment, just watching as Naomi carries on feeding the baby. A blush rises from the collar of her T-shirt, flushing her neck and cheeks a rosy pink.

'Allie, do you want to take him?' She nods down at the still feeding baby, her eyes flicking away from mine. 'He was crying his eyes out and I … We didn't know how long you would be.'

'I only went to get nappies,' I say, taking the baby from her. He grizzles as the teat is wrenched from his mouth, and when I pull my shirt up and place him at my breast he wails angrily and twists his head away from me.

'Come on, baby,' I mutter, trying again, but he only cries louder, the shrill sound scraping across the surface of my skin, down to my bones.

'Maybe let him finish the bottle?' Rav says tentatively, and I snatch it up, blinking away tears when the baby starts to gulp greedily. 'That's better.' He leans over and kisses the baby's head, seemingly oblivious to the rage I am sure is emanating from my every pore.

'Rav was trying to cook and Leo just wouldn't stop crying,' Naomi explains, taking a sip of her wine. The air is thick with tension, the echo of their words reverberates around the small kitchen and I imagine them bouncing off the roughly plastered walls, the edge of the butler sink, settling on the table in front of us.

Instead, all I say is, 'I fed him before I put him down. Before I went to the shop.'

'That was nearly an hour ago,' Rav says. 'I thought you'd run off and left us.' He tries a laugh, but it comes out flat and heavy.

'I bumped into Miranda,' I say as an explanation. 'What are you doing here, anyway?' I raise my eyes to Naomi's, but she is looking at the baby, watching him feed.

'I wanted to see how you were,' she says, finally tearing her eyes away, 'after this morning, you know.' She flicks a quick glance towards Rav, but he has his back to us, stirring what smells like a risotto. 'I wanted to make sure you were OK,' she whispers.

'I'm fine,' I say at normal volume. 'I told you earlier I just lost track of time. I didn't realize how late it was, and my phone was on silent. That's why I missed Rav's call.'

'Are we … OK, though?'

'Yes. Why wouldn't we be?' *Aside from the fact that you think I'm going bonkers, and although I can't prove it yet, I think there is something going on between you and my husband.* I meet her gaze head on, rearranging my face to clear any animosity from it. It's unsettled me, seeing her sitting at my spot at the kitchen table, my baby in her arms, discussing with my husband how I could be crazy.

'No reason.' Naomi shakes her head slightly and I watch as she glances at Rav, who gives me a small smile. There's something wary on his face mixed with something that could almost be guilt.

'Mummy!' A shout comes from upstairs, a piercing cry

from Mina's bedroom. The baby isn't finished with his bottle, and I dither for a moment, trying to weigh up which child needs me most. Before I can decide, Rav speaks.

'Naomi, would you just check on her? Allie's still feeding and I have to keep stirring this.'

'Of course, no problem.' Naomi jumps to her feet. '… Unless you want to go, Al? I can give him the rest, there's only a tiny bit.'

I shake my head, watching as she bounds up the stairs, hearing her voice murmur to Mina and then the sound of footsteps overhead as Naomi leads Mina back to bed. I turn my attention to Rav.

'You could have texted me, told me Naomi was here. I would have hurried back.'

'It's not a big deal, is it?' Rav keeps stirring the saucepan. 'She only got here about twenty minutes before you came home; she wanted to check on you. As soon as she leaves, you and I can sit down together and talk.'

'OK.' The baby finishes the bottle and I stand, laying him over my shoulder and patting his back to bring up any wind. 'I wasn't expecting Naomi to be here, that's all. She was at the preschool this morning, when I was … when I was late.' The baby burps contentedly and I lay him gently in the Moses basket.

'Yeah, I asked her to go, because you weren't answering your phone.' Flicking a tea towel over his shoulder Rav turns to me, before his gaze moves past me and I realize Naomi must have returned.

I turn and say, 'Naomi, you'll stay for dinner, won't you?'

Chapter Twenty-Four

Rav gives me a hard look as he passes Naomi three sets of cutlery, and I use Mina as an excuse to get some space. As my feet reach the bottom step, I hear the murmur of their voices coming from the kitchen and the rattle of plates being removed from the cupboard. I pause for a moment, that same unsettling feeling washing over me, before I climb the stairs, taking them carefully as a sharp pain bolts through my ankle on every step.

Mina is asleep again, one arm flung over her head. I tiptoe into the room, dodging the plastic bricks that have tumbled to the floor and a naked baby doll, its eyes wide and unblinking. Her breath whistles slightly as she breathes in and out, still stuffy from crying and I lean over and press a tiny kiss against her forehead. Naomi got her to sleep much more quickly than I would have been able to, and a splinter of resentment pricks its way under my skin. Satisfied that she is settled, I creep back out, pausing on the landing to look out of the window. It's getting late, the sky a dark purple as the last vestiges of sunlight have disappeared over the horizon. The moon is making her way up the clear, velvety sky, tiny pin pricks of stars beginning to show. As soon as the sun disappears, I can't walk past this window without looking out into the woods as if there is some magnetic pull, my nerve endings on red alert. The trees are silent now, the air still, and I let out a breath I don't realize I have been holding. The woods are dark and it is as though I am watching a frozen tableau, the scene in front of me paused, until movement catches the corner of my eye. The fox, his bushy tail up, runs from the shadows alongside the oleander tree, something small and furry dangling from his mouth. I let out an involuntary gasp, and he pauses as if he has heard me, dropping whatever creature he has caught, his face turning to the window where I stand. His muzzle is ringed a rusty red, the maroon of slowly drying blood, and I press my hand to my throat, aware that in the dusky light I shouldn't be able to see him as clearly as I do. A cry comes from the woods, a sharp, piercing shriek. The cry of a terrified child. I close my eyes, exhaling slowly, counting to ten to compose myself before opening my eyes. A face is reflected back at me in the black canvas of the glass, and I stifle a shriek. It's not my face. *It's hers*, I think. *Agnes*. Her skin is alabaster white, her long hair hanging over her forehead in thick, pale hanks, her mouth downturned. Her eyes are black holes in her face, and I grit my teeth together hard to hold in the scream that burns at the base of my throat, stepping back, away from her furious glare.

'Allie?' Rav's voice makes me jump and I turn to where he stands at the top of the stairs, watching me. 'What are you doing?'

'Shit, Rav. You scared me.' My eyes go back to the glass, but she is gone and my own face stares back at me, pale and wide-eyed.

'You OK? You look like you've seen a ghost.'

I ignore Rav's choice of words. 'Just checking on Mina.'

'We've been waiting for you. Dinner's getting cold.'

'I'm coming now. Sorry.' I could have sworn I was only watching the fox for a few minutes before Agnes's face appeared in front of me. I turn back to the window, but the fox is gone, taking his quarry with him.

Naomi is already sitting at the table when I get back downstairs, a plate of risotto in front of her. She has also topped up Rav's wine glass and her own while mine stands empty. 'I didn't know if …' She waves her hand towards my glass.

'Just water for me,' I say. 'I'll need to feed the baby later. I don't want him to have another bottle.' I didn't want him to have one in the first place.

'Oh, of course.' Naomi picks up her fork and begins to eat. 'How are you feeling now, Allie? Is that ankle OK?'

'Fine.' I push the food around my plate, not hungry. 'I was just late this morning, that's all. I don't know why either of you have made such a big deal out of it.' They exchange a glance and irritation begins to make way for real anger. 'I was up late. Rav, you know I was tired, you're the one who left me sleeping. Mina was fine.'

'Yes, I know she was,' Rav says quietly. 'We're … I'm just a little concerned that things are getting a bit much for you, that's all. It's tough with a newborn baby and a toddler.

And you're not … I mean, you just don't seem yourself at the moment.'

'I only want to help you, Al,' Naomi butts in. 'I'm your friend, you should feel able to rely on me.'

I say nothing for a moment, weighing up how to respond. In the end I say, 'I know. Thank you, but I don't need any help. I just overslept today. You know I haven't been sleeping enough' – I nod towards Rav – 'and it all caught up with me. I'm fine now, really.' I return to pushing my food around, forcing in small bites as Rav looks at his own plate, his eyes coming to rest on me at intervals as I turn the conversation to more mundane topics. When Naomi gets up to use the bathroom, Rav gives up any pretence of eating and lays a hand on my arm.

'Did you have to invite her to stay for dinner?' His tone is sharp, and I raise an eyebrow.

'Excuse me?'

'Don't think you can wriggle out of talking about this, Al. We need to talk about things, about how you've been.'

'I've been *fine*,' I snap. It's on the tip of my tongue to say something, to tell him I overheard them both, but I don't think it will do me any favours. He'll deny it, try to tell me that I misheard or imagined it. Try to make me feel like I am mad. 'I was late, it's not a big deal.'

'It is a big deal,' Rav says. 'You left Mina. And it's not just that you were late, it's all this stuff with the house. The bones. Doing all that last night with the chimney. Hounding the old lady who used to live here – you're becoming obsessed.'

I open my mouth to argue but Rav cuts me off. 'I know

I should have told you about the history of the house, but I didn't want to upset you and clearly I made the right choice – ever since you found out about this bloody Pluckley Witch story you've been … not yourself.'

'Rav, I know I saw something out in the woods, whether you like it or not.' I hiss back at him, aware of Naomi above us. 'You can hardly blame me for wanting to find out what happened if I'm going to bring up our family here.' I watch as Rav almost flinches at those words, confirming to me that I did hear correctly. He is concerned that the children aren't safe with me.

'That's my point! You were so focused on the house you forgot about Mina. Allie, listen, it's not that—'

'Is everything OK?' Naomi has appeared in the doorway, her perfectly groomed eyebrows knitted together in a frown.

'I was just moaning about Avó,' I say quickly, not meeting Rav's eye. 'I was just complaining about her bringing over potatoes so I could make Rav dosa.'

'Oh yum, I love dosa. Don't complain, Al, I'd love it if I had a mother-in-law like Avó.' She flashes a smile at Rav.

'Why don't you two go through into the living room.' Rav shoots me a look and gets to his feet. 'I'll clear up and bring you some tea.' He starts stacking the plates together, waving Naomi away as she tries to help. I push my chair back and walk into the living room, choosing the same seat on the sofa where I always sit. I didn't mention it, but Naomi had sat in my usual seat at the dinner table, directly across from Rav. Rav hadn't mentioned it either.

'Lovely dinner.' Naomi plonks herself down on the

sofa next to me. 'You're so lucky Rav can cook. Jason was totally useless. You're lucky to have Rav, full stop.' Her face clouds over, and she picks at the tasselled edges of her cardigan. 'I really am sorry about this morning, Al. I wouldn't have gone over to get Mina if I had known you'd be upset.'

'I was upset, I wasn't expecting you to be there,' I say, but I am already thinking about Tara, how Naomi knows her. 'It was just a bit of a shock, that's all, especially in light of the things I've told you lately.'

'The house. Rav told me that you found something in the chimney.'

'Did he.' The statement comes out flat, and a flicker of rage bursts into flame low down in my belly. 'You two must have been having quite the cosy chat while I was out.'

'Not really.' Naomi looks down, starts to pick at the perfect polish on her nails. 'He's worried about you. We both are, to be honest.'

'I told you everything is fine. I am fine. More importantly, the children are fine. What is it you want, Naomi?' Something chimes in the back of my mind and I think maybe I know what she wants. She's the one who put the idea in Rav's head that the children are not safe with me. Does she think they would be safer with her? Is that it?

'What I want? I don't …' She blinks and gives a slight shake of her head. 'What do you … ? Allie, I don't want anything.'

'I know you're friends with Tara Newman – is she the one who made you think like this? Is she the one who made you think I can't cope?'

'Allie, I don't understand what you mean.' Naomi is on her feet now, her keys in her hand. 'I don't want anything. You're my friend, you're important to me, and I want to help you.' She reaches out a hand but doesn't touch me. 'It's hard work looking after little kids all day, I thought you might want a break. Give you a bit of adult conversation when you're on your own at home all day. It's not as if I have anything at home to rush back to, is it? I might as well help you out where I can.' Her voice thickens and she looks down at the keys in her hand, running the keychain through her fingers.

'I told you before, I'm fine, I don't need any help.'

'I think I should probably go,' Naomi says. I don't follow her into the hallway, instead my gaze is fixated on the set of keys in her hand. 'We can talk tomorrow.' Something crosses her face, something I can't quite read.

'Naomi?' Rav appears, two cups of tea in his hands.

'Naomi's going now,' I say, taking the two cups from him. 'Thanks for coming over, but everything is perfectly all right.'

Rav looks from me to Naomi and back again. 'I'll see you out,' he says, his hand on the small of Naomi's back as he walks her to the door. She doesn't leave immediately and peering around the doorframe I see Rav's head lowering to hers as he says something to her. Her eyes flit towards me and she bites on her lower lip before nodding, her hand lingering for just a moment too long on his shoulder. I feel sick at the intimate gesture, closing my eyes against the image as I hear her say goodbye. Rav closes the door and then leans against it, his back against the old, solid oak and he sighs.

'What's going on, Al?'

Maybe I should ask Rav the same thing. 'Nothing. Nothing is going on.' I go back into the sitting room, taking care not to stomp my anger and fear out across the floorboards. I need to keep calm. As I lower myself back against the sofa cushions, a single *scratch* comes from the chimney and my breath catches for a moment in my throat.

'I'm worried about you.' Rav comes and sits next to me, pulling me against him. I lean my head against his shoulder, feeling my whole body unstiffen, even though I am still furious with him for what he said to Naomi. 'So is Avó. Naomi is too. You're not yourself.'

'I told you, Rav, I'm tired. I told you that things were worrying me, and you just laughed it off.'

'Is this about the bones? And the stuff in the chimney?'

I nod, but don't speak, not trusting my voice. 'I'm not mad, Rav. I know what I saw, whether you believe me or not.'

'Al, this place is old, really old. There are going to be some stories about it but honestly, there isn't anything for you to worry about. You don't believe in all that stuff, do you? We laughed about it before.' He kisses the top of my head and there is silence for a minute. I say nothing, the article about Lillian Sparks still fresh in my mind, Elsie's adamance that the charm needed to be replaced. That's not just a story.

'Al, would you think about maybe seeing the doctor? Just for some peace of mind?'

'The doctor?' I pull away, twisting my face up towards his. 'Rav, I'm fine. I promise. I don't need to see a doctor.'

'It couldn't hurt though, could it?' Rav says, pulling away from me now, sitting forward on the edge of the sofa. 'I mean, you say you're fine, that there's nothing wrong. If that's the case, the doctor can confirm it.'

I sigh. I don't need a doctor, I know I don't. But if it means that Rav will start listening to me when I say things aren't right, maybe I can suffer a quick ten-minute appointment. 'OK,' I say reluctantly, 'I'll make an appointment. For you though, I'm doing it for you. I know I don't need to see him.'

'Really?' He turns to face me and for a minute he looks like the old Rav, the Rav I met on the beach. 'And no more talk about witches or anything?'

'Nope,' I say, lies bitter on my tongue. I wonder if Rav and Naomi get that same bitter flavour when they lie to me. I saw Naomi's keyring when she got her keys out of her bag. The keyring with a silver pentacle dangling from it, even though she says she doesn't believe in all that stuff. The pentacle, that according to my book represents all the necessary elements required for witchcraft – earth, air, water, fire and spirit. If Naomi thinks witchcraft is all a load of nonsense, then why is she carrying a pentacle around with her? I saw the way their heads angled together at the door, heard the way they spoke about me when I wasn't in the room. I know there is something going on and it's all connected somehow to the vision – the memory – I keep having. I just have to figure out how.

Chapter Twenty-Five

The sensation of someone sitting on the edge of the bed wakes me, a similar sensation to before, only this time something is different. This time I open my eyes and stare up at the ceiling, my scalp tingling as if someone is stroking a hand over my hair. *Once, twice, three times.* Goosebumps rise on my arms as the sensation fades to be replaced by the pressure of a hand on my chest, making me feel breathless, although for the moment I am still calm. I wait, my breath coming in shorter and shorter gasps as the pressure increases, as if someone is leaning over me, pressing down hard on my chest and the feeling of calm is replaced with panic, as I fight to catch my breath. *I can't breathe,* I think, suddenly desperate to sit up, to heave in great gulps of air but my body doesn't move. Distantly, there is the cry of a child, chilling and desperate, and I try to push myself up, to push back the covers and get to my feet but I can't move my limbs, my hands and fingers are numb, as if I am frozen. My pulse soars, my heart crashing against my ribcage like a caged bird, and I open my mouth to gasp.

'*Please,*' I manage to whisper, closing my eyes against the dizziness that washes over me, Rav breathing heavily beside me. '*Please.*' As quickly as it starts, the pressure eases and there is a lightness on the mattress beside me, as if whoever it is has got up from the bed. I push myself on trembling arms into a sitting position, one hand resting against my chest as if I can still feel the pressure of that unseen hand. There is the scent of rosemary in the air, thick and heavy. The real thing, not a cheap, imitation manufactured smell and I look towards the window, expecting the curtains to sway softly in the breeze as the rosemary is carried in, but the window is closed, the curtains are still. The cries have faded, and the room is filled with a thick silence.

I don't sleep after that, feeding the baby and standing on the landing, looking out over the trees, waiting to hear the cries from the woods until an hour before Rav's alarm is due to go off. I managed not to wake Rav up and was back in bed before he woke and caught me roaming the landing, and when his alarm does go off, I feign waking from a deep sleep. Rav has a big meeting apparently, so although he kisses the top of my head and asks me how I am feeling as he gets dressed, I get the distinct impression that he is already miles away before he has even left the house. Before, this might have upset or annoyed me a little, the way he has the ability to leave us while we are still in the same room as him, but today I feel relieved, as though the spotlight has been switched off.

As I walk through the village towards the preschool my phone buzzes with a text, and when I check after dropping Mina off, I see it's from Naomi, asking how I am. I pause, one hand on the handle of the pram, as I try to decide how to respond. She must have sent it as we walked past The Daisy Chain and my eyes go to the now open door, the buckets of flowers arranged outside. Ten minutes ago, when we walked past, the door was closed and the windows were dark, but she must have been inside.

'All absolutely fine,' I type back. 'Sorry about last night. Was utterly shattered, I didn't mean to be weird x' The words are far breezier than I feel, and there is no sense of the weight of suspicion I am currently carrying. I wonder if she'll report my reply back to Rav. Mere seconds after I send the text, my phone rings.

'It's me,' Naomi says.

'Hi. I did text you back.'

'I know you did. Look, Al, I shouldn't have texted, I should have rung you in the first place. Do you want to come to the shop for coffee? We can talk properly.'

'I ... can't. I have to drop Mina off and then I have an appointment.' I cross my fingers against the lie. I don't want to see Naomi. I still feel odd, remembering the way they spoke about me, the way her hand rested on Rav's shoulder. My mother's words come back to me. *Be careful who you trust.*

'I'll just say it to you now, then,' Naomi says. I hear a rush of air, as if she has just drawn in a deep breath. 'Allie, I don't know what is going on with you, but there is something that isn't right. All I want to do is help you. Why is it so hard for you to accept that?'

'Because I don't need any help.' My voice is sharp. 'I'm

fine. I don't need you hovering around, poking your nose in all the time. I can manage on my own.'

'But that's just it, Allie, you're not on your own. I don't think you quite understand how Rav feels at the moment.'

The image of her and Rav in the pub, her face breaking into a smile as she laughs, Rav leaning in close and putting his arms around her swims in front of my eyes. Rav talking with her in our kitchen, the pair of them discussing my mental state. *Keep the children safe.* 'And you do understand how Rav feels, I suppose? You know what Rav is feeling? Rav and I are fine.' The lie slices across the top of my tongue, a physical pain.

'You're pushing him away, just like you are with me.' Naomi lets out a bitter laugh. 'I don't think you understand quite what you have there, Al. Rav is a good man, a perfect husband, you have two beautiful children, a lovely house. I know this whole thing about Agnes Gowdie has got you unsettled, and I would be too, especially finding what you have, but, Al, it's all superstition, a story.'

I don't respond for a moment, biting my tongue against the sharp words that rise to my lips. 'Naomi, a child died in my house. There is *something* in my house, I can feel it. I've tried to talk to you and Rav about it, but neither of you want to listen, you just make out that I'm mad. I'm going to get rid of the witch's ladder, the bones, then everything will be fine.'

'You're getting obsessed with the house! We're concerned about you. Rav is worried. We're both worried that you're not coping.'

'I am coping fine. I haven't asked you for help. If I did need help, I would have asked, so why don't you back off? Or is it that you want me to be mad? Would that make things easier for you?'

'I'm sorry, Allie. I didn't mean to lose my temper.' Naomi lets out a long sigh. 'I don't know what you're talking about, and I don't want to fall out with you, OK? If you want me to keep my distance, then I will.'

I don't know what I want. Exhaustion makes my head feel muddled and confused, and while I think Naomi is keeping things from me, there is that other part of me that still instinctively wants to go to her first. I want to tell her what happened last night as I slept, the feeling of the hand in my hair and on my chest, but I no longer know if I can trust her.

'It's not that,' I say eventually. 'There are things … I don't want to talk about it, anymore, OK? Rav and I are fine. We always have been, and he would tell me if he was that concerned. There is nothing to worry about – I've told Rav I won't look into the house anymore. Just believe me when I say I'm OK; that's what a real friend would do.' And I hang up.

Sliding my phone back into the pocket of my skirt, I see Tara on the other side of the road, one hand raised to get my attention. She waits a moment at the crossing, then almost jogs over towards me and I wonder for a moment if she is going to ask me about the blanket she left at the house. I don't know how I'll respond if she does.

'Hey.' She is a little out of breath from the short jog. 'I thought I must have missed you this morning. My turn to be late.' She laughs, and I try to smile, her words a jab against my skin. I should have realized that the other mothers would have known that I wasn't there to collect Mina yesterday. I feel my cheeks start to burn with embarrassment. 'Are you coming for coffee this morning? I won't be staying too long as Rufus is still a little under the weather and I promise I won't let Miranda start talking about anything weird.'

Right on cue, the baby starts to fuss in the pram, giving me the perfect out.

'Sorry' – I pull a face – 'not this morning. I've been up all night with this one.' Not strictly true – the baby slept for a glorious three-hour stretch, while I lay wide awake, unblinking, next to Rav, not wanting to sleep or to dream, imagining I could still feel the pressure of a hand on my chest.

'You do look tired.' Tara peers at me, and I get that feeling again of being under a spotlight. 'OK, we can catch up next week. I have to pop across the road before I head to the café anyway.' She glances over her shoulder, but I am not sure whether she is looking at The Daisy Chain or the small supermarket next to it. 'See you at pick-up?'

I nod, and say goodbye, moving off in the direction of my house before I allow myself a quick glance over my shoulder. Tara is bumping the travel system over the threshold to The Daisy Chain. I try not to read too much into it.

Tired as I am, I don't go straight home. The baby has settled again so I follow the path past the turning into the lane our house is on and carry on walking, round to the entrance to the woods that back onto the garden. Pausing as I come to the edge of the woods, I see that Tara is right about the trees. There isn't really an entrance as such, just a place where the branches aren't so tightly tangled together. There isn't a path, although where the branches are thinner it does look as though someone has walked through, but not enough to be a proper, well-used path. It is overgrown this end, more overgrown than it is at the edge of the garden and I peer between the trees, looking for signs of life. It's impossible for me to push the pram between the branches, and I don't think I'd want to take the baby inside anyway. That strange oozing malevolence that I felt from the witch's ladder is present here too, stronger, if anything. The hairs on the back of my neck prickle, and I feel as if someone is watching me, eyes on my skin. *There's someone here.* The voice is in my head not in my ear, but the breeze ruffles my hair and I shiver, my blood running cold as I hear another, familiar sound. A child crying. It is coming from deep inside the trees, louder than I have heard it before on the other side by the house. I wait a moment, my heart in my mouth when it comes again, the distinct sound of a child, lost and afraid and calling for her mother.

Ducking under a low branch, I step just inside the trees, on to the crackly, brown forest floor, the child's cries a siren call. Leaves crunch beneath my feet, decades of winter seasons lying dead on the ground as I dodge the sharp ends of branches that threaten to tangle in my hair, following the distant cries. Brambles claw at my legs as I take another step in, trying to follow the sound but the further in I go, the quieter the cries become until I can no longer hear them. I find I can see the house from here, can see how close someone would need to get before they could watch us. A bird calls from high up, a monotonous ringing shout and I take one more step deeper inside. I feel that tugging in my lower belly, the way the witch's ladder called to me when Rav threw it out, the urge to go deeper into the shadowy, damp-smelling trees almost overwhelming.

'Excuse me?' A shrill voice reaches my ears and for a moment I almost laugh, thinking it's coming from my house, that I am calling to myself, both the watcher and the watched. 'Hello? Are you there?'

Turning and peering back through the trees, I see there is a woman standing next to the baby in the pram, her hand on the handle, a worried face peering back at me. *Shit. The baby. I forgot about the baby.* Heart thundering in my chest, I run the few metres back towards the edge of the woods, branches snatching at my clothes and pulling at my hair.

'Sorry,' I pant, emerging from the trees like a mad woman. The lady, a woman I don't recognize, looks at me in shock. 'Sorry, I'm here now, you can let go of the pram.'

'Is this your baby?' She frowns at me, and I raise my hand, brushing back my hair. 'Are you all right?'

'Yes, fine.' I try to smile, try to stop my breath from catching in my throat. 'Sorry, I thought I heard something in there. A child. I live the other side, you see ...'

'Right.' She looks me up and down. 'Well, you can't go

haring off and leaving your baby by the side of the road. Anything could have happened.'

'I was only a few paces in, I was gone for a few seconds.' Tears fill my eyes and I blink rapidly. By trying to protect my family, I have done something completely stupid and put my baby at risk. 'I didn't mean …'

'No, well …' The woman looks into the pram, seemingly uncomfortable with my tears. 'Maybe you should get him home now, eh?'

I thank her and walk away quickly, limping on my still sore ankle. Stumbling over branches and twigs in my short sprint back to the baby didn't help it. By the time I open the front door to the house I am ready for some strong painkillers, my throat thick with unshed tears. I lift the baby gently out of the pram, holding him close and inhaling his scent as my eyes fill, and I feel that familiar sting in the bridge of my nose. I can't believe I did something so stupid. So risky. God forbid, if Naomi or Rav hear about this, I'll really be in trouble. I make little shushing noises at the baby, holding his head close to my shoulder, feeling the weight of his tiny body across my chest. He snuffles, twisting his head away and I kiss his downy hair. I can't let anything happen to either of my babies. I have to follow Miranda's advice and get the bones and the witch's ladder out of the house, or least get them out of my bedroom away from the baby. I feed him, blinking and shifting in the feeding chair so that I don't doze off, and once he is finished, I lay him down in the cot and then pull out the book on witchcraft from under the mattress. Pausing briefly at the page on the witch's ladder, I keep flicking through until I find a section on bones.

Bones can be used as part of a binding spell. It is believed that a witch can tap into the energy of the bones, thereby enabling her to use the bones to capture part of the spirit, binding them eternally. To break the binding, the bones should be buried in the earth, capturing the witch's spirit and preventing her from doing further harm.

I feel cold, goosebumps rising on my arms as I push the book to one side and move to the drawers where I have hidden everything. Miranda said, to break the curse on the witch's ladder a spell should be said over it as the knots are untied, but I don't know any spells, and I don't know if I can bear to touch it long enough to unpick the knots. Would burying everything work? If it works for the bones, then perhaps that will work for the witch's ladder too.

The blanket is still on top, the bones and the ladder tucked underneath, but the moment I open the drawer it's as if I can feel them. The air changes around me, growing thick and heavy and I think I can smell lavender again. I gingerly reach in and scoop up the bundle, making sure my skin doesn't touch the hair or the feathers. I take it along the landing, without pausing to check on the movement in the woods below, and down the stairs out into the garden. The weather is still unseasonably warm for May, and the rosebush on the edge of the border is looking wilted and brown. Neither Rav nor I have thought to water the garden, and while the rosemary and mint are still going strong, some of the other plants are starting to look as if they are dying off. At the far end of the border, closest to the woods, I stop, laying the bundle on the ground. I will bury it all, I think, bury the bones and hair deep under the earth so that I don't have to feel it anymore. *Capturing the witch's spirit and preventing her from doing further harm.* Surveying the border, trying to ignore the overwhelming feeling of heaviness hanging over me, I look for the right spot to bury the items. I don't want to bury them under the roses, chamomile or lavender – they are the healing plants of the garden and I don't want the hair and bones to contaminate their goodness. I choke back a laugh. I sound like Miranda, believing in all this good and evil, witchcraft and superstition, but if I hadn't felt the suffocating malice coming from the witch's ladder, I probably wouldn't have believed in it at all. It's probably best to bury them at the opposite end of the garden, among the oleander, the foxgloves and the aconite. Rummaging in the tiny, run-down shed at the opposite corner to the border, I find a pair of old gloves, stiff with dirt and age and with a feeling of distaste, I slip them over my hands. I can't risk touching most of the plants in that area but Rav will be less likely to notice that I've dug it up. He doesn't seem to spend much time on the border, preferring to sit by the pond instead. I skirt my way past the pond, ripples shattering the surface as I disturb something, and then I begin to dig, in a small patch of earth between the foxgloves and the oleander bush. The faint scent from the flowers fills the air and I find myself taking shallow breaths, not wanting to breathe in their perfume. I have dug a small hole, the earth I've removed mounded up beside it, when my phone rings. Glancing down, I see Rav's name. I have to take the call;

Rav never calls during the day, he's always too busy, and after what happened yesterday … I yank the gloves off, glad of the touch of a breeze that runs over my sweaty skin, and sit back on my haunches.

'Hello?'

'Al, it's me.' His voice crackles down the line and I shift slightly, looking at the screen. Only one bar of reception. 'You sound out of breath. What are you up to?'

I realize I am panting slightly from the effort of digging and take a second to try and regulate my breathing. 'My phone was downstairs; I was putting the baby down for a nap.' I cross my fingers against the lie.

'I just wanted to let you know, I made a doctor's appointment for you. He can see you tomorrow morning.'

'Rav …' Irritation prickles and I have to temper my tone. 'I can make my own doctor's appointment. I'm not a child.'

'No, I know,' he says. 'I just thought that maybe you—'

'That I wouldn't do it? That I'd go back on my word?' My voice rises sharply and something behind me splashes into the murky water of the pond. Turning, I see more ripples, bigger this time and I turn my back, not wanting to see what it was. 'Jesus, Rav, I said I would do it.'

'I was going to say,' he says, his voice tinged with impatience, 'that I thought you might forget, that's all. I thought I was doing you a favour. Had you already booked it?'

'No,' I say, shoving the small trowel into the dirt, 'I hadn't.'

'Well then,' Rav says, 'good job I did, eh? One more thing you don't have to think about today. Listen, how about we go out for dinner tonight?'

'What about the children? The baby?' Panic flutters in my chest at the thought of them being in the house, at night, in the dark, without me there to protect them. Without me there to watch over them all as they sleep, keeping an eye on the woods.

'I'll sort it, leave it all to me. I think we need to spend the evening together, on our own. I think perhaps I've not been as understanding as I should have been.'

'No, Rav—'

'I've got to go – I popped out of the meeting to call you. Leave it all to me, OK?' The phone beeps in my hand. He's hung up. I let out a long breath and pull the gloves back on. I'll just have to go along with it and pretend it's all OK. If we go somewhere close by, and only have a main – skip the starter and dessert – I can be back home within the hour. If I don't go, then Rav might think that I am not OK, that I really do need to see the doctor – before all of this I would have jumped at the chance for the two of us to spend the evening alone. I dig the last few centimetres down into the dirt and lay the bones in first, followed by the pearls, then the witch's ladder on top, taking care to make sure that the hair and feathers are tucked in neatly. I hold the blanket in my hands, tempted to throw that in too, before remembering that it belongs to Tara. What if she realizes she left it here, and comes back for it? I can't exactly tell her I buried it in the garden. Instead, I fold it neatly and put it to one side, and begin to fill in the hole, watching as the grains of dirt tumble over the hair until it is buried completely. Nausea washes over me as they disappear beneath the soil, and for a fleeting moment there is a crushing heaviness, a sense of sorrow that is so acute I feel it as a pain in my chest. As I tamp over the loose soil, careful not to catch my skin on the toxic leaves of the aconite plant, I think I can feel eyes on me and I pause, sure that I hear my name whispered on the breeze. I peer into the trees from where I sit, my trowel in my hand, but there is nothing, no movement, no flash of white. Hurriedly, in a sudden spurt of panic, I get to my feet, convinced that despite the lack of movement in the trees, I am not alone. With one last glance over the border and sure that no one can tell that the earth has been disturbed, I hurry back inside, the blanket under one arm.

I hear the wailing as soon as I step into the kitchen. Raw, angry cries, desperate and ragged as if he has been crying for a long time. I forgot about him, the baby. Again. I left the baby monitor upstairs, so eager was I to get the bones and the ladder out of my house. I rush now, limping slightly, and throw the blanket onto the bed as I lean over and pull him close to me, his tiny body hot and damp with sweat.

'Shhhh,' I whisper, bouncing him in my arms. 'I'm so sorry, baby, I'm so sorry.' Sinking into the nursing chair, I latch him on, his cries stopping abruptly as he begins to feed. I rock slightly in the chair, my throat thick with grief, tears running down my cheeks. Maybe Rav is right, maybe there is something wrong. I left the baby and the monitor, left myself with no way of knowing if he was OK. *But*, a voice reasons at the back of my mind, a voice that sounds suspiciously like my mother's, *you were doing what was right for the baby and Mina. Getting those horrible things out of the house, away from the children.* I relax, nodding to myself. I was doing the right thing, getting rid of it all. Now I am inside, away from the disturbed soil, it's almost as if a weight has been lifted and the air in the bedroom feels lighter somehow, like the air after a storm.

Chapter Twenty-Six

I bend forward, peering into the mirror as I try to perfect my eyeliner, Mina bouncing on the bed behind me. I feel out of practice, it's been months since I bothered with make-up, not since my last day working at The Daisy Chain, and my hand wobbles ever so slightly as I run the black pencil over my eyelids. Rav must be concerned about me, as he made it home early and is lying back on the bed, the baby sleeping across his chest.

'Stop, Mina,' I say, watching in the mirror as she starts to bounce again. 'Daddy and the baby are lying there too.' Rav holds out a hand and she scrambles over to him, tucking under his arm and nestling against his shoulder. 'We don't have to go out, you know,' I say, turning to face him. 'You guys look very comfortable there. I could go and get fish and chips and we could all snuggle together.'

'Looking like that?' Rav says, waggling his eyebrows at me. 'No chance, lady. I want to take you out and show you off. Make all the boys jealous.' He tickles Mina as he says it, making her giggle and squirm.

It was worth a try. Holding in a sigh I turn back to the

mirror, brushing the mascara wand over my eyelashes. I've managed to find a dress that fits me, a dress from before I was pregnant. It actually fits surprisingly well and when I examine myself in the mirror, I realize that perhaps I have lost more weight than I first thought. I still have the smallest remainder of a belly, but my arms look thin and there are shadows in the hollows of my collarbones. Slicking pale pink lipstick over my mouth, I hold my arms out and walk over to the bed. Rav reaches up as if to pull me down.

'No!' A laugh bubbles out, surprising even me. 'I've just got ready! Give me the baby, I'll put him down.' I take him, holding him close for a moment before laying him in the cot. 'Won't be long,' I whisper, hearing Rav saying goodnight to Mina, the bedroom door closing until only a small gap remains. I meet him on the landing, let him take my hand and lead me down the stairs. Everything feels wonderfully normal for the first time in months – or at least, it would if I could erase the memory of Rav and Naomi, the words *postpartum psychosis* hanging in the air between them. I am making a concerted effort tonight to not mention the house, Agnes, or any of the strange things that have happened.

'What time did you book the table for?' I ask. Rav has booked a table at a pub nearby, one that was a favourite of ours before we had the baby.

'Eight o'clock,' he says. I glance at the clock on the sitting-room wall. It's already seven thirty.

'What time will Avó be here? She's cutting it a bit fine.' I would have thought she would have arrived long before now, in time to help – or rather interfere – with the children's bedtime routines. I expected her to arrive before dinner, bringing food for Rav with her, as she has done so often before. She doesn't approve of my 'bland' cooking.

'Oh, Avó couldn't do tonight. She's annoyed with me, of course, for wanting to go out on her bridge night. She can't let her partner down apparently.' Rav shrugs and opens the door to the understairs cupboard, rooting around for his new trainers.

'Avó isn't coming?' I raise my eyes to the landing, to the rooms where the children are sleeping. 'I thought you said leave it to you. Bloody hell, Rav, who have you got to look after the children?' *Please don't let it be Naomi.*

'Evie,' he says, finally pulling his head out of the cupboard, trainers dangling from his fingers. 'Evie said she was free and she's looking for some extra money. She's saving to go travelling, Naomi said.'

'Oh.' I don't know how I feel. I would have preferred Avó to come. In fact, I'd now quite like to tell Rav that that's it, I definitely don't want to go out. 'Are you sure?' I catch sight of his face. His expression is mild annoyance – perhaps at the realization of what I am about to say – mixed with something else. It's the something else – fear? Suspicion? – that makes me keep my mouth shut. The children are asleep, they won't even know that Evie is here. And at least it isn't Naomi. I couldn't bear to come home and see her holding the baby, looking for all the world like she belongs here instead of me.

Before I can say anything, the doorbell rings and Rav

opens the door to Evie on the step. It's the first time I've met her properly and she looks even younger than I imagined.

'Come through.' I force the words out, trying to smile, dropping it when it feels tight across my face. 'Let me just show you where everything is.' I wait until we are in the kitchen before I ask her, 'Do you have any experience? I don't mean to be rude it's just …'

'I know, they're your babies.' Evie smiles. 'Yes, I have lots of experience. My aunt has two children that I babysit a lot, and I am the eldest of six, so …'

'Six? Gosh.'

Rav appears, sliding his hand around my waist. 'So, nothing to worry about, Al. Evie has tons of experience and she has my number if anything happens. Shall we go?'

I have no reason to say no. But that doesn't stop me from turning back and watching the house as we drive away, out of the village, a sensation like an itch between my shoulder blades telling me that I shouldn't be leaving the children. That I've made the wrong choice.

The pub is dimly lit, and I am glad of it, hoping that Rav can't tell how jittery and anxious I feel. My knee bounces under the table as I wait for him to return from the bar and I lay my hand on it in an effort to stop it.

'I ordered you the fish pie, is that OK?' Rav hands me a small glass of white wine as he sits opposite me, a pint of ale in his other hand. I nod, but I have no appetite. 'This is nice, eh? Just the two of us. It feels like it's been ages since it was just us.' His hand slides across the table and I let his fingers squeeze mine. 'I love you, Al. Whatever happens, remember that.' He raises my hand and presses his lips to my palm. As he does so, a shadow flickers across his face in the dim lighting and for a moment he is unrecognizable.

Whatever happens? What does that mean? I open my mouth to ask him, but he is talking again, about the case he's working on, generic stuff, and I tune out letting my mind wander. *What does he mean by that?* Maybe it's nothing, but still, it's an odd thing to say. The waitress brings our food. By the time it arrives I think I am hungry, the wine enhancing my appetite, but when she lays the plate in front of me the scent of fish and cream wafts up and I think for a moment I'll be sick.

'Excuse me, I just need to …' I get up, head to the ladies'. The air is cool in the bathroom, and I splash my cheeks gently with cold water, careful not to smudge my make-up. The nausea dies away as I draw in some deep breaths and I grip the sink tightly with both hands until I feel ready to face Rav again. *It's fine, everything is fine.*

'OK?' His phone is in his hands as I approach, and he drops it to the table, clicking the side button to darken the screen. His steak sits half eaten on the plate, and my fish pie is cold and congealing.

'Yes. Fine. How's your steak?' I pretend I haven't seen him on his phone and pick up my fork, taking the tiniest bite of mashed potato.

'Really good, I've missed this place.' He spears a piece of meat and I keep my eyes on my plate, the nausea still not quite gone for good. Rav starts talking again, but I can't concentrate. My mind is at home with the children, wondering if they are OK, if they are still asleep. *Wondering if Agnes is walking the landing, filling the space left by my absence.* I glance towards the window, to where the sky is turning a deep indigo. I wonder if the fox is in the garden, if the trees are silent. I wonder whether Evie has heard the scratching, what she thinks of it.

'… Naomi.' Her name is the only part of Rav's sentence that I catch.

'Sorry, Rav, what did you say? I was miles away.' I give a small apologetic smile, shedding any pretence of eating and laying my fork down. Rav's eyes flick towards my plate but he says nothing.

'I was just saying that I hope Evie is getting on OK. It would be quite nice to have an extra babysitter on hand if Mum is busy, or Naomi.'

'Mmmm,' I say non-committally. I am not in any hurry to leave the children again any time soon.

'Have you spoken to Naomi today?' Rav asks, as he finishes his last mouthful of food.

'Yes,' I say, 'she called me earlier. Everything's fine.' I wonder now if I should have gone into The Daisy Chain when I received her text this morning, spoken to her face to face instead of over the phone, but I still feel odd about the way I felt seeing her with Rav while I was outside, looking in. 'What about you? Have you spoken to her today?'

Rav shakes his head, pushes the breadbasket towards me. 'If you won't eat the fish, at least have some bread.'

'I don't want any, I'm not hungry. So, you didn't speak

to her at all today?' I thought he would have – it wouldn't surprise me to learn that the two of them had talked about Rav making my doctor's appointment before he booked it, after what I overheard yesterday evening.

'No, Allie, I didn't speak to her. Maybe you should mention your appetite to the doctor when you go? I thought you needed the extra calories when you feed the baby yourself?' He frowns, his voice holding a vague note of concern and I feel a pang of guilt before I chase it away with a swig of wine. Anyone can fake concern. I reach for a small piece of bread, buttering it slowly.

'I had a big lunch,' I lie. 'Listen, I told you yesterday, you don't need to worry. I am absolutely fine. Tired, but that's to be expected. I honestly don't need to see the doctor.' He opens his mouth and I hold up a hand. 'But if that's what you want, I'll go. I haven't mentioned anything about the bones, or being watched, or anything else weird, have I?' A bite creeps into my tone, irritation leaching through.

'No. No, you haven't. Of course, you know how you feel better than I do. You know best.' He shrugs, but there is something off in his tone. He doesn't believe me. 'Do you want to split a pudding, or should I just get the bill? You do look tired. I shouldn't have made you come out.' He gets to his feet.

I put the bread back on the plate, relieved I don't have to force it down. 'Let's get the bill and go home.' I watch as he makes his way to the gents', not sure how I feel about this evening. I thought maybe he wanted to cheer me up, but it almost feels as if he brought me out so he could examine me at close quarters. See how I reacted to leaving the children, see how much I ate, see how I behaved when it was just the two of us without the distraction of the house and the children. Something crackles under my skin, a nervous energy. His phone lies on the table next to his empty plate, and I picture him turning the screen dark as I approached from the ladies' earlier in the evening.

Maybe he was checking to see if Evie had contacted him. I lift the phone, entering his passcode. Our wedding date, the same as mine. The picture on his lock screen is of Mina, holding the baby on the day we brought him home. *No signal*. The pub is in a dead zone, there is no way for Evie to contact us if she needed to. I feel the first wings of panic flutter in my chest, butterflies beating hard against my ribcage. I swipe across, and there is one unread WhatsApp message. Maybe that is from Evie – there is one weak Wifi bar in the pub. I tap on the WhatsApp icon to open the app, but the unread message isn't from Evie. It's from Naomi.

Glancing up to check that Rav isn't yet at the bar, I open the message, my pulse thudding loud and hard in my ears. Somehow, I think I already know what I will find.

> Yes, I feel things are escalating. You're doing the right thing.

This, from Naomi. I scroll back to see what message Rav wrote that she is replying to.

It's the children I am worried about – whether they are safe or whether I need to remove them. Passports are sorted.

Oh God. Reading Rav's words to Naomi makes bile rise in my throat. *Passports. Whether I need to remove them. He's going to take my children?* I am still, iced water in my veins as I re-read the message. I think of the two of them talking in the kitchen while I was out, the way Naomi slid into my seat at the table. It's as if she's inching her way into my life one tiny step at a time. Has she put the idea in his head that I am mad? Does she want him to remove the children so that she can take my place? I can't believe that Rav, *my Rav*, would come to this conclusion of his own accord – he knows how much he and the children mean to me. The door to the gents' swings open at the far end of the bar and Rav comes striding out. I lay his phone down, pressing the side button to turn the screen dark just he did barely an hour ago. Instead of going to the bar he comes back to the table.

'Shall we have a nightcap? Do you have enough milk pumped to have a drink?' There is no sign of his betrayal on his face; if I hadn't read the messages, I never would have known.

'No, thanks though.' I get up and pick up the tiny hand-bag that feels alien to me now I am used to carrying a huge nappy bag around with me. I feel disconnected from my body, my feet numb. 'There isn't much reception here, we should get back.'

Rav's eyes flick down to his phone on the table and he

278

snatches it up. 'Yeah, you're right, we should probably get back.'

Rav is quiet all the way home, his hands light on the steering wheel as the radio plays softly in the background. I don't even attempt to make conversation – all I can see is the stream of WhatsApp messages on his phone screen. A whole thread of betrayal and deceit. Now I just have to decide what I'm going to do about it.

Chapter Twenty-Seven

Stepping into the hallway, I shrug off my light jacket, relieved to be home. The house is quiet, no sound of children, and I breathe out – at least they slept through my not being there. It's only as I walk into the sitting room that I realize something is wrong.

'Naomi.' A stirring of unease rolls in my belly. 'What are you doing here? Where is Evie?' I turn to look at Rav as he follows in behind me.

'Hello Naomi.' He stands in the doorway, his back reflected in the mirror in the hallway behind him. 'What's going on? Evie was meant to be watching the kids.'

'She had a bit of a problem.' Naomi gets to her feet in one fluid motion and I am reminded of a cat, a sneaky, stealthy feline. 'Her nephew is poorly, and her aunt needed her help. She tried to call you guys but there was no reception, I'm guessing. She said it just went straight to voicemail. She didn't know who else to call.' She turns to me and gives me a nervous smile. 'Al, how was the meal? You look lovely.'

I am thrown. After reading the messages, in the car I had

built her up in my mind to be some sort of Cruella de Vil creature, but she's still the same Naomi, the Naomi I have shared secrets with, laughed with, cried with. The Naomi I made my friend. 'It was fine,' I say.

'Do you want to check on the children?' Rav asks, and I shake my head. There is no way I want to leave the two of them alone together and it makes me feel confused and wrong-footed.

'I'll check them in a second. Let me see you out, Naomi.'

'Oh.' She looks surprised and turns her face to Rav. 'Well, I'll see you later.'

Rav stares at me. 'Don't you two want to have a cup of tea together before Naomi leaves?'

'Rav, I'm really tired. Sorry, Naomi. Do you mind if we catch up later?' I am already standing by the door, watching as she fumbles around for her cardigan, her shoes, her bag. I can't bring myself to thank her for stepping in so Evie could rush off. I can't thank her for worming her way into my house, my life, again.

'Thanks for coming over, Naomi,' Rav says. 'Poor Evie, I hope her nephew is better soon.'

'I hope so too,' Naomi says, pulling a sad face. 'He's had to go to hospital, I think. Some sort of gastro thing. But it was no problem, you two should have called me in the first place.' She looks directly at me. 'I told you, I'm always happy to help with the kids.'

'Bye, Naomi.' I open the front door and she sidles out, waving her fingers at Rav, who just smiles wearily. He waits until the door is closed before he speaks.

'I thought you two were OK? You said that you spoke to her today and everything was all right.'

'It is.'

'Really? Because that just felt really, really awkward. Are you mad at her for something? I know you were annoyed that she picked Mina up the other day, but that was my fault, not hers. Why aren't you cross with me about that?'

Why are you defending her, Rav? 'I'm not cross,' I lie smoothly, 'I'm tired, Rav, that's all. This is the first time I've been out in months. I just didn't fancy sitting there with a cup of tea making idle chit-chat when I can catch up with her properly tomorrow. You don't need to make a big deal out of things.'

Rav looks at me hard for a moment, as if debating whether to call bullshit on what I've said. In the end he just says, 'OK. Fair enough.'

He walks away towards the kitchen, and I debate for a moment whether to follow him. My reflection in the mirror is haunted, for want of a better word, my eyes fiercely dark thanks to the make-up, the pale of my cheeks almost glowing in the dim light. I close my eyes for a moment, tears stinging, before breath on the back of my neck makes them fly open. *I see you*, I think, a dark figure on the stairs watching me in the glass. *I feel you. I know you're still here.* My heart starts to bang in my chest, painfully hard and I turn slowly, my mouth dry. The staircase is empty.

The air is cooler tonight, as I stand watch over the garden from the landing window. There has been a brief shower bringing some break in the weather and the clouds have disappeared now to leave bright moonlight behind. The grass sparkles, and I know in the morning my feet will be wet the moment I step onto it. Mina sleeps soundly in the room to the right of me. I had leaned over her after Naomi left, and kissed her sweaty forehead, her dark curls sticking damply to her skin. I had breathed her in, the scent of the baby shampoo I used on her only a few hours earlier, and her own natural scent, something like fresh peach. The baby is fed and changed and sleeps soundly in the cot beside my side of the bed, Rav sprawled across the other side, snoring heavily.

The fox slinks through the garden, skirting the edge of the woods and the pond, hurrying, urgent, as if he has somewhere important to be. The water on the pond is flat and lifeless this evening, no sign of life. I wonder again how it would be to sink my toes into the cool, flat mud under the water. To step further and further in until the icy cold water closes over my head, clearing away the hot, sweaty, uncomfortable tumble of thoughts that roam around in my mind. *Rav. Naomi. The children. The blanket. The figure on the stairs, always reflected back in the darkened glass.* I can't swallow, my body burning from the inside.

'Allie? What are you doing?' Rav is beside me, his arms wrapped around his bare torso against the persistent chill that swirls about the landing, no matter how warm it is outside. 'God, you're freezing.'

I press my hand to my face, feeling the chill of my fingertips, white in the milky moonlight, against my hot cheek. 'I didn't realize how cold it was.'

'Come to bed, come on. You'll catch your death out here. I'm going to call a guy, get someone in to sort these windows out before the winter.' Rav takes my elbow and begins to steer me towards the bedroom. I stop, the thought of lying next to him, thinking over the message thread between him and Naomi, like nails catching on my nerve endings. Sharp and raw.

'Wait …' I stop him before he can lead me any further. 'The baby is going to be up again soon, you're going to be exhausted for work.'

'I'm more worried about getting you back into bed and getting warm at the moment.' He rubs his hand briskly over my shoulder, and I stifle a wince, my skin feeling as if it is snagging on his.

'I'm OK, I didn't mean to wake you up.' I form the lie before he can ask me what I was doing. 'I got up for a glass of water, and there was a fox in the garden. I was just watching him.' To his credit Rav doesn't pull me up on the fact that I don't have a glass of water in my hand. 'I can catch up on my sleep when Mina is at preschool tomorrow, but you can't. Maybe you should sleep in the spare bedroom tonight?'

Rav opens his mouth as if to speak before thinking better of it. He nods slowly, removing his hand from my shoulder. 'If that's what you want.'

'Just for tonight. So you can catch up on your sleep.' Before he can respond, I go to the cupboard that holds the spare sheets and towels and start looking for a fresh set.

Rav is already in the spare room when I bring in the sheets, standing in front of the unmade bed. We haven't really used this room at all, and haven't even begun to start decorating it, focusing instead on the living room, the bathroom, and Mina's bedroom when we first moved in. The carpet is threadbare, the walls uneven and lumpy, with old curtains hanging at the windows, the fabric so thin they barely keep the morning light out. It's not very inviting and for a moment I feel a shard of guilt until I remember the WhatsApp thread.

'Here.' I shove the duvet cover towards him and yank the pillows off the bed.

'I thought this was a spontaneous event,' Rav says, with a trace of bitterness in his voice.

'What?' I pause in my attempt to stuff the pillow into the case and follow his gaze. 'It was spontaneous … oh.'

A vase sits atop the battered chest of drawers that was in the room when we moved in. Neither of us thought about getting rid of it, as we didn't have anything to replace it, although Avó had given it a good going over with the Dettol before she allowed us to keep it. The vase is one of ours, one that I believed to be empty in the cupboard under the kitchen sink. Only it's not. It's here in the spare room and it is filled with flowers.

'Like you were expecting me,' Rav says, with a bark of laughter. He reaches out with one finger to touch the petals.

'Don't touch that!' My voice rings out, loud and crashing in the silence of the house. 'It's poisonous.'

I can smell it on the air, now that I think about it. The fresh, apricot-like scent of the oleander flowers. They are mixed with the pink bells of columbine, a plant that is toxic if even touched, let alone ingested. I have seen columbines somewhere before recently, their fragile heads bowed under the weight of their bell-like petals, but I can't place it.

'Fucks' sake, Allie.' Rav is furious, a twitch in his jaw and the fact that he swore at me belying his calm façade. 'The kids are in the house. What are you doing bringing toxic plants into our home?'

The petals of the flowers are wilted slightly, the water only two thirds of the way up the glass of the vase. 'I didn't,' I whisper. My hands are shaking, and I turn my frightened gaze to Rav. 'I didn't bring them in.'

'Well I didn't,' Rav snaps, 'who else could it be, Allie? You're the only one who's here all day long.'

'I promise you, Rav, I would never bring those plants into our house. If Mina touched them—' I break off, not wanting to think about it. If she touched them, their pretty, pink, irresistible bells, then put her hands in her mouth …

'If not you, then who?' Rav's voice softens. 'Maybe my mum thought she was doing something nice; you know she hasn't got a clue about plants and flowers. I just hope she washed her hands after she touched them. I'll call her in the morning and warn her not to pick stuff. These grow in our garden, don't they?' He comes to me, but there is a wariness in his eyes as he wraps his arms around me. I stand stiffly, not taking my eyes from the vase.

That's where I have seen the columbine. They grow on the far side of the pond, away from the house. 'Naomi.' The words rasp out of my throat and I have to swallow. *Or Agnes.* But I can't bring myself to say her name.

'Naomi?' Rav pulls away and the chilly night air hits my skin in the gap between us. 'Don't be silly, she wouldn't pick stuff like that, not if it was poisonous. And she would know, wouldn't she?'

Yes. She would know. 'I'll get rid of them,' I say. 'You make the bed up and I'll get rid of them. I promise you, Rav, I didn't bring them in.'

Chapter Twenty-Eight

There are none of Rav's usual light snores from the spare bedroom as I lie awake, waiting once again for the sun to creep its way up the sky, and I wonder if Rav is lying there as sleepless as I am. The flowers are stuffed deep inside the outside bin, as far away from the children as I could get them. It was only as I shoved the stems deep down into the bin, the hardened leather of the gardening gloves scratching at my wrists that I thought about what columbine could mean. It can mean love, strength, wisdom, given as a gift for a birthday in May. Or it can mean foolishness, deceit, errant lovers, unfaithfulness. Flowers can tell a thousand stories, if you'll just let them speak.

Foolishness. Deceit. Unfaithfulness. I turn over onto my side, gazing through the bars of the cot at the sleeping baby. Given what I read on the message thread on Rav's phone, I could assign all of those to him and Naomi. I imagine her stealthily creeping through the garden, my gloves on her hands as she snips, snips, snips, before tiptoeing upstairs to put the stems where I wouldn't find them immediately. Where I wouldn't find them until the smell of decaying petals led me to them. I blink slowly, hoping that sleep will come, but my eyes ping open, gritty and dry. I picture the dark figure on the stairs, gliding towards the spare bedroom, flowers in hand. Waiting for Mina to find them, to reach out and grasp the deadly petals. The baby snuffles and raises a fist in his sleep. *A gift for a birthday in May.* Allowing the thought that has been ricocheting around in my mind to formulate fully, I roll over, away from the baby's innocent form. I could smell the oleander on my hands, as I watched Rav and Naomi through the window after my return from the local supermarket. It was on the air, and I thought then, for a moment, that I could smell it on my skin. Was Rav right? Was it me who picked the toxic stems and brought them into our house? A single tear slides from the corner of my eye, running a sticky, salty track down my cheek. Wouldn't I remember picking them? There are so many things I am not sure of, I don't know what to think anymore. The movement in the woods, the feeling of eyes on me. I'm sure – positive, even – that I wasn't the one to pick those flowers, to bring them into our house where our children sleep. Sitting up, I wipe my hands over my face, and turn to Rav's side of the bed. *Deceit, unfaithfulness, errant lovers.* I want to read the messages again, the thread in which Rav mentions passports and getting away. But the cord of the phone charger lies curled sadly on the top of Rav's bedside table. He has taken his phone into the spare room with him.

I hear the shrill beep of the alarm coming from the spare room – from Rav's phone – a short while later. I haven't slept, I haven't even tried, but when Rav stumbles in, creases on one side of his face from the pillow, I fake stretching, yawning, rubbing my eyes as if well rested. Rav eyes me warily.

'Did you sleep in the end?' he asks, his voice hoarse. He coughs and reaches for the glass of stale water on the table.

'Yes, like a baby.' I give a small laugh. The baby had only woken once for a feed, but he stirs now as if sensing I am awake. 'Did you?'

'Hmmm.' Rav looks washed out, his skin sallow. 'A little. Can I use the bathroom first? I have an early meeting.'

I glance at the clock – it is barely six thirty. Early even for him. I hear the shower run, and the baby starts to grizzle so I lift him gently from the cot and pull up my nightshirt. I am still feeding when Rav comes back in.

'I'm off. I won't be late back this evening.' He leans over and kisses the baby's head but doesn't kiss me. He smells of tangerine shower gel and a fresh citrusy aftershave. There is nothing odd that I can tell in his tone, it's as if it's business as usual. The only way I know he isn't his usual self is his failure to mention our evening out last night – he always thanks me the day after, whenever we have an evening meal or drinks out, and he has done ever since our first date, on a hot, sandy beach in Goa. Instead, he says, 'Don't forget you have a doctor's appointment at eleven thirty.'

'I won't.' I keep my eyes on the baby's face as I feel Rav pause in the doorway.

'See you later then.' And a few seconds after, the front door slams.

I hurry Mina to preschool as she grumbles and whines alongside me. On the way home, I rush past The Daisy Chain, the buckets already outside. I would have stopped usually, but I keep my eyes down, hoping that Naomi doesn't come out and see me. Once inside, I lay the baby down to sleep and step out into the garden, to where the flowers of the oleander tree almost glow in the bright sunshine. Ragged stems show where the flowers have been snipped, and I feel a hot gush of tears sting my eyes as I look over the bush. It wasn't me. I'm sure it wasn't me. There is a dull throbbing at the back of my head, an ache that thuds with each beat of my pulse. I step away, my chest tight, as my eyes rake over the disturbed earth where I buried the bones. I can still feel them, beneath the soil, can still feel a thick malevolence pulling me in and I step back, towards the pond, my arms wrapped tightly across my body. Turning my back, I look out across the pond. It lies at the very edge of the woods, half of the water covered by shade from the trees, the other half sunlit but still murky, reeds growing from the clay edges, the mud drying and cracking around it from the long spell of warm weather. Rav should have filled it in, months ago. I asked him to when we moved in, afraid the children would be drawn to it, but this morning it offers a sense of peace. I have a strong urge to feel the cold water and the cool mud beneath it on my skin and I glance towards the house. The baby monitor is silent, the house quiet. I slide my shoes off and sit on the grass, inching forward until my toes sink under the water. Closing my eyes, I lean back on my elbows, letting the water lap around my calves and let out a long breath. *What am I going to do?* The message on Rav's phone from Naomi burns brightly behind my eyelids and sticks in my throat. *They both think I'm mad. They think the children aren't safe. They want to take the children away.* I feel it again then, the breath on the back of my neck and sit bolt upright, catching my foot on something hard under the water.

'Shit.' I breathe, raising a shaking hand to my mouth. I've never felt her outside before, only in the house. *She's everywhere.* I hear the words in my head as clearly as if they were spoken directly into my ear. I scrabble to my feet, still in the water, my toes sinking into the mud just as I imagined they would, when I feel it again under the water. Something smooth and hard. Reaching down, my fingers disappearing into the silty water disturbed by my own movements, I fumble around until I find it, my hand closing over the cold surface and I slowly draw it up. *A silver baby's rattle.* The handle is an ornate twist of silver, the top a smooth oval. I rub at the metal, wiping away the mud to reveal an intricate pattern of flowers and swirls, before giving it a small shake. There is the thin rattle of a bell, as though water and mud have found their way inside to dull it. Holding it tightly in my fist, I have an overwhelming sense of grief, a sadness so strong that I sit back down on the grass to steady myself. A wave of rage follows this, an anger so fiery that I have to close my eyes against the red mist that descends. *It's hers*, I think, the image of a small girl rising in my mind, dressed in white, calling for her mother. This belongs to Agnes's child. I don't know how I know, but I know that it does. Clutching it tightly I get slowly to my feet, my head thumping and nausea swirling in my belly. *You have to stop them.* The voice in my ear comes again, clear and knowing.

I clean the rattle, running my fingers over the intricate pattern, until the crushing sadness and following rage that descends every time I touch it becomes too much and I wrap it in a tea towel and hide it in the pantry. Then I go to the laptop and click on the icon for Rav's screen. A lock screen comes up with a password box and I falter for a moment. Would he have changed it? It was always AllieVero2 – my first and middle names, Vero for Véronique – and 2 for the fact that there was just the two of us when he set it up. I type in the words and wait anxiously, suddenly convinced that he will have changed it to try and keep me out. After a few seconds, the screen changes and I am in. The screen fills with a picture of the two of us, taken on the beach at Colva on our last day there together. Before we were married, before the children. His arm is slung over my shoulder and I am looking up at him, laughing. Rav is laughing too, his eyes crinkled, his hair swept back by the sea breeze. I think of the way we were before we moved here, before all of this. Before he was caught up in cases he is desperate to win, too busy to spend time with his family, before I felt constantly watched, before Agnes. I resist the urge to lay my head in my arms and cry. Instead, I look to where the baby lies in the Moses basket, his breaths deep and regular as he sleeps. *Passports are sorted.* Rav's message to Naomi is illuminated in my mind. They are planning to take my children, I think, certainty making my senses feel sharp and alert. They are going to take them away from me. I pull up Safari and open up Rav's search history. I hit the jackpot straight away, he hasn't even tried to hide his tracks. *Why would he?* I think. He doesn't know that I have any idea what he is planning. The website for the airline is the first one that comes up, and thanks to cookies on the laptop, I can see exactly what he has been searching for. Flights to Goa, to Dabolim Airport, for two adults and two children, leaving on 18th June. He hasn't entered a return date, only one-way details. The breath is knocked out of me, and I feel winded. How could he – the only man I have ever loved – do this to me? Take our children from me. I wonder whose idea this was – Rav's or Naomi's? Maybe this is what Naomi wanted all long. *Rav is a good man.* Maybe this is why she has planted the idea in his head that I am going crazy. I picture the way she is with the children, the way she always goes to Mina when she falls, jumping up before I can even realize something is wrong. I imagine Naomi being the one taking the baby to his first day at school, talking to Mina about boys, sitting beside Rav in a fancy hat as Mina walks down the aisle. My fingers are cold, so cold they feel numb and I rub them together to get some life back into them as I stand and start to pace the sitting-room floor. Does Avó know about this? Was she trying to warn me the other day, when she said that I looked as if something was wrong, that I looked unhappy? A *scratch* comes from the chimney, making me jump. Dialling with shaky fingers, I call my mother's number, even though I know she won't pick up.

'Mum, it's me. I need you. I … I need to talk to you. Please.' I hang up and scrub my hands over my face. I can't let this happen. I can't let them take Mina and Leo.

Maybe I'm wrong. Maybe it's all wrong and I jumped to conclusions. These are the things I am running over and over in my head, mumbling them to myself as I hurry towards preschool to collect Mina. I am late again, but if I hurry, I think I can make it.

'Allie? Al, wait!' A voice calls as I enter the High Street in the village, and I turn to see Tara headed towards me. 'Where are you off to in such a rush?'

'To collect Mina,' I say in confusion. 'Aren't you late for James? We'd better hurry.'

'We still have fifteen minutes,' Tara laughs. 'I've left Karl at home with Rufus – he's been really unwell, a gastro thing, we had to take him in to the William Harvey last night.' She looks tired as I look more closely at her. There are dark circles under her eyes and her mouth looks drawn. 'I just wanted to get out for a few minutes, you know.' I realize now for the first time, she has no pram with her.

'I'm sorry. I hope he feels better soon.' Something chimes in the back of my mind when she mentions a gastro thing, but I can't put the pieces together. All I can see is the screen on the laptop: two adults, two children, Dabolim Airport.

'Oh, he's on the mend,' Tara says, flicking her keys in her hand. My eyes are drawn to the keychain that dangles there. 'He'll be right as rain in a day or two.' The keychain is a silver pentacle, identical to the one Naomi has on her keys. As if summoned, Naomi steps out of the doors of The Daisy Chain, her purse in one hand as she walks towards the supermarket next door.

'You know her, don't you?' I nod in Naomi's general direction and Tara turns to see. I watch her to see her reaction, but she gives nothing away, no sign of guilt.

'Naomi? Yeah, I know her a little. Not terribly well though.' *Well enough to invite her to your house*, I think. 'Isn't she a friend of yours? I thought you two were quite close. Good friends.'

'We are,' I say. *Were.*

'I thought so.' Tara starts walking towards the preschool as Naomi disappears inside the shop. 'I knew I knew her from somewhere, and then I saw her and Rav having a drink in the pub not long after the baby was born. Wetting his head, no doubt,' she laughs.

'Really? Which pub?' There is a roaring in my ears and I suddenly feel very hot.

'The village pub. The Black Horse. Must have been, oh … last week sometime?' She looks at my face. 'Oh shit, have I put my foot in it?'

'No, not at all.' I rearrange my features, leaning down and fussing with the baby before pasting a smile on and straightening up. 'I sent Rav out for a bit, told Naomi to meet him so he wasn't a billy no mates. Just celebrating this little one, that's all.'

'Oh, phew.' Tara pretends to swipe sweat from her brow.

'You should have seen your face – I thought I'd put my foot right in it!'

Tara chatters on about everything and nothing as we walk the last few metres to the preschool, but I don't hear a thing she says. All I can see is Rav telling me he was working late, that the case was a nightmare. And now I know he was with Naomi, just like he was the night Mina was ill. I wonder if that was when they first decided that something wasn't *quite right*. I wonder if that's when they decided they were going to take the children.

Chapter Twenty-Nine

Rav is home early, just as he said he would be, but I busy myself with the children and at dinner the air between us feels crackly and tense. I don't trust myself to speak, so I don't, not directly anyway – I find myself doing that awful thing that I swore I never would – using Mina to talk to Rav. Rav opens his mouth as if to say something a few times, and I can feel his eyes on me as I rinse the dishes before scooping up the baby and taking him up for a bath. Once Mina and the baby are in bed, I head outside to the garden while he is still reading to Mina, stepping outside into the cool May evening and finding myself breathing more easily as soon as my feet touch the lawn. Fussing with the border, I prune back the dead leaves and stems, even though it is the wrong time of year to do it, and march backwards and forwards with the watering can in an attempt to revive the wilted plants. I don't look at the pond, where the columbine grows, and I avert my gaze from the oleander tree as I splash loosely around it with the water. As the soil beneath the tree turns dark and damp, I think of the bones and feathers buried beneath it, the idea of them a solid and heavy weight, the malevolence I felt from them only slightly dulled by the dirt. *I should have burnt them*, I think, although the idea of breathing in the smoke they would give off makes my stomach roll.

'Here, I brought you some tea.' Rav appears beside me, a mug in each hand. He has changed out of the suit he wore to work this morning, but he somehow looks older. The lines around his eyes look deeper, and tiredness radiates from every pore. It must be exhausting plotting against your wife. I take the cup, peering into it suspiciously. 'It's chamomile,' he says. 'Mum gave it to me for you, she said it might help you to sleep.'

I take the tiniest sip, floral steam swirling around my head. It tastes slightly bitter and I run my tongue over my lips in an attempt to dispel the taste.

'How did your appointment go at the doctor's?' Rav watches me as he sips from his own cup. His thick, dark brows knit together in something I assume he thinks is concern, and I imagine dark horns sprouting from his forehead, his tongue split like a snake's. I blink, and they are gone.

'Fine,' I lie. I had forgotten all about the appointment in the event of what I had discovered on the laptop, although deep down, I know I had no intention of going anyway. 'He said it's just normal postpartum hormones. That everything will settle down soon enough and not to worry. Shane O'Neill, known to everyone as Blackie.' The words trip easily off my tongue as if practised.

'Really?' Rav looks sceptical. 'I don't remember you being ... like this when you had Mina.'

'Well, it's easier with one child, isn't it?' I say brightly. 'Less to juggle. I told you I was fine, Rav, and now the doctor has said it too, so maybe you'll believe me.'

He moves towards me, and my pulse flutters, although not in the way it used to when he moved closer to me. Then, it was the very idea of him that set my heart racing, now it is fear, the fear of what he is planning that makes my heart thud and my breath come short in my throat.

'Well, if the doctor says you're OK …' Rav pulls me to him with his free hand. I lean against him, slightly stiffly, as he strokes my hair. 'I guess you're OK. Finish your tea.'

I feel drowsy, the motion of his hand in my hair running tingles across my scalp. My eyes are heavy, and I stifle a yawn. 'So Avó brought me tea,' I say, my tongue feeling clumsy in my mouth. 'Avó never brings me things, she must be worried.'

'We all are.' Rav's voice is quiet, his breath tickling my ear. 'Come on, time for bed.' I follow him on leaden feet, a dull ache in my twisted ankle. In the bedroom, I can barely lift my arms to pull off my T-shirt I am so exhausted, my limbs feeling languid and heavy, and it comes as a relief when my head finally hits the pillow, the cotton cool on my cheek. I don't think about the vision, or Rav and Naomi, letting sleep pull me under.

Mummy! Mina's voice is shrill, pitchy with fright and my eyes snap open. *Mummy!* I hear it again, and I am fully awake now, my feet already on the chilly floorboards, the duvet thrown to one side.

'Mina, I'm coming.' I can hear her crying, the sound

growing fainter as if she is moving away from me. I pull on a jumper that hangs over a chair in the bedroom, not bothering with shoes as I hurry out onto the landing.

Mummy! Her voice floats up to me again, laced with panic, and I stumble towards the top of the stairs, a glimpse of white appearing in the landing window. I pause, my pulse crashing in my ears, my breath steaming in the icy chill of the hall. It is cold out here, abnormally so, and I shiver, my muscles tensing in reaction to the change in temperature, but I don't move, frozen for what feels like hours but is probably barely seconds. Out in the garden, the shadowy branches of the trees at the edge of the woods reach out, long, bony fingers cutting into the glow cast by the moon overhead. A small figure, dark haired and wrapped in white fabric runs towards the trees, dangerously close to the edge of the pond, before disappearing behind the tall reeds that decorate the edge of the water.

'Mina, no!' My hand slaps against the icy glass of the windowpane, my eyes straining to see her, to see the white fabric of her nightdress as she runs, but there is nothing, just the branches swaying gently in the wind. Ignoring the dull ache in my still slightly swollen ankle, I hurry down the stairs in the dark, fumbling with the keys to the back door, Miranda's words running on a loop in my brain. *Legend says, Agnes still haunts her old home to this day.* Finally, I manage to slot the key into the lock and, yanking the door open so hard it bounces back on its hinges, I run out into the garden. *I am not Agnes. I will not lose my child.*

'Mina!' I call out, desperation causing my voice to come

out ragged and sharp. 'Mina? Where are you?' Turning in a circle I scan the garden, barely aware of the dampness beneath my bare feet, the air that grazes my cheeks so much warmer out here than it is inside the house. 'Mina?' Quieter now, I start to follow the path I saw her run along, around the pond and towards the woods. Did she see someone in there? A flash of white? Perhaps she thought it was me. She isn't calling for me anymore and my entire body trembles as I creep towards the darkened edges of the trees, my heart in my mouth.

'Mina … it's Mummy. Come out, come to me. I'm right here.' My feet don't want to go into the woods, but I force myself on. I have to find her. I have to save her.

Mummy. Where are you? Mina's voice is behind me now, and I whirl on the spot, dizziness making me squeeze my eyes shut. In that brief second there is a small splash from the pond, followed by the clear jangle of a bell and my eyes fly open to see ripples bouncing across the surface of the water. There is no sign of Mina.

'Oh God, no, not the water.' I am running before I have even finished processing the thought, my feet flying, my hair whipping across my face. At the edge of the pond I keep going, sinking into the mud beneath the surface. The shock of the water as it hits my thighs takes my breath away, and I strip off my jumper before diving under the water, groping blindly in the dark for any sign of her. My lungs bursting, I surface, gasping and shivering.

'Mina!' I shout, looking around wildly. There is still no sign of her. 'Please,' I whimper, before gulping in a huge breath and ducking back into the dark, weed-ridden water. I dive down and resurface again and again, my legs getting weaker and my voice hoarser with every try. My toes sink into the thick, claggy mud, weeds wrapping themselves around my legs as I reach out, swiping and groping, desperate for my fingers to snag on anything other than reeds. The pond isn't anywhere near as deep as a lake, but it's still over a metre and a half to the bottom, plenty deep enough to take Mina. I feel my nightshirt billowing around me, my lungs aching and stars starting to burst behind my eyelids. If I can't find her, I think, what is the point of coming back up for air? I hear the bell of the rattle again, not understanding how. Didn't I leave it in the pantry? How can it be under the water with me? *I'm going to lose her. Agnes has taken her for her own, just like the others.* I close my eyes, arms still outstretched and let myself sink further towards the bottom. *Mina, I'm sorry.*

A hand latches itself around my wrist and yanks me unceremoniously back to the surface. As my face breaks through the water, I gulp and then start to cough, dank, dark pond water scorching my throat as I cough it from my lungs.

'Allie, Jesus Christ, what the hell are you doing?' Rav has pulled me from the water and now sits behind me, his legs either side of my body as both arms snake around my waist, clutching me tightly.

'Let go. Let me go!' I wriggle, fighting back against him, but he holds me tighter. Panic overwhelms me and I claw and scratch, anything to get him to let me go, let me back into the water to find Mina. 'She's in there!' I shriek finally, unable to fight him off. 'Mina is in there! Agnes has her! In the water … please, Rav, let me go, I have to get to her, it'll be too late …' Sobs wrack my body, but still Rav doesn't let me go.

'Shhh, Allie, please, you have to calm down.' He doesn't relinquish his hold, drawing me even tighter to him if that's possible. 'She's not in there. Listen to me – Mina isn't in the water.'

'What?' I go still, my face still anxiously searching the body of water in front of us.

'Mina isn't in the water, Al,' Rav says quietly. 'She's asleep in her bed.'

'Did you …' My teeth begin to chatter violently.

'Did I check? Yes, of course. I just checked on her not five minutes ago – I heard you calling for her. She's tucked up in bed, fast asleep.' He rests his head against mine, and I soak up the warmth of his body behind me. I am cold, so cold. My arms and legs are aching as my muscles go into a shivering spasm. 'I need to get you inside, Allie. If I let you go, will you follow me?'

I nod, tears starting to run down my cheeks, scalding hot after the icy water of the pond. Rav picks up the jumper I cast off earlier and tugs it gently over my head, and then I lean on him as we walk slowly back to the house. Once inside, Rav nudges the thermostat up in the kitchen and sets the kettle on to boil before he turns to face me. I sit at my spot at the kitchen table, still shivering, confused and exhausted.

'Allie, what on earth were you doing? Were you … I mean, did you mean to …' Rav sighs, his words thick in his throat.

'I thought she was in the water,' I say, forcing myself to blink. 'I heard her calling for me, and I looked out the window and she was outside. In her nightie. She ran towards the trees and then there was a splash …' I break off, wracked by shivering. Rav fills a hot water bottle and lays it gently in my lap before pouring more water for tea. 'I thought she was in the water, Rav. I was trying to save her.'

'It was a dream, Allie. A nightmare. You were sleep-walking.' Rav pauses. 'I think you need to go back to the doctor, Allie. This isn't normal, even after having a baby. Something isn't right. Your dreams, and now sleepwalking. I don't think that's normal.'

'It wasn't a dream,' I say flatly. 'I saw her out there. And the other dream … it wasn't a dream either, it was something else, something more.' *A memory. A memory of something awful that happened in this house.* Rav's expression changes and he turns his back to me, using the tea as a pretence to hide his face. When he turns back, his face is neutral.

'Here, drink this.' He hands me the cup, but I don't drink from it. 'It was a dream, Allie,' he says firmly.

Neither of us sleep much the rest of the night. I check on Mina myself as Rav follows me up the stairs towards bed, needing to see her with my own eyes before I can settle. As I step past the mirror that hangs in the hallway, I see her, a dark shape behind Rav, her face pale, half covered with her hair. *Agnes.* I shiver again and deliberately turn my back, my heart hammering hard in my chest as I walk into the bedroom and slide beneath the covers next to Rav, both of us careful not to move too close to each other for the rest of the night.

The door slams somewhere below, and I freeze, my entire body tensing. I wait for a moment before the panic kicks in fully, my breath rasping in my ears, my heart pounding as the blood courses through my veins. Quickly, quickly. I have to finish this, before it is too late. They are coming for the children, for me. My steps are silent across the floorboards, as I hurry across the room towards the bed, towards the humped mound beneath the duvet. Her shoulders rise and fall with every breath and I stand for a moment, mesmerized, knowing that that rise and fall will soon stop, that the body will become still and the light will go out for good. And with no light, there is no threat, no fear, no pain. There is silence now, no sound of footsteps, no more slamming of doors. I imagined it, I think, blinking slowly, feeling as if I am underwater, fighting against a tide that no one else knows is there. The smell in the air is thicker now, heavier, and my temples throb, a wave of nausea rising in my stomach. I am so tired. My eyelids are heavy, my limbs like lead. I just want to sleep, the image of my bed in my mother's house rising to the front of my mind, the thick blankets, the soft, downy pillow, the way it feels to sink into that bed. But I can't sleep. Not yet. There is still too much to be done. Once I am finished, when this is finally over then I can sleep, for the first time in so long. As my hands reach for the pillow, cast aside at the end of the bed, it's as if my arms are moving independently of my body. I am not really there, my body just a shell. I pick up the pillow, hold it to my chest, digging my fingers into the soft feathers, feeling the sharp press of a stray quill against my palm. Will they fight? I wonder, as I draw the pillow to my own face, gently pressing it against my nose. I can still breathe, for now. Will they scratch and bite? Will they struggle and try to push me away? Or will it be peaceful, a tiny movement beneath my hands before the breath runs out and there is only stillness? Clouds thicken and gather across the moon and the room is pitched into darkness once more. I let out a breath, my throat sore, my chest restricted. It's better in the dark – I can't see their faces in the dark. I lean down over her dark head, sleeping soundly, the pillow gripped tightly in my hands and I begin to lower it, my arms rigid to stop the trembling. They shouldn't have cast me out. It's time for all of this to be over.

Chapter Thirty

Rav is gone when I open my eyes. My entire body aches and for a moment I wonder why before remembering the events of just a few hours before. A thick, purple bruise has formed around my wrist where Rav yanked me from the water, a sore, twisted bracelet made of finger marks. I push myself up the bed, the dent of Rav's head still on the pillow next to me, and from the bathroom I can hear water running. The remnants of the dream still swirl in my mind, so real I can almost feel the fabric of the pillow in my hands. I feel sick and my head throbs, just as it did in the dream, and I swallow down the bile that seems to creep up my throat. Rav has left his phone on the bedside table. With a stealthy glance towards the still sleeping baby, as if worried he'll see me, I reach over and pick it up. I flick quickly to his WhatsApp messages. Sure enough, there is another exchange between him and Naomi.

Can we meet?

This from Rav, sent at four o'clock this morning, just a couple of hours after he had pulled me from the pond.

Something has happened with Allie. It's really serious this time.

Of course.

Naomi had replied at a little after five thirty this morning. She would have been on her way back from the flower market, I think.

Meet me at The Blue and White at 7.30 a.m.?

I'll be there.

The Blue and White is a café around a twenty-minute drive from here – in the opposite direction to Rav's office. Naomi and I used to make a point of meeting there at least once a week after Mina was born, leaving Rav to look after her while we caught up with each other. Naomi used to moan every week about the fact that I left Mina behind, but I needed that hour to just be Allie, not Mina's mum or Rav's wife. Now I wonder if she was planning this even then. Rav must be keen to cement his plans if he's prepared to meet her there, and at that time, meaning he will be late for work. I glance at the time on the phone screen. It's a little after six thirty. The shower turns off and I hurriedly lay the phone back on the bedside table, closing my eyes as if still sleeping.

'Oh.' I blink groggily as Rav enters the room, a towel around his waist. His face looks grey with exhaustion, despite the hot shower. 'You're up early. Meeting?'

'Yeah.' He reaches for a polo shirt, then changes his mind and swipes a white Ralph Lauren shirt off a hanger. *Nearly, Rav,* I think, *you nearly slipped up.* 'How are you feeling this morning?' He buttons the shirt, then perches on the side of the bed, taking my hand in his. I have to fight the urge to recoil.

'Oh, better,' I say. 'I'm sorry I frightened you, I scared myself if I'm honest. I've never sleepwalked before.' And I haven't. I remember the bitter taste of the tea; the way exhaustion had overwhelmed me. 'I think maybe I'll steer clear of the tea before bedtime in future.'

'Might be an idea.' Rav tries on a smile, but it doesn't stick, his brows coming together in its place. 'Will you be OK today? I was thinking I would go to the meeting this morning, and then come back here. Work from home. We could go for lunch after you pick Mina up. We need to talk about what happened last night, don't you think?'

'I'll be fine, Rav. You're busy, you won't get anything done here and I know that case is important to you. Last night was a one-off. It won't happen again.'

'What about Naomi? Or Mum? She could come over and spend some time with you.' A pulse flickers under his eye, a persistent twitch. He doesn't want me to be alone with the children, I think. Maybe he's worried I'll take them before he does. I smother the urge to laugh at the idea that Rav has the same fears I do. I need things to be normal. I need Rav to believe me when I say I am OK.

'Honestly, Rav, you don't have anything to worry about. I sleepwalked – that's all. If you call Avó she'll only make you drive her over.' I slide my hand out from under his, push back the duvet. 'It was just a stupid nightmare, Rav. You go. You'll be late if you don't get a move on.' Rav frowns and gets to his feet. I shouldn't have said that about being late.

'If you're sure?'

'Positive. See you tonight.'

The mirror. I stand in front of it now, waiting for that dark, sinister shape to appear in the reflection behind me. There is nothing. The air remains still, there is no breath on the back of my neck, no sign of Agnes on the stairs. The house is quiet, the baby fed and back to sleep, Mina still slumbering on in her bedroom, the duvet tugged right up to her dark curls. The mirror is where all this started – finding it in the attic and then discovering the feathers beneath the floorboards. Once the mirror was hung that's when Agnes made her presence really known. I think of Lillian Sparks, of her baby and how they took her away, called her mad. Agnes is part of it all, I am sure, just like Elsie Sparks was sure. I don't have the first idea of how to make a charm to protect the house, but I can get rid of the mirror. Taking a deep breath, I grip the frame on either side of the glass and lift it from where it hangs. It's heavy, and I remember how Rav and I struggled to get it down the stairs, me laughing as he called out instructions. Was that the last time Rav and I laughed together? Somehow, I manage to manoeuvre the mirror out to the kitchen and through the back door, where I lean it against the house. It occurs to me that maybe I should smash it – would that stop her, or is it too late? I am still so cold, despite the warm sunshine that is beginning to peep through the trees, and I rub my hands over my arms. Maybe removing it from the house will be enough. Please, let removing it be enough.

An hour later, I have every intention of taking Mina to preschool, despite my sluggish tiredness, but everything changes on our walk to school. As we turn into the High Street, I see Tara, with the pushchair this time, talking to Evie outside The Daisy Chain. At first glance I don't think too much of it, until Evie goes inside, and Naomi comes out. I can't hear their conversation, but the way Tara kisses Naomi warmly on the cheek tells me that both of them have lied to me about how well they know each other. I freeze, pulling Mina close to me.

'I need to tie my laces,' I lie. 'Hold on to the pram.' As Mina wraps her tiny fingers around the handle of the pram, I crouch down and fiddle with my shoes, straining to hear what they are saying. I can't make out the words, but I can read their body language easily enough. Naomi peers into the pram, cooing over Rufus who is clearly much better. Tara says something and they both laugh, in that comfortable way that confirms to me they aren't simply acquaintances, they are more than that. Tara speaks again, and Naomi's face grows serious. She looks towards the end of the road, towards our house, and she shrugs, shaking her head. She rubs the tops of her arms with both hands as if cold, and as Tara reaches out a hand as if to comfort her, I get the unmistakable feeling that they are talking about me.

'Mummy, come on,' Mina grumbles.

'Just a sec.' I keep crouching, watching, as Tara pulls Naomi in for a hug. They hold each other for a few seconds, and I feel a pang. Naomi and I would hug like that before, but I haven't let her for weeks and I miss the feel of her arms around me, the scent of her perfume, before I remember that only a couple of hours ago, she was meeting my husband behind my back. Tara and Naomi say goodbye now, Naomi stepping back inside the dark, cool air of The Daisy Chain, while Tara turns towards the village, walking towards the preschool.

'Shall we stay home today?' I say to Mina, standing up. My lower back throbs where I have been crouching, my thighs burning. Everything feels too bright, too loud. 'We can play in the garden, have a water fight.'

'Yay!' Mina cheers and starts running along the pavement in the direction of the house. I heave a sigh of relief to myself that she is so easily led and follow her, as fast as I can on my sore ankle. When I turn to look back, the street is empty.

I set Mina up in the garden with a plastic paddling pool and a tiny watering can. The sight of her sitting in just a couple of inches of water is enough to make my blood run cold after the previous evening, and I have to keep telling myself that it wasn't real, that Mina was never in the pond. Even so, I drag the pool close to the edge of the border where I weed between the plants, close enough so that she is in my eyeline the entire time, and far away from the mirror that leans against the wall of the house. She sings as she plays, water sparkling in her hair, as I prune and weed, pausing only momentarily at the oleander tree, at the snipped ends of the stems where flowers have been cut. I shake away the memory of the scent of them on my skin, instead focusing on Tara. Clearly Tara and Naomi are more friendly than either of them cares to admit, and when I think of them standing together in the street earlier, I feel a crawling sensation like ants on my skin. Tara hasn't asked me for the blue blanket back – it is still tucked away in the drawer of the spare bedroom. Why do I see that blanket in my dream? Is Tara the one who has put the idea in Naomi's head that I am going mad? Everything feels as though it is connected but I can't figure out how. I sit back on my haunches, my eyes going to the mirror at the other end of the garden, expecting to see Agnes's face reflected back at me.

'There you are, I was knocking and knocking, and you didn't answer. I knew you must be home.' My eyes fly open as Avó waddles into the garden, looking immaculate in a gold and red sari.

'Avó!' Mina jumps from the paddling pool and barrels into her, wrapping her arms around Avó's knees and soaking the fabric of her sari.

'Avó.' I get creakily to my feet, dusting my hands over my shorts to hide my displeasure at Rav calling her behind my back. 'I didn't know you were coming. And how did you get here? Is Rav here?' Avó doesn't drive, can't walk far and flat out refuses to take the bus, although she will occasionally deign to take a taxi. When Rav is home – and sometimes, even when he is not – he is summoned to drive Avó to the various places she wants to go to, while she phones through her shopping requirements to me to drop off on my way back from the supermarket.

'I brought her over.' Naomi appears behind Avó, looking fresh and perfect in a short linen dress, her hair tied back in a swishy ponytail, her lips painted a nude pink.

'Yes, Naomi came to get me.' Avó sighs, waddling over to the garden chairs and stiffly lowering herself into the nearest one. 'Be a darling, get me some water, won't you?'

I move towards the open door into the kitchen, before I realize it isn't me she's talking to but Naomi. Naomi darts inside and Avó and I are alone.

'Did Rav ask you to come over?' I ask as she taps the seat of the chair next to her. Despite not wanting to sit, Avó is a woman who commands respect, so I sit.

'I can come and see my own daughter-in-law, can't I?' She tuts. 'You are always so touchy, Allie. Always asking why do you do this, why do you do that. I have come to make sure you are OK.'

'I'm fine,' I say, but tears sting my eyes. 'You have been speaking to Rav. It was just a nightmare, there's nothing to worry about.'

'Of course I have. He's my son. When you are old, like me, you will speak to Mina and Leo often as well.'

I think of my mother, never one for telephone conversations, unless she was calling to check on me to see where I was. As a teenager we never needed long telephone conversations, as she would never let me leave her for long enough to require it. Now, I wish she was here every day.

I wish she didn't hate Rav, I wish she could come for dinner, and ask for lifts, and spoil the children the way Avó does.

'Yes, you're right.' The prickliness in me subsides and I attempt to change the subject. 'Rav gave me the tea. Thank you for sending it over, it was very thoughtful of you.' I don't mention the sleepwalking. If Rav hasn't told her everything, there's no need for me to mention it.

'Oh, that wasn't really from me.' Avó flaps a hand. 'I got it from Naomi – she comes to visit me sometimes. I told her you weren't sleeping so well and so she brought the tea the next time she came. She said I would probably see you before her, that she was working so hard in the shop without you there.'

'Oh. Well, thank you anyway.' My mind is whirring away nineteen to the dozen. *Naomi gave her the tea. Gave ME the tea. Does Rav know it came from Naomi?* I think of the exhaustion, the way it came on so quickly. *Was it just tea? Or was there something else in it?* The last time she made me tea, when I twisted my ankle, I had fallen asleep after drinking it. I swallow, suddenly feeling very hot.

'Ravi just wants to do the best by you,' Avó says, as I try to focus on what she is saying. 'And for the children. The children are so important to him, but you must know this. He has everyone's best interests at heart and what he is planning …'

I switch on, her words snagging. 'What he is planning?' I hardly dare breathe as I wait for Avó to elaborate. I can't believe he has told his mother what he plans to do – would he tell her? Perhaps she thinks I know; she doesn't realize that I have been left in the dark.

'Ahhh, here we are.' Avó turns as Naomi appears with a jug of iced water and three glasses on a tray, a carton of juice for Mina on the side. She must have gone through every cupboard to find the jug; it was in a box in the pantry, still packed from when we moved in.

'Here we go, ladies.' She pours for each of us but as Avó gulps greedily, I leave my glass untouched.

'You're looking very smart for the shop, Naomi,' I say. 'Did you have an important meeting or something?'

She colours, her cheeks a glowing shade of pink. 'No, nothing like that. Just the flower market, and obviously it gets warm in the shop. This was the coolest outfit I had.'

'Avó was just about to tell me about Rav's plans,' I say, keeping my face neutral. I give nothing away, as Naomi's colour subsides, and she turns a watery pale. Avó is preoccupied, cooing over the doll Mina is showing her.

'Oh?' Naomi says. 'That sounds intriguing. I love what you've done with the border, although I'm not sure that keeping that oleander is such a good idea. What if Mina or Leo get hold of it? It's toxic, you know.'

'I know. I shouldn't be surprised that you know that too.'

'You should plant the hibiscus,' Avó butts in. 'I miss the hibiscus. My mother used to grow it all over our garden in Margoa. Why don't you plant that, Allie? Take that horrible white one out.'

'Yes, Margoa,' I say, without taking my eyes from Naomi's face. 'You must miss it Avó. I know I do. It would be lovely to take the children there for a long, extended holiday.' Naomi stills, her glass halfway to her mouth. She only pauses for a matter of seconds, if that, but I see it. 'Perhaps I should sort out a passport for Leo, if Rav could get the time off over the summer we could go back, stay a while, visit with the aunties and uncles.'

Avó opens her mouth to speak, but Naomi jumps up, spilling water all across the garden table. 'Oh shoot,' she says. 'Let me get a cloth and clean that up.'

Mina giggles as water runs off the edge of the table, sitting beneath it so that it drips over her hair. I close my eyes, the image of her running across the lawn to the pond as vivid as it was last night. 'Let me help you.' I get up and follow Naomi into the kitchen.

She is on her phone, texting madly as I walk into the cool air of the kitchen. 'Texting Rav?' I say casually.

'What?' Naomi looks up, her eyes wide. 'No. Why would I be texting Rav?' I have to hand it to her, she's an excellent liar. 'Allie, are you OK? You look like you've lost even more weight.'

'Thanks for the tea,' I say shortly. 'So kind of you to make sure Avó gave it to me. It had the desired effect. I'd better get that water cleaned up.' Something glints at her throat, and I lean in to get a closer look, reaching past her for a roll of kitchen towel. It's a pearl. A single pearl in a simple gold setting, hanging on a slim gold chain around her neck. 'Where did you get that?'

'What?' Her hands go to her throat, her fist closing around the pearl. 'It was a gift. My mother bought it for me, after my brother died. I've had it for years. Allie, I don't know what is going on—'

'I think you do,' I hiss. 'I think you do know. And I know, too. I know what you've been saying to Rav.' I eye the necklace closely, wishing the pearl would scald her skin the way the ones I found scalded mine. 'I won't let you get away with this. Either of you. I think it's best if you leave now, don't you?'

Naomi stands, her phone in her hands and her mouth open, as I breeze past her back out into the garden. As I swipe at the puddles on the glass table, I feel her behind me and almost flinch as her voice comes close to my ear.

'Avó, do you mind if we leave? I just had a text from Evie to say the shop is getting busy and she can't manage the orders alone. I really need to get back and help her.'

I don't look up, still dabbing at the water. The sun has gone in and there is a chilly wind now, the leaves of the trees rustling and swaying. Shivering, Avó gets to her feet, and Naomi holds out an arm for her to lean on.

'Thank you for coming over, Avó, I'll let Rav know you came.' I lean down and kiss her wrinkled, raisin-like cheek. 'Goodbye, Naomi.' Mina fusses at my legs and I lift her into my arms so she can wave goodbye to her grandmother. As they reach the garden gate, my mother appears on the other side of the road, checking for traffic before she starts to cross. She raises her hand to me as Naomi lifts the latch on the gate to let Avó through, Naomi throwing a brief smile in my mother's direction before she hurries Avó to the pavement.

I stand at the garden gate, watching as she helps Avó into the car, before getting in herself and driving smoothly away. Avó looks back and waves, but Naomi keeps her eyes on the road.

'Penny for it?' My mother walks up the path to stand beside me before turning back, raising one hand to shield her eyes as she joins me in watching Naomi drive away.

'It's a penny for *them*,' I say. She never could get her head around English idioms. 'I thought you'd left. I haven't seen you.'

'I've been busy, lots to do.' She looks older today, her shoulders slightly bowed and thin lines radiating from her mouth that I haven't noticed before. 'Was that Avó with Naomi? It's a shame I missed her; I would have liked to have seen her.'

'You would?' I frown. My mother never had time for Avó before.

She shrugs, a familiar gesture. 'It's been a long time. It would have been nice to catch up. Maybe next time.' She peers closely at me. 'What about you? How are things? You don't look so good.'

I smooth down my hair, press a hand to my cheek. I don't feel so good, either. I turn and lead her through the garden and into the house, waiting until she is seated at the table and Mina is preoccupied with the TV before I say, 'I think Rav is going to take the children away.'

Mum reaches for her cigarettes, runs one through her fingers as she eyes me closely. 'Why do you think this?'

'I found flight searches on his computer. A message thread on his phone to Naomi about me, and how he has sorted out passports. I think they're planning it together.' I blink back tears, still not wanting to cry in front of her, a hangover from my teenage years. Tears don't get you sympathy with my mother. 'Things have happened since you were here last …' I explain about the toxic flowers left in the bedroom, the tea, how Rav had found me in the pond. How everything keeps coming back to me, and how I feel there is a connection between what is happening now and the past.

She is quiet when I finish speaking, the only sound her nails tapping on the table. 'This is not good,' she says eventually. 'They think you are crazy, no?'

'I don't know. I overheard them talking … they mentioned postpartum psychosis. I think they think that I have it … or some sort of postpartum depression anyway, and that I am a danger to the children,' I say, a bloom of hurt bursting in my chest. 'I think that Tara mentioned it to Naomi, and Naomi has told Rav that she thinks there is something wrong with me.'

'What do you think?' she says quietly, giving in and lighting the cigarette. I open the back door pointedly but she still sits at the table. 'What do you think is going on?'

'I think all of this is connected to Agnes Gowdie. She was a witch, she took children, hurt them maybe. And I think she is still here.' My hands go to my arms and I rub at the skin there. I am so cold, all the time.

'Still here?'

'Yes. I think she is still here, and I think she is the one who is a danger to the children, not me.' I tell my mother about Lillian Sparks, of how she was accused of smothering her child. Of how they took her away and didn't believe her, even though Elsie tried to tell them. 'I found her child's rattle in the pond; I hear her crying for her mother at night.

I see Agnes in the mirror. I've removed it, but I don't know if that worked, I think she's still here. I'm going to ask Miranda about a charm to go back under the floorboards, but I need Rav to believe me. I can't let him take them away.' I swallow back that hard lump in my throat. 'I don't know what to do, Mum.'

'Do you want to bring these children up alone?'

I shake my head. I don't want my children to feel the way I did growing up, suffocated by a mother who couldn't bear to be left alone. Who couldn't bear to let go. I want things to be as they were, before – me, Rav and the children.

'You have to show him that you aren't crazy. You have to show him that it's not your fault, what has happened.'

Maybe she has a point. He won't believe that Naomi has manipulated him – and me – if I tell him that straight out, he'll just think I'm acting crazy again. Despite it all I love Rav, and if I can just show him that I am the Allie he knows, the Allie he met on the beach all those years ago, maybe I can fix this. I love my family. I don't want to end up like my mother. 'How do I do that? How do I show him that Naomi is wrong, that there's nothing wrong with me?'

'You need to show Rav that this was just a temporary thing, that you are all right now,' she says. 'You need to behave the way he would expect you to behave before. Sleep at night, don't stay awake worrying about things. You need to do something that will reassure Rav that you are back to the old Allie again.'

I think for a moment, my mind a terrifying blank. All I can see is myself thrusting the poker into the chimney, the bones and debris all over the floor. Then it comes to me. 'The mural,' I say. 'I was going to paint a mural on Mina's wall before the baby was born but I just ran out of time. It's the kind of thing I would have done, if I hadn't been so preoccupied with everything that has happened. If he sees me doing that, then maybe he'll think it's all OK. I haven't mentioned the sounds from the chimney or the witch's ladder for a while, even though I still hear it.' And it's been an effort not to involve him, the weight of it heavy on my shoulders.

'This is perfect. Paint the mural.' My mother gets to her feet. 'You will be fine, ma chérie. You will figure this out, you must just go one day at a time.' She lays a gentle kiss on my hair. 'I will see you soon.'

After she leaves, I think about Naomi and the glistening pearl sitting at the base of her throat. Is she the one who did this? Did she leave the pearls in the house knowing the story of Agnes Gowdie?

Chapter Thirty-One

I feed the baby and lay him in the cot, then give Mina a sand-
wich and some more juice before I head upstairs to search
out the paint that I bought months ago for the mural, my
mother's advice buzzing around in my head. *Act normal.
Don't mention Agnes. Don't give them any opportunity to say
that you aren't a fit mother.*

As I push open the door to the spare bedroom, I fancy
I can still smell the oleander flowers on the air and I find
my gaze drawn to the top of the chest of drawers, where the
vase sat. It is empty, of course, the only sign that the flowers
were ever there a slight ring on the varnish.

Grabbing the loft pole from the spare wardrobe, I hook
it into the hatch and twist, suddenly feeling apprehensive
as I recall the last time I was up in the attic. There is a faint
scratching sound as I pull the stiff door down, the hinges
squealing, and I pause, feeling my pulse speed up. There is
silence again and I brush my nerves away. It must have just
been the hinges. Clicking on the torch app on my phone,
I slowly climb the ladder and peer inside, relieved when I see
the tins of paint stacked neatly against the wall. I tug

them out, reaching in to find the rollers and trays that we also bought, when I notice the small stack of suitcases that Rav brought up here. Solid, sturdy fabric, the area around them disturbed. I move forward, casting the beam from my phone over the suitcases. There is something odd, something different about them and it takes me a moment to figure out what it is.

Scratch. Scratch. A scratching comes from the walls, the same as the noise that comes from the chimney. I blink, taking a moment to try and regulate my breathing, waiting for it to come again. Silence. And then all at once I know what it is that is different about the cases. There is no dust on them. Everything up here is covered with a few months' worth of dust, everything except the suitcases, and I am sure that they were just as dusty when Rav and I came up here to bring the mirror down. *He's been up here*, I think. *Rav has been up here and he has moved the suitcases. He's packing to take them, he must be.*

Holding my breath, I unzip the suitcase, but I know what I will find. Clothes. Rav's clothes, Mina's clothes. All summer items, tiny skirts and vests for Mina, thin linen shirts for Rav, ones that he bought at the market the last time we visited Goa. I rummage through the tiny dresses, the thin, soft linen, before plunging my hands into the inside pockets, not sure what it is exactly that I'm looking for. Something rustles inside the pocket and I slow down, letting my fingers grasp it and pull it out. It's a thin sheet of paper, folded in half, and when I open it, I immediately wish I hadn't. The paper shakes slightly in my hand as I read over the words handwritten in black ink on the page.

*Baroque pearl/gold inlay – 24ct,
£495 – to be collected. PAID*

It's a receipt, from a costly independent jeweller in Maidstone and the date on the paper is a week before the baby was born. *Pearl. Gold inlay.* I feel slightly sick, the words swimming on the page in front of me. This receipt must belong to Rav. I close my eyes and the image of the glistening pearl, set in gold on a thin chain around Naomi's neck fills my mind. My throat thickens and hot tears sting the back of my eyes as I remember her hand going to the chain, her long slender fingers enclosing the pearl in her fist, hiding it from sight. *My mother bought it for me,* Naomi had said. *I've had it for years.* But I don't remember ever seeing her wear it before, and I would have remembered that – I know I would. Naomi is lying – Rav bought it for her, he must have done, and then he hid the receipt where he thought I would never find it. He thought he and Naomi would have packed up the children and gone, and I would have been none the wiser of their plans. Maybe they have been having an affair the entire time. Maybe that's what all of this has been about. My eyes wander back to the open suitcase, to the now jumbled clothing, and I shove the receipt back into the pocket I found it in, scrubbing my fingers over my jeans as the air moves around me, as if someone has brushed past me.

Freezing, my hands still on the lid of the closed suitcase, my breath catches in my throat. I can feel someone, *her,* watching me, the hairs on the back of my neck tingling, as if a hand is being held close – but not quite touching – my skin. My eyes comb the attic, hoping to see a trapped bird, a stray cat – hell, I'd even take a rat over the threat of Agnes Gowdie – but there is nothing in the dim, shadowy light. I inch away, my feet silent on the boards as I move towards the trapdoor, my hands shaking as I fumble with the light on my phone, my eyes never leaving the suitcase.

I can't let this happen. I can't let this happen. The same thought revolves round and round in my mind as I descend the ladder, and I have to force myself to try and think rationally. It doesn't have to happen. Rav hasn't booked the flights yet, as far as I could tell when I searched his account on the laptop; he's only looked at flights. My mother is right. If I can show him that I am fine, that everything here is fine, I can stop him from taking them. I'll ask Miranda to help me make a new charm for the attic, I'll get rid of the mirror, I'll make sure that Agnes Gowdie is banished forever. *I'll die before I'll let him take them.* I think of myself walking purposefully into the pond, letting my feet sink into the mud until the water closes over my head. The image is as clear as if it is happening on screen in front of me, only it's not my face. It's the face of Agnes Gowdie. I blink the image away and let my eyes wander to the cans of paint stacked against the wall. *I'll start the mural, and he'll see then that I'm trying to make things nice for Mina, that I am a good mother.* I push the trapdoor closed and use the hook to lock it, then ferry the cans of paint into Mina's bedroom.

I had already sketched the artwork lightly onto Mina's wall in pencil before the baby was born, and now I pull her bed into the middle of the room and stand back to get a good look at it. It's an underwater scene, inspired by her favourite movie, *The Little Mermaid*. Fronds of seaweed rise from the skirting boards, as tiny fish swim in between them. At the end of the wall, a mermaid sits on a rock, her long hair drawn over one shoulder. A fishhook dangles from the ceiling, a worm baited on the end as a hungry fish eyes it, a shoal of smaller fish behind him. A shark's snout peeps out from behind a lobster pot, and I have managed to arrange the coral and sea plants so that when the sun streams in the window it will bring life to them. The air is cold in Mina's room and I shiver slightly, refusing to acknowledge that whatever usually chills the landing has moved, has followed me into Mina's room. Swallowing down the fear that bubbles beneath the surface, humming under my breath to break the heavy silence, I begin to paint.

'Allie? What in God's name are you doing?'

I stop muttering to myself, one paint brush clamped between my teeth as I dab frantically at the walls with another. I have painted in all the seaweed fronds in varying shades of green, the mermaid is brought to life with Ariel's trademark red hair and clam shell bra. I am fully immersed under the sea.

'Allie. Stop.' Rav moves forward, a crying Mina on his hip as he takes the paintbrush from between my teeth. 'Look at the state of you, you're covered in paint. How long have you been up here, doing … this?'

I glance towards the window. Earlier, the sun had been

breaking through the clouds, now it is barely above the horizon. The room is still cold, but it is a natural cold and my skin prickles with sweat and heat, my cheeks burning. My reflection in the glass is unkempt, my hair sticking to my sweaty forehead, paint daubed on my cheeks and splattered across my T-shirt. 'I … not long.' I become aware of a thin wailing, a ragged and exhausted cry. Rav glares at me for a moment before hurrying from the room, Mina still snuffling in his arms. I lay down the paintbrush, feeling disorientated and off kilter. Rav's voice filters through from our bedroom, where he is murmuring to the baby, who in turn responds with more angry cries. Quietly, I walk through to where Rav is leaning over the bed, changing the baby, as Mina sits next to them, her eyes red and her breathing hitching in her chest.

'Shall I do it?'

'No.' Rav's tone is short, his face white with fury, and I blink, sure that I am about to cry. 'I've nearly finished.' He stuffs the baby's legs into the Babygro and snaps the poppers closed. The baby continues to wail, and the sound is like nails on a chalkboard in my ear. 'Fucking hell, Allie. What were you thinking? I found Mina sobbing her heart out outside her bedroom door because she couldn't get in and the baby in his cot screaming his head off.'

'I'm sorry, Rav.' I reach out to Mina but she pulls away, leaning against Rav. 'I lost track … I forgot I moved the furniture in front of the door. I didn't think—'

Rav cuts across me. 'When was the baby last fed?'

For one terrifying moment I can't remember, and

I almost say 'last night'. 'Earlier, not too long ago, when Avó left.' I hold out my arms and Rav lays the baby in them, so I can feed him. He latches on immediately, not like before when he has fussed and rooted for ages, always after someone has given him a bottle. I sigh, relieved the screams have stopped. The baby's skin is hot and clammy, his eyes squeezed tightly shut as he drinks. A low *scratch* comes from the wall to the left of me and I turn my face away, looking at Rav who stands in the doorway with Mina.

'What time is it?' I ask, suddenly aware that the sun has dipped completely behind the trees.

'Just gone seven.'

'Oh gosh!' I look away, training my eyes on the baby's head. I feel exposed, as if my nerves are electrified. 'I didn't realize it was so late.' No wonder the baby was screaming, this is the longest he's ever gone between feeds. I can't believe I didn't hear the children crying. I feel sick at the idea of Mina calling for me and not getting a response.

'I take it you've fed Mina?'

I swallow, feeling the shame rise up my cheeks. 'I'm sorry, Rav, I got lost in the painting. You know how I lose all track of time when I get involved in something creative.' I couldn't tell you how many times he's had to come and draw me away from the shop.

'I know.' His voice softens slightly, and I think that maybe, just maybe my mother was right. By starting to paint the mural, Rav will believe me when I say I'm back to my old self. 'I'll go and make her something to eat, if you don't mind packing your painting things out of the way so she can go to bed.'

'Of course.' I breathe out a sigh of relief as he leaves.

I bath the baby and lay him in the Moses basket that I have left in the corner of Mina's room. I want our bedroom to be just ours for a while tonight, to spend some time alone with Rav. I have to talk to him, to clear the air. I push the thought of the suitcase in the attic out of my mind. He hasn't used it, not yet, and if I can make things right, he won't need to. When Rav comes back down from putting Mina to bed, he doesn't comment on the fact that the baby is sleeping in the Moses basket instead of the cot.

'Do you want some tea?' Rav asks. 'Or are you hungry? I can cook.'

I shake my head to both. I don't have any appetite and the very thought of the tea makes me feel nauseous.

'OK.' Rav comes and sits opposite me. 'Allie, we need to talk, don't we? You seem …'

'I feel better. Much. I'm sorry about today, about the painting. I lost track of time. You know I wouldn't have let Mina cry deliberately.' I meet his eyes, almost daring him to look away first. He does. 'I saw Avó and Naomi earlier.' I tuck my hands under the table and give in to the urge to pick at the skin around my nails. The thought of Naomi, standing here in my kitchen earlier today when just a few hours before she had been meeting Rav behind my back, makes me jittery and anxious.

'Oh?' Rav tries to look surprised, but he doesn't make

a very good job of it. 'It was good of Naomi to make the time to bring Avó. She must be really busy in the shop, it's wedding season, isn't it?'

'I never said Naomi brought Avó over.' Something stirs in my gut, putrid and poisonous. They have spoken since this afternoon, Rav and Naomi. They must have.

'I just assumed … Mum didn't call me to come and pick her up so I thought Naomi must have brought her over.' His face is guileless and if I hadn't seen the message thread, seen the suitcase in the attic, then I would have no idea that he was planning to take the children. 'What happened to the mirror? I noticed it wasn't in the hall when I came home.'

'I took it out,' I say. 'It's in the garden for you to take to the tip when you get a moment.'

'I thought you loved that mirror?' Rav frowns. 'Are you sure you don't want to try it in another room?'

I shake my head, my lips clamped together. I can't tell him why I don't want the mirror in the house. 'I fancied a change.'

'OK …' Rav gives me a long look, while I rearrange my face to look as pleasantly *normal* as possible. 'The mural looks really good by the way. Mina's going to love it. What made you start the painting today – I thought you would have been exhausted after last night?' As he finishes speaking his phone pings and he pulls it from his pocket, frowning down at the screen.

'It was my mother's idea,' I say quietly as he stares at whatever message he has received. *Is it from her?*

'What?' Rav looks up from his phone and I can't read the expression on his face.

'She always wanted to paint a mural in my room, and I wouldn't let her. It was her idea for me to paint one for Mina.'

Rav lays his phone on the table, and I think that for a moment his hands look a little shaky. He folds them in front of him as if he knows they are shaking too. 'When … When did your mum suggest that?'

'Does it matter?' I don't understand what the big deal is. I'm just trying to do something nice, something normal, although of course, I don't say that to him.

'I just wondered. You know it's been a long time since you were able to speak to your mum, so this idea seems to have kind of come out of the blue.'

'It's not been that long at all actually.'

'Allie, when did you speak to your mum last?'

He knows. He knows she's been visiting me. I should have known he would have smelled her cigarette smoke. 'Today. She told me today that I should paint a mural on Mina's wall.'

Rav's face changes colour, pale beneath his tanned skin and he looks for a moment as though he might be sick. I don't understand what the problem is – it's just a lick of paint on the walls. If he hates it that much, I'll paint over it. I'll do whatever he wants, as long as he doesn't take them. 'What did you say? Is that meant to be funny, Allie?'

'I said, it was my mother's idea for me to start painting the mural today. She suggested it.'

Rav stands, running his hand through his hair, never taking his eyes off me before he moves forward and crouches next to me. He covers my hand with his. 'Allie, why would you say that?'

'Because it's true. She told me, here, in the garden today that I should start working on the mural for Mina.'

'Allie …' Rav pauses, takes a deep breath. 'Allie, your mother couldn't have told you to start painting the mural today. Al, your mother died almost two years ago.'

Chapter Thirty-Two

'I knew that,' I say shakily, pulling my hand out from his and pushing my chair back. I feel sick. 'I knew that, I didn't mean it. It was just a joke. No one gave me the idea, I just decided on my own.'

'Allie …'

'Sorry, I need to use the bathroom.' I push past him, leaving him standing open mouthed as I head upstairs, locking the bathroom door behind me. *She died almost two years ago … but how could she have been here today, when she is dead?*

I run the tap, holding my hands beneath the icy stream before splashing it over my face. The shock of the chill helps to refocus my mind, bring me back to Earth. My mother was here, I know she was. I spoke to her, listened to her advice. I raise my eyes to the mirror, where my reflection stares back at me. My eyes are huge in my face and ringed with dark purplish circles from lack of sleep. My cheekbones are sharp and prominent, exaggerated by the recent weight loss, a daub of dark green paint staining the skin there. I can't remember the last time I ate a full meal, can't remember the last time I felt hungry. My skin is washed out, pale, almost corpse-like and my blonde hair lies flat against my scalp. If anyone looks as if they should be dead, it is me. I think of Rav's words and try desperately to recall the last time I saw my mother before she appeared at my kitchen table just a matter of days ago. I would know, wouldn't I? If she was dead.

She isn't dead. She can't be. I don't remember a funeral — there would have been a funeral and I would have been there, as her only child. But I don't remember it. I remember her apartment in Paris, and our last visit there when Mina was only a few months old. My mother wasn't there, and I had wandered around her tiny flat, picking up ornaments and jewellery before laying them back in the precise spot I found them, not wanting to upset her by moving them. She is particular, my mother, and she would know if I had been touching her things. There had been a sense of loss in the apartment, a gaping hole in my heart. Rav had wanted to visit the Sacré-Coeur, the Eiffel Tower, all those touristy things that English people do when they visit France, but I had been too tired, unhappy, adjusting to life with a small child. There is a black cloud over the memory — Mina had been fractious and unsettled the entire weekend and I had ended up starting to bottle feed when we arrived home. Was it that that clouded the weekend? Or was it the absence of my mother, the knowledge that she was gone? Everything is a blur. I lean my forehead against the cold glass of the mirror, leaving a greasy smudge behind. As I pull away, I see her in the mirror, feel her breath on my cheek as her gaunt face is reflected next to mine. *Agnes.* She pulls her lips back in a semblance of a grin that shows uneven teeth, her stringy hair hanging limply on either side of her hollow cheeks as she moves her face towards mine, her lips forming words to whisper in my ear.

'No!' I gasp, squeezing my eyes closed as I grope with shaking hands for something, anything, to throw. My fingers close around the ceramic hand soap dispenser and I hurl it towards the mirror, opening my eyes in time to see my face shatter into fragments as the glass breaks into a thousand tiny pieces.

'Allie? Are you all right in there?' There is a pounding on the door, Rav's voice filtering through. *Rav.* I grip the sides of the sink, staring down at the shards of glass that litter the porcelain. *Rav is lying. My mother isn't dead.* Shock at the realization makes my throat close over and I cough before I can speak. 'What's going on? Was that glass I heard?'

'I'm fine. I'll be out in a minute.' My voice is strong, no hint of the shakiness I am feeling. He *wants* me to think I'm going mad, why else would he tell such an awful lie? If he makes me think that I am mad, that I am seeing things that aren't there, then it will make it all the easier for him to take Mina and the baby. *Mina and the baby.* I can't believe I left them crying like that – will he use it against me now? Will he say that the children are safer with him, that I am neglectful? All I wanted to do was show him that I am a good mother, that I love Mina and Leo. I have to get into his account again, I have to find out exactly what he is planning so that I can see how much time I have left, so I can stop him. *You will figure it out.* It is my mother's voice I hear. Splashing my face once more, brushing away the tiny shards of glass that sit in my hair as my pulse ratchets in my ears, I throw open the door to see Rav still on the landing, his face wary.

'Al?' He steps towards me, slowly and gently with one hand out as if taming a wild horse. 'I'm sorry. I didn't mean to upset you.'

'It's ... I'm OK. I got confused.' The lie is already formulating on my lips. Two can play this game. 'Did I say my mum? I meant your mum. Avó. Avó suggested getting Mina's room painted. A good idea, hey?' The landing is growing dim now, the sky outside darkened by thick clouds. The trees whisper to me, but I keep my attention on Rav.

'Right. Yeah. My mum.' Rav follows me as I walk down the stairs, into the sitting room. 'Listen, Allie, I have to pop out, just for half an hour. Will you be OK?'

'Of course, Rav, I'll be fine.' I reach for the remote, switch on the television. Some intense drama begins playing, a man shouting at a woman. 'I'll just watch some telly for a bit.' I debate whether to ask him where he is going, even though I know he will only lie to me. Would I usually ask him? Yes, I think, the usual Allie would ask him, because the usual Rav very rarely goes out in the evenings, not spontaneously anyway. 'Where are you off to? I didn't think you had anything planned.'

'I ... er, I'm just going to check on Mum. Seeing as I didn't see her today.' Rav stumbles over the words slightly, a blush appearing beneath the dark skin on his neck as he inadvertently glances upwards, to where the children are sleeping. 'I won't be very long – you stay there.'

'OK.' There is something off in the way he speaks to me, and I rearrange my features to mask the doubt that surely must be written all over my face. 'I'll wait up for you.' Pasting on a smile, I turn back to the television, my mind going at nineteen to the dozen. If he's gone, then I can check his account on the laptop. I wait until I hear the front door slam behind him.

Watching from the sitting-room window as Rav drives away, I make sure he really is gone before I grab the laptop and quickly sign into his account. I don't know how long it will be before he returns from Avó's, if indeed he has even gone to see her, so I work quickly, signing directly into his Gmail account. Straight away, I see I was right all along. He is going to take the children. A flight confirmation sits in his unread messages, from British Airways. I click on it, my fingers shaking, as I scan the contents. Two adults, two children, flying to Mumbai on June 23rd, with a connecting flight to Dabolim. The total price is at the bottom, with the details of the credit card he has paid on. It's an American Express card, a card that he must have ordered without me knowing. I feel sick, dizzy, and I have to close my eyes and press my heels into the floor, to try and ground myself. How could he do this to me? My eyes ping open, and with a heavy heart I go back into his emails, trying to see what else I can uncover. There is nothing sinister – apart from the flight booking – and I sit there, letting the heat of the laptop battery burn into my thighs.

There is a *scratch* from the chimney, and I grit my teeth

together until they ache. A murmur comes from the baby monitor and I wait, expecting the baby to start wailing but he settles himself, and the only sound is my ragged breathing, interspersed with the scratching from the chimney. My nerves are electric, ants buzzing beneath my skin, the air around me charged with static. Agnes was here, I saw her, properly, reflected back in the mirror upstairs. I thought she was tied to the mirror from the attic, but she isn't. *I am not crazy*. Naomi thinks I am crazy, has told Rav that there is something wrong with me. All she's ever wanted is a family of her own, and now she has persuaded Rav to take mine. Shoving the laptop to one side I start to pace, my hands raking through my hair, the scratching in the walls insistent now. It follows me from the sitting room, into the kitchen, out into the garden, a buzzsaw running along my nerve endings. The sun has disappeared completely, the garden various shades of purple darkness. The trees sway, whispering to me, calling to me and I press my hands to my ears, trying to drown out the constant noise. There is a flash of white through the trees, moving quickly as if running through the forest, and my heart leaps into my throat as I try and follow the movement through the thick tangle of the trees. My eyes come to rest on the border, on the snipped stems of the oleander bush. It wasn't me; I knew it wasn't me. I never brought those poisonous blooms into our house – Naomi did. It has to have been her. Why? Was she trying to make Rav think that I was trying to hurt him? She said herself that she didn't believe in all the stories about Pluckley, the legends that haunt the village, but I saw the photo of her at Tara's, sage burning in the background. I know that Agnes is here, that she never left, but is Naomi using her as a way to turn Rav against me to get what she wants? It's not just the chilly evening breeze that makes me shiver now — how much does Rav have to do with it all? My brain feels foggy and jumbled, nothing making any sense as sparks try to connect. My mobile rings in my pocket, startling me, a shriek escaping from my lips before I can stop it. Naomi's name glows bright on the screen and I scan the woods before I swipe to answer it. They are still, dark, no hint of movement, no sign that someone was moving through the trees just minutes before.

'I know what you're doing.' I don't let her say hello, the words tumbling out in a landslide of icy granite. Naomi is silent on the other end as the words hit her.

'What?' she says eventually. 'Allie, what are you talking about?'

'I said, I know what you're doing. I won't let you take them!' I shout into the phone, the wind whistling through the trees, whipping my hair across my face. I hear a low rumble through the thick cloud that has gathered, hiding the moon from sight.

'Allie?' Her voice is faint, the growing wind making it difficult to hear. 'I don't know what you mean … you're scaring me. Where are you?'

'I know you told Rav that I was crazy, that the children weren't safe. I know that you were the one who put the idea of postpartum psychosis in his head, and I know it was you who told him to take the children away from me.'

There is silence at the other end of the phone, and I know I am right. 'Allie, where are you? Where are the children? Are they safe?'

'It doesn't matter anymore.' The first splatters of rain hit my shoulders, my hair, my face. '*I know what you're doing*. I'll die before I let you.'

'Allie, I don't know what you're talking about. No one wants to take the children; we both just want you to be safe.'

'They are safest with me!' I shriek into the phone. 'I have to protect them from Agnes. From all of you.'

'Allie, stay where you are, I'm coming over.'

I hang up without replying. Of course, she's coming over. The panic subsides and all at once I feel calm. Resigned, almost. Turning back to the house I look up at the windows. Dark. Rav has forgotten to leave Mina's night light on. There is only one way that this can end, and as the thought forms in my mind I feel a strange sense of acceptance. I have to save the children. I have to take them first, to save them from Naomi, to save them from Agnes Gowdie. Stepping across the patio I leave the rain outside, heading into the kitchen. The heating hasn't come on, it's too warm given that it's May, but I am cold, right down to my bones. I don't bother to turn the light on, enjoying the peace that the darkness brings, the shadows that flicker in the corners of the room. There is a murmur from the baby monitor and then a rustling as the baby moves, but no cries come, not yet.

I know what this is. Suddenly, it all seems so clear. The dream, the way it feels like a memory as though I have lived it before. It's not a dream, it's not a memory. It's an echo. Agnes lost her child, and she took revenge, and she's carried on doing that for four hundred years. I think of Lillian Sparks being hauled away, one child dead, the other kept from her forever, all because of Agnes and her inability to leave, her insistence on repeating the past over and over.

How long do I have? I look at the clock on the kitchen wall, my head seeming to move as if in slow motion. Everything feels heavy, blurry, as if underwater. Rav won't let me go. If I stay here, Agnes will always be there, watching, waiting, ready to take her moment to take them from me forever, just like she did to Lillian Sparks's children. Lillian's baby died, and Elsie never saw her mother again. There is only one solution.

The scratching starts as I move on leaden feet towards the fake Aga. *Scratch, scratch, scratch.* It comes from the walls, the ceiling, underneath the floorboards. It's inside me and all around me. Slowly, I turn the knobs at the front of the range, the hissing of gas filling my ears, yet still not drowning out the sound of the claws scratching, scratching around me. The air seems to thicken, time slowing down even further, and I think for a moment I can see the gas escaping, lying thickly in the air above my head. Sparkly threads wisping in the breeze from the open door behind me, as I move silently towards the staircase. My heart is hammering in my chest, but I can barely hear it over the roaring in my ears. I feel the creak of the tread of the stairs beneath my feet rather than hear it, and as I reach the landing I stand in a puddle of moonlight. Cold, so cold that goosebumps rise on my arms and the balls of my bare feet ache. I pull the pilled sleeves of my linen shirt over my hands and pause, listening. Silence. Just faint breaths coming from the darkened room ahead of me. I trail my hands over the warm wood of the banister, stopping to look out of the landing window, as I have done for so many nights previously. The fox, my old friend, steps out of the shadows of the trees and stops, sniffing the air. He raises his face to the window, his eyes meeting mine. His head dips in a quick nod, as if acknowledging what I am doing and giving his blessing. I watch him go on his way, waiting until his tail rounds the pond and he disappears from sight, before I move forward to the doorframe, knowing I won't see him again, he won't be back. I clutch it tightly, my vision suddenly blurry and when I blink, the room is unfamiliar. Shadows dance across the wall in the thin light of the moon that trickles in from the landing and my hand goes to the light switch before I drop it. I blink again, nausea rising hard and fast in my stomach and saliva floods my mouth. The shadows on the walls become clear — the fronds of seaweed, the mermaid perched atop a dark rock, tiny fish that are just dark smudges on the wall now. I step onto the bare floorboards as the scratching starts up again, over the head of the bed this time, and I see her, the dark figure standing over the bed where Mina sleeps. I move closer, seeing the baby's fists appear over the edge of the Moses basket, tiny and plump. There is an urge to pick him up, bring him close to my chest and inhale him one last time but I don't. I step over the toys on the floor, moving closer to the bed. Mina is asleep on her back, her breath whistling in and out in light snores, and my eyes drop to the end of the bed. To the blanket that Rav has laid out over her feet. Blue, knitted, with a trailing edge where the satin has become unravelled. To the empty cup lying on its side, next to the bed, discarded by Rav after putting Mina to bed. She stands there, Agnes Gowdie, dark and shadowy, a pillow clutched in her hands. She turns to look at me, her eyes strangely blank, her mouth twisting in that familiar grin as she raises the pillow and brings it down, slowly over Mina's face as a sob erupts from my chest. *I am too late.* I reach for her, my hands scrabbling for the pillow to seize it from her. Somewhere, far away, a door slams.

Chapter Thirty-Three

Six weeks later

Postpartum psychosis. The words still feel thick and unfamiliar on my tongue as I wait for Rav to bring the car round. I am finally leaving the secure psychiatric unit at Maidstone and going home to the children, six weeks after they brought me here. My heart rate increases when I think of Mina and Leo. I haven't seen them since that day, the day Rav came home to find me standing over Mina with a pillow in my hands, the gas blazing away merrily downstairs. Thank God he came back when he did. Thank God he stopped me.

It wasn't a dream. I blink back tears, smiling at a woman who comes out of the automatic double doors, a cigarette already halfway to her mouth before she is completely outside. I don't want to be seen crying out here, I don't want them to think that I'm not ready to go home. The woman lights the cigarette, a look of bliss on her face as she breathes out a plume of smoke. She reminds me of my mother, and I step away from her and the grey wreathes of smoke around her, towards the kerb as Rav brings the car to a stop.

'Ready?' His face is still creased with worry lines and there is a smattering of grey at his temples now which was never there before.

'Ready,' I say, trying not to let my nerves betray me. I slide into the passenger seat, the two car seats in the back catching my eye. I wonder how Mina will respond when I get home after six weeks without me. Will she be shy? Or will she throw her arms around me the way she does to Avó when she visits? The baby won't even know I've been gone, I tell myself, even though Rav keeps telling me Leo misses me.

As if he has read my mind Rav says, 'Avó will be there when we get home, will that be OK? I had to get her to watch the children.'

'Of course.' I smile, wishing Rav would put the radio on. Anything to break this awkward silence that fills the car every time Rav stops talking. 'Have you seen Naomi?'

'Yes.' Rav keeps his eyes on the road but stretches out a hand to squeeze my knee. 'She's had to move back in with her mum. I think she'll be there til the end now, until her mother passes.'

I am not sorry. I am sorry that Naomi's mother is dying, but I am not sorry that Naomi is not there. She visited me in the hospital a few times with Rav, awkward visits full of stilted conversation and things left unsaid. Then finally, the week I was told I would be able to come home, she came to visit me alone. I think of that visit now, as Rav tries to make small talk, eventually falling into silence as we pull on to the M20.

'Allie?' I roll over in my bed as I hear her voice from the

doorway. Maybe, if I lie still enough, she will think I am asleep. 'Allie, I know you're awake.'

I roll back to face the door. 'Where's Rav?'

'He's not here, he'll be along later. It's just me.' Naomi walks across the room, her shoes squeaking slightly on the lino. She looks like she always does, perfectly made up and immaculate. I am plain-faced, my hair pulled back in a simple ponytail. 'I wanted to talk to you alone.'

'Why?' I push myself up the pillows, making sure I am as far over on the bed as I can get. It feels odd, stiff and formal between us. There is none of the usual ease there was between us before, and as Rav was always here on previous visits I never realized quite how stilted it would be. I don't know if it's because I am ashamed of the way I behaved towards her, or if she finds it hard knowing that she was right. Even though I know I was wrong about things, it's difficult to let go of something that I believed was real.

'I wanted to apologize.' Her cheeks burn red and I feel some satisfaction that this is as difficult for her as it is for me. Her fingers pluck and worry at the smooth white sheet on the bed, wrinkling it. 'I'm sorry, Allie.'

'What for?'

'For ... pushing you.' Naomi reaches out now for my hand. I let my fingers lie limp in her palm, too tired to try and pull away. 'I'm sorry for a lot of things. That I didn't try and talk to you more about it, that I jumped to the conclusion that the children weren't safe with you.'

They weren't. That is the most frightening thing. At first, Naomi thought I was just becoming obsessed with Agnes

349

Gowdie, with the cottage and what had happened there over the years. It wasn't until Tara saw her and mentioned that she thought I might be suffering with postnatal depression that Naomi became really worried. And then when Tara told Naomi outside The Daisy Chain that she almost met my mother, that's when Naomi began to think that perhaps things were escalating. Now, when I think of Tara, I think of the blue blanket, left entirely by accident on the floor by the baby's changing station. I'll have to give it back to her, I think, and I wonder if she will still be my friend after all of this.

'Allie, please talk to me?' Naomi's dark eyes fill with tears and I feel a small pang of guilt.

'I know you were worried, that you were just trying to do the right thing. I was sick, I didn't know what I was doing,' I say eventually. 'But I'm better now. I'm going home soon.'

'You are?'

'Yes. The doctor told me this morning that all being well I can go home next week.' I glance down at my hand, at the brand-new ring on my finger, given to me by Rav last night. A single pearl inlaid in gold. An eternity ring made with the pearl I found on the bathroom floor all those months ago. An eternity ring to celebrate the babies, to celebrate us and what is ahead of us. I hadn't wanted to wear it at first, scared that the stone against my skin would evoke all those feelings from before, but Rav had looked so sad, and so desperate that I had let him slide it onto my finger. And I felt nothing. It was just a ring. Whatever it was that had made me feel that way was gone. The receipt I found in the suitcase was for the ring, not for the necklace that hung around Naomi's neck. I see the glint of gold as she shifts on the bed, reaching across the stark, white duvet. She's still wearing it.

'That's brilliant news.' She smiles, and I feel the pressure of her hand on mine. 'I'm so pleased. I'm, errr, I wanted to let you know that I'm not going to be around much when you come home.'

'Oh ...' I look down at our joined hands, not sure why I feel such a rush of relief. Naomi had nothing to do with any of this, I shouldn't be feeling relieved that she won't be around.

'My mum is sick. I'm going to go home and take care of her for a while.'

'I'm sorry. I didn't know. Rav never said.'

Naomi gives a tiny shrug, but it is as if there is a heaviness to her shoulders. 'Just one of those things. She's been poorly for a while but it's not getting better so ...' She stands, the removal of her weight reminding me of that night in the house, the pressure on the bed beside me. 'I just wanted to tell you. Go well, Allie.'

I had watched her walk away down the corridor, and then moved to the window to watch her get into her car, parked below. I had hoped that she might look up at the window before she drove away, but she didn't, instead just leaving without a backward glance. I had stood there for a few moments longer, not sure why I felt such grief at her going when I have spent so long carrying such anger towards her, before getting back into bed and crying until it was dark outside.

I stare out of the window now as the familiar sights of the village whizz past, even keeping my eyes open as Rav drives past the woods. A few minutes later Rav pulls the car onto the drive and I sit for a moment, my heart pounding in my chest as my hands fumble for the clip of the seatbelt.

'Are you OK?' Rav asks. 'Do you need a minute?'

I shake my head, finally managing to unclip myself. 'No, it's fine. I want to see them.' I get out of the car on shaking legs, hoping that I don't look too nervous when Avó appears in the doorway with Leo lying in her arms and a smile on her tiny, wrinkled face.

She holds out the baby and with a flutter of fear, I take him, the weight of him in my arms familiar and comforting. I press my lips to his head, breathing in his soft baby scent and then I lean down to kiss Avó, anxious about how I will be received. She raises her hand to my cheek, holding it there for a moment, and I breathe in her familiar scent of coconut hair oil and incense. 'I am so glad my daughter is home,' she says, and the pair of us blink back tears, Avó sniffing and dabbing at her nose with a tissue, flapping her hands at Rav as he tries to hug her.

'Mama!' Mina's voice shrieks from the sitting room, and a streak of pink tracksuit hurtles towards me, arms and legs tangling around mine as I crouch down to scoop her into my free arm, barely able to breathe she holds me so tightly.

Later, when the children are bathed, fed and asleep and Avó is safely tucked up in the spare bedroom, Rav pulls me towards him and I settle into his arms on the sofa. I find myself trying not to tense, waiting for the sounds of scratching to come from the chimney, but there is nothing, only the muted sounds of the lowered volume of the television.

'I'm glad you're home,' he whispers into my hair. 'Are you sure you feel OK? You will tell me if you … if things don't feel right.'

I press my head against his chest. 'Of course, I will. I'm glad to be home too,' I say, honestly. Twisting round, I lift my face to his and accept a kiss. 'I'm sorry.'

'What for?'

'For everything. For what I did.' I pause, my throat thick. 'For what I thought was happening. For doubting you.'

Rav shifts his body so that he is facing me, the light glowing behind him reminding me of the day I first saw him on the beach, the sun in his hair. 'Allie, I don't blame you for doubting me. You were sick, tired, alone with the children and struggling to cope. I wish I had realized – I should have talked to you about things, not Naomi. I shouldn't have put work before everything else.'

Naomi hadn't been lying when she said she knew how Rav was feeling. The day I saw them together in the pub was the first time he had asked to meet her, telling her he was worried that I wasn't sleeping. She had become upset, confessing that she too was worried about me and he had put his arm around her to comfort her, nothing more sinister than that. As my behaviour had become more and more erratic, he had met with her more and more often, trying to understand what was happening to me, why I was behaving the way I was.

'I'm sorry anyway,' I say. 'I should have known you wouldn't have done anything like that.' Rav leans forward and I let him kiss me, my breath coming short in my throat. It's been a long time since I let him kiss me like that.

'Are you coming up to bed?' Rav asks. 'It's been a long day for you, and I don't want you to overdo it. I was thinking we could start packing tomorrow.'

Packing. For the trip Rav booked for the four of us to Goa. The four of us – not Rav, the children and Naomi. Another thing I got wrong. He thought booking us an extended stay in India with his mother's family would help me, give me a rest and enable me to cope. After I was admitted to the hospital, he rearranged the flights – only this time we discussed it before he booked anything.

'I'll be up in a minute.' I smile up at him as he leaves, and then wander through into the kitchen, happy to be back in my own home. The chimney is silent, not a single scratching noise since I got home.

I pour myself a cold glass of water and take my medication, my feet seeming to move of their own accord towards the pantry. I never told Rav about the silver rattle, and I find it stuffed where I hid it, still wrapped in a clean tea towel. I unwrap it carefully, my heart starting to thump hard in my chest. The cool silver feels familiar under my fingertips, but when I shake it gently there is no sound. There is no ring of a bell, no dull thud of movement inside. It is silent. I rewrap it and carefully place it back in its hiding place before heading back into the hallway. At the foot of the stairs the mirror hangs in its original position, the glass clear and the frame gleaming. Rav must have rehung it, and I'm sure the cleaning is Avó's handiwork. I step closer, peering into the glass, waiting for her to appear, but there is nothing. The staircase is empty, there is no breath on my neck. Goosebumps prickle on my arms and I look down at the new ring on my finger, the pearl a misty white under the yellow warmth of the overhead kitchen light, imagining it sitting around Agnes Gowdie's neck as she fled Scotland for Kent. *She was never really here.*

'Allie?' Rav's voice floats down the stairs, and I tear my eyes away from my reflection in the glass. As I climb the stairs to our bedroom, Rav is on the landing in a pair of pyjama bottoms, closing the door to Mina's room.

'Everything all right?' he asks, as I go to him, wrapping my arms around his waist. He smells of toothpaste. 'You didn't hear anything down there, did you?' I can hear his heart thudding in his chest, his pulse rapid.

'No,' I say, letting the relief wash over me. I am tired now, genuinely ready for sleep for the first time in months. 'There's nothing down there.'

'No more talk of spirits and witches?' Rav asks warily.

'No more talk of anything like that.' I shake my head, his chest hair tickling my nose. 'I know now there was nothing like that. No Agnes Gowdie, no ghosts in the trees. None of that was real.' I pause, breathing him in. 'Do you think Naomi will be all right?'

'Naomi?' Rav pulls away and looks down at me. 'I don't know. I hope so. I mean, it's tough isn't it? Nursing someone you care for.' I look away, my cheeks warm, even though

I know he's not referring to us, to him taking care of me. 'And after the way she was when Jason left, well, she's always been a little fragile, hasn't she? But, Al, you can't worry about her, not now. You have to focus on you.'

I lean against him again, breathing in his warmth. He's right, Naomi has always been fragile. I was always the strong one in our friendship, the one mopping up the tears and fixing things. The coper. Perhaps that's why part of me couldn't let myself lean on her no matter how much she offered to help.

'Come on. It's late. Let's go to bed.' Rav walks into the bedroom and I move to the light switch on the landing to put out the light.

Moonlight streams in through the landing window, and I can't help it, I go to look out one more time, as I did so many nights before. The leaves on the trees wave silently, the moon shining a fat, white circle on the area where the pond used to be. Rav has finally filled it in. The fox appears, slinking his way along the border and I suppress a smile, pleased and a little comforted to see that my old friend is still here. I turn, ready to join my husband in bed for the first time in six weeks, when I catch movement out of the corner of my eye. A flash of white, a blank oval of a face looking back at me, before it begins to move through the trees, quickly, silently.

Acknowledgements

Pluckley is a real village in the heart of Kent and, according to the *Guinness Book of Records*, is said to be the most haunted village in Britain. I have taken some liberties with regards to the layout of the village (there isn't a Co-op, but there is a good butchers), and while the other ghosts mentioned are believed to haunt the village, Agnes Gowdie is a figment of my imagination (I hope). Her sister, Isobel Gowdie, is not – she was a Scottish woman who confessed to being a witch in 1662. So, thank you, residents of Pluckley (both living and not) for lending me your village as the perfect setting for Allie and Rav's story.

Thanks as ever to Lisa Moylett and Zoe Apostolides – your ability to see the things I can't (including the ghosts) and pushing me towards them makes for a better book every time.

Thank you to Kate Mills for your insight, and to Becky Heeley for all your hard work. And always, to Lisa Milton.

Thank you to my mum for reading early draft after early draft, telling me each one was brilliant. Sometimes you just need your mum to tell you you're ace. To Kate and Amy,

Natalie and Charlie, for listening to me when I'm trying to hash out plot points and telling me when I'm not making any sense.

And thank you to Nick, Geo, Missy and Mo, for everything.

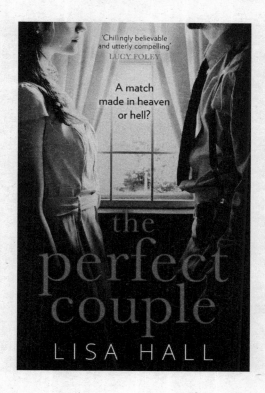

ONE PLACE. MANY STORIES

Bold, innovative and
empowering publishing.

FOLLOW US ON:

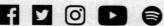

@HQStories